THESE BITTER BLOOMS

ALSO BY EMMA HAMM

The Otherworld
Heart of the Fae
Veins of Magic
The Faceless Woman
The Raven's Ballad
Bride of the Sea
Curse of the Troll

Of Goblin Kings
Of Goblins and Gold
Of Shadows and Elves
Of Pixies and Spells
Of Werewolves and Curses
Of Fairytales and Magic

Dragon of Umbrar
Fire Heart
Bright Heart
Brave Heart
Torn Heart

and many more...

VI

Your soft heart is not a weakness.
Your warm soul is not a burden.
Your quirky nature is your gift, not a curse.

There is magic in you, my darling.
Never deny it release.

VII

1. WILDECLIFF
2. SUNSPELL ACADEMY
3. ORBWEAVER MANOR
4. CEREDWIN'S ALTAR
4
3
2
1

RIVER DANU
7
8
5
6
1. WATERDOWN
2. STRONG MEADOW
3. BRIAR BEACH FARM
4. PILLARS OF LUGH

CHAPTER 1

Today, she became a witch.

A real witch, like her sisters and mother. True, it had taken Thea a little longer than the rest of her family. Her sisters had bled early, but Thea's body wasn't normal. And every time she felt horrible about making everyone wait, her mother would remind her that everything happened for a reason.

Hekate looked after the daughters of the moon. If she wanted Thea to endure until she was sixteen for her first blood, then there was a good reason for that.

She'd wanted to bleed for so long, and now everything felt strange. Like someone else was inside her body, or maybe that wasn't right. She was hyper aware of the area between her legs and the blood that dripped down her thighs. When she'd come into the kitchen, her mother had been so pleased that she'd squawked like the crows that lived around their home. Her sisters had laughed at the expression Thea had made, and both of them had shouted, "Finally!"

And though she should celebrate with them, Thea just felt uncomfortable.

She was sixteen. She shouldn't feel surprised when her moon blood came. But… Well… Maybe it could have waited for a day other than her birthday.

Her mother had sent her to the stream to wash. Almost as though Máthair had known how much this made her youngest daughter feel strange. Thea didn't want people to know that she was bleeding. She didn't want anyone to see her, touch her, or even talk to her.

Sighing, she stooped and scooped handfuls of water. Her long, woolen skirts swung around her legs and got in the way of cleaning, though. Tears of frustration pricked her eyes, and then she couldn't prevent them from running down her cheeks.

"Stop it, Thea," she whispered, angrily dashing away the drops. "You're being a baby."

The words could have worked if a sudden cramp hadn't burned through her stomach. Hissing out a long breath, she sat down on the edge of the stream and pressed her hands to her belly.

"If the bleeding came without pain, I might not hate it so much," she muttered. Or fear it. How was she supposed to find peace in knowing that every month she would have a wound between her legs that refused to heal? Why couldn't it have just never come?

She laid on her back and flopped an arm over her eyes. The sun was too merry and the feelings inside her were too dark for blue skies. Thea wanted to hide and then maybe everything else would disappear.

An hour passed by the river while she listened to the quiet sounds of nature. The burbling of the brook never changed, and of course it didn't. There was a deep natural spring that fed the stream near their home. Her family drank clean, fresh water rather than having to boil the seawater on the other side of the ridge.

Something nudged her hand, hard. When Thea sat up, she made eye contact with a bright green snake. She froze, entranced by the yellow eyes and flicking tongue that tasted her scent. The snake nudged her hand one more time, gave her a disappointed look, and then slithered toward the stream.

"Brighid," she breathed.

The goddess came to those in need. Brighid was the goddess of healing, sometimes, other times of poetry or smithcraft. A woman with many talents and no interest in staying put when others told her to. Thea's mother adored her.

But she was also the goddess of fertility, and Thea could tell the snake came with a message. *Get up. Go home. Stop moping that you've become a woman. You knew it would happen, eventually.*

"All right," she muttered, pushing herself upright and dusting her hands off on her skirts. "I'll stop."

The snake seemed to nod before it disappeared into the waters and never came back up. *Goddesses and their messages,* she mused. They were never very clear, but sometimes they were forceful in their opinions.

She wandered toward the small home where her mother and two sisters waited for her. They were all witches, though much more powerful than Thea. Her mother's ability to manipulate the weather made her a dangerous woman to cross. Her sister, Marigold, conjured plants that grew from nothing. Even barren soil could not deny her magic. Belladonna could heal rotten food with a single touch. They kept the village well fed, adequately stocked, and healthy with their powers.

And Thea?

She sighed and blew at a lock of dark hair that fell in front of her face.

She ate plants.

Perhaps that was oversimplifying a power that might become helpful, but she had yet to find a use for it. On her way to the house, she snapped off a sprig of lavender from her mother's prized garden and popped it into her mouth. Instantly, all the anxiety and fear of the day disappeared as the herb melted on her tongue.

No matter what plant she devoured, it always melted. It sank into her skin and she used that power to her advantage. They'd discovered the gift when she was a little girl and she had taken a bite out of her mother's prized sword lilies. The alliums were known to be poisonous, but Thea hadn't fallen ill. Instead, she'd been much stronger than before. Her mother had made her pick up the stove as a toddler, and then they all realized what her powers were.

But she couldn't help anyone. She didn't save villages from a blighted crop with a single wave of her hand. She didn't make plants grow or bring in the rains during the middle of a drought. Many other witches were inhumanly strong, or capable of so much more.

Thea was the weakest of her family, and that made her fade into the background.

She rounded the corner of their home and unlocked the front gate. Their father had hand built the quaint little farmhouse when he first moved to this area of Waterdown. It was far from the village, but had given his wife plenty of room for her magic and for the gardens that spread out like a spiderweb from the front door.

He'd been given a small gift, just like Thea. Her father gifted homes with a personality. In a sense, he turned inanimate objects into thinking, feeling beings. Not much of a gift. But still, one worth remembering.

The house shifted at her approach. Smoke spewed out of the chimney, and Thea knew that it had put on a pot of tea for her. Their home always did that when it sensed discomfort.

"Thank you," she said as she walked through the slanted front door. "You always know how to help."

A deep hum echoed down the hallway and a breeze kicked up to toy with the strands of her hair before disappearing. Their crooked little farmhouse with mismatched windows and doors of every color had soaked up so much magic throughout the years that no magic was too difficult.

The short hallway led into their kitchen, where a cauldron large enough to bathe in bubbled with some dark liquid. Most likely the anise scent coiling out of it was a spell Belladonna was working on. The cast-iron stove on the opposite corner had twin teapots on the top. Steam already rose out of one of them, though the other had recently been added and was yet to boil.

Thea ducked as a sharp knife came careening off a shelf and floated over her head.

"Marigold!" Thea shouted, spinning on her heel. "What did I tell you about summoning knives when other people are in the house?"

"Sorry!" her sister called back, her voice muffled from the rear of the house. "I forgot!"

She wouldn't forget when her spell cut Thea's ear off. Now would she? Living in a home full of witches had its dangers, she supposed, but she would appreciate not having to worry about losing an eye in her own kitchen.

The cramps tightened her belly, again. Wincing, Thea sank into one of the rocking chairs by the stove and put her head in her hands. When would this get better? She had heard her sisters complain about these pains before, though she'd never realized how painful they were going to be.

"Here." Her mother's voice filtered through the anguished thoughts like a glass of cool water on a hot day. "Drink this."

Straightening, Thea took the tea without even looking at it. The faint scent of licorice tickled her nose. Steam rose over the chipped teacup that Thea had painted with tiny thistles when she was three. The plant was her namesake, after all.

"What's in it?" she asked, sipping at the hot liquid.

"Ginger, fennel, and a little black tea." Her mother sat down in the other rocker, her own dark hair a plume of curls around her head. "The ginger will settle your stomach and the fennel will help with the cramping. I remember when I had my first blood. I felt the same as you do now."

"Like you wanted to die?"

"So grumpy and sorry for myself that a goddess had to intervene." A twinkle in her dark eyes, her mother leaned forward and whispered, "So, which one was it?"

How did....?

Thea shook her head at her thoughts. Her mother knew everything, always. Was she really surprised that this powerful witch knew a goddess had visited her?

"Brighid," she muttered into her teacup. Thea slouched in the rocker so far that the small of her back touched the seat. "She wasn't pleased with the theatrics, apparently."

Her mother tilted her head and let out a bark of laughter that filled the entire room. She'd always thought her mother's laugh sounded like thunder banging against the roof of the house. And while some people found the sound utterly appalling, Thea had always loved knowing where her mother was.

"Brighid?" Tears in her eyes, her mother wrangled herself to stillness. "The goddesses were not kind to you today! They must have plans for you, my darling, if they were so forceful that they sent the Bright One!"

Thea doubted that. The goddesses were likely disappointed that all she'd gotten for a power was an ability to eat plants. Or maybe Thea was just upset that all of this had to happen today, and her thighs were still sticky with blood.

"Do we have to go to the altar tonight?" she asked, even though she knew the answer. "I can wait until next year."

"Absolutely not, dear one." Máthair reached forward to grab onto her hands and gave them a tight squeeze. "You will not wait a moment longer for your familiar. You know how important they are to your magic. Besides, don't you want someone to be with you? To be your best friend and only yours?"

Sometimes. She watched her sisters with their familiars and it made her a little jealous to see how close they were. Marigold and her hare with velvet soft ears and claws the size of a cat's. Belladonna and her butterfly that glowed in the dark so she could read all the grimoires their father had left behind. She'd always wondered what kind of creature she would get, and how they would improve her life. Her magic.

Even her mother's black cat, which saw the world with human eyes, made her want a creature of her own.

Thea licked her lips and nodded. "I suppose we can go, then. But are you so sure that Ceridwen will even gift me with a familiar?"

"You are more powerful than you know." Máthair released her hands and tucked a strand of hair behind her ear. "The goddesses have their eye on you, Thea. They have seen into your brilliant heart and they know you will serve them well. Mark my words."

She wanted to. Thea really did.

Maybe the lavender kicked in. Or maybe some goddess had wrapped her in a warm hug. Either way, Thea's spirit swelled as she looked into her mother's eyes. The same eyes she had, the same heart-shaped face, the same brightly colored lips. Máthair said Thea was her reflection. Though Thea sometimes worried that meant she would always be a disappointment in comparison.

The doors to her sister's rooms burst open and slammed against the walls. The house shuddered in anger, reminding the other two girls how important manners were.

"Sorry!" Marigold shouted. She had her hands behind her back and a bright grin on her face. Her yellow dress matched her golden hair, and a matching silk sash was tied tightly around her waist. "Bella, are you ready?"

Her other sister stood to the right, dressed in a deep emerald green with long skirts that dragged on the ground as she moved. Bella's oak colored locks were darker than Marigold's, but they both had their father's bright blue eyes and his square jaw.

Bella gave Marigold a quick nod, and together, they raced into the room so quickly that Thea nearly spilled her tea. They converged upon her like a storm cloud with sudden shouts and whoops of glee as they sprinkled pine needles over her head.

"What are you doing?" she shouted, standing up while trying not to spill boiling water all over her hands.

"Birthday blessings!" Her sisters crowed as they threw more pine needles in her face.

Once they quieted down, and emptied their pockets, Marigold held out a tiny pot filled with the smallest rose plant she'd ever seen. The single blossom was the size of the nail on her thumb and bright pink. "We made this for you."

"Oh," she breathed. Her sisters had spent all this time working on the perfect birthday gift? Thea hadn't thought they would do anything. After all, they celebrated most birthdays devouring a dinner their mother would make. She hadn't gotten them anything for their special days.

Thea took the offered tiny pot and the little rose that seemed to turn its blossom so she could admire how lovely it was.

"We never give each other gifts," she said.

Belladonna chuckled. "And we won't ever get you another one. This is your first blood, little sister, and the day Ceridwen provides you with a familiar who will walk through life with you, hand in hand."

"Or paw in hand," Marigold said with a bubbling laugh. "Perhaps flipper in hand? We won't know until you have one."

Her heart could burst with love for these women. She looked between her sisters and then glanced over at her mother, who wore a soft smile.

Thea burst into tears. "I love you all so very much!"

Why did that make her chest hurt?

The three witches gathered her up in their arms, all laughing at her antics, and Thea was reminded how very lucky she was.

CHAPTER 2

The icy drafts of the manor never ceased. Perhaps that was his family's penance for all the dark magic that swelled within these walls.

Alistair Orbweaver was the forgotten son of a very influential man. Wildecliff only valued those with power, however, so he supposed it wasn't unexpected that his father would forget the boy whose only gift was to see through the veil of the world. Alistair saw the faerie creatures, gods, and goddesses, as though they were in the same realm. Most others only ever felt the faintest impression of being watched.

He saw their true forms. And while that was terrifying to such a young man, it had made him quieter than his brothers.

He peered out of his bedroom, eyeing the cold hall to make sure that neither Lysander nor Cassius were waiting for him. They were relentless with their pestering, no matter what time of day it was. Sometimes, he swore they had placed a tracker on him so they knew when to exit their bedrooms and how to find him in the corridors beyond.

The dark floors reflected no shadows of people, however. The black wallpaper didn't ripple with any spells, though the hand-painted lilies looked a little too awake for his liking.

Still, he was hungry. He hadn't gone to breakfast with them because he knew their torment would be endless on a day like today. With clouds in the sky and rain on the horizon, his brothers would stay inside all day. Boredom bred madness with Orbweaver men.

He twisted the knit hat in his hands and reminded himself that he couldn't starve. All he had to do was make it to the kitchens, and then he could sneak back before anyone saw him. What reason would they have to be out of their rooms?

Alistair pulled the hat down over his ears so he didn't freeze them off and nodded. He would be brave. He could walk out of his own room and to the kitchens without feeling like his heart would beat out of his chest.

The second he put one woolen sock on the floor of the hallway, he heard two doors creak open.

Alistair winced and squeezed his eyes shut. He had known they would watch for him, yet still, he had taken the risk.

His brothers descended upon him like vultures to their prey.

"Look who it is," Lysander hissed. His eyes were so pale they were nearly yellow and glinted in the torchlight like a snake's. "What do you think you're doing? Walking out of your room in the middle of the day like this seems like you're planning trouble."

"It's not the middle of the day," Alistair muttered, marching down the hall as though he wasn't terrified of them. "I'm going to the library."

He'd learned a long time ago never to tell them what he was actually doing. Otherwise, they would follow him, hounding him until he snapped. That's what they wanted, after all. They wanted to see him at his worst and to encourage behavior that made their father angry. They loved watching their father punish him.

Cassius waited for him midway down the hall, his arms crossed over his chest and a disgusted expression on his face. Lip curled, nostrils flared, he looked like he'd smelled something rotten. "What are you wearing, whelp?"

Alistair slipped as one of his large socks slid from his knee to his ankle, causing the toe to be floppy. He righted himself quickly, but not soon enough to escape his brother's laughter. "It's cold in here," he muttered.

"Cold is good for you." Cassius was the oldest of the brothers and had spent more years with the icy drafts. Even he wore a woolen coat, and his fair hair covered his ears.

"I'm sure it is," Alistair replied as he tried to skirt past his brother. "I'm just getting a book to read, so if you'd let me pass..."

With the speed of a viper, Cassius shoved Alistair against the wall and slammed his hands on either side of Alistair's ears. "What's the truth, then? You're hungry, is my guess. You weren't in your seat for breakfast. But don't you remember? If you don't eat with the family, you don't eat at all."

Why were his brothers so vicious? They were cruel just to be cruel, and he hated every second of being around them. The way Cassius's lip remained curled, like the mouth of a wolf, let him know how much danger he was in.

Until he saw the shadows on his brother's shoulder. He blinked a few times, letting his eyes go slightly cross so he could see outside of his world and into the other.

Their bean-tighe had her hand on Cassius. The elderly fae looked after their house, although he couldn't imagine why. Her kind frequently took to thoughtful families who remembered they existed. Her wrinkled face had creased with anger, and the tattered edges of her old-fashioned gown blew in a wind he could not feel. She stood on a small stool usually strapped to her back for sweeping far off cobwebs, but today she used it to grab the boy who threatened young Alistair.

"Alistair," his brother hissed.

He wasn't paying attention anymore. Not to his brother, at least.

"Cream and berries?" he asked the bean-tighe. "I saw raspberries in the kitchen two days past."

The grin on her face was all the answer he needed. But then the faerie woman who came up to his chest snapped out her clawed hands, grabbed onto Cassius's ear, and yanked so hard his brother nearly fell over.

He saw an opening and took it. He darted away, though he heard Lysander trip the moment he tried to run after him. Likely the bean-tighe as well.

Thank goodness for the kindness of faeries. Or he'd have died here a long time ago.

He ran past the library where he'd told his brothers he planned to go. The dust-covered books were rarely touched by anyone but himself, and even then, the grimoires liked to scream if someone stroked a finger down their spines. He sprinted past the corridor that led to his father's wing because Balthazar Orbweaver never left that side of the house unless it was for family business. Past the dining room with its massive chandelier decorated with spider webs and tiny crystals carved to look like knives.

Alistair didn't slow down until he reached the servants' quarters and the section of the house that disappeared underground. His father liked to believe that the help didn't need light, but Alistair knew they'd found other ways to illuminate their way.

The stairs leading down into the kitchens were always slick. Two doors leading outside hit the cold air of this home, making water pool and drip down the stairs. They were horribly dangerous. He'd heard of too many servants falling and injuring themselves.

He took his time getting downstairs, one hand on the wall and socks soaking up the water until his steps were wet slaps echoing around the stones. But he made it down without slipping, then rounded the corner into the massive kitchen that made up most of the underbelly of the manor.

Food filled one long table to the brim with all they would need this week. Four butlers ordered the maids about, each telling another person where the food items should be stored to keep everything edible for the longest amount of time.

Two chefs stood on opposite ends of the kitchen, each one manning a massive stove that burped and belched like monsters devouring everything put inside them. Alistair used to fear those horrible contraptions. Even now, he knew better than to stand next to them. They spat coals at people they didn't like.

A hand clamped down on his shoulder, and he flinched in fear. Had his brothers found him again? He thought the bean-tighe would keep them busy for a little while, at least.

Instead, the hand softened around the joint and gently squeezed him. "We were wondering if you'd make your way down here, Master Alistair. We didn't see you at breakfast!"

He looked up at one of the maids who had always been kind to him and felt all the tension in his body ease. "Hello, Nora."

"Hungry?" she asked.

Vigorous nods were her answer, and he knew he didn't have to tell her why he hadn't been to breakfast. All the servants knew their place in this home, but they also knew his. They'd seen how his father reacted to Alistair's mere existence. The last thing he wanted was to see his father if he could avoid it.

Alistair trailed her through the kitchen, dodging maids with arms laden with food, butlers with scowls and pressed suits, and the chef on the right who tried to pop him on the head with a spoon. At least they weren't afraid of him like they were the rest of his family. He considered that a good sign.

Finally, they made it to the back of the kitchen. Nora whirled around and put her hands over his eyes. "Wait! You aren't supposed to see this yet."

He lifted his own hands to cover his eyes and sighed. "Why not?"

"Because, little master."

Right. If anyone else had talked to him like that or said it in front of his father, they would have their tongue cut out. Balthazar would have used their entrails in his next spell.

He sighed and waited while a commotion whirled around him. Though there were noises he recognized, like footsteps and the clattering of dishes, there were also a few sounds he didn't. Like... feathers? Was that ruffling feathers?

"All right!" Nora called out. "You can look."

He lowered his hands to stare at the empty table in front of him. There was nothing there but the worn oak and stone wall behind it. Screwing up his face in confusion, he pushed at the edges of his knitted hat to see better. "Nora?" he asked, then turned around.

The staff had rushed to get rid of the food on the table behind him, or at least some of it. They'd pushed most to the back and now stood around the end near him with a tiny honey cake set up at the edge.

A single flame flickered atop a precious candle, clearly made with the leftovers of others. There were at last twenty different wax colors in it, but it still burned for him, and that was special.

Nora clasped her hand at her heart and grinned. "Happy birthday, Alistair. Many blessings to you for this year."

It was his birthday?

Sixteen years felt like a milestone he should have remembered, but the days passed either too slow, or too quick, in this house. He'd forgotten. Somehow.

Apparently, no one else had remembered either. Other than the servants.

A tiny faerie shuffled forward on the table with a flower hidden behind his back. The brownie was one of his favorites, although the only way he could tell the difference between the mouse-like creatures was the color of their hats. This one had a bright red cap on top of his head. He dragged a daisy into view and let the glamour fall away from it so the rest of the staff could see it.

The red-faced chef noticed it first. He let out a boom of laughter and pointed to the flower. "Even the real help of the manor agrees! Happy birthday, dear boy."

The servants knew about the fae just like he did. They were the only ones who made him feel sane when he was just a little boy and first started seeing faerie creatures that crawled up the wallpaper and hissed at his attention.

They'd all come a long way from those first few moments.

Nora gestured for him to come up to the table. "Come on, Alistair. Blow out your candle and then the rest of us will get back to work. No need for you to wait much longer, otherwise your father will find out."

He'd find out no matter what, Alistair thought. Balthazar had eyes in every part of this manor and always knew what the servants were doing. Though, he'd never said anything about them paying extra attention to his youngest son. Maybe the old man had a heart, after all.

Lungs filling with a deep breath, he blew out the candle and tried hard not to let his cheeks turn bright red as the servants all cheered quietly around him. He failed. The brownie laughed at him, although it was a sweet sound and not filled with malice. The tiny mouse-like man gave him a little bow and pointed at the flower. As though it was important.

Alistair picked it up and twirled the long stem between his equally long fingers. The petals billowed out from the bright yellow center, and a sweet scent like honey filled the air. The fae had always taken good care of them. They wanted him to be happy, but sometimes he worried they stayed in this crypt of a house because of him.

The other servants started off so they didn't fall behind on their work. But Miss Nora stayed right beside him and then leaned down to squeeze his shoulders in an awkward hug.

"Are you doing anything fun for your birthday?" she asked.

He shook his head. "I didn't even remember it was my birthday, miss."

"Oh," she breathed. Then straightened with a determined expression on her face. The maid ripped off her apron and yelled to the cook, "Didn't you say we needed to get more milk?"

The cook gave her a startled look before he noticed Alistair still standing beside her. With a soft smile on his face, he replied, "I did."

She held out her hand for him to take, palm up, cheeks bright red. She had to know the rules that she'd break by taking him out of the house. And yet, Nora still said, "Why don't you come with me, Master Alistair?"

He shouldn't. He'd get her in trouble. and his father might even fire her. It wasn't easy in Wildecliff to get a job, let alone in a house as prestigious as this.

And yet... It was his birthday. And his own family had forgotten that.

Alistair slapped his hand down on hers and nodded. "I'd like that, Miss Nora."

CHAPTER 3

Thea tilted her face toward the silver rays above her and closed her eyes. She could almost feel the caress of the witch mother. Many witches called upon Hekate, so Thea rarely felt as though the goddess was with her. But tonight? She was certain the touch of the wind was Hekate smoothing her hair over her shoulders, so she looked perfect when they reached the altar.

She rubbed the embroidery along the hem of her sleeves. Her mother had spent months working on the tiny herbs and blue flowers that decorated all the edges of her fine white muslin. Calming spells were woven into every little detail covering her from head to toe. Thea didn't feel the soothing effects that much. All she felt was love.

Their boat coasted over the river with no sails and no oars to make ripples. Standing at the bow with her arms held up toward the sky, her mother's silhouette created a picture of magic and power that filled the air with electricity, as though lightning had struck nearby.

Thea's mother was beautiful. Her dark hair coiled in tight ringlets all the way to the small of her back. Usually, she kept her hair tied away so she could work in their gardens, but tonight was special. Her mother let all those curls fly wild in the slight breeze.

Thea felt a swell of magic as her mother whispered an incantation. The lily pads surrounding the boat flipped over and gently pushed them forward again. The faint slaps of greenery against the wood were the only sounds this late at night. Even the seabirds had gone to sleep.

Then her mother turned, and Thea saw her future in the heart-shaped face that grinned at her.

"Are you ready?" her mother asked.

"I am, Máthair." At least, she thought she was.

Thea had magic. She'd had magic her entire life. But this was the moment when she would become a real witch. She'd gain a familiar who would stay with her until the very end of her days. This creature would be like an extension of herself, and as such, it was very important for the goddesses to give her the right one.

When she was little, she thought her mother could see through her familiar's eyes. The black cat had followed her everywhere as a toddler. Máthair might have that power, but she never admitted to it, even when they talked about the ceremony she'd undergo.

Smoothing her hair away from her face, Máthair removed the looser curls from sticking to her forehead. "Ceridwen is not as kind as Hekate, my daughter. You must be respectful and listen to what she has to say to you. No matter what familiar you are given, be grateful that you were given any at all."

Thea had heard of another girl from the village who was denied a familiar. Apparently, Ceridwen had looked into her powers and thought she was not strong enough.

Reaching into her pocket, Thea pulled out a small sprig of lavender and set three buds on her tongue. Immediately, the calming magic of the flower soaked into her. She no longer felt her stomach rolling in her belly as though she might be sick. The tension in her chest eased, and her heartbeat slowed to a steady, lulling thump.

"I'll be all right either way," she said.

"I know you will, sweet girl." Her mother turned her attention back to the front of the boat, but not fast enough to hide the worry on her face.

After all, if the gods thought anyone had a small gift, it was Thea.

She thumbed the handful of plants in her pocket and sighed. Vervain to ward off ill will, dill for good spirits, and pansy blooms for happy thoughts. The effects only lasted for a half hour or so. She'd yet to find every combination that would make her feel certain ways, but these she knew would be helpful.

It wasn't much of a gift. Still, she appreciated having anything at all.

The boat hit the other side of the river with a dull crunch. Máthair leapt out and reached out her hand for Thea to take. "Come, little thistle. Shall we meet a goddess?"

Thea gulped but took her mother's hand.

Together, they hauled the boat up onto the shore and followed the winding path which would lead them to Ceridwen's altar.

The two goddesses had very different backgrounds, but they were intrinsically woven in the way of the witch. Hekate gave her daughters the powers they were born with, and Ceridwen decided what familiar would guide them through life. She hoped they would be kind to her, together. Thea had tried very hard to worship them correctly.

Reaching ahead of them, her mother brushed aside a large branch that had fallen over the path to the altar. "Here it is," Máthair breathed; her words were reverent.

A spear of moonlight illuminated three large stones surrounding a flat pillar in the center of the clearing. The standing stones cast long shadows that crept toward her feet and stroked her bare toes with icy darkness. The fluffy clouds overhead seemed to glow with magic. She could feel it in her chest—an electric thrum, like the beat of a drum rocked through her body with each heartbeat.

She had a hard time brushing aside the stray thought that her power wasn't strong enough to give her a familiar. She'd prepared for the nerves, though. Thea reached into her pocket for a strand of dill and chewed it. All that negative energy was banished by the burst of flavor.

The leaves beyond the altar shifted, and strangely, a man walked out. Thea thought, for a moment, that this was part of the ritual until her mother squared her shoulders. The curls along the sides of her head lifted with static anger.

"Balthazar," her mother practically hissed. "What are you doing here?"

The man was... strange. That was the only way Thea could think of him. Creamy blonde hair was slicked back to his skull, and his clothing was so fine she wondered why he'd walked through the woods in it. His pressed black suit jacket looked like it could stand on its own, and the pale-colored vest beneath it appeared more suitable for a wedding.

Three other men stepped out behind him. Two looked exactly like their father, with matching scowls on their faces and hands raised as though they were ready to let spells fly. The third, the youngest, looked nothing like the rest. His blonde hair was burnished gold and red with smatters of orange streaks that flopped over his face in unruly locks. Freckles dotted over his cheeks. She could see them from across the entire altar space, and his bright green eyes were like a meadow in direct sunlight.

"Fenna Earthshaker," the older man replied. His voice sounded too smooth, unlike any human she'd ever heard. "You are interrupting our ceremony."

"Your ceremony? It is my daughter's birthday after her first blood. We are here to get her familiar." Her mother crossed her arms over her chest, immovable as a mountain. "You will have to wait."

"I don't think it will take long for my son to be given the powerful familiar as he is due." Balthazar snapped his fingers at his son, who stepped forward hesitantly before being shoved toward the altar. "I'm sure it will take Ceridwen hours to decide what paltry familiar to give your daughter. She has a small gift, doesn't she? Hardly worth a familiar at all."

"How dare you?" Máthair shoved Thea's shoulders, sending her careening toward the altar as well. "She will go first, as we arrived before your family."

Thea's eyes widened with every word as the two parents suddenly stalked toward each other with raised voices, pointing fingers, and more anger than she'd ever seen up close. Her mother had never mentioned knowing anyone from this side of the river, but Wildecliff and Waterdown had never gotten along.

Her heart skipped a few beats, then thudded so hard against her ribs she thought it might stop. Thea pressed a hand against her chest and willed the thumps to slow. They didn't. She sighed and reached into her pocket. Again. Another few lavender buds should do the trick, otherwise, she'd have to eat the pansy.

Her mother could handle herself, so she turned away from their parents to get a good look at the altar. Then her eyes were so arrested with emeralds looking back at her that Thea forgot to breathe.

Oh, but he did have such pretty eyes.

The young man in front of her cleared his throat and held out a hand. "Alistair."

Scrunching her nose, she wondered if she should ignore him, considering the fight going on behind her. Still, he seemed harmless enough. She shook his hand and forced a smile. "Thea."

"I'm sorry for my, uh, my father." He stuttered over the words. "He can be a little entitled."

"My mother can be quite loud." She winced at a high-pitched shriek. "It's just because they love us."

His face went so pale that she could count the freckles like stars on his face. "Maybe yours does."

What did he mean by that?

A clawed hand clamped onto her shoulder and dragged her away from the altar. Thea angrily hissed out a long breath, grappling with whoever tried to manhandle her until she was tossed toward her mother.

"Wait your turn, girl," Balthazar snarled. Then he snapped those horrible fingers at his son again. "Get on with it."

"Yes, sir."

Her heart broke for the young man, who shook while he did his best to cast the summoning circle. She wanted to watch and see what he did. Every family's spell was unique, but her mother cupped her cheeks and forced Thea's eyes away.

"Don't you take an ounce of interest in Orbweaver magic," Máthair said. Her words were intense, and Thea could feel her hands trembling. "They are not a family you are ever to emulate. Do you understand me?"

"Of course I do."

But the young man didn't seem all that bad. Alistair had meadow eyes and a tentative smile that never really reached past the very edges of his lips. She wondered how long it had taken him to get those freckles or if he'd been born with them. She didn't have any freckles, and she spent hours in the sun every day.

Alistair finished quickly. His father stood right next to the altar with his arms crossed over his chest until a horrible scream filled the clearing. A raven flew overhead and then landed on the altar next to Alistair's hand. It hopped a few times, turning its head to meet the young man's gaze.

The raven didn't have only feathers, as most corvids did. This one had thorns down its spine and around its head like a lion's mane. The sharp edges glinted in the moonlight like the spikes of some macabre knives had been thrust into the poor beast's hide.

"You see?" Balthazar opened his arms wide and laughed. "I told you my boy would get a strong one. It's hardly even from this mortal realm!"

Thea held her breath, waiting for the young man to move. Would he leave the bird on its own and join his family? Victorious that his power had been confirmed?

No. Alistair wasn't like them. He moved his hand slowly and brushed the soft feathers on the raven's chest. That slight brush of comfort to an innocent creature told her everything she needed to know.

He was a good person. Somehow.

Her mother nudged her forward, and Thea gulped as she realized Balthazar and his children were staying to watch her cast her own summoning circle. As she passed Alistair, he whispered, "Good luck."

Those freckles were bright against his pale skin again. She wondered if he was nervous, and her hand moved of its own accord. Thea reached into her pocket and handed him a small sprig of her remaining lavender.

"You can chew it, and it eases the nerves." She shook her head, remembering that not everyone was like her. "Or smell it. I suppose most people might find it a little bitter."

As he walked by, he gave her a strange look, and the raven left the altar to perch upon his shoulder.

Now it was her turn. Thea stared down at the ancient stone and reminded herself that she'd practiced this for hours. Witches did this every month of every year, and so few of them had been turned away by the goddess. A small gift didn't matter. Her heart did.

She lifted her hand toward the right side of the altar, palm flat to the stone. "Spirits of fire, I call upon thee. Seek out the bravery in my heart and see the steadfast desire there to do right by this world." A small flame burst to life on the altar and remained there like she'd lit a candle.

Thea turned and flipped her hand, so her palm was to the sky. "Spirits of air, I ask thee to feel the adventurous heart that beats in my chest. Guide Ceridwen to know I seek a familiar who will stand beside me in all adventures now and to come." A small funnel of air swirled near the top of her hand.

Flicking her fingers over the top of the stone, she pressed her thumb and forefinger together. "Spirits of earth, I honor you. My feet remain solid on the ground and I wish you to help me walk a just path." The stone shuddered under the slight pressure of her magic.

And the last, the spot in the middle of the altar. Thea had saved water until the end of her spell because she had always felt connected to it. She curled her fingers as though beckoning something forth from the stone. "Spirits of water, I ask of you to give me a familiar. One worthy of my heart, my soul, and my magic." Water bubbled out of the pillar and fell onto the ground in loud plops.

Long moments passed. Only silence answered her spell. Thea's stomach twisted into a tight knot with each moment until she couldn't breathe.

One of the older boys behind her snickered, and her cheeks burned at the sound. Would she have to suffer such an injustice? In front of them?

But then she heard it. Everyone did. The loud croak startled her so much that all her magic disappeared, weak as it was. Thea looked down at her feet and saw a toad larger than a dinner plate staring up at her. He was a lovely mottled yellow color, with moss growing on his back and tiny fireflies floating above him.

"Oh," Thea whispered, trying her best not to scare him. "Are you here for me?"

It croaked, and that was the first moment she knew what love felt like for something outside of her family. Delighted, she hauled the toad into her arms and stood with him as though she had been given a human baby.

The toad let out another loud croak, likely at the men behind her, and Thea could not be happier. He was handsome. Rather girthy, but they'd work on that. And his back was soft with spongy moss that tickled the palm of her hand as she petted him.

Ceridwen hadn't forgotten her at all. Instead, the goddess had given her a gift of unimaginable wonder.

"Thank you," she whispered reverently to the altar, knowing Ceridwen listened. "This is more than I hoped for."

The man who had snickered behind her burst into laughter. "More than you hoped for? You realize that's a toad, right?"

She turned around with her new familiar in her arms. "Of course I do. He's quite handsome."

The two older brothers held onto each other as they laughed. Even Balthazar had a small smile on his face.

He covered that smile, wiping it clear of his expression before he replied, "A toad is a grotesque animal. But I suppose I expected nothing more from a daughter of Fenna."

All the men filed out of the clearing, but Alistair remained a few moments longer. He petted the soft feathers of his raven's chest, and it almost looked like he wanted to say something. Then he turned and disappeared into the forest with his family.

"Oh, Thea." Her mother wrapped an arm around her shoulders. "Toads have been witches' familiars for centuries. It is a good familiar. Don't let them ruin tonight."

"I won't."

And she didn't. She held her toad a little tighter and walked with her mother back to the boat. Her mind, however, remained on the young boy with bright green eyes and a hundred freckles she hadn't counted yet.

CHAPTER 4

Alistair followed his family through the woods to the clearing that led toward their home. His stomach rolled with the injustice he'd seen at the altar.

No one should endure the horrible things his brother and father had said. She had such a bright look in her eyes the moment she realized the toad was hers, and he'd watched that light die while his family made fun of her.

And it wasn't such a terrible creature. Toads were perhaps the most traditional familiar given to witches, and that very ancient history would serve her well as she honed her magic into a sharp edge. Of course, he had no idea what she could do. His father had made it very clear that he didn't think anyone in her bloodline had any power. In fact, Balthazar had practically attacked her mother from the onset.

Lysander still snickered, coughing every now and then into his hand.

The motion and noise caught their father's attention. Balthazar's wicked gaze turned toward his middle son, and Lysander stopped laughing. "What has you in such a good mood?"

His brother gulped. "I'm still surprised those witches were proud of a toad, Father. That's all."

With an arched brow that called his son's honesty into question, Balthazar let his gaze wander back to the clearing before them. "Keep your mind in the now, boy. Apparently, you have forgotten that there needs to be at least an ounce of decorum among Orbweaver men."

That saying made Alistair flinch. How many times had he heard Orbweaver men were supposed to be a certain way? His father wanted them to reflect upon society that they were terrifying creatures who would tear the world down to get what they wanted, but... Alistair wasn't like that.

His brothers might be. They had followed in their father's footsteps a little too willingly, and he supposed that was to be expected. Their powers also leaned toward darkness, just like his father. And though he had never seen them weave magic—the way Balthazar claimed they could—he knew they enjoyed hurting people. Hunting people.

Gulping, he trailed along behind them to the wall that loomed around Wildecliff. No one came into the city other than through the port. At least, that's what the officials claimed. Everyone who was anyone knew that there was a small crack in the wall on this side, which led to the altar should anyone need to seek guidance from the goddess.

Deities were unlikely to step foot into Wildecliff. The men who ruled their city said they never understood why, but Alistair knew better. The black magic within those walls would banish any magical creature who tried to enter or leave—even a goddess or god.

His father walked right up to the crack in the wall, then looked at his youngest son. Alistair was pinned beneath the sharp, angry gaze.

"You," his father snarled. "Keep that familiar out of the house. You know it goes in the barn with the rest of them."

Alistair had no intent on doing so. The raven on his shoulder had chosen him. Didn't his father understand how rare a circumstance that was for the forgotten son of a very powerful man?

He knew better than to say that to Balthazar Orbweaver. Instead, he nodded his head and dropped his chin down low. Better to tell his father he would do it and then ask for forgiveness later.

Apparently, he would not need to argue tonight. His father gave another nod to his boys and then they all clambered over the rubble, slithered between the heavy stones of the wall, and then out onto the street beyond. It was a forgotten street of Wildecliff, but it still looked like the rest of them.

Magic made the cobblestones sparkle as though someone regularly ran over them with a broom and a mop. The empty homes, for no one wanted to live this far out in the town, were made out of white marble with black windows stretching up four stories. The houses were just boxes, which Alistair had always thought was rather boring, but they were all the same and immaculately kept. Even the black tin roofs gleamed in the moonlight, and a single chimney poked out of each home in the exact same spot.

A carriage waited for them. The well-oiled mahogany exterior showed their wealth without making it too obvious for vagabonds and thieves, as his father worried about. However, Alistair had never heard of a single instance of robbery in Wildecliff. The inhabitants here were far too powerful, and no one could ever guess when the person within the carriage could set the entire thing on fire.

His father got inside, then his two brothers. Alistair looked up at the top of the carriage to see a terrifying creature looming over the edge. The beast had the head of a coyote, although its mouth had nearly split to its ears. It had the tail of a horse that lashed about, while the rest of it looked like a black cat.

Pooka.

Apparently, the faerie creature hadn't decided what it wanted to look like tonight and instead had gone with the macabre amalgamation of many.

Alistair hooked his raven's claws with one hand, then held the squawking creature up toward the pooka. "Take care of him for the ride, will you? There's plenty of milk in our area of town you can curdle. I think the maids would all be quite put out."

That horrible grin split even wider. But the pooka reached out with gentle claws, took the familiar from Alistair's grasp, and set the bird on its own shoulder. The raven let out another disgruntled squawk before patting its feet a couple of times on the pooka's back. Apparently, the familiar decided this was comfortable enough.

If he had his choice, Alistair would have stayed on the roof with them. Instead, he was forced to go inside with his horrible family.

For a few moments, it seemed like they might have a quiet ride back. Maybe none of his family had anything to say, and that meant he could focus more on thoughts about that young woman.

Instead, his family were the cruel beings that they had always been. And the ones he knew so well.

Balthazar was the first to speak. "You know, Lysander, I've heard that toads are frequently given to young witches who exemplify what it truly means to be a witch."

His brother's face paled, and Alistair knew they shared the same thought. Their father had just told him to stop talking about the girl, and now he brought it up again? This had to be some sort of trick. The punishment that would come afterward would be swift.

Until Cassius spoke up with more venom in his voice than Alistair had ever heard before, "The day that is the truth will be the day I swallow my own tongue. That girl had no power; even I could see that. Small gifts have no place in Wildecliff. The altar is on our side of the river, so I don't see why they had to come here in the first place."

Why did they have to torment the young woman this much? There was nothing wrong with a toad!

Balthazar snorted. "Just mark my words, Cassius. You'll have to deal with this long after I'm gone. The weak in Waterdown will never stop coming to our lands and never stop distracting our goddesses from their real work with pleas for familiars. They think it makes them more powerful to have one. But they know they are too weak to use the powers that familiars give them."

"That girl didn't deserve anything better than a toad," Cassius agreed. "But she should have had nothing at all."

Normally, Alistair would lean his head against the window of their carriage and ignore the acidic insults his family threw so easily. He'd tell himself that he was nothing like them. Words like that would never drip like poison from his tongue. He wouldn't let himself become them.

But, as he looked out the window, it had started to rain. And the color of the sky paled to a shade like her skin, clouds faintly tinged with blue. The water drops on the window seemed to reflect her expression when they had insulted something she was so excited about. And those drops glimmered like the tears that had gathered in her eyes.

The young woman hadn't snapped at his family. She hadn't argued with them like her mother or even tried to defend herself. She'd gathered up the little life that had meant something to her, held the toad against her heart, and walked away as though they had no control over her happiness.

"Thea," he whispered.

All the other men in the carriage stopped talking. Cassius glared at him, and his eyes turned that horrible shade of yellow. "What did you just say?"

Oh, he hadn't meant to say that out loud. He'd just been thinking about how pretty her dark eyes were and how brave she had been in the face of his family when he hadn't ever been brave around them at all. Maybe around his brothers, considering he had to fight with them on a regular basis. But she'd looked his father in the eye and hadn't shown an ounce of fear. He didn't know how to do that.

Or maybe he did.

"She said her name is Thea," he said, straightening his shoulders. "You don't have to be so hateful anymore. No one is ever going to see her again, so why are you still talking about her?"

Cassius looked like the thought of punching him was rolling around in his head, but it was their father who leaned forward to answer.

"Alistair," Balthazar said. His voice was a low simmer of poison bubbling in a cauldron. "We talk about those people, so we never forget who is more powerful. So we never forget that they are using our home to get what they want when they should stay on their side of the river."

"I don't see any reason why they cannot seek what they need outside of the walls." Alistair gulped but kept going forward. "We stay within the sacred walls and they are outside of them. Who cares what they do near the altar? It's not ours."

"All of this is ours, Alistair. Every rodent, insect, and all the fish that should be in our port alone." Balthazar waved a hand in the air and leaned back on his cushions. "You're too young to understand. You still have a few more years at the university to learn, and then perhaps you will come around to the right way of thinking."

"I don't believe there's any right way of—"

His father twitched his fingers, and webs wove themselves over Alistair's mouth. They were sharp and pointed, anchored to the sides of his cheeks where he felt warm blood well and drip down to his jaw. Touching the sticky webbing with his fingers, he frantically tried to pull it off, but he already knew he wouldn't be able to.

The magic that silenced him was old magic. Spider magic that his father had always wielded. His father was the Orbweaver incarnate. Webs were his power, and Alistair should be thankful he only wrapped his son's mouth and not the rest of his body.

Alistair remained silent for the rest of the ride home. His cheeks burned, and more blood welled so much that he had to cup his hands underneath his chin to catch all the droplets before it ruined his clothing.

His family continued to laugh. They kept insulting the young woman and her mother because they knew it had made him angry. For the remainder of the ride, Alistair had to sit in his own anger that they would be so cruel to someone who had done nothing to them.

Finally, the carriage rolled up to the front door of their manor. As one of the wealthiest families in Wildecliff, their exterior was permitted to differ from the rest of the white marble homes. His father had chosen black, fitting for their family colors. The wrought-iron fence outside depicted spiders and their webs all around the property, which led up to a black manor larger than life with three steeples on the roof.

His home looked like a gothic prison. And to Alistair, it was.

No one waited for him as the carriage stopped. His father and brothers stepped out and walked toward the house as though they had forgotten he existed. Perhaps they had. His father didn't even take the spell off Alistair's face.

He eased his aching body out of the carriage and suddenly felt like he was so much older. His cheeks hurt. Every part of his soul throbbed, knowing that his family had been so cruel to that young woman, and he hadn't been able to do anything to protect her honor.

Turning to the roof of the carriage, he looked for his familiar. He'd thought the pooka would have taken off by now. But the faerie creature still clutched the wood with its massive paws, and it looked down at him with pity in its eyes. Rain had soaked its fur into a matted, flat tangle all along its back and face. The familiar's talons were sunk deep into its shoulder, but it didn't seem to mind.

He would have reassured the pooka that he was all right. His father had done this before, and the pain had dulled a bit. The magic of the webs couldn't hurt him forever, after all. They had a salve to take care of the wounds or any scars they might leave behind. The last thing Balthazar needed was someone else sticking their nose into "family business."

The pooka lifted a long arm and sliced through the webbing that covered Alistair's mouth. It fell away in a sudden tangle of magic that sparked with flames before disappearing.

"Thank you," Alistair said.

Eyes overly large and watery with emotion, the pooka reached up to the raven and let it step onto its hand. Water sluiced off the familiar's wings as it shook hard, sending droplets flying. Its loud caw would have woken the neighbors if a crash of thunder hadn't boomed at the same moment.

The pooka handed the familiar over to him, dangling precariously off the roof.

"I can't leave you out here," Alistair muttered, placing his familiar on his shoulder. "Not either of you. This storm will freeze you to the bone."

He gathered the pooka up in his arms as well, though the creature weighed as much as a small child. Grunting, he had to keep using his thigh to nudge the pooka up higher because apparently, it had decided it quite liked being carried. It didn't help him in the slightest as he snuck into the house and brought both of the creatures down the long hall to his room.

By the time he closed the door behind him and deposited them both onto his bed, they shivered so hard they made the frame quake.

"Right," he muttered. "Let's get a fire going."

Though his father would prefer it if all the fireplaces in the house were unused, Alistair ignored that rule more often than not. He stayed in his room mostly because of the flames that crackled and warmed up the air.

It took him a bit to get the fire going since he was shaking quite badly himself, but he got it going. Then he grabbed two of his knitted hats on the way back to his bed and jammed them down on top of each creature's head. For good measure, he wrapped the pooka up in a blanket as well.

"Better?" he asked.

Both of them looked at him. Miserable and sodden. He knew how they felt, and unfortunately, there wasn't much more he could do for them.

Flopping onto the bed beside them, he stared up at the ceiling and linked his fingers over his belly. "I hope she's not upset about what they said. I wish I'd said something in the moment. I could have stopped them if I tried."

The lie sizzled over his head. He wouldn't have been able to stop them because his father would have done the same thing to him. Only he'd have to endure the pain in front of her. His cheeks still hurt from the sharp points of that spell.

His new familiar hopped over and stood on top of his thigh. It crowed for attention until he sat up on his elbows and asked, "What?"

The creature turned its head to the side, and he saw something in its eyes that made him pause.

"Could you..." He hesitated, then continued. "Could you get a letter to her, by any chance?"

The familiar nodded.

And suddenly, he felt hope bloom in his chest for the first time in a very long time.

CHAPTER 5

Living with a familiar was different. Thea had thought it would be similar to having a pet, but he wasn't that at all. The toad, who she had named Browning, had a mind of his own.

He wandered through their house like he was their king. Her sisters nearly stepped on him all the time, and she would wake up to their screeches that she had to close the door to her bedroom, or they would accidentally kill her familiar. But that was the thing. Thea always closed her bedroom door. She'd even tried locking it.

Somehow Browning always got out. She knew he wasn't tall enough to reach the doorknob, and she didn't think he had control over his hands so well that he could unlock it.

Her mother just shrugged and said familiars had a mind of their own. If Browning wanted to spend his days indoors, then her sisters would have to get used to it. But a week after she got him, Thea could already feel trouble brewing.

The last thing she needed was her sister's snapping at her poor familiar, who just enjoyed wandering around the house while it was quiet.

"Are you ready?" she asked her toad, who looked unhappy sitting on top of her bed.

Thea had made a little sling for him to sit in since he wasn't very good at keeping up with her long stride. The plaid tartan had once been her mother's, an only family heirloom that sat in a trunk until she'd wanted it. She had sewed it at the top so she could throw it over her head, then Browning could sit in the sling portion at her hip. She'd read somewhere that women used to carry children like this.

If it was sturdy enough for a baby, it was sturdy enough for her familiar. Although, he disagreed with her if she had to guess. The look on his face was enough to make her reconsider.

"Come on, now," she said, disappointed he'd try to worm his way out of the walk. "You know Marigold and Belladonna are angry with you. If we give them the house, then they might not be as angry with you tomorrow."

She scooped him up underneath his armpits and popped him into the sling. And though it took him a while of circling to find a comfortable spot, he did eventually lay on his back with a sigh. He looked a bit like a rather large baby in a hammock that was too small for him. Adorable. Even with the fuzzy moss that covered his body from his back to his belly.

"Not so bad after all, is it?" She arched her brow. "And to think, you were complaining about it so horribly."

Browning huffed an angry breath at her, then looked at the door as though he were telling her to get a move on. He didn't have to tell her twice.

Thea burst out of her room, shouting to her mother along the way, "Browning and I are going for a walk!"

"Where are you going?" her mother shouted back.

"Just to the old mound!" Thea caught herself on the door and grabbed a floppy sun hat that would keep her wild tangle of dark curls away from her face. "We'll be back before dinner!"

She didn't give her mother time to argue. She knew that Máthair hated that mound. There were bodies buried underneath it, the stories claimed. But Thea had never gotten an ill feeling anywhere near that place. Sure, it was on the edge of the forest where they were only supposed to enter during festivals. She never broke those rules. The forest was off limits unless there was something to celebrate or honor.

Toad swinging at her hip, she fled from the house with a speed that would have made an eagle proud. Thea pumped her arms at her sides, going faster and faster until her lungs ached in her chest and the wind had lashed her cheeks bright red. She hadn't felt so free in a while now.

Every hour of every day was supposed to be spent learning how to cast spells from her mother. She had a duty to be a good witch and that required practice. Of course, Thea understood that. But she was only sixteen once, and now that she had her familiar, there was so much out there that she hadn't discovered. Like what would happen if she ate grass?

Hair blowing in her face, she skidded to a stop in the middle of the path that led back toward Waterdown. Frantically, she picked up a blade of grass and held it up to the sunlight.

"What do you think, Browning?" She twirled the blade. "Should I try it? Maybe it'll surprise us, and I'll have some wonderful power that

I never could have guessed!"

The toad croaked loudly, and she swore it sounded like, "Or you'll get a stomach ache."

Blinking, she looked down at her familiar in shock. "Did you just talk?"

The strange sound he made was definitely not talking. But she heard him in her head. "No."

She frowned. "There you went again. You talked."

Browning struggled to sit up in his sling, then eventually gave up. Falling onto his back again, he then placed his webbed hands behind his head as though he were reclining in the fabric. "Ribbit."

"That was definitely the voice of a person trying to impersonate a toad." She dropped the blade of grass and moved to yank him out of the sling. Hands underneath his armpits, she swung him out before her, dangling his legs over the open air. "Can you actually speak, or am I the only one who can understand you?"

He croaked again, and this time she paid close attention to his mouth. He definitely wasn't talking. She could see that he had made the noise just like a regular toad.

And yet, she heard, "Sometimes talk."

Thea let out a startled sound that echoed so loudly that a few robins flew out of the surrounding fields. The green grass swayed in the wind, tangling her hair in front of her face. But all she saw was the giant toad in her grasp who could talk to her.

"So you really understand me," she whispered.

"Always."

She bit her lip. "So you're a real friend, then? I always thought familiars were... servants."

At the word, her toad wiggled until she lost her grip on him. One moment, Browning was in her arms, and the next, he had fallen onto the ground with a heavy "oof" sound and hopped away from her.

"Browning?"

"Not servant!" he shouted while croaking and disappearing into the waving fields beyond. "Go away!"

"Browning!"

Thea couldn't lose her familiar this quickly. The last thing she wanted was to lose a new friend only a week after finding him. And now that she knew he could talk? She wanted to talk to him all the time! What might he have to tell her about magic? Where had he come from? Had he ever met a goddess? Did he know Ceridwen personally?

She took off after the surprisingly quick toad. Those short legs should make it difficult for him to gather up any speed, and he wasn't exactly the lithest toad she'd ever seen. Browning had taken to her mother's cooking in the week he'd been with them, and it showed.

"Wait!" Thea's feet pounded on the ground. The tall stalks of grass and wheat slapped against her thighs, but the wind pushed her on. She was so close! All she had to do was find the perfect timing to leap onto his back, and just as she thought she might catch up with him....

Her foot caught in a rabbit hole. The fields always hid them well, and she should have remembered her mother's warning. Racing through a field of grass and wheat without looking at her feet was bound to end in injury.

The horrible snapping sound made her wince. But worse was the fire that spread up her leg from her ankle as though the myths of burning witches were true. She let out a little cry as she tumbled to the earth, hitting hard on her forearms and coming to complete stillness.

Breath ripped from her lungs, ragged and aching. She couldn't quite keep herself from panting through the pain that swelled around her ankle. This was her own fault. She knew better than to careen through the fields like a child when she wasn't anymore. What if someone had seen her?

Wincing, she sat up and then looked down at her leg. Not broken, or at least, it didn't have any bones poking through the skin. She'd gotten lucky.

Gently pulling her ankle out of the hole in the ground, Thea took her time. The rabbit had been thoroughly making its home, and a flare of guilt made tears prick her eyes. She'd ruined its home. Where would it live this winter?

Then she heard a horrible croaking sound next to her and saw Browning sitting beside her elbow.

"There you are," she muttered, pushing her stockings down so she could see how swollen her ankle was.

"Crying because hurt?" he said with multiple ribbits laced together.

"No, I'm sad because I hurt this poor rabbit's home." And maybe a little because she was in pain too, but she would not admit that. Only children cried when they got hurt.

Thea prodded at her already swollen ankle and winced. Even the slightest touch hurt. Now she would have to walk all the way back home, limping the entire time, and her mother would scold her until she turned bright red with embarrassment.

"My own fault," she muttered, wiggling her shoe off so she could try to move her toes. "I shouldn't have run after you."

Browning maneuvered himself within reach, and for a moment, she thought he would scold her too. But all he did was tilt his enormous head back, opened his maw of a mouth, and then sat there with his jaw wide for her to look all the way down his throat.

"What are you doing?" she asked.

He kept the same position but shuffled slightly closer to her.

"Browning, what?" But then she saw there was something in the back of his mouth. Something that glimmered in the light, as though it was... metal?

Did he want her to reach inside? What had he swallowed?

Her first thought was that he might have hurt himself as well. Perhaps he tripped at the same time as her and somehow jammed a forgotten piece of farm equipment inside himself. But then she reached into his mouth and pulled out a tiny bronze tin with little lily pads on the top.

"What's this?" She held it up for his inspection.

Browning moved his jaw a bit from side to side before he croaked, "Healing."

She could have found the right herbs for healing back at their house. They had septic weed growing in the garden for situations like this, but they didn't let it grow far because of how poisonous it was to cattle. She only had to make it home.

Turning the little jar over in her hand, she lifted the top and let the smell waft up to her nose. There was no herbal scent or even medicinal qualities to it. But as soon as the scent hit her, she knew the salve was full of magic.

"Where did you get this?" She dipped her finger into the clear balm and a numbing coolness spread through her hand.

"Familiar magic," Browning replied. His stomach bloated up with pride. "Ankle."

Who was she to argue with the magical salve that came out of a toad's mouth? Thea shook her head while slathering it onto the areas that hurt, musing at how strange her life had gotten in such a short amount of time. She'd known having a familiar would be odd, but she hadn't realized it would be.... well. This odd.

The cooling sensation that had numbed her hand spread through her ankle as well. Strangely enough, the glistening salve soaked quickly into her skin until there appeared to be nothing on her ankle. The swelling disappeared before her eyes too, which was enough magic on its own. Rotating her foot in a slow circle, she let out a choked laugh when there was no pain with the movement at all.

"Well," she breathed. "You're more useful than I gave you credit for."

Again, her toad puffed himself up so large that he looked more like a bullfrog than a cane toad.

She stood and picked him back up. "Into the sling with you, though. No more running, okay?"

Browning nodded and then lounged in the sling with his back legs sticking straight up. The toad was too comfortable with her hauling him around like this. She supposed he'd earned the luxury, though. Healing her had been helpful.

A crow screamed over her head. Normally she'd ignore the sound. There were crows everywhere, but that one sounded a little different from the others. When she glanced up, she noticed the thorns that trailed down the creature's spine. It circled underneath the clouds and landed on the packed dirt path in front of her.

"I remember you," she said.

What was the young man's familiar doing here? Alistair. She'd never forget his name. The way he'd lingered while she received her familiar and how his eyes had shown a tortured hatred for his family. It was strange, really, to be so interested in a young man she'd only met once.

But they shared the same birthday, so she told herself she was only interested because of that.

The beast on the ground wasn't a crow, she realized. The familiar was too large for that. A raven? It hopped closer to her and lifted one of its legs. Someone had tied a tiny piece of rolled-up paper to its leg with a black ribbon. The note was surely from Alistair, but for some reason, she didn't want to untie it.

What would it say? Was it more insults like his brothers had thrown at her?

She couldn't stand here all day wondering about it, she supposed. Thea marched over to the raven and untied the note on its leg. She gave it a quick pat on the head in thanks and then walked back to her toad while unraveling the paper.

His handwriting was impeccable, she mused. The looping swirls were so... pretty. She'd never thought handwriting could be pretty.

Thea,

I hope this letter finds you well and you don't think this is all too... awkward. I'm certain you never expected to hear from me again.

My conscience would not let me rest until I apologized for my family's behavior. They were cruel and heartless, and I wish I were in a better position to have defended you at that moment.

I suppose a note isn't a sufficient way to say I'm sorry, but I am. And I hope you can sense the sincerity in this letter in some small way.

~~Perhaps you would be interested in~~

You would do me a great honor if you would answer a question for me.

How is your familiar? I named mine Atlas. He's a rather stoic fellow, and it seemed to fit him. If you feel comfortable, you may write me back.

Alistair

She pressed the letter to her chest and tried to still the butterflies dancing in her belly. He'd felt badly enough to write to her? And to send his familiar to find her rather than send it through the mail?

That was silly, she told herself. Of course, he didn't know her address, so the familiar was the only option.

Still, it all felt rather secretive, and that was wonderfully romantic. She shouldn't think of it like that, but she did.

Thea looked at the raven still standing in the dirt and sighed. "Well, you'll need something to eat, I suppose. If you don't mind staying for me to write him a letter back?"

The raven clacked its beak at her and then imperiously looked down its nose. How it did that on the ground, she had no idea.

She picked it up and let the raven perch on her shoulder. "You fit right into his household, don't you?"

With another croak, the raven stopped looking at her.

"Yes, you do," she muttered, turning around and heading back home.

CHAPTER 6

His father always said that Sunspell Academy took in mediocre witches and turned them into legends.

Of course, Alistair didn't care to be a legend. He didn't plan to use his particular brand of magic that much, either. The fae were entertaining to see, yes, and he'd always enjoyed his interactions with them. But he was safely within the walls of Wildecliff. The moment they realized what he could do, his teachers would send him out into the fields and forests beyond.

Mischievous fae were nothing compared to the dangerous monsters that lived outside these walls. Nor did they compare to the gods and goddesses that could rip his head clean off his shoulders for saying the wrong thing. The other fae had warned him about them.

There were rules he didn't know. Traditions he had to follow that were different with every deity. If Alistair ever came upon one of them, he would need to tread carefully to keep his life.

Sighing, he watched as the butlers pulled his and his brothers' things out of the carriage. This was Cassius's extra year. He had agreed to come back after his last year to teach some of the students and work with a professor who got along with him. Lysander was in his final year of senior cycle, and of course, Alistair still had a few more.

They all arrived together, though, much to his elder brother's embarrassment. Already, they both stood to the side so no one would see who they'd arrived with. Starting now, they were unlikely to speak to Alistair unless forced.

None of them wanted anyone at school to know they were related. Even Alistair agreed with that. The last thing he wanted was for the bullies in his own year to think he could stick up for himself in a fight when he would most certainly end up with a broken jaw.

"Thank you," he mumbled to the butler, who placed his trunk on the ground in front of the school.

"Don't thank the help," Cassius snarled as he waved a hand to levitate his own trunk. "People will think you're weak."

Good-hearted people would think he cared about the well-being of his staff, but sure. Weak. Cassius could believe that's what kindness made him. They were at school, and now he didn't have to pretend to care about his brother's opinions.

Shaking his head, he tried to remember the summoning spell that would lift his own trunk. He cast the spell, but nothing happened.

"Levō," he said again. And still, the trunk remained right where it was. Heavy as always.

One of the oldest professors in the school walked up to him and stood behind him. The old man had a neatly trimmed white beard and eyes like black chips in his head. The hair atop his head was black other than two pale wings at the temples, and his cruelty showed through in his horrible expression.

"Professor Burns," Alistair said with a nod.

"Again."

All the other students had their trunks floating already. Only the first years weren't required to float their own trunks, and they watched everyone walk by them with awe. Alistair had been that student. He'd done this already and had learned how to channel his magic into something this simple. He knew how to manipulate his power into a spell that would work for him.

Every good witch did. He took another deep breath and then flicked his fingers at the trunk as though the magic didn't bother him at all. "Levō."

Again. Nothing. The trunk didn't even rattle.

Professor Burns sighed and pressed his fingers to the sudden wrinkles between his eyes. "Your father could do this spell in his first year. You know that, don't you?"

"I've heard all about my father's magical talents."

"Then how have you proven to be such a failure in your father's shadow?" Professor Burns shook his head and turned toward the looming school behind them. "You're not allowed inside until you levitate that trunk, Mr. Orbweaver. You can stay out all night for all I care."

The other students walked past him until Alistair stood alone. Even the second years gave him a look as though they were shocked he couldn't do this on his own. He was frustrated, too. Alistair had been casting this spell for ages, and nothing made any sense of why he couldn't do it now.

Angry now, he muttered "Levō," over and over again. He said it so many times that his face burned with embarrassment, and he never cared what others thought.

His familiar shrieked above his head, and Alistair blew out a breath toward the hair that had flopped in front of his face. He looked up at Atlas wheeling in a circle like a bird of prey.

"You don't have to tell me when you find carrion," he called out. "Eat what you want!"

Apparently, some people limited what their familiars could eat. At least, that's what Cassius had told him. His eldest brother had no problem advising him on how to take care of his familiar in the weeks he'd had the beast.

But, as he looked back toward his trunk, he suddenly realized a tiny boggart sat on top of it. Boggarts weren't naturally mean beasts, but they were more apt to bite rather than help. At one point in their lives, they were brownies—helpful household spirits who would clean and put things in order during the night. If they were underappreciated or not given gifts, they would grow angry and turn into boggarts.

The little one on top of his case had seen a fight recently. Its eyes were blackened and a small cut bloomed bright red on its shoulder. The rodent-like creature had arms longer than its body, with short little legs that lacked any hair. In fact, its entire body was hairless, rare for their species. But the pointed features and overly large ears were of the boggart kind.

"Can I help you?" Alistair asked.

Frowning at him, it pointed to the trees on the right side of the Academy. As if it wanted him to go over there and leave his trunk alone.

Peering around them, he hissed, "Were you stopping my spell from working?"

The boggart shrugged, then jabbed its fingers toward the trees. As though he had something important to see and he was stalling.

Alistair pointed at it with his best angry expression. "We're not finished with this. You and your kind cannot get involved in my schooling. Do you know what that might do to me?"

Saying the words made him feel better, but he knew he couldn't argue with the faeries to get what he wanted. The fae had minds of their own. He was a vessel for them to speak through, sometimes. Other times, they just enjoyed pranking someone who would know it was them.

Frustrating. It was all so frustrating.

But he knew the little boggart would hold his luggage captive until he did what it wanted him to do. Alistair looked behind him to make sure that Professor Burns wasn't looking anymore. And he was pleased to find that no one was outside with him at all. They'd left him out here to his own devices.

Though, there was likely someone inside who had been told not to let him in if he wasn't carrying his trunk. He'd figure that out when the time came.

Alistair sighed, dropped his bag beside the boggart, and started off in the direction the little beast had pointed. Clearly, there was something he had to see, and if he didn't go over to look, then he'd be stuck out here until it rained.

The outside of Sunspell Academy was covered with trees. Even though they weren't trees that anyone would see in a forest. The Headmistress enjoyed color when she looked out of her office window, and color meant lots and lots of cherry blossoms. Someone enchanted the trees to bloom year-round, even when the snow came during winter. The pink petals blanketed the ground that led up to the precipice, looking out over Wildecliff.

Hence Wildecliff, he supposed. Although, he wasn't very familiar with the lore surrounding the name of his town.

Sighing, he turned around in a circle in the cherry blossom forest. "All right," he called out. "What did you want me to see?"

He spun in a slow circle, peering up into the branches as though another boggart would be there. But then he heard the soft sound of a snort behind him and the pawing of hooves at the ground.

"Oh, no," he muttered, quite unsure of what he was about to find behind him.

Alistair held his breath until he found the strange creature waiting for him in the cherry trees. A fiadh ruadh stood between the branches of a trunk that had split in half. The red stag's antlers spread out impressively at the top of his head, at least thirty points and a clear sign this creature was old. Very old. Moss hung from each antler, and cherry blossoms stuck to the emerald trails. As he watched, a few other faerie creatures he didn't recognize revealed themselves. They'd been hidden in the moss and among the flowers. But they unfurled their dragonfly wings that glittered in the dying sunlight, and he knew they were as special as the beast they rode.

He bowed low to the ancient creature of the forest. Fiadh ruadh could sometimes be heard over the wall. Their roars were like thunder in the mating season, and he used to be terrified of them as a child. Even now, he feared the beast that looked at him with black eyes.

"It's an honor," he said, eyes still on the ground. "I did not know you had come so far from the sacred lands."

He heard its voice in his head as though someone had spoken into his ear. "Protect my people. It is your duty, son of the web."

His people? Alistair didn't know what the faerie beast spoke of. He'd been able to see the faerie creatures his entire life, but that didn't mean he knew how to protect them. And why would he need to? They were more powerful than him.

Alistair looked up and met the creature's intimidating gaze. "Protect them from who?"

Ravens flew overhead, screaming up into the sky in a circle of dark feathers and ill omens. He feared what that meant, even as he stared into the abyss of the fiadh ruadh's eyes. What monstrous being would attack the fae?

An icy chill danced down his spine, and he immediately straightened. Alistair spun to look up at the windows of Sunspell Academy, right into the windows of the Headmistress, who so enjoyed looking out over this field of pink flowers. The curtains in the metal framed windows shifted as though a breeze had touched them.

Had she been watching?

She couldn't have been looking out the windows. The Headmistress had a lot of things to do today, especially with all the students arriving at her doorstep and needing to be greeted and then settled into their rooms. Besides, she couldn't have seen him out here on his own. He was too far away from her window.

Still, the icy feeling didn't go away. His teeth chattered, and he didn't know if that was with cold or fear. Swallowing hard, he said,

"I'll do my best to look after them, but I'm only one person."

He turned to find that the fiadh ruadh had disappeared. Though he could still see the scrapings on the ground where the creature had dug into the earth, leaving deep furrows with its hooves.

It was time to go inside, lest someone else comes looking for him who was worse than Professor Burns. But the closer he got to the front of the school, the worse he felt. Alistair's stomach twisted into a knot. His heart beat so quickly that he could feel it skipping beats. And his palms grew so sweaty he was afraid to touch anything in case he left a wet handprint behind.

He needed to get control of himself, or they would notice. Everyone noticed weakness in this place.

A horrible caw echoed overhead, and then Atlas soared into his line of sight. Without thinking, Alistair held out his arm for his familiar to land. "There you are," he muttered as he approached his luggage. "I was looking for you."

The raven climbed up his arm to his shoulder and then held out his leg. A single note was attached with a pretty green ribbon.

Just like that, some of his nerves eased. He might not be able to save all the faeries as the fiadh ruadh wanted him to, but, at the very least, someone in this ridiculous life wanted to see him. Wanted to talk with him. And she had responded to his letter.

He hadn't even dreamed she would do so. Alistair had no right to ask her to give him any time of day, and yet here she was. Writing him back after his family had been so cruel to her.

Now his stomach twisted for another reason.

He surveyed his trunk, making sure the boggart had left before he tried the spell one more time. "Levō."

This time, the trunk lifted with no issues. And though he felt a small amount of his power drain, that didn't matter much. He'd lifted the trunk. He'd done what they thought he couldn't do, and it was all because a single boggart had wanted to talk to him.

The entrance to the Academy loomed over his head. The twin doors were carved with all the most impressive students that had come out of this school throughout the centuries. His father was on there. He'd seen the web tangled around the figure of his father so many times now, and it never failed to remind him that Balthazar was always watching. Even in the walls of this school.

"Ah, you finally figured it out." The young woman at the front of the door was one of the few who had been accepted to work for the school right after her graduation. Her long black hair was pin straight, and she wore it in a long braid to her waist. "Took you long enough, Orbweaver. I thought I'd miss dinner waiting for you to do simple magic."

"Figured it out," he replied, his eyes darting through the shadows for his brothers. They usually liked to wait for him at times like these.

She sniffed and tilted her nose up into the air. "Dormitories, Orbweaver. Go."

She said his last name like he didn't deserve to be called that, and he supposed compared to all the others, he might not. They'd all done a lot more impressive things, while he just lied and said he didn't have any special ability at all.

Further into the Academy, he went with a slight nod at the young woman who had guarded the door. Four winding staircases led in opposite directions. One for classes, another for the food hall, one for dormitories, and another for staff. He'd been here so many times; he knew this entire place like the back of his hand. He could probably walk through the halls blindfolded and never hit a single statue or scuff the mahogany floors.

His trunk glided along beside him as he wandered up the stairs toward the rooms. At least this year, he got a room to himself. Only the students in senior cycle were allowed that, and Alistair had always had the worst bunk, usually because he was the last one to get to his room.

Finally finding a little privacy, he walked into the room marked with his name. The bright blue tapestries that hung around the bed were woven with the gold sun symbol of the school. A single window showed the grounds out beyond, and he had a pretty good view of the city itself.

He let the spell go, and the trunk hit the ground with a dull thud.

"Not bad, don't you think Atlas?" Someone had set up a small stand, likely having been told he had a bird for a familiar, so he deposited Atlas on top.

Giving his familiar a light chest rub, he bent to work and gathered the letter off his familiar's leg.

The goosebumps that rose on his arms as he unraveled the ribbon were from the chilly air in the school, he told himself. Not because he was ridiculously excited to see what she had to say. Still, he wrapped the green ribbon around his finger before he rolled the small piece of paper open.

Her handwriting was horrible, he realized. He could barely read the words this chicken scratch made.

ALISTAIR,

I'LL ADMIT, I WASN'T EXPECTING TO GET A LETTER FROM YOU. I'M SURPRISED YOU FOUND ME! YOUR BIRD MUST BE A VERY INTELLIGENT FAMILIAR INDEED.

YOU DON'T HAVE TO APOLOGIZE FOR YOUR FAMILY. I KNOW YOU AREN'T THEM, AND THEY AREN'T YOU. SO WHY WOULD I ENDEAVOR TO PUNISH YOU FOR THEIR MISDOINGS? CONSIDER ALL FORGIVEN, ALTHOUGH THERE'S NOTHING TO FORGIVE YOU FOR. YOU WERE QUITE POLITE.

THANK YOU FOR ASKING ABOUT MY FAMILIAR. I'VE NAMED HIM BROWNING, AS MANY WITCHES DID WHEN TOADS FIRST BECAME OUR FAMILIARS. HE'S VERY HANDSOME AND GETTING ROUNDER EVERY DAY. PERHAPS SOMEDAY YOU'LL MEET HIM.

I'M NOT CERTAIN THAT HE'D MAKE IT TO WHEREVER YOU ARE, THOUGH. HE'S QUITE AVERSE TO PHYSICAL LABOR.

WHERE ARE YOU, ANYWAY? I ASSUME WILDECLIFF, BUT I DON'T KNOW MUCH ELSE ABOUT YOUR CITY.

EXCITEDLY WAITING FOR YOUR NEXT LETTER,

THEA

He pressed the letter against his chest and fell back onto the bed. A single letter shouldn't excite him quite so much, and yet... goodness. She'd written him back even when he didn't deserve it.

Somehow, that made being in this horrible place a little easier.

CHAPTER 7

H ave you heard parents in Wildecliff pay to have their children taught magic?" Belladonna asked. She tugged on her white gardening gloves and then looked them over one last time for any lingering dirt on the pristine fabric. "I think that's absurd."

Marigold stood next to her, tying her apron around her yellow dress so she didn't ruin yet another gown their mother had made for her. "Why would they send them away? Isn't their magic passed down through the families like ours?"

"One would assume."

"Then wouldn't learning from the people practicing the same magic give them better results?" Marigold finished her outfit by placing a single yellow daisy behind her ear. "Since they're all so obsessed with being powerful."

Thea reached into her pocket and thumbed the most recent

letter that Alistair had sent her. He'd made it very clear that what her sisters said was true. Sunspell Academy stood on the edge of a cliff that overlooked the town. It was a monolith and a terrifying place where their professors wore smiles that never reached their eyes, and the students were all freezing in their beds every night.

She never wanted to go there. All her letters with him had only reminded her how lucky she was to learn magic in the old way. The best way, if someone were to ask her opinion on the matter.

"Are you ready?" Belladonna asked, her vivid green eyes catching upon Thea. "You're the one who's watching today, you know."

"I know." Thea shrugged. She'd never be able to make flowers or plants grow, and that's all what today was about.

Once they were grown, she could trial her own magical powers. Her small gift. One that she was slowly learning how to be proud of.

Thea looked down at the gloves in her hand and sighed. She wouldn't need them. She wouldn't be sinking her hands into the earth to make anything grow, and she wouldn't try to convince anyone other than herself to use her powers.

Tapping the gloves against her side, she decided it would be better to put them in her crossbody sling. "Browning," she said. "Would you look after these for me?"

Her toad reached for them with his webbed fingers and hugged the gloves to his chest with a decidedly impressive look on his face. She'd even suggest that he appeared rather fierce, if it was possible for a toad.

"I'm ready to watch," Thea said. Then followed her sisters out the door of their home.

The house unfurled the stairs for them and then let out a little rumble as it reordered some of the rooms. Thea wasn't sure why it had started doing that, unless it wanted to confuse anyone who walked into their house looking for information about the family. But there was no reason to do that, was there? Her mother hadn't gotten involved in any of the local politics, and she was well known for being a kind woman willing to help any who needed it.

Still, her stomach twisted into a knot every time the house made that noise. It made her think the house was preparing for something she didn't know about.

Their mother waited for them in the gardens. Máthair's wild hair was unbound, and the loose curls blew in the wind around her. Her back was to her daughters, arms raised as she spoke to the elements. Thea could already see a cloud in the distance, ready to rain upon the earth that her sisters stirred up and prepared for harvest.

There was a lot of work to do today. The village had been unfortunately invaded by weedles, which had destroyed many of their crops for the year. Not theirs, though. Never her family's.

Her mother turned, and it was like the sun had come out on a stormy day. The bright smile on her face illuminated the world. The way magic coiled around her fingers in green tendrils of vines reminded her daughters how powerful she was.

Thea took a deep breath and let it out with a long sigh. She'd always been so fascinated by her mother. This was the powerful witch she'd always hoped to be someday. And even if her powers would never compare to her mother's exceptional abilities, she hoped she'd get a fraction of it.

"Daughters!" Máthair called out, opening her arms wide. "I hope you're ready to learn magic today!"

Belladonna and Marigold walked through the garden, each of them ready to cast spells that would feed the entire village for the winter. Thea sat down nearby on a small hill where she wouldn't get in the way.

Just watching them was enough, she told herself. She should be happy with the chance to watch.

At least, that was until another body hit the ground beside her. The young woman lay on her stomach, chestnut-colored hair brightly illuminating her face as she chewed on a small strand of grass. The sun had turned the ends of her curls bright orange this year, Thea noticed.

"What are you doing here?" she asked, hoping her mother didn't notice that they had an unwelcome visitor. "You know mother doesn't like it when people watch."

The young woman looked up at her, and all the freckles dotting her cheeks had spread even further until there were hundreds across her cheeks. "So? If she doesn't want me here, she can kick me out. I just wanted to fill you in on the newest and brightest love interest in my life. I know how you so enjoy listening to all my wild and crazy tales."

"Clodagh," she hissed. "I'm supposed to be paying attention."

"To what?" Clodagh waved a hand at her family. "You're never going to do what they're doing. Not unless you go to Wildecliff and get their kind of magical instruction, which I don't think any of us want."

Did Clodagh... Did she know about the letters Thea had been sending? Was that why she brought up Wildecliff?

Shifting on the grass, Thea focused all her attention on her lifelong friend. "Why would you mention Wildecliff?"

"Because everyone knows they teach them to do more than their small gift."

No one knew that. Thea had only heard it from Alistair, which made her even more suspicious that her friend had been sneaking into her room and reading the letters. And maybe that was why the house had started rearranging itself because this little freckled imp was getting into Thea's things!

"If you've been sneaking again—" she started, only to be interrupted when Clodagh lifted her hand.

"I know, I know. I've suddenly become so much more knowledgeable in a short amount of time. And if only you would listen, then you would understand why. There's a lovely young lady in Wildecliff I met the other day while my Da and I were delivering goods across the river. She's got eyes like the sky and skin so smooth you'd think it was porcelain." Clodagh touched a couple of fingers to her freckled cheeks before sighing. "My skin will never look like that."

"Maybe if you became a cave person." Thank all the gods and goddesses she'd been wrong. Thea would have had to slap Clodagh for going through her things, and she didn't want to do that. "What's all this about a lovely lady?"

"I thought you'd never ask." Clodagh rolled onto her back and spread her fingers up to the sky. "We've been meeting in the river almost every night this week! You know how Da doesn't mind if I take the boat at night."

That wasn't true at all. Clodagh's father had tanned her hide the last time he'd found out she'd stolen his boat. Thea would never forget the bruises on Clodagh's back that had looked so horrible and purple for weeks.

But Clodagh had never feared her father. She would rather go against everything he wanted her to be rather than follow any of his words to the letter. And that was how their relationship went, apparently.

"All right," Thea muttered. "So you've met another person to fill your empty head with thoughts. I thought you were interested in Callum, down the way. The baker's boy, wasn't it?"

"Tsk." Clodagh hissed out a long breath as though Thea had suggested she be interested in a goat. "He smelled of brine all the time. He's a baker's boy! Shouldn't he smell rather sweet? The boy was disgusting, and I had forgotten that I sometimes find boys to be all too sticky for my tastes. Women, however, now those are the ones who smell like flowers and sweetgrass."

Not true at all. Thea had smelled herself after a hard day in the gardens, and she reeked. She could clear a crowd with that smell; she was quite certain of it.

But her friend was in another one of her trances and found herself, yet again, in love with another person who likely wouldn't ever fall in love with her. Clodagh liked the impossible partners, which meant people who didn't give her a second thought unless she stood right in front of them.

"So, what are you going to do about this one?" Thea asked. She glanced over at her mother and sisters, but they were so busy weaving magic out of thin air that they didn't even look at her. Thea flopped onto her back beside her friend, resting her head on Clodagh's stomach.

"Well, to start, she says she loves flowers. Which is why I'm here. And second, I thought maybe I'd see if Marigold could make a new flower based on her name."

"Well, that's quite romantic for you, actually." Thea was impressed. This young woman had really wiggled her way into Clodagh's thoughts. "What's her name?"

"Odharnait," Clodagh breathed as though she were casting a spell.

Right, well, that didn't sound like a flower. And she already knew that Marigold would want a pretty name for a brand new species—

especially since it might grow out of control and take over yet another field by the house. Flowers were tricky and aggressive little buggers.

"Maybe we should just pick her a pretty bouquet," Thea replied. "Marigold is busy, after all. And they'll be busy for quite some time."

"Oh, right. The weedles." Clodagh sat up onto her elbows, looking down at Thea's head on her belly. "So why are you out here if this is going to take them all day?"

"I watch."

"And learn what?"

Patience?

Kindness?

Temperance?

She didn't know what the point of watching was, other than her mother knew that Thea might get into trouble if she wasn't within her eyesight. If she wasn't watching her family, then her mother had no idea where she was. And that would make Máthair worry, and worry for a witch who controlled the weather could sink the entire town into a horrible thunderstorm.

Speaking of... Thea lifted her head and glanced back at her family. And there were Máthair's eyes watching her, as she had known her mother eventually would. But instead of a scolding expression, her mother merely smiled and lifted her chin.

"Go," she said without having to say a single word.

Thea mouthed the words, "Thank you," before sitting up and reaching for Clodagh's hands. "Come on, I know where there is a splendid patch of wildflowers that your new lady will love."

Clodagh clapped their hands together, and away they raced. Away from the horrible feeling of never being enough for her family, even though she knew they didn't agree with those thoughts. They loved her.

They would never be disappointed in her. It was just... well. Sometimes she was a little disappointed in herself.

When they reached the meadow of wildflowers, she skidded to a halt and inhaled the salty scent of the sea. The wildflowers grew best next to the river, which was really a small channel that led out to the ocean. Seagulls flew over their heads, and their screeching calls filled her ears with a terrible kind of music. But the sun sparkled on the faint waves in the river, and she could see the other side from where they stood. Wildecliff.

It was so far away, she knew. It had taken her and her mother quite a while to paddle over to where she had gotten her familiar.

Where she had met Alistair.

Clodagh pressed her hands to her mouth. "Wow, you weren't kidding, Thea. This place is amazing."

Hundreds of wildflowers dotted the landscape all around them. Every color imaginable was here, and they would have to be very particular about what they plucked from the ground. A wildflower bouquet took time and talent to create. Thankfully, those were both things that Thea had in abundance.

"What message do you want to send her?" she asked.

"What?"

"Bouquets have meaning. All flowers do." Thea tucked a strand of her dark waves behind her ear, then crossed her arms over her chest in thought. "Blush roses, I think. That means you're looking for a blossoming romance."

"Well, I am." Clodagh bent down and plucked a handful of roses, hissing as their thorns cut into her palms. "All right, what's next?"

"Umm... Cornflower?"

Clodagh made a face. "They're boring."

"They mean you have hope for love." Thea snickered as Clodagh dashed to collect them. "Don't forget Sweet William!"

"Whatever for?" her friend called out.

"Gallantry, and to show you'll be respectful. Oh! Honeysuckle too. Honeysuckle for devotion and to say you have eyes only for her." It took the two of them quite a while to find the last one, but then they were finished. Thea tied a bright red ribbon around the bundle and nodded. "That'll do."

"Do you think she'll like it?"

"I know she will." Thea wrapped an arm around her best friend and hugged her close. "Come on, let's head back and get those in water or they're wilt."

But then, at the worst moment, she might add, a cawing noise echoed overhead. Thea looked up to see Atlas circling above them. The raven was clearly agitated that there was another person with her and that she had her arm around said person.

"Is that a familiar?" Clodagh asked.

"Um..." She didn't know how to answer that. Especially not when Atlas landed in front of them and held out his leg with a disapproving look.

"Is that..." Clodagh pulled away from Thea's arm. "Is that a letter? Have you been writing to someone through their familiar?"

"Um, no." Thea lunged for Atlas and pulled the letter off his leg before her friend could get it. Then she sent him off into the air without an answering letter. "Off you go. Sorry!"

The squawk Atlas let out before flying off clearly stated he didn't like this plan and didn't appreciate how forcefully she'd thrown him into the air. But Clodagh would never let her down if she didn't hide the letter...

That was snatched out of her hand the moment there was an opportunity to do so.

"Give that back!" Thea shouted, sprinting after her friend, who had already ripped the black ribbon off.

"Thea," Clodagh shouted back, reading the letter as she ran wildly through the field. "It has been too long since I've last heard from you. How strange it feels to miss such awful handwriting!"

The shriek that followed those words made Thea's cheeks burn. He wasn't exactly the most romantic of men, but he'd been writing to her for weeks now! And how nice was it that someone cared enough to write to her at all?

"Clodagh!"

"You said you're teaching Browning a few tricks. I'd love to hear more about that process," Clodagh spun around, so she was running backward. "Are you talking to a boy, Miss Thea? Regularly?"

That was enough. Thea tackled her friend into the dirt and wrenched the letter out of her hand. "Stop it!"

"What? Why! I just want to know! I tell you all about my failed love stories."

Because this was a secret. Because it was hers and no one else's and because she didn't want anyone to know about Alistair just yet. She'd never had something that was just her own and didn't have to be shared with everyone in her family. Even Browning sometimes slept in Marigold's room.

But Alistair was hers. And hers alone.

Or at least, that's what it felt like.

She sat with the crumpled letter in her lap. How had the page gotten so mangled already? She wanted to bind them all into a journal someday, but now it was so wrinkly... Sighing, she tried smoothing the edges out with her thumb. "Because I don't... He's a friend."

"A friend, huh?" Clodagh sat up, and a streak of dirt had smeared her right cheek. "Then why are you writing him back so much?"

"He's a friend." She repeated, but her fingers lingered on the crumpled edges as though they would never smooth out again.

And she wanted them smooth because... because...

Well, she guessed it was because the letters made her feel special. As impossible as that was.

CHAPTER 8

Weeks came and went after the letter he'd written to her. Alistair wondered if he'd gone too far in mentioning that her letters had gotten him through some tougher parts of school.

He hadn't meant it as though she were required to write him letters or even to continue talking to him. In fact, he'd thought it was honest and sweet of him to say such things. Instead, he realized that maybe he had pushed her a little too far.

Sighing, he juggled all the books piled high in his arms from the library. He'd collected all the books required for his classes at the same time. He should have gotten something to carry them with, and yet... here he was. Struggling to even see over the wall of books that obscured his vision.

"Well, well, well," the voice was all too familiar. Cassius hadn't said a word to him at school so far this semester, but Alistair had known he wouldn't be so lucky as to avoid his brother's long reach. "This is how the Orbweaver name is being upheld in this school? Embarrassing."

Lysander snickered, not far from the oldest as always. "And here I thought we were required to at least look the part. Do you see how dirty his nails are, Cassius?"

Of course, his nails were dirty. Alistair had taken a class on herbs and medicine. As such, he was required to have his hands sunk deep into the ground, pulling out weeds while the rest of the class sat around trying to figure out a spell that would do the work for them.

He'd never been afraid to get his hands dirty. Especially since the faeries teased him mercilessly if he didn't use his hands. That was part of what he had to do as their guardian. Or at least, that's what they said.

He wasn't sure how much of a guardian he was. He was only seventeen, after all.

"I just got all the books for my classes," he muttered, trying to walk around his brothers. "I need them to study. "

Cassius moved in beside him, and Lysander flanked the other side. He was bracketed by his brothers, his own personal escort from hell now that they were insistent on following him back to his room.

"Lysander," Cassius asked. "How much studying did you do in his year?"

"Not much. It all came rather naturally, if I remember right."

"That's what I thought." His brother leaned closer and whispered, "Orbweavers don't have to practice, whelp. The fact that you're studying at all to learn the most basic of magic is an absolute disgrace."

Alistair gritted his teeth and told himself to keep moving. He didn't have to listen. He didn't have to let their words sink into his skin or remind him how much of an embarrassment he was to his family.

There was a young woman out there who considered herself his friend. Or at least, he thought she did. Thea had taken the time to write to him, and even though that must have been a hard thing for her to do, considering his family, she'd still thought he was worth the risk.

All those details had to crowd out what his brothers were saying. He couldn't let them get underneath his skin, or he'd never finish out his senior cycle, and then he would be stuck in this damned school for all eternity.

The thought of Thea gave him more courage than he should have had. Alistair straightened his shoulders and looked Cassius straight in the eyes. "At least I won't have to stay another year after graduation. The rumors going around the Academy are that you're here because you didn't learn everything you had to do, and now you're just pretending to be a professor's assistant."

The moment he said the words, he knew how much of a mistake that was. He should never have threatened Cassius, let alone ever suggested that people were talking about him. Cassius wanted, no needed, control over his image. His older brother was a younger version of their father, and he knew what Balthazar would do to anyone who suggested what Alistair just suggested.

Alistair didn't have time to brace himself before the books in his arms went flying. They cascaded in a wave of leather, scattering pages down the hall to the stairs where they floated down like someone had laid out a carpet of white and black. The books fell all the way to the first floor that would lead him back to the library.

And here he was, the fool who now had to pick them all up and put the books back together, or the professors would leave scars on his knuckles.

Cassius slammed his hands into Alistair's shoulders, and he careened back. He lost his footing, and the only thing that saved him from falling to the first floor was the flimsy railing he hit. Alistair wrapped his fingers around it and held on for dear life. If the old wood gave, then he'd hit the ground, and he could only imagine the pain would be unbearable.

His siblings wouldn't help him. They wouldn't even shout for anyone to gather up the splattered remains of their brother. They'd just leave him there until someone found him, writhing in pain and likely broken in many places.

Both of his brothers converged on him, stealing all the air from his lungs as they pushed him to focus on them and them alone.

Cassius spat, "Don't embarrass the family name anymore, whelp, or I'll tell father how poorly you're doing here. It sure would be a shame to be the only Orbweaver to not finish his schooling. Don't you think?"

He didn't agree, actually. Not having to finish out his years here in the Academy would give him much more of an opportunity to use his powers in a better way. The fae had already made it very clear they had a plan for him. Their illustrious gods and goddesses had already mapped his future out. Who was he to change that?

Of course, his brothers didn't know anything about the fae. They never would. If they found out what his powers were, they would have him summoning all manner of dark beings so that they could use them to their own advantage. It was a nasty path that he knew would only end poorly.

Lysander gave him one more shove with a raised eyebrow that dared him to say anything about it. And though the worn wood behind him creaked dangerously, it held his weight.

His brothers disappeared down the hall, likely to find some other younger students to torment. Which left Alistair alone.

Swallowing hard, he stared into the eyes of the portrait of the fourteenth Headmaster. The man had eyebrows like wings, and his yellow eyes were a little too all-knowing. He stared into Alistair's soul as though saying he was disappointed in Alistair as well.

"Everyone is," he muttered, bending down to gather up the pages. "Everyone and their mother, it seems."

A tiny faerie hand reached for one of the pages and shoved it closer to him. He was so surprised by the size of the hand that it made him pause before he looked at the little creature. The brownie was quite possibly the most adorable one he'd ever seen before. She wore a tiny daisy as a cap, and her bright yellow dress was made from more petals than what he thought might be a rose. Her pointed face was nearly perfect as well, though the crow's feet at her eyes some might consider a flaw. He thought they were beautiful.

"Are you the only brownie taking care of the Academy?" he asked. She shook her head.

So there were many here. He had always thought a building this large with this many children must have brownies. The entire building was far too clean, and besides, none of the professors or even the Headmistress were the type to waste good magic on a cleaning spell.

"Thank you for all your hard work," he said while piling up all the loose papers near him. "The Academy is spotless all the time. I assume there had to be some like you in this building."

The brownie's face blossomed with a bright, radiant smile. He'd known the compliment was likely something she hadn't heard before, and it broke his heart to see that no one had given her or her people any of the recognition they deserved. Brownies weren't around forever, after all. Look at the boggart who caused so much trouble with his trunk.

The little faerie turned around and lifted her arms over her head. All the papers that had cascaded down the stairs came rushing back up and then neatly piled themselves beside his legs. Each pile had already been ordered by the title of the book, and he thought perhaps they were also in order by the page as well.

"Wow," he whispered, then stacked them all together. "I have to bring these to my room. Thank you so much for the help. I don't think you know how horrible this year has been already. I mean—"

All the books and pages floated out of his arms and into the air. The brownie gave him another bright smile, then started down the hall while waving a hand over her head for him to follow her. Apparently, the brownie wasn't finished with him yet.

Swallowing hard, he looked through the hallway to make sure no one had noticed the strangeness of the situation. Thankfully, most students were either in an early class or still in bed. He only noticed a single other student sitting on a bench down the hall, but it appeared that the young man was asleep. His head rested against the wall, and his jaw had opened in a soft snore.

No one would see him if he followed the brownie wherever she wanted to take him.

So, he followed her. Alistair trailed her down the carpeted hallway, where the blue carpet turned green, a marker that the classrooms were nearby. He didn't want to run into his brothers again and opened his mouth to say so, but she stopped in front of a well-known tapestry that showed the history of Sunspell Academy.

He'd seen it countless times. It showed the Academy starting out as nothing more than a small hut outside the walls of Wildecliff. Then it had been brought inside, and the secrets were taught only to a few select students. Eventually, the upper class of the city discovered the use of having their children instructed by professionals, and suddenly, the Academy inherited the rather large building from an admirer who had had no children.

And then he heard Cassius's voice. His brother was already bragging about how he'd put his little brother in his place, likely to one of the sixth years who wanted to suck up to the Orbweaver who had stayed in the school. Everyone wanted a job at the Academy, after all.

Frantic, he looked down at the brownie and whispered, "What are we doing?"

She arched a delicate brow and then waved her hand again. Though she only came up to his knee, her magic was more powerful than he'd thought. The tapestry shifted to the side, revealing a small stone stairwell that spiraled out of sight.

She brought the books with her, snapping her fingers like they were puppies who needed to follow her every whim. Alistair assumed he had little choice in the matter now. He followed after her as though she'd cast a spell on him, just like the books.

The stairwell was dark and gloomy. A few cobwebs caught at his hair, and he felt horrible for ruining the spider's nest, which had likely never been disturbed before. Or not for a very long time. Small slats in the wall showed through to other rooms. They were nearly the same width as a needle, so he didn't worry too much that others would see him.

A servant's stairwell, he mused. Perhaps this was where the servants had once struggled through. Now, it had been forgotten and left to the fae who really took care of this building.

They reached the top of the stairwell, and Alistair spilled out into one of the many attics at the peak of Sunspell Academy. Piles of old school materials, desks, books, and even some old banners that looked like they might have been used for particular outings were haphazardly thrown about.

He wouldn't be surprised if no one remembered this room existed. He'd heard that there were nearly a hundred small attics like this throughout the school. He wondered, sometimes, if there were hidden treasures that no one had seen for centuries.

Obviously, those curious thoughts had been correct. There were plenty of hidden secrets within the walls of this ancient building.

The brownie weaved through the clutter with a deft skill that made him wonder if she might live in this attic. It was a far cry from the kitchens, where he'd always assumed brownies usually were. That's where he'd always found them, at least.

She set the books down on the floor in front of herself and then sat down. Without even looking at him again, the brownie got to work, weaving the pages back into the bindings of every book they had fallen out of. She even had a needle and thread in her hands that she used to patch the pages which had ripped. He'd never seen anything like that silver, glimmering thread that healed the pages of books without leaving a single mark.

Was this why she'd brought him here? Was he supposed to wait while she fixed his books? That was all well and good, but he couldn't be gone that long. And though he appreciated her help, he also knew that he needed to get back to classes today or the professors would punish him.

"Um, miss," he started, clearing his throat in what he hoped wasn't a rude manner. "I need to get back to my room and…"

Wordlessly, she pointed over to another corner of the room. And if Alistair had learned anything about the fae, it was that he needed to listen to them.

He trudged through the piles of brick-a-brack and then made it to the back corner, where he was shocked to find a rather fat toad with moss growing on its back. The creature looked up at him with yellow, watery eyes. And he realized that he knew this ugly little creature.

"Browning?" he asked, hesitant to think this might be the same creature. After all, Thea had said the toad didn't like to travel far. And it had been weeks since he'd last received a letter.

The toad let out a ribbit and then hopped to the side to reveal the letter it had been sitting on. Even though it was a little moist, he could see the smudged ink on the outside that said his name.

Alistair lunged for the letter and tucked it against his chest. "Thank you."

The toad glared at him but then hopped off into the clutter of the attic and disappeared. He should have offered the familiar some kind of food, he supposed. Or something to help get it home to its witch.

But he couldn't think of anything other than the letter in his hands.

Undoing the gentle folds, he opened it up to reveal what she'd written to him.

ALISTAIR,
I'M SO SORRY I DIDN'T WRITE TO YOU SOONER. UNFORTUNATELY, ONE OF MY FRIENDS CAUGHT YOUR RAVEN BEFORE I DID, AND I DIDN'T WANT TO SUFFER THROUGH HER UNBEARABLE TEASING, SO I SENT ATLAS OUT WITHOUT ANOTHER LETTER. HE DIDN'T COME BACK, SO I SENT BROWNING IN HIS PLACE. HOPEFULLY, HE GETS TO YOU BEFORE YOU HAVE DECIDED IT'S NOT WORTH WRITING TO A GIRL YOU'VE ONLY SEEN ONCE IN WATERDOWN BUT...

The letter continued on to describe how she was learning more about her gift and then detailed accounts of her mother and sisters growing their gardens.

He ate up every single word. His eyes couldn't read fast enough, and sometimes he thought he could hear her voice. Even though he didn't remember what she sounded like, he thought perhaps there had been a rasp to her words. A deepening tone that hadn't quite appeared yet.

Oh, she'd probably changed since the last time he'd seen her. He had. Alistair knew he'd gotten taller and lankier. She'd take one look at him compared to his handsome brothers and find him lacking.

Or perhaps there were some farm boys in her hometown who were more muscled. More burly if that was what women found attractive. He didn't know. It wasn't like Alistair talked to any of them regularly.

But... she'd written to him.

To him.

The unwanted son of a horrible man. Her kindness meant something.

He spun and caught eyes with the brownie. "Was this what you wanted to show me?"

She nodded, and the bright smile on her face spread again. As though she knew the contents of the letter and how happy it would make him. And, of course, he was happier right now than he'd been in a while.

Because Thea existed. And if she wrote to him, then he existed as well.

CHAPTER 9

Months flew by as Thea learned to be the best green witch she could be. Her mother always pushed her a little harder. To taste more plants. To discover more about her magic and who she was. All that was fine and good, but Thea sometimes wished the time wouldn't pass quite so quickly.

She got her letters from Alistair as the winds grew cold and the fields turned to gray. His letters were how she marked the time now, as silly as that might be. She waited until she heard from him to realize that another week had gone by.

And now they were almost two years away from having met each other for the first time. She felt as though she knew him quite well. He'd become part of her day-to-day life, especially since she kept all his lettersin a box underneath her mattress. Thea had taken to reading them when she was upset.

But she didn't really know him. She'd only seen him once, and without seeing him again, she feared the friendship between them would fall apart. They'd become strangers who were stuck in some obligatory cycle that had no end.

Sighing, she tucked her coat a little more firmly around her shoulders. She'd come with her mother to town, knowing that there was plenty for them to figure out before the snows came down from the sky.

Namely, they needed a better heat source. Her mother had hoped they could make a deal with the shopkeeper to give him a certain amount of grain, and in turn, they would get a new wood stove. Theirs had cracked down the cast iron back.

Along the way, her mother had bought her this new coat. The fur-lined collar tickled her chin and nose when she buried her face in the white mink fur; it was nicer than anything she'd ever owned.

"Wait here," her mother said with a bright smile. "I'll go talk with Herbert."

Herbert had been the shopkeeper in Waterdown for as long as Thea had been alive. Probably longer. His prices were fair, even if he wasn't easy to haggle with. He always made her mother pay more than what she wanted, but Máthair knew that going in.

"I'll wait for you here!" Thea replied with a quick smile to ease her mother's mind.

At least Máthair wouldn't have to worry about Thea while she was in the shop. That much she could promise.

The cobblestone streets of Waterdown Square gleamed in the sunlight. Four people had earned the job of street sweepers, a rather sought after position considering it was so easy and they only had to do it once every other day. But they had outdone themselves today. The street lamps were a glistening gold and ready to be lit tonight, where their torchlight would merrily fill all the glass windows with beacons for shoppers to come back tomorrow.

Even where she stood, Thea could see countless items that piqued her interest. A florist with twenty pretty bouquets. The dressmaker with three gowns that could be worn to any function in Wildecliff and still be more beautiful than any made there. A spellcaster with items that would help keep your house clean, convince the fae to visit your abode, or even spell the entire house like theirs was.

The air was filled with the fresh scent of baked bread, and a clean linen scent as everyone came to wash their laundry in the well at the center of the town.

A few soap bubbles floated by her head, and she reached up to pop one of the iridescent circles.

As the bubble popped, she looked through the splatter of soap to a shop that she hadn't noticed before. Probably because she did little writing before Alistair, but now she did often. Feathers decorated the interior of the shop, each one more lovely than the last.

She crossed the street, waving at a carriage that passed by before she stood in front of the window. There, a single raven feather had been carved into a golden tip for writing letters. The black of the feather was so dark it seemed almost blue and purple at the edges.

The owner of the shop had set it up to entice. The black feather quill laid on top of a bunch of handwritten letters, and she could just make out the lovely poetry that had been so painstakingly written by hand. It was... perfect. Everything about it was perfect.

Yule was coming soon, and she could use that as an excuse to give him a gift. Not that Alistair needed anything from her. He looked as though he came from a very well-to-do family, and a gift even like this wouldn't impress him.

But she was thinking of him and wanted to get him a gift. His letters had meant so much to her these days and, well... he deserved it.

She glanced over her shoulder to see that her mother was still deep in arguments with Herbert. Máthair wouldn't notice if Thea slipped into this shop. And she had a few coins of her own from helping a neighbor who hadn't been sure what plants were in her herb garden. The woman had been terrified she'd poison her own daughter with the tea she made, and she'd paid Thea to help figure out and label all the plants.

She just hoped the coins would be enough to buy the lovely quill. The feather looked like it came from his familiar, after all.

A bell above the door chimed as she stepped into the shop. The lights were dim in this room; shadows lingered along her sides and deep into the hidden secrets of the store.

As she watched, a man emerged from those shadows. He had a drop of ink smeared on his chin, and his dark eyes wildly searched the store until he saw her standing in the doorway. He had jet black hair plastered to his skull, although she couldn't be certain if that were the color of his hair or ink he had smeared into the locks.

"Good evening," he said after clearing his throat.

"It's morning," she corrected.

"Ah. Well." He blinked at her a few times with an owlish gaze before nodding. "Morning it is. What can I do for you, miss?"

She shouldn't have disturbed him. It was quite early in the morning, but he seemed like he was awake at the very least. She pointed to the dark quill in the window. "How much is the black and gold quill?"

"Ah, that's a very special quill." He tucked his hands behind his back and approached the window. "I'm sure you know Dame ó

Dubhghaill?"

Of course, she did. The Dame was one of the most powerful spellcasters in their town, and she was particularly known for giving inanimate objects the ability to do other things. Mostly stoves that cooked on their own. Tea kettles that boiled water on request. Thea had even heard of a few mops that cleaned the floor without the owner ever having to even ask.

"I know of her," Thea replied, trying her best to be very polite. "I've never had the honor of meeting her, though. My mother and I live up on Briar Patch Farm."

His eyes widened even further. "Your mother is Fenna?"

Why did so many men make that face when her mother's name was brought up? She'd have to ask because this was getting ridiculous at this point. Her mother was the same as any other woman. And yet, some of these men treated her like she was a goddess herself.

Thea nodded. "She is."

"Oh. Then your sister is Bell.. Belladonna." He seemed to shake himself before realigning his hands. "That quill was spelled by Dame ó Dubhghaill so that any time the writer makes a mistake, the ink disappears. It's quite the invention, if I do say so myself."

"It is." She thought back to all the ink blotches on her letters and how meticulously Alistair wrote every single word as he responded in his letters. Did he rewrite everything if he made a mistake? Every time?

This really was the perfect gift for him. And it was a gift he didn't even know he needed.

Oh, but something like that was bound to be more expensive than she could afford. She reached into her pocket where she had placed the coins in case she wanted to buy something with her mother. Four silver coins, not much in the slightest. And a quill like that....

She bit her lip. "How much is that quill?"

"Oh, quite a bit. I couldn't part with it for less than six golds, if I'm being honest." Although, he gave her a sidelong glance. "Were you thinking of buying it?"

"Well there's... There's a boy, you see. We've been writing back and forth for a while now and Yule is coming up." She tucked an unruly curl behind her ear and sighed. "I wanted to impress him, I suppose. I haven't seen him in a very long time and I worry very much that he'll forget about me. A letter isn't the same as actually seeing someone. You know?"

The man seemed to hang on to every word she said. A single oily lock fell in front of his eyes, and he brushed it back. But not fast enough for her to see that it was ink in his hair. The strand had left a smear on his forehead.

"Young love?" he asked.

"Oh, I wouldn't go so far as to say that. We're friends, you see." She thought, at least. "Friends."

He hummed low under his breath before nodding. "For a daughter of Fenna and for young love, how much do you have?"

Thea drew the four silver coins out of her pocket and held them out in the palm of her hand. "Not much, sir. Not enough."

The wince he made when he saw how little she had made her feel even worse. It wasn't that she wanted to make him come this low on his price. He'd probably paid Dame ó Dubhghaill over four silvers just to enchant it.

Thea closed her fingers around the coins. "It's not enough. I know. I'll try to make more with odd jobs here and there and then come back?"

"It's a popular item." He blinked a few times in sadness. "I can't promise it'll be here long."

"Of course not," she whispered. But then Thea forced a bright smile onto her face. "It wasn't likely I could afford it, anyway. I thought that he might like it. Thank you anyway. I do appreciate your time!"

The bell chimed behind her, and Thea found her mother standing behind her with a determined expression. She'd only seen that look from her mother a few times, and it always meant trouble. Or at the very least, that her mother had something on her mind.

"Fenna!" the man said. He shuffled his feet awkwardly before taking two large steps away from Thea. "Your daughter and I were just talking."

"How much is it?" her mother asked.

That seemed to stump the man. He cleared his throat and croaked, "What?"

Thea stared as her mother looked down at her with a soft smile on her face. "How much is the quill she wanted to buy?"

"Six golds," he managed. But then he stammered, "For you, I'd let it go for two."

Thea swallowed hard as her mother bent down to whisper in her ear, "How much do you have, daughter?"

"Four silvers."

Máthair held out her hand for the coins in Thea's pocket, which she quickly deposited. And then, to her shock, her mother pulled out her own coin purse, which looked far too light. She counted out the rest of the six golds and then handed it all to the shopkeeper. "I won't take any discount, Hugo. You know that."

He nodded, but his lips quirked to the side as though he were unhappy about getting the full price. "I'll go package it up for you,

Fenna."

As the man gathered up the quill and disappeared into the back, Thea stood frozen in shock. Had her mother really bought the quill for her? They didn't have that kind of money. And she'd already bought Thea this jacket...

"Máthair," she said quietly so she didn't disturb the man behind the counter. "Can we afford this?"

Her mother wrapped an arm around her shoulders and tugged her against her side. "I heard what you said, daughter of mine. A young man who deserves such high regard from my youngest daughter deserves a good Yule gift. And you'll pay me back."

She would. Thea would work harder than she ever had before to ensure that her mother got every single coin back. "I will. I promise. You'll get all of it back by the end of the year."

"I know." Máthair squeezed her again. "Now, care to tell me who this boy is? I've never heard you talk about anyone with such..."

Apparently, the word even escaped her mother. But Thea knew how she sounded when she talked about Alistair. The sense of wonderment he shared with her bled into the tones of her voice. She adored him. And that was so strange to say about a young man she'd only met once before.

His letters spoke of a young man who struggled in life, however. He made few connections with people, and somehow, that made her feel special. She was one of the people he talked to. He gave her time and space in his life because he trusted her not to squander it.

Besides, she quite enjoyed reading about the world he described. Wildecliff sounded like a terrifying place to live, and the stark difference between his home and hers fascinated her.

Thea dropped her gaze to the toes of her brown boots. "Do you remember the boy at Ceridwen's altar? The one who received the raven familiar at the same time as I got Browning?"

"How could I forget? Those Orbweaver men are always so ridiculously pompous..." Her mother paused, then touched a finger underneath Thea's chin and tilted her head until their eyes met. Her voice hardened. "You're talking to Balthazar Orbweaver's son?"

"His name is Alistair. And he's quite kind, Máthair." Thea tried to pour all of that into her gaze. "He's been writing me letters since we both got our familiars. He used his, the raven's name is Atlas, to apologize for his family's behavior. They sound awful, Máthair. And he's so lonely."

Her mother sighed. Her lips pinched together in a thin white line, but then something softened in her gaze. "Lonely, you say?"

"He doesn't fit in with his family. He hates them, although I don't know if he'd ever admit it. They're so cruel to him, Máthair." She pressed a hand to her chest. "He tells me all about it. I'll show you the letters, if you want. Please don't make me stop talking to him, though. He's... He's..."

"Kind?" her mother asked.

"Yes."

"Thoughtful?"

"He remembered Browning likes crickets and sent me a bunch of them with his last letter that he'd gathered from the gardens at Sunspell Academy." Thea took a deep breath and then forcefully added, "He's my friend, Máthair. I like him."

Her mother absorbed her words and then nodded. "I suppose there's no reason for me to deny your contact with him. But be wary, Thea. Sometimes your heart is too big for your mind."

The man who owned the shop interrupted them with a happy

chirp. "All wrapped!"

Thea gathered her gift up from him and held it against her heart. She would be mindful of Alistair. Of course, she would.

But some part of her soul whispered that she didn't have to be. He was careful with her, after all, like he thought she would disappear on a gust of wind.

CHAPTER 10

So many of the students were happy to return home for Yule. He heard them chattering about the halls, even in the carriage that took him, his brothers, and a few of the neighbor's children back to the street where they lived. Everyone wanted to guess what their parents had gotten them for Yule. Who would have the largest log, and whose would burn the longest?

These were all usual stories of children excited about a holiday break from their schooling. He knew that was the normal way to think.

But all he cared about was how deep the snow would be outside his window. How the desolate white landscape would make it even harder for him to get to sleep at night when he lay shivering in his cold bed. Balthazar didn't care if it was winter outside. The colder it was in the house, the better.

At least Cassius and Lysander were busy talking with the other students about what they would get for Yule. His brothers were easy for their father to buy gifts for as they mimicked their father in everything. If Balthazar wanted it or particularly liked an item that he already owned, he would get one for his two children. But Alistair? He was harder. Eventually, his father gave up on trying to find something his strange son would like.

Now Alistair knew gifts would be waiting for him that Cassius and Lysander would steal. They were magical items that Alistair would never use or have any interest in—rare potion ingredients, sometimes the hides of famous animals, all the normal items that a boy his age and power should enjoy.

Or at least, that's what everyone claimed.

The carriage rattled to a halt in front of their house, and his brothers said their goodbyes to the other students in the carriage. Even Alistair tried to give them all a nod, but his hair flopped in front of his eyes at the wrong moment, and his knit hat followed it, obscuring his vision.

He had the decided impression that the other people in the carriage weren't interested in his goodbye, anyway. He was wasting his energy on them.

Hopping out of the carriage, he reached into his pockets and pulled on the hand-knit fingerless gloves that the brownies in the Academy had made for him. They'd noticed how purple his fingertips got in classes while trying to take notes. Apparently, it was worrisome enough for them to make a brand new pair of gloves that he could write with.

They weren't made to capture attention. The brown yarn didn't stand out, nor did the strands of earth green and deep blue look out of the ordinary. He thought they matched his hat quite well, and the brownies had done a decent job.

The carriage driver summoned their trunks down from the back and traded the magic off to all three of them. Even Alistair caught the trunk without too much difficulty.

Of course, Cassius sneered. "You can cast the spell at home but not at school? What is it, you've got some kind of performance anxiety? Your future wife will sure love that."

How dare his brother even suggest that a wife wouldn't be happy with a husband like Alistair? He already knew how different he was from everyone else in their family. Goddess, he was different from everyone in Wildecliff! No one needed to point that out.

Curling his hands into the gloves, he made fists at his side and retorted, "At least my wife won't be married to a sadistic bastard like you."

It was the first time he'd ever sworn at his brother. And though he'd stuck up for himself a few times before, no one could ever say that Alistair had been particularly brave. But right now, returning to the place he hated so much, he didn't mind if he got knocked into the dirt for saying something Cassius didn't like.

His brother let out a little snort while Lysander stared at him with his jaw wide open.

"Is that how it is?" Cassius said another huff of breath following his words. "So the whelp has a voice, after all."

And then he walked away. Just left Alistair standing in the knee-deep snow with his trunk hovering next to him. Lysander quickly followed his brother.

The snow fell around him as the carriage moved to bring the other students back home. He'd never felt more elated than in this moment right now when he had stood up for himself and hadn't gotten a black eye for it.

Atlas circled overhead, then landed on Alistair's shoulder.

"Did you see that?" he asked his familiar.

The raven gave an uncomfortable squawk that suggested he didn't think this was over. And maybe it wasn't. Maybe Cassius would attack him in his bed tonight. But right now? He felt like he'd accomplished something.

Alistair made his way toward the looming dark house, staring up at the slate tiles on the roof that were already piled with snow. He'd found out the hard way that the snow could fall at any time and bury whoever was underneath it.

The front door stood open, just waiting for more cold air to blow through the entryway and make it even colder inside. He tucked his wool coat a little tighter around himself and ducked his head as he walked in. He didn't want to see the portrait of his father looking down at him in that disappointed manner. Nor did he look at the wooden accents that made the dark walls somehow even darker. And he definitely didn't want to see any of the dead flowers that his father insisted the maids leave because they were proof of the dark magic that went on within these walls.

He kept his head low through the hall, then turned right toward the stairwell that led up toward the family's private chambers. At least the "children's" wing would keep him safe. The stairs were icy even through his thick boots.

A gust of stiff wind blew through his jacket, and he shivered as he reached his door. How was it possible that the wind had gotten through his wool jacket? The blue fabric had never let him down before, but now even the neck didn't seem high enough to keep him warm.

Or maybe it was just that knowledge that he'd returned. He'd come back to this horrible place that he hated. And that icy chill would never leave him as long as he was here.

The trunk bumped against his bedroom door, and he winced. At least no one yelled at him from inside their rooms or warned that if he kept making noise, they would come out there and deal with it themselves. Still. He hated being in a home where he had to fear what someone would say to him for as innocent a mistake as that.

Carefully opening his door, he stepped into the cold room and sighed as his trunk hit the floor.

His father had left the window open. Or maybe one of the maids had done so and forgotten that he hated the cold. Either way, snow had drifted through the window and would leave a wet spot on the floor once he got the fire going.

Alistair shuffled over to the window while Atlas leapt from his shoulder to his perch right in front of the chilled breeze.

"Sorry," Alistair muttered, "I know it's not what you expected either."

Atlas squawked. He'd fluffed up so much that his feathers looked like he wore his own wool coat. Those dark eyes stared at him, thorns poking through as though he were a particularly angry, frustrated bird whose owner had forgotten him.

"I am sorry," Alistair repeated. "I have no control over what happens in this house, you know that. If I could get my father to light every fireplace in the house, I would. I know you hate the cold just as much as I do."

He paused in his apologies to listen. Why was there a scraping noise outside his window?

Alistair stopped mid-rant and peered out the windowsill down the building. Somehow, impossibly so, a toad clung to the side of the wall. And not just any toad.

"Browning," he gasped before scooping the familiar up with his arm and dragging him inside the house.

Browning plopped onto the ground, breathing hard and covered in... winter clothes? Alistair's jaw fell open as he finally noted the warm jacket wrapped around the toad like he was a child, the mittens on all four of his feet, and the hat shaped like a lily pad that had been tied around his thick neck.

She'd taken great lengths to ensure her toad companion had stayed warm, and now it was up to him to warm the toad back to life.

"How did you even get here?" he muttered as he slammed the window shut and rushed over to the fireplace. "It's the middle of winter! What was she thinking? Atlas would have made it to her once the snow stopped, and she already sent me a letter. I haven't replied to her yet because we were coming home from school, but I'd have told her all of that."

Damned girl, she needed to learn some patience. He had half a mind to yell at her the moment he had the chance to, but when was he going to see this mystery girl from the other side of the river?

Browning hopped up to the fire and sat down on his back haunches, neck enveloping the tie of his hat. Those big, watery eyes watched each of his moves, and he made a little grunt every time Alistair stacked the wood in a way he didn't like.

"I've been lighting fires in this room since I was five years old," he muttered. "Stop critiquing my skills."

Even Atlas glided down from his perch and landed next to the toad. The two familiars were quite particular in the way they wanted the fire lit, and then both of them scooted far too close to the flames.

"Here." Alistair reached underneath Browning's chin and untied the warm hat. "You'll get too warm."

He didn't enjoy touching Thea's familiar. Sure, there was always something interesting about all creatures, and he hated to think he'd insult the toad. But the little thing was sweaty sometimes, and he had clearly sweat on the journey and now was a little too toasty here by the fire.

The moment the hat was off, Browning opened his mouth as wide as possible and tilted his head back until he resembled some kind of planter he might have seen at school. The toad looked like he wanted Alistair to give him something, but he didn't have any food here that would satisfy a curious toad like this one.

"Um," he muttered. "I don't know what you want."

Browning shuffled closer to him.

"I really don't have any food here, bud. I can go get some, perhaps in the kitchen? But I'm not sure we have anything that you'd like to eat." He scratched the back of his neck. "I wasn't expecting you or I would have foraged a bit. Bugs and worms are harder to find in winter."

But the toad only got closer until Alistair realized something was inside Browning's mouth. It glistened, dark and smooth like a stone, but not quite that hard. He had no idea what was in that toad's mouth, but he supposed if something horrible was inside the poor familiar, he should help ease the discomfort.

Sighing, he rolled his sleeves up and steeled himself for what would likely be one of the most disgusting experiences of his life. Alistair kept his eyes open for as long as he could stand and then grabbed what was inside Browning's mouth.

He tugged, and then it just kept coming—more and more of what revealed itself to be a long, smooth box. There was a black velvet bow around it that had been ruined by Browning's saliva and a letter that was also wrapped around the box.

"Why?" he muttered. "Why couldn't she have waited for Atlas?"

He shook some of the slobber off the box and then peeled the letter off. All the while, he did his best not to gag or make it more dramatic than it already was. Poor Browning thought he'd done a good job. He'd tried his best, after all.

He opened the letter to find her chicken scratch handwriting waiting for him.

ALISTAIR

I KNOW I ALREADY WROTE YOU, BUT I FOUND THIS WHILE OUT SHOPPING WITH MY MOTHER, AND I COULDN'T RESIST. IT JUST LOOKED SO PERFECT FOR YOU!

AND... WELL.

HAPPY YULE.

THEA

She'd gotten him this gift for Yule? He hadn't known they were getting each other anything for Yule, or he would have spent some of his allowance on her. But now he would look like a fool because he hadn't gotten her anything at all.

Still, he stroked his fingers over the box, cleaning it one last time before he opened the lid.

Golden letters on the inside told him it was a mistake erasing quill. His eyes, however, couldn't stop looking at the beautiful black quill with a golden tip that would make writing letters and even taking notes in his classes so much easier.

The thought that went into this gift nearly stopped his heart in his chest. It meant so much to him that she would take the time to even think of him at all, let alone buy him something with her hard-earned money.

He lifted the quill out of the box, and both familiars made little sounds of awe.

"Isn't it lovely?" he asked them. "She got this for me."

If possible, Browning puffed up even more in pride for his witch, who had done everything right. The familiar was a loyal one. Even Alistair could see that just by looking at him.

Now he wanted to get her something. He wanted to make this festival special for her too, but he didn't know how. She'd seen something that made her think of him, and the honor of that... well, he didn't know if he could match it as easily as she had done.

He never went shopping. He rarely went out of the house when he was home.

But he wanted to find a gift that screamed "Thea."

He set the quill down on his bedside table and focused on Browning. "I'll admit, I don't know your witch as well as she knows me. But I want to get her something special in return, Browning. Something she'll like."

The toad focused on him and gave him a little nod.

"Will you help me?"

Remarkably, the toad held out its hand and waited for Alistair to shake it. This little creature was more human-like than his raven. Although, in looking at his own familiar now, he wondered if he simply hadn't treated Atlas like the family member he was.

"All right, you two. Let's figure out the best gift for Miss Thea. It is Yule, after all."

CHAPTER 11

Their house was filled with the sweet smoke of burning pine needles and cedar logs. Thea sat at the kitchen table with her mother and two sisters, laughing as they each picked through the mound of food in front of them.

Yule was always about food, small gifts, and rituals to welcome the sun's return.

She loved this time of year. Yes, of course, she was ready for the sun to come back and the snow to melt away. But this was the time when they all got to celebrate the return of longer days, warmer weather, and soon everything would be green again.

They'd already exchanged their own gifts. This year, Thea had chosen Marigold. She'd painted her sister the prettiest new vase for all the flowers they would create this year. And Belladonna had chosen Thea, so she'd received a brightly colored felt hat in every shade of purple. Her favorite color.

It was the first year Thea was old enough to drink the hot buttered rum her mother had always made for Yule. Surprisingly, it tasted much better than she'd thought. Thea still remembered Marigold trying it for the first time last year and declaring it was far too bitter and burned her throat. But Thea kind of liked the burning.

Belladonna snorted into her cup. "Drink that slower, little sister. You'll wake up with a headache tomorrow."

Was she drinking it too fast? Thea laughed into her own cup and then set it far away from her so she wouldn't be tempted to gulp more of it down.

"You've got a mustache!" Marigold chortled.

A mustache?

Thea wiped away the foam on her lip and endured her sister's laughter. Even her mother grinned at her, and the happiness of the moment felt so warm. It heated her right into her very bones. Or maybe that was the buttered rum.

"It's Yule," her mother said, reaching across the table for Thea's hand. "You drink as much as you want. But I can't promise Belladonna is wrong. Your head will hurt in the morning."

They all dissolved into giggles around the table, and Thea was reminded of how much she loved this family. How much she never wanted to leave them or any of them to leave her. They should stay like this. Forever.

"Oh!" Thea stood up from the table, then braced herself on the edge. "I forgot! The quill shop owner gave me something for you, Belladonna. He said to tell you Merry Yuletide."

"The quill shop owner?" Belladonna blinked at her. "Why would he have given you a gift to give to me?"

Thea shrugged. "He said you helped him out with something, I don't know. Hugo isn't the most chatty person I know."

Immediately, the other two women in her family descended upon Belladonna like a duo of wolves. They wanted to know everything about her interactions with the quill shop owner. Was he sweet on her? Had they been talking for a while now, or was this a rare thing that even Belladonna hadn't expected? He seemed like a kind young man. He'd even offered to give Thea the quill for nearly free.

She left their chattering behind her and weaved down the hallway toward her room. It was now a curved hallway, like the body of a snake, all the way to the end of her room where she had slept alone the past few nights. Dear Browning had taken her gift all the way to Alistair, and he had yet to return. She hoped he was all right, considering how awful the snow had been on the night she sent him out.

Sighing, she rubbed the back of her neck and strode into her room. She almost didn't notice the two pairs of eyes watching her until the very last second. Thea gasped and leaned away from the window where both Browning and Atlas must have let themselves in.

"You two!" she said, fanning her suddenly hot face, which tingled from fear. "What are you doing here?"

They both blinked at her again, but then Atlas lifted his foot. A small bag hung off it, wrapped with a black ribbon and a letter attached at the end.

Of course. They were here because Alistair had gotten her gift, and he wanted to say thank you. But she hadn't expected to see an answering gift attached to his familiar's leg.

Had he gotten her something the same way she had? Did he see something in a store and think of her?

Her cheeks burned. The likelihood of that was very small. She had no reason to assume that he thought of her in any way other than as the strange pen pal he'd had for almost a year now.

But still. She liked the idea of him thinking about her. Maybe even more than just waiting for a letter.

Crossing the room, she forgot all about Belladonna's gift. Instead, she pulled her own from Atlas's leg and opened up the letter.

You surprised me!

I didn't think we were getting each other anything for Yule. To be honest, my family doesn't do much for it. My father will have a few gifts, but mostly that's up to us to celebrate how we want to celebrate it.

Thank you for thinking of me. I'm writing this letter with the new quill, and it is just... exquisite. You're so thoughtful, and I wish I could say the same about myself.

But, I will be honest. Browning and Atlas helped quite a bit in the design of your gift. You should thank them both with a sweet treat (Atlas craves caramels most days).

Anyway, it took me a while to make your gift, so I'm sorry it's a bit later than you might have expected. But it's a way to give you a glimpse of how I see the world.

I hope that's something you'd like.

Yours,

Alistair

"Yours," she whispered, then pressed the letter to her heart.

She didn't mean to let herself get so far into this. Writing back and forth with Alistair was supposed to be nothing more than making another friend who lived across the river. But the more she wrote to him, the more she built him up in her head.

He had to be handsome, of course. She remembered him as being a little on the thin side, but those freckles had caught her attention. She wanted to count each one until she knew the specific number.

Her hands shook as she opened up the bag and dumped out a tiny necklace onto her palm. It was a thin vial of metal, like a tube. One side had been slightly crushed, so it was thinner than the rest. Holding it up to the light, she noticed a few tiny holes drilled into the thin pipe.

"What is this?" she whispered.

Atlas nudged her hand closer to her mouth, and she realized it was a recognizable shape. It looked like a miniature flute or perhaps a whistle.

Holding the necklace up to her lips, she blew upon it and watched as the world in front of her changed. The whistle made no sound, but it didn't have to make a sound for the magic of this gift to unfurl.

The world suddenly seemed dusted with tiny sparkles. She peered out the window and noticed snowballs were rolling themselves. Then, as she looked closer, she realized there were tiny beings rolling the snow into little snowmen that would end up outside. Her mother had always said the snowmen were made by brownies, but now she could see them!

Tiny creatures with little woolen caps tromped through the snow outside her window. They'd come up to her knee if she stood beside them, and each one was more lovely than the last. Their long fingers were covered with little mittens, and they wore knit dresses.

Thea let out a little sound of surprise as she recognized the colors of the yarn. She'd had so many pieces of yarn going missing lately, but she'd always assumed that she had misplaced them on her own.

Each one of those brownies wore an outfit made of her yarn. And they all looked so happy. A new one appeared through the snow. It trudged closer to the others while holding up a raspberry she'd left out overnight for them. One of the sisters always left a gift for the fae. Cream, berries, sometimes a pile of sugar. No matter what, they always knew to take care of their house fae.

And they were so happy dancing outside while the snowflakes fell.

The moment her lungs ran out of air, the faeries disappeared again. Frantically, she inhaled and then blew again. The moment she used the silent whistle, she could see them.

"What a gift," she whispered, then blew on it again.

This time, her attention turned to the familiars in her room. Shocked, she watched as Atlas blinked his eyes, and a third one appeared in the middle of his forehead.

"Were you hiding that?" she asked.

He squawked, then gave her a low bow. He apparently had finished his duty because then he hopped over to the window and pecked at it.

She knew it was Yule and that Atlas would want to be with his own witch. And poor Alistair was alone tonight while he waited for his familiar to return. She'd known that this would be a difficult holiday for him. She just hadn't been able to guess how difficult.

"Oh!" She pulled the door to her bedside table open and fished out a little caramel candy. Her mother had given her a whole bag of them, though she'd nearly devoured them already. "Here. For the flight home."

Atlas grabbed the candy, gave her a nod, and then flew out the window the moment she opened it.

She couldn't help herself. Thea blew on the tiny whistle again and watched as the brownies pointed up at Atlas and giggled. She caught the slightest hints of their words. How pleased they were that the youngest daughter was talking with a boy. How even that worried them, because they all had such a soft spot for Thea.

Eventually, she couldn't look at them any longer. Thea gathered up Belladonna's gift from her own beau and then tucked Browning into the sling around her waist. He dramatically flopped onto his back with a webbed hand over his eyes.

"Yes, I'm certain you are tired," she said with a soft giggle. "You've had quite the journey! I'm sure mother will have something sweet for you to eat, though. Only the best familiars get sugary treats during Yule."

She wandered into the kitchen with the gift in hand. Without even looking up from Browning, she handed Belladonna the package.

Her sisters were still talking about the possibility of a romance blooming between Belladonna and the quill shop owner. Marigold's rabbit sat in her lap; her eyes rolled back with the luxury of having her ears pet. Her mother's cat stalked through the house with its fur fluffed as though hearing something in the walls.

Thea listened while her sisters revealed more secrets about Belladonna's mystery man. Hugo wasn't from either Wildecliff or Waterdown. Which made him a little interesting in these parts, considering they rarely saw someone out of either town.

Thea stroked a finger between Browning's eyes, and he let out a happy little grunt at her touch. He'd gone a long way for her, through the snow even, and that wasn't natural for a familiar of his species. But he'd still done it, and she didn't know how to thank him for that.

"How did I get so lucky to have a familiar like you?" she asked.

"Because Ceridwen saw how kind your heart was," her mother replied. Máthair scooted her chair over to the same side as the table as Thea and looked down at Browning with her. "The goddess knew my daughter knew how to love regardless of appearance, and that no one else would have given him a life like you."

"Máthair," Thea said, followed by a giggle that she hoped sounded kind. "He's a good familiar. I don't have to be kind for him to be good."

"You do. Some familiars will even leave their owners if they are not respected enough." Her mother touched a finger to Browning's nose as well. The soft boop made the toad snort. "I am ever so proud of you, daughter of mine. Now I do believe you have your own gift in your other hand, do you not?"

Thea narrowed her eyes at her mother. "Have you been spying on me?"

"The brownies tell me everything." Her mother winked, even though that gave away nothing.

Her mother couldn't see the fae. The brownies were no more talking to her mother than they were talking to Thea. Or at least, before the gift of the tiny whistle.

Still, she knew better than to keep a secret from her mother. Thea opened her hand and showed her mother the little handmade gift. Of course, her mother took it. No magic existed in this house without her knowing about it.

Considering the last time Marigold brought in an enchanted teapot it exploded green goo all over the kitchen, Thea couldn't blame her.

"This is well made," her mother said. "Who did this?"

"Alistair. He said he made it himself." She tucked a strand of hair behind her ear. "If you blow into it, you can see the realm of the fae. Like he does. That's his power, although I don't know if I'm supposed to tell you that."

Her mother's eyes widened with every word. Hesitantly, she placed the whistle to her own lips and blew into it. Still, Thea couldn't hear a sound. It was as if the air went into the whistle, and that was the price to see into the faerie realm. The breath from her lungs created the magic. Or perhaps fed it.

Considering how much her mother's eyes were darting around the kitchen, Thea could only assume they weren't alone.

Finally, her mother stopped and then handed the whistle back to Thea. Her hands were shaking. "Keep this very safe, daughter of mine. There are plenty of people out there who would love to get their hands on that."

"Why?" She lifted the necklace over her head and hid it underneath her clothes. "It just shows you where the brownies are. And we all know they exist."

"Not all of us," her mother whispered. "There are some who would stop at nothing to look into the other realm and greet the gods and goddesses on their own terms. Those are the people to watch out for, my daughter. And if they know you have magic like that, I fear you may be in grave danger."

Thea felt all the blood drain out of her face. She held her hand over the gift where it hid beneath her clothing, but... some part of her still wasn't afraid of it. Not yet, at least.

Alistair had given her the whistle. He'd made it. It couldn't be that dangerous.

Could it?

CHAPTER 12

The weeks turned into months, and Alistair realized far too late that he marked the passage of time by when he got a letter from her. And that was silly, really. He had other things going on. He had his classes and the fae who had awakened at the Academy. They needed his help with all manner of things, so he was quite busy. So busy, in fact, that he staggered to his bed at night in complete exhaustion.

But every time there was a letter waiting for him and Atlas standing in the window, he felt all that exhaustion disappear. His raven knew, it seemed. Atlas always had a rather sad but also pleased expression on his face when Alistair staggered into his room to find a letter.

Sometimes they gave Atlas a break and used Browning, but most of the time, they tried to stick to the familiar who could fly. Poor Browning had lost weight, and that made Thea nervous. He couldn't blame her for worrying about the little man. He might have as well if he'd been given a toad for a familiar.

All those busy weeks passed into the end of the semester, and then suddenly, he was home again. The summer came, and with it, the sensation of knowing that he had made it through the year. That summer was rather busy. His father wanted them to go on trips to visit the best and brightest in Wildecliff, likely seeking a job for Lysander now that he had graduated.

Near the end of the summer, though, he realized it was close to their birthday. Almost two years since they had met each other. Two years since they had first realized that they were two sides of the same coin who would stay in touch for a very long time, despite the physical distance between them.

And he did not know how to celebrate that with her. She deserved more than another letter and another present. He'd been showering her with gifts lately. But the summer had forced him out of the house with his family, and he hadn't been able to send her as many letters. He feared she'd forget about him.

Wildecliff was known for its artisans and spellcasters. He'd found so many items and objects that reminded him of her. Flowers pressed into bookmarks. Pretty baubles for her hair. Little things, certainly, because he didn't want his father to realize what he was doing.

But all of it made him think of her. And these days, he was always thinking of her.

Alistair popped his chin onto his clenched fist and stared out the window of his bedroom. He needed advice; he decided. He didn't know enough about women to guess what she would want on this special day. If he wanted to do this right, and he did, then he would need to ask an expert.

Nora.

The maid might not want to tell him much about the world of romance, considering how awkward the conversation might get, but he hoped she would have some magic trick up her sleeve. Some gift or situation that would make Thea realize she wanted to keep him around.

Alistair spent many hours every night staring up at his ceiling, wondering if she was doing the same thing. Thinking about him. Hoping he was thinking about her.

"Ugh," he grumbled, standing.

Atlas opened his wings wide and flapped them angrily.

"Sorry, I didn't mean to startle you." Alistair groped for something on his desk that would give him a reason to go down into the servant's quarters.

If his father or brothers saw him wandering around, they'd have questions. And he didn't want to answer any questions of theirs because he knew they would think that asking a servant for romantic advice was the most foolish thing they'd ever heard.

Then he remembered that he'd ripped a shirt outside the other day while chasing down a drunken clurichaun who had stolen more wine from his father. He'd caught the faerie and made sure that no one would notice the missing alcohol, but only after sacrificing one of his last remaining shirts without a rip or stain.

That would do. If anyone saw him going to the servant's quarters, they would note the shirt in his hands and assume he needed it mended. While he did that work himself, no one would be the wiser.

He snatched the shirt off the bottom of his bed and raced out of his room.

At this time of day, Cassius and Lysander were bound to be in the library. He had to sneak past them, of course, to get to the other side of the house. But if he were quiet enough, then his brothers wouldn't notice him.

He'd gotten better at sneaking the older he got.

As he passed the library, he paused at a strange word.

"Wedding?" Lysander hissed, then a bubble of laughter escaped from his mouth. "You?"

Alistair pressed his back against the wall beside the door, craning his neck to the side so he could hear better.

His eldest brother didn't laugh in response to Lysander's words. "Yes, wedding. You know father is ready to have a grandson, and she's the best witch in Wildecliff. Her parents are ridiculously wealthy and she had good grades at the Academy. She's a good match."

"But have you met her?" Lysander asked. "She seems awfully young. Isn't she only eighteen?"

"One doesn't have to meet a wife to get married." Cassius snorted, and then the chime of glass bumping against glass echoed. Were they drinking? This early? "A wife is only there for her duties, just as the husband is. I'll find someone else to entertain me once she's served her purpose."

An icy shiver traveled down Alistair's spine. He pitied the poor girl who would be traded off to his brother like cattle, but he also knew that most families in Wildecliff used each other like this. She was probably elated to be marrying into the Orbweaver family.

Like her family, they were also filthy rich, and most of them were very powerful. Disregarding Alistair, of course. But no one talked about Alistair.

He ducked into the shadows and crossed the hall to the servant's wing. He couldn't let that distract him from his purpose of leaving his room. If he could save the girl from his brother, he would have. But there was no proof that the young woman didn't want to marry Cassius.

Perhaps the fae would look into that question for him, just to make sure.

The kitchens were bustling at this time of day. Preparations for dinner were already well underway, and the two chefs were bright red in the face as they hurried throughout the kitchen, barking orders wherever they went. The entirety of the butler's staff were lined up for the house manager to survey their uniforms for serving. And, of course, the maids were behind. They scurried from room to room, shouting about their next plan of where to clean, what linens to prepare, and did the master want them to take care of the basement this year or would they put it off again?

He spotted Nora in the distance. She stood in front of a worn oak door, patting her hair underneath a horrible looking bonnet that didn't suit her features at all.

"Nora!" he called out, waving his hand in the air with the shirt clutched in it.

The moment she caught his eye, she rolled her own. He could only imagine there was a small part of her that lumped him in with his brothers. Yet another self-righteous Orbweaver boy who thought his problems were more important than the rest of them.

But then, a bright smile beamed across her features and he knew that she hadn't forgotten the young boy who had trailed her through the house. She hadn't forgotten him, and that meant more than she could ever know. He wasn't alone in this house, at least.

"Mister Alistair," she said, approaching him while still fixing the cap on her head. "How do you like our new uniforms?"

"What was wrong with the last ones?"

"Your father thought this would seem more appropriate when visitors came to the house. Apparently, the last uniforms were too simple." She shrugged. "We're all trying to get used to them. Anyway, young man, what can I do for you?"

He liked to think that Nora wasn't that much older than him, but Alistair always forgot that she had seemed to be the same age for years now. She'd been around when he was just a kid, after all.

Clearing his throat, he wrapped the tangled mess of the shirt around his hand. "Well, I... I..."

She noticed his shirt right away and then held out her hand for it. "How badly did you tear it this time? You don't usually ask for me to fix things, but I can have it done for you before dinner if that's what you require."

"That's not..." He cleared his throat. "That's not why I'm here, actually."

The silence rang between them louder than if he'd struck a gong in the middle of the kitchen. She lifted a brow, waiting for him to continue.

And he should. He needed to. This was the plan, after all. He would ask Nora what she thought he should do with this lovely young woman in his life so that he could convince her that he wasn't a terrible person, that he was more than just someone she wrote to.

Alistair had nightmares every night that he received a letter from her, talking about a young man who had caught her eye. Or worse, that she wouldn't tell him about the other option at all until it was far too late. Maybe she'd send him an invitation to the wedding.

No, they were far too young for that.

But then he remembered Lysander's words.

"Isn't she only eighteen?"

And they were almost eighteen. They shared the same birthday. They'd gotten their familiars at the same time, so was it all that unlikely that she would get married when there was already a woman her age marrying his brother?

He swallowed the anxiety and fear of the situation and met Nora's curious gaze head-on. "There's a young lady I've been writing to for almost a year now and I'd like to ask if you could help me plan something special for our birthday." He caught himself, stuttered, then corrected, "Her birthday."

Nora's expression softened into something quiet and subtle. She looked at him with the eyes of a woman. A woman who appreciated him going out of his way for another, and perhaps even a little jealous that he would do so.

"You've met a girl?" she asked.

"A long time ago, actually." He lifted his hand to rub at the back of his neck, only to realize he had wadded up the shirt and now looked like he was dabbing sweat off his neck. "We received our familiars together almost a year ago now. We've been writing to each other ever since."

"Well, that's rather sweet." She crossed her arms over her chest and cocked her hip out to the side. "And how am I supposed to help you?"

"I want to do something special for her. Something that will make her see..." Damn it, how was he supposed to say this without sounding like an absolute idiot? "I like her very much, Miss Nora. We've been writing for... a while."

"Yes, you said that."

"And for most of that time, I've thought she was the funniest girl

I've ever met, and that I admired the way she took care of her familiar who might not have been the easiest kind to get. She looks at life through happiness while I don't do that, and I think every time I get a letter from her, I get to soak up a little of that happiness." He looked back at Nora and met her gaze with more confidence than he felt. "She makes me happy, Miss Nora. I want to make her feel the same."

The maid pressed a hand to her heart and sighed. "So that's the way of it, then."

He waited for her to say more, but she said nothing else. Nora kept looking at him with that strange expression on her face, like he'd brought her a kitten. Why was she looking at him like that?

"Stop that," he muttered. "I don't like it when you make that expression."

"It's just that you're all grown up," she replied. "And I suppose there was always a part of me that was afraid you'd end up like your father, or worse, those spoiled siblings of yours. Don't tell anyone I said that. But you turned out to be a good man, Alistair Orbweaver. I'm quite proud of you."

His cheeks burned with embarrassment while his chest swelled with pride. He'd never thought about it that way, but now that she said it, he was pleased he'd passed her inspection. "Thank you, Nora."

Tears welled up in her eyes for a moment, but then she dashed them away with a quick nod. "I think the answer is rather simple, Alistair. You should tell her what you told me. But, I think the most important part of that will be that you stand in front of her to say it. Just like you're doing right now."

How? How could he do that? They lived on either side of the river, and it wasn't as if he knew anyone with a boat. He couldn't cross the river Danu without stowing away on some fisherman's boat, and then his father would find out from someone who talked too much. And if that happened, then Alistair wouldn't be let out of the house for weeks on end!

Unless...

He remembered she'd gotten over the river with her mother that night. The moon had lit their path, but he hadn't thought for even a second about how it was possible for them to travel over the river.

She must have access to a boat. Thea's mother must have something that Thea could use to come to him.

He snapped his fingers and pointed at Nora. "That's a great idea! Nora, you're a genius."

She shrugged. "I know, and yet I'm still here."

The elation built in his chest so great he could have kissed her. Instead, he rushed out of the kitchens with a plan rattling around in his head.

Alistair would write her a letter. He would use the best penmanship he had and her quill that would allow no mistakes. The words had to be perfect. Absolutely perfect. She needed to know that he had important things to say to her and that she had to be secretive. They'd meet at the same place where they first met—Ceridwen's altar. No one would suspect a thing, and then they could finally see each other again. After all these years.

All those thoughts rushed through his mind so quickly that he didn't notice his father standing in the hallway. Alistair crashed into Balthazar's broad chest and bounced off it as though he were nothing more than a flea.

He hit the ground hard on his backside, wincing as a spike of pain traveled up his spine.

"Just what do you think you're doing?" Balthazar snarled.

An icy chill always traveled with his father as though he were never very far from the grave. The white stripes at his temples had gotten a little wider in the past year or so, and his father's face had become more gaunt. Whatever magic he practiced in his wing of the house was dangerous and slowly, eating the old man alive.

Swallowing hard, he tried not to stammer as he replied, "I—I—"

Helplessly, Alistair held up the shirt in his hand.

"Did you rip another?" his father said. "I will stop giving you clothing altogether, boy. Take better care of what I give you. And no running in the halls or I'll tie you up in your room, so I don't have to listen to that incessant noise."

He had no doubt his father would do just that. Balthazar swept down the hallway toward his private wing, and Alistair noticed his father was limping.

Why? He couldn't guess.

Seeing the old man was a stark reminder that he needed to be more careful. Balthazar didn't need any excuse to ruin this plan of his, and Alistair couldn't let anyone in the household know what was happening.

No one but Nora, of course. He trusted she'd never give up his secret.

Alistair hauled himself off the floor and limped back to his own room. His back ached from hitting the hard floor, but he ignored it.

After all, he had a letter to write.

CHAPTER 13

The wind blew too loud today. It slapped against Thea's ears and made her hair dance around her face in such a crazy pattern that she feared what would happen if she untied her locks for a single second. Still, it made gardening a little more entertaining. She had to get creative and put rocks on the seed packets she was planting, even though they were well out of season, and she had to figure out the best way to keep her hat on.

Her mother had said the hat was a ridiculous addition. Thea's face was adorable with freckles, and no matter how hard she tried, the sun always gave her a few of them.

But Thea wanted to look like the young woman Alistair had met a year ago. She couldn't help but compare herself to that moment. Even though she wouldn't be likely to see him again soon, she wanted to feel like she was the same young woman who had made an impact on his life.

"Growing up is hard, Browning." She shoved the trowel into the earth and leaned back on her haunches. "I don't want to grow up and differ from the woman he expects, but I also don't want to stay a child because that would make everything rather awkward. Don't you think?"

He burped and then shoved his hands into the small cup of blackberries she'd placed next to him. He'd been stuffing his face all morning as though he knew something she didn't.

"Why are you eating so much today?" she grumbled, then returned to digging in the earth. "There are plenty of raspberries in the house for you. Or better yet, those mealworms that Marigold bought and you refuse to eat."

Toads were supposed to eat hardier stuff than just sugary treats. But Browning wasn't a regular toad, she supposed.

"You know, if you eat too many sweets, all the teeth in your head are going to rot out." The warning was one her mother used to give her and not one that Browning cared about at all.

He rolled his eyes at her and popped another juicy raspberry into his mouth. The munching sounds made the hairs on her arms stand up, but she'd endure it for him. He was so rarely happy, after all. Her grumpy familiar could have a few moments of happiness, even if they were unhealthy.

A black feather floated down from the sky and landed in front of her. Smiling, she reached for it and ran the soft feathers through her fingers.

"Atlas?" she asked, peering up at the bright blue sky with not a cloud in sight. She should be able to see the magical familiar if he were here, but... Well, she couldn't find him at all. "Atlas, where are you?"

The answering squawk came from behind her. Thea gasped and

turned so quickly she almost slapped his beak.

Breathing hard, she pressed her hand to her chest. "Where did you come from?"

Another loud noise was her answer until she was treated with a rare comment from her Browning.

"Alistair." Browning smacked his lips loudly and then rolled onto his back. The moss cushioned him as he rubbed his extended belly with a webbed hand. "Extra letter."

She glared at her familiar. "Thank you for being so eloquent while giving me poor Atlas's words." Thea stroked a hand down the raven's back, careful to avoid the thorns. "You are much more charming than him, I know. I'm so sorry you have to deal with him as much as I do."

Browning snorted while she shared a look with the handsome raven.

Sighing, she untied the letter around Atlas's leg and unrolled it. This was an unusual time for them to be sending letters, and her stomach twisted with the fear that something might be wrong. What if Alistair's father had decided to move them? Or what if he had to go back to the Academy and something terrible had happened?

Too many situations could happen to him without her knowing, and she didn't know what she'd do if he just... disappeared.

Thea,

I'm sure you haven't forgotten our birthday is in two days. I took such a long time trying to figure out the perfect gift to give you or a special moment, but honestly, there is nothing I want more than to see you.

If possible, can you meet me at Ceridwen's altar? Just like the last time.

Perhaps it's too much to ask but.... come? Please.

I haven't seen your face in so long, and I fear I might have forgotten what you look like.

Yours,

Alistair

He wanted to see her? For their birthday?

"Oh," she whispered. "Oh I..."

Helplessly, she looked at Atlas, who seemed to preen now that she had read his master's words. At the look on her face, he shook his head a bit and took a couple of steps away from her. Disappointed, perhaps?

"It's not like that," she was quick to say. "I want to see him too, Atlas. More than anything. But look at me."

She stood to make her point. The dress she wore was a hand-me-down from Belladonna, who had given it to Marigold, who had then given it to Thea. She couldn't remember the last time she had brushed her hair but knew it was in a billowing, tangled nest on top of her head. There was dirt smudged on her cheeks and wedged so far underneath her nails that even a bath couldn't fix the problem. Not to mention she had so much work to do, and running off with the boat would make her mother suspicious.

Two days. She only had two days to fix all this, and what would she do if she couldn't?

"I look like a creature who walked out of a swamp!" she exclaimed before throwing her hands up into the air. "I'm supposed to look beautiful to him and here I am, just a monster from a lagoon who has no right to even stand in front of him. He's an Orbweaver, for goddess sake!"

The two familiars stared at her with equal expressions of horror and realization. There was a lot of work to do if she wanted to impress him, and Thea only knew of one person who could help her with that.

Belladonna.

Her sister had spent her entire life making herself beautiful. Everyone knew her name in the town, and everyone said she looked like her mother when Fenna had been her age. Their mother was known for being a beauty. Marigold looked like their father, who had been a striking man until an accidental spell had caught him the wrong way. And Thea? Well... Thea was just Thea.

"Oh dear," she muttered, then dropped all her gardening things onto the ground. Gardening could wait when something as important as this came up.

She raced back to the house, slamming into the gate and wrenching it open. The magic of their home grumbled at her, but she didn't pause to see if it would punish her or not. There was so much she needed to do.

"Thea?" her mother asked as she ran by.

"No time to talk, Máthair! Where is Belladonna?"

Her mother wordlessly pointed toward Belladonna's room, so that's where Thea ran. Meanwhile, she sent her thoughts to the house and begged it to run a bath for her. A long one with more soap than she usually used. She might need two baths if she were being honest. It had been a long day in the garden, after all.

Slamming her fists onto the door, she banged over and over until Belladonna opened up. Her sister wrenched the door open with an angry snarl and shouted, "What? What could you possibly want, Thea!"

She held out the letter to her older sister. And while Belladonna took her time reading every single word that Alistair had written, all the anger in her expression disappeared by the second time she looked up.

"Who's this?" Belladonna asked.

"Alistair." As if that answered everything. Clearing her throat, she tried again. "I've been writing to him for over a year now. And he wants to meet."

"He's from Wildecliff?"

"Why does that matter?" Thea gestured up and down her body. "Would you look at me? I can't go see him like this! Help!"

At least that got through Belladonna's head. Her sister eyed her and then snorted in agreement. "You can't see anyone like that. Not if you want them to give you any respect. Do you have to look like a goblin every time I see you?"

"I'm asking for your help."

Her sister lit up as though Thea had told her she'd found the spell for immortality. "Say it again."

"I'm asking for your help, Belladonna." She lifted her hands from her hips and then dropped them again. "Make me pretty. Like you."

The squeal from her sister's mouth made her other two family members come running. Máthair's face was creased with worry as she sprinted into the hallway, hair flying in all directions and eyes wide. "What's wrong?"

Thea couldn't breathe as Belladonna wrapped her arms around her. "Too. Tight," she wheezed.

"Thea's finally asked me to make her pretty!" Bella shrieked again. The sound nearly burst Thea's eardrum. "We're going to shove her into the bath. We're going to brush her hair. Oh! I can try the new facial cream on her that I've been dying to try. It'll make her skin so rosy!"

Their mother sighed and pinched the bridge of her nose. "Is that worth waking the entire house for?"

Belladonna glared at their mother with more venom in her gaze than Thea had ever seen before. "Yes!"

With that, she yanked Thea into her room and slammed the door in their mother's face.

"Is that worth waking the entire house?" Belladonna repeated with a low hiss. "It's like Máthair has never looked at you."

Thea had to repeat to herself that Belladonna meant nothing by it. She hadn't intended to insult Thea when she said those things. It was just that Thea and Belladonna had very different opinions about what made a person pretty. Unfortunately, Belladonna's opinions matched those of the men in their village.

"House!" Belladonna ordered. "Two baths, all the soap you can conjure, and make sure to get some of that lavender scented hair soap I bought. Seven sponges, please, each one with varying levels of roughness. Perhaps we could also use a nail file, but I haven't looked yet." Thea tried not to flinch when Belladonna snagged one of her hands and held it up to the light. "Yes, nail file. Two probably. I think we'll break the first one trying to fix all this."

"Bella," Thea whined.

"You're the one who asked for this, so settle down, would you? At least two brushes. We'll need more, but we'll start out with two. Those tangles are going to take me forever."

And that was precisely how Thea found herself sitting in a boiling hot tub with her knees drawn to her chest while her sister piled more and more soap in her hair. Belladonna claimed the soap she used for

Thea's hair was supposed to soften the knots and make her curls stand out better. But Thea didn't have curls. She had waves, unlike their mother's pretty ringlets. No soap was going to make her hair turn into their mother's.

She shivered every time Belladonna hit a bad knot.

"Oh stop doing that," Belladonna said, but her brushing turned a little more gentle again. "There's nothing wrong with the way I brush your hair."

"I know there isn't," Thea whispered. "I should have brushed it a long time ago."

She heard nothing but the slight sloshing of water against the sides of the tub. This was the second round of water they'd used, and at least there wasn't dirt sitting around her feet now. She'd been shocked at how much grime had come off her body on the first round of scrubbing.

Belladonna brushed her hand through Thea's long hair and let it slap back down into the water. "When you were very little, Máthair used to let me brush your hair like this. I don't know if you remember, but you always complained everyone but me was too rough with it."

"Did I?" She was sad she didn't remember. But her memories as a child weren't all that clear. She remembered their father only in one snippet. A big man with bright blue eyes, who laughed so loud it scared her sometimes. That was all.

Her sister ran her fingers through her hair one last time. "I used to treat you like a little doll. And it never used to scare me how quiet you were. Not until I got older and remembered you'd just sit there and let me do whatever I wanted. You were such a solemn child. Quiet. Still. I'd never seen a little girl be like that before. Or any child."

Thea didn't remember that either. But why would she? Glancing over her shoulder, she saw tears in her sister's eyes. "And that makes you sad?"

"Only because you're all grown up now." Belladonna stood and held out the towel for her. "And we won't all live together forever, so don't mind me getting all emotional that this might be the last time I get to do this."

Thea rolled her eyes and stepped into the towel. Tying it down around her chest tightly, she shook the wet strands out of her face. "Oh, you'll do it again. I'll call you when I'm old and disgusting and remind you of this moment. You can hobble your way over here with two canes and then brush my hair again."

Though her sister laughed, the sound wasn't as happy as she'd hoped. Instead, Belladonna ran her hand over Thea's head and brought her close for a quick hug. "Can I pick out your dress, at least? I know you aren't leaving tonight, but..."

"Go ahead."

If Belladonna was a little too nice for the next couple of days, Thea tried to ignore it. But she felt especially pretty sitting on their boat in the middle of the night two days later.

Her hair, though never curly like their mother's, blew about her face in gentle waves as dark as the sky above her. Bella's magic cream really did make her skin glow like the full moon, and her cheeks appeared even plumper.

The dress that Bella had chosen was quite pretty. Baby blue and fitting on the top, it hugged her tiny waist and fell into a full skirt that darkened into midnight blue by the bottom. It was lovely and a perfect dress for a witch. She hoped she didn't ruin it by the end of the night. There were a lot of thorns and mud on the path to the altar.

Every dip of the paddle in the water made her stomach churn with anxiety. What if she wasn't as he remembered? What if she didn't hold a candle to all those pretty women in the Academy? Thea had seen a few of the visitors from Wildecliff in the town before. The women were especially perfect.

As her boat hit the rocky shore of Wildecliff, she stepped into a puddle of mud that soaked the right side of the dress's hem.

"No," she whispered, then sighed.

It was bound to happen. She couldn't hide who she was from him forever.

Thea reached into the boat and swung Browning's sling over her shoulder. The toad let out a little grunt of surprise as he too was swung up in the air but settled down quick enough.

"I couldn't go without you," she said with a soft laugh.

Thea patted his back on the short path to the altar. She told herself it was to soothe him because Browning must be a little nervous about the whole situation. But really, she needed to pat him to make her own nerves settle.

She paused on the path that led to the altar. Leaves obscured her view but also hid her from any prying eyes.

Thea moved the leaves just a bit to look into the clearing. And there he was. The freckled boy she remembered with burnished yellow hair and freckles all over his face. He'd gotten taller, she realized. Lankier too, and his shoulders were broader than she remembered. He wore dark green pants and a white shirt with buttons halfway down it.

Alistair had his hands tucked into his pockets as he stood beside the altar. He leaned against it, then stood up, then leaned against it again. As though he didn't know what was the best way to wait for her.

"He looks quite handsome, don't you think?" she asked Browning.

Her toad didn't reply, of course. But she thought Alistair painted quite the picture. He was tall, handsome, and so uncomfortable waiting for her by himself. Even from this distance, she could see the freckles on his cheeks, and she wondered if his eyes were as green as she remembered.

Taking a deep breath, Thea stepped off the path and into the moonlight.

CHAPTER 14

Alistair's nerves were getting the better of him. How had he been so confident that he could ask her to see him? They had only been writing back and forth for a very short amount of time. Together, their letters had soared up into the stars and told a story of romance and wild abandon that could only be seen in the handwriting of children.

But in person?

He was a man now. His father was all too pleased to remind him of that with every chance he could. Alistair was a young man with a wide future in front of him, and that meant that she was a woman.

A woman.

A real-life woman with curves and dark hair, and what if he had remembered her incorrectly? What if he turned around to see her, and everything came crashing down around his shoulders?

Gooseflesh rose on his arms as he heard the sound of a twig breaking. She wasn't being all that quiet. And then he had to scold himself for even considering she'd want to sneak up on him. He was the one who had invited her. She knew he was waiting for her and that she didn't have to hide her approach.

Glancing at the altar, he muttered, "Ceridwen, give me strength."

Alistair turned around and watched as a pale hand moved the branches out of her way. And then she stepped out of the mist, all wild dark hair and dark eyes. Her long skirts swayed around her ankles, and the half smile on her face was both tempting and terrifying.

She wasn't just a witch. She was the witch.

He had the terrifying realization that she was everything he'd been looking for. Not just a woman. Not just the kindly girl who had sent him letters since they had first met on that ill-fated night. Thea was everything his soul had been searching for and desperately needed.

And now he had no idea how to talk to her.

His face flamed bright red, and his hands shook because what if he said something stupid? What if she laughed at him as his family always had? What if he tried to talk about something that he loved, and she thought that he was a fool? He'd never survive the embarrassment.

Sweat slicked underneath his arms, and he worried he would smell. She'd find him disgusting then and would turn right back around.

Thea paused on the other side of the center altar. She tilted her head to the side, clearly waiting for him to say something, and yet... What could he say? What did a scruffy young man like him say to a woman like this?

Swallowing hard, he dug his hands down into his pockets, shoulders lifting to his ears. "Thea?"

Her laughter bubbled up into the air and floated on the faint breeze. "Were you expecting someone else?"

That blush spread up to the tips of his ears until they hurt. Of course, he wasn't expecting someone else; it was just... well... He realized he didn't know how to talk to a woman.

His brothers were much better at this, even though they eventually got a lot worse. They knew how to make a woman laugh and giggle. Then they would put an arm around her and draw her into the shadows. Usually, those same young women came back with a frown on their faces, but at least his brothers knew how to make them smile for a little while.

Alistair didn't even know how to do that. And it frustrated him because he'd talked to her for so long! They knew so much about each other, and yet he didn't think he could bring up her frustrations with her sisters or how her mother had been acting. He'd never spoken to her much face to face.

She opened her mouth, closed it, and then looked at him with a begging expression that he knew meant she expected him to start this conversation. But how did one talk to a young woman he'd put up on a pedestal of starlight and magic?

"I—Uh—"

Thea looked away from him, back to the safety of the woods, and he knew she wanted to leave. She'd rather return to the boat that had taken her across the river Danu than stand here right now, awkwardly staring at each other while he had turned as red as a tomato.

Damn it. He was muddling this all up, and he'd looked forward to seeing her so much.

"I—" he tried again, even though the words coming out of his mouth didn't seem to match the ones in his head.

He should say that she looked even more beautiful in person. He wanted to say that her letters had kept him going when the entire world felt dark and gray. All the words he'd prepared, the ones that had been locked up inside him because a letter simply couldn't convey the correct emotions, pressed against his throat and jostled to be the first to be said. Instead, the only sound that emerged was a faint croak.

Or perhaps that sound wasn't him at all.

His eyes trailed down past her shoulder until they followed the blue plaid that she'd wrapped across her body. Then he peered down into a wart-covered face that was much more familiar to him. One that, despite his ugliness, Alistair had grown rather fond of.

"Browning!" he exclaimed, significantly more like himself. "I didn't think you'd bring him with you, or I would have brought Atlas."

"Oh!" Thea looked down at Browning as well, then patted her familiar on top of his head. "He goes everywhere with me. He gets angry if I don't bring him, you see. I'm quite afraid of him when he's angry. It's nearly impossible to control him."

The snort that echoed out of his mouth was undignified, but he knew what she was talking about. "The last time he came to my house, I caught him in the kitchens with all the maids. They were hand feeding him flower petals."

"His favorite snack." She nodded, perhaps a little too vigorously. "He'll eat anything, of course, but he has a soft spot for flower petals."

This was awkward. They were talking about a toad rather than talking to each other, but at least he could feel himself loosen up a little. The tension between his shoulder blades eased enough for him to drop his shoulders away from his ears.

If only he could think of something else other than the way her curls coiled around the seashell of her ear. Or how she shifted from foot to foot as though she were dancing and had no idea that her body moved of his own accord.

He'd wanted this night to be special. He wanted this moment to show them why they'd been writing to each other for months on end. Over a year, now. He wanted to know that she felt the same strange feelings for him even though they were impossible and awkward and... and...

Thea held her hand out for him to take. Her fingers were long and pale. There was dirt underneath her fingernails, just like there was always dirt underneath his.

He looked up to meet her eyes through the lanky fall of his hair.

She smiled and wiggled her fingers. "Altars are so depressing, don't you think? They suck all the energy out of the air."

"Where would you rather go?"

"Anywhere."

And that sounded quite nice. He'd let her take him anywhere she wanted if she didn't stop looking at him with that sparkle in her eyes.

He slipped his hand into hers and let the witch draw him away from the shadows that lingered around the altar and into the woods beyond.

He'd never gone anywhere other than the altar on this side of the wall. His father claimed it was a dangerous place, full of ancient gods and goddesses. Beasts that would tear him limb from limb if he thought he was important enough to disturb their peace. Everyone in Wildecliff was warned away from the terrifying outside of the wall.

But the moment they stepped away from the altar, the world burst into life. She drew him underneath branches that creaked with the wind. Tugged him over logs with moss that glowed in the moonlight while eyes blinked open from their nests deep inside the wood. Finally, she brought him to a small ring of mushrooms that had cleared out a space on the forest floor. Even the trees had moved their branches so the moon could see the white caps in a perfect circle.

He almost stepped inside it before she tugged him back. He lost his balance, tumbling dangerously until she caught him in her arms. Her chest pressed against his back, and her strong arms wrapped around his waist. Surprisingly strong for a girl who didn't come up to his shoulder.

"Don't step into a faerie ring," she hissed. "You'll be taken into the other realm and then no one will ever see you again."

That wasn't true. "Actually, as long as you don't eat or drink anything, you'll be fine."

"Except time passes differently in that realm! A few days before you figured out how to get back might be a few years here, or a few centuries!" She shuddered against his back, and her fingers curled protectively in his shirt. "Best not to try your luck. Even if you can see their kind."

"Worried about me, are you?" There was the faintest hint of his brothers in his voice, one that he didn't necessarily like but also knew had worked.

Her fingers spasmed in his shirt before she drew away from him. Thea had moved her grip to the plaid and frowned at him. "If you want to try your luck with the fae, then by all means. I just don't think they're likely to give you back."

They would. The fae had little use for him in their realm. They enjoyed ordering him around in this one far too much to waste him in their own realm. Still, he thought it was adorable that she'd worried for his safety.

Looking over at the faerie circle, he muttered, "Why don't you ease her mind a little?"

Faerie lights rose from each mushroom. These were little will-o'-the-wisps, faeries that she could see without the gift he'd given her. They floated up to about the same height as Alistair and then gently bobbed from side to side.

"Oh," Thea breathed. "They're so lovely."

The faeries loved compliments. At his nod, they rushed toward her and settled in her hair, on her shoulders, down her arms. One even landed on top of Browning's head. He went cross-eyed, trying to see the flying light that he obviously wanted to eat.

Thea froze where she was, holding her arms out at her side and the lights dancing in her eyes.

"Look," she said. "I think they like me!"

"I think so too," he replied with a chuckle. He tucked his hands into his pockets, more naturally this time, and leaned back a little to get a good look at her. "You look pretty decorated in faeries. What shall we call you? Mistress of the wisps?"

She crossed her eyes, mimicking her toad, and stuck her tongue out. "Now that would be a gross exaggeration and an insult to these lovely fae. If anyone were their mistress, it would be someone much more important than me."

But he wasn't so sure about that. The way the lights danced on her features only proved how lovely she was. The shadows along her nose were aristocratic, and the smooth globes of her cheeks made him want to touch them to see if her skin was as soft as it looked.

Goddess divine, she was more than he'd ever expected. Here Alistair had been, waiting to meet a toadstool when he was waiting for a faerie princess to step out of the wood and draw him deeper into her world.

He tilted his head to the side and smiled at her. Not a full grin because he hadn't done that in years. But a half smile that was more than he'd felt on his face for years.

"Oh, I think important people forget they aren't the only ones here. You'd remember them, Thea. That's more important to the fae than wealth or beauty."

"Why's that?"

He took a step closer to her, and the faeries lifted off her, returning to their watch over the faerie circle that needed guarding.

The look in her eyes was one of apprehension but also something that was akin to excitement. He hoped she wasn't nervous anymore or afraid. Alistair wanted her to see him for who he really was.

Maybe it was the forest. Maybe it was the faeries surrounding them. Whatever it was around them that encouraged bravery to bloom in his chest, he would never know.

But Alistair stepped up to her and hooked one of those dark waves around his finger, and now he knew that her hair felt like silk. "The fae have learned that being remembered is more important than wealth or power. For if you are remembered, then you've already discovered immortality."

"Immortality sounds rather boring to me," she whispered, wide eyes staring up into his. "I'd rather live a wild and untamed life than be so concerned with forever that I forget to live."

He didn't understand this magical woman in front of him, but he wanted to. Alistair wanted to dive into her mind so he could live a few moments like her. Without worrying about honor or greatness, not having to worry about how her family name would live on.

She lived. Just like she said. And he wondered how it would feel to be less of a tamed pet and more of a wild animal whom no one could control.

Thea bit her bottom lip, brows furrowed as she looked up at him. "Do you not agree?"

The lock of her hair slipped from his fingers, and he sighed before shrugging. "I don't know. I've only grown up with the laws my father has put in place. He told me for years that I had to uphold a legacy that he and his father had built. And the father before that, etcetera."

"That sounds very heavy to carry."

"It can be." Again he shrugged. "But I am the youngest of his sons, so I have the least amount of expectations on my shoulders. My brothers will uphold my father's history, so I suppose I have less to worry about. That's probably why my father has let me live on the sidelines for such a long time."

Why was he talking so much? These were personal thoughts that she likely didn't care about at all. And yet, he wanted to tell her. He wanted to let his deepest, darkest secrets pour out of his mouth so that he could purge them from his soul.

She reached up between them and placed her hand on his jaw. "When we are here together in the woods, you can leave that weight somewhere else. To me, you are just Alistair."

Just Alistair.

He liked that.

"Sound good?" she added.

"Yes," he replied. "I think I would like that very much, if you feel comfortable with that."

"Why wouldn't I be? After all, I've been writing with Alistair, not the youngest son of the Orbweaver family." She chuckled as though the thought amused her. "I've always wanted to know you for who you are, Alistair. I don't care about your family or what everyone else thinks you're supposed to be. Caring about any of that is a waste of time."

He supposed she was right. He took a step back and held out his hand. "Will you walk with me back to the wall? I'd like to talk about Browning more, and perhaps learn a little about your family. And once we're there, I have something to show you."

And so they walked.

He took her around the paths that led to the wall, but then he rounded them back to the altar a few times as though he didn't quite remember how to get home. Mostly because he enjoyed listening to her talk. There was a musical quality to her voice, as though she were always just moments away from bursting into song. He wanted to hear her sing. He wanted to hear her talk. All her stories were filled with so much detail it was like he had been there. Right beside her.

Eventually, however, the sun peeked out on the horizon, and he knew they both needed to get home.

As the sky turned pale and the moon set for the evening, he drew her to the wall and pointed out what he wanted her to see. "There, do you see it?"

The crack in the wall had recently been patched, but it never lasted long. Already, some Wildecliff citizens had pulled the stones away to reveal the hidden entrance into his city. The crumbling edges were just big enough for someone larger to fit through.

"A hole in the wall?" she observed. "My mother said that was impossible to find because people from Wildecliff are terrified of the wilderness entering their home."

"Not impossible," he corrected. "Just unlikely. But this hole has been here for centuries. It's a way for us to get to the altar and back, but if you ever needed me..."

She bit that lip again, white teeth flashing to hide her smile. "And why would I ever need to find you, Alistair Orbweaver?"

His cheeks turned bright red again. "Just in case."

She nodded, still grinning. "If something horrible happens and I need an escape, I will come to you first. I promise. Goodbye, Alistair."

There wasn't anything else to say, he supposed. She turned to go back into the woods and the wilds, and he should have gone home to the safety of his dark manor. Except this wasn't right. Not yet.

He spun around, eyes seeking her disappearing shape. "Thea!" he called out.

"What is it?" she asked, turning around with her eyes still wide.

"When will I see you again?"

She tucked a strand of that lovely hair behind her ear and smiled in a way that nearly sent him to his knees. "I'll tell you in a letter."

CHAPTER 15

Thea almost didn't want to leave him, and that was an unusual feeling for her. She'd always wanted to go home, even when she was a tiny baby who was at other children's houses. Her home with her mother and her sisters was the only safety she felt. So to not want to leave him at all?

She didn't know how to process that.

"Do you think I'm mad?" she asked Browning as she paddled them across the river. "I can't imagine staying with him would even be possible! His father would turn me away, and besides, I've never been interested in Wildecliff. Mother says there's something wrong with everyone who lives there."

Maybe that wasn't fair. There wasn't something wrong with them, per se. It was more that they didn't want to be connected to the earth.

To someone from Waterdown, the mere idea of not being connected to the earth should make them sick. Her stomach should turn thinking about living on those cobblestone streets, surrounded by rock and smoke. But the more she thought about living with him, the more she wanted to give it a try.

Would it be all that bad? Maybe she'd find something to love there, just like she'd found many things to love about Alistair.

She chewed her lip until it bled as they paddled their way across the river Danu. A few fishermen were already out in their boats, and they gave her a strange look every time they floated by. A young woman in a canoe wasn't something they often saw, especially in deeper waters like this. But Thea still gave them a wave and a bright smile, and they shrugged off the oddity of the sight.

Most people did, after all. She'd gotten quite used to people looking at her strangely. Thea never did what others expected, and that had started when she was very young. How many children put flowers in their mouths and then said how delicious they were?

The canoe hit the sands on the other side of the river. She got out, tied Browning safely around her waist again, and let herself look one last time at Wildecliff. It was so far, but she swore she could feel him looking back at her.

Sighing, Thea started up the mound and down the long walk home. It would be breakfast time once she made it, and she hoped her mother had made blueberry pancakes. They were Thea's favorite.

She'd been much too hopeful, however. Her legs ached, and her lungs burned when she made it back to their little cottage, and there was no sweet scent of syrup in the air. There was only her mother, standing in the doorway with her arms crossed over her chest and a disappointed expression on her face.

"And where were you?" her mother asked.

Ah. Thea supposed she hadn't been so sneaky that she'd gotten away from her mother's wrath. Even if she were supposed to meet a boy, she wasn't meant to spend the entire night with him.

"Máthair," she muttered, trying her best not to sound like she was also angry. "I didn't mean to stay out all night. I'm sorry. But we weren't in any danger at all."

"Not in danger? My youngest daughter is meeting with one of the Orbweaver boys in the middle of the night and then doesn't come home? Do you think I'm not supposed to worry about that?"

She hated it when her mother used his last name as some kind of insult. Alistair wasn't just some "Orbweaver boy." He was nothing like his family, and the mere fact that she slapped that title onto him was rude.

Thea drew herself up straight and tall, squaring her shoulders so she could look a little more intimidating while meeting her mother's angry gaze head on. "His name is Alistair, Mother. He was a perfect gentleman and was quite kind the entire time I was there with him. I'd appreciate it if you didn't insult him to my face."

"Insult him?" Her mother quirked a brow. "And how did I insult him?"

"He's not an Orbweaver boy. He's nothing like his family at all, in fact. And he requested that while he stands before me, I think of him as nothing more than Alistair. No last names required." She crossed her arms over her chest. "I'd like it if you did the same while speaking about him."

She'd never stood up to her mother like this before, and she supposed it surprised Máthair. There was a moment where they stared at each other, neither of them knowing what to do with what was said.

The words hung between them until her mother let out a little sound close to a laugh.

"Well, then," her mother said, her posture loosening. "You have strong feelings for this boy, I understand."

"I just..." It wasn't that she had strong feelings. Thea didn't know how to say the words. "He's been a very close friend for a long time now and..."

Her mother held up her hand for silence. "A close friend requires more than letters, little one. I know you think you're an adult, but meeting someone in person differs greatly from reading their words. You know there is a lot of interpretation in the written word, and I would hate to think you fell under this boy's spell because he has a quick wit and a talented quill."

Somehow, it felt as though her mother was saying something other than Alistair was good at talking.

"He's not charming in the slightest," she corrected. "He's quite awkward, in fact, and I thought for a bit that he wouldn't even speak to me after asking to meet me in person."

"That's unusual."

"He is." She nodded. "But I do like him, mother. Perhaps even more now that I've met him in person."

"Then that is a good sign." Máthair stepped aside and gestured for Thea to step into the house. "I only wanted to warn you that I don't think this situation is wise before your sisters sank their claws into you."

"What?" Thea barely got the words out before both of her sisters launched themselves out of the door.

They grabbed onto her arms and dragged her into the house, asking a million questions at once.

"Was he handsome?"

Thea shook her head. "Not really. I mean, in a quiet sort of way."

"Did he kiss you?" Belladonna waggled her eyebrows.

"No! Of course not!"

Marigold stuck out her tongue. "Did he at least try to hold your hand?"

Her face burned at the memory of how she'd held him away from the faerie ring. Maybe they hadn't held each other's hands but was there another way to talk about how her fingers had brushed against his stomach, and the thin lines of his ribs had touched her knuckles?

Apparently, her blush was all her sisters needed to know about what had happened between them. They both burst into laughter like the harpies they were and then yanked her toward her bedroom.

"Tell us everything! Everything!"

She supposed it was only fair to tell them what they wanted to know, especially since Belladonna had been the one to help Thea get ready.

She let the entire story spill out of her mouth and held nothing back. Her mother would likely be horrified at the things she and Alistair had talked about, but Thea trusted him not to run back and tell his father everything. Besides, what man cared about the daily life of a young woman? It wasn't like she'd told Alistair anything about affairs of the estate or manners of the city. She wouldn't know the first thing about dangerous details to tell someone about Waterdown, anyway.

Marigold laid on top of her bed and dramatically draped her arm over her eyes. "It's so wonderful and I'm horribly jealous. Why is it that you find someone handsome and kind before me? I'm older than you!"

Thea pointed at her eldest sister. "Belladonna is older than both of us, and she's not yet married."

"Perhaps not for long," Belladonna muttered.

Both of the sisters stared at her with wide eyes until Thea blurted, "What?"

Though Belladonna shrugged, as though unaffected, the sparkle in her eyes was one that Thea had never seen before. "I quite like the quill maker, I suppose. And we've been talking. It's not the right time, but soon... If we're lucky..."

Now it was Belladonna's turn for her sisters to leap onto her and shriek until their ears nearly bled. A wedding! Oh, how Thea had always wanted to see a wedding. They would have it in the cottage, of course. Their enchanted home would make the most lovely place for a wedding. They'd have honey cakes and so many flowers. One couldn't have a wedding without flowers. And... and...

"Stop it!" Belladonna said, laughing hysterically with her sisters. "We're not talking about me!"

All the attention swiveled back to Thea, which she discovered she did not like. It was easier to have all the attention on Belladonna, who was older and more likely to handle it correctly. Thea turned bright red and cleared her throat.

Belladonna let out a little laugh. "So, when are you going to see him again?"

At the time, Thea had thought she sounded rather mysterious, telling him she'd write to him. She had stepped into the shoes of so many women who had wooed men with a chase and a thought that maybe, just maybe, he could catch her. Except now she wondered if she shouldn't have set up an exact date and time.

She tucked a strand of hair behind her ear and muttered, "Well, I don't know."

The silence in the room became deafening.

Marigold planted her hands on the bed and shot straight up. "What do you mean, you don't know?"

"We didn't set up another time to see each other. I told him I'd write to him and let him know when I wanted to see him again." The hairs on her arms rose as both her sisters groaned. "What? Should I have said something else?"

Marigold heaved a long sigh. "He probably thinks you don't like him now. You decided to tell him that you were not interested in saying that."

"How?" she exclaimed. "We both know how long we've been talking with each other, and that will not change any time soon."

"But he asked you to meet with him in person," Belladonna interjected. "Did you not think that maybe meant he was no longer satisfied with the letters and wanted to see you in person? He likes you, Thea. He wants to be around you more, and here you are, unwilling to even mention when you want to see him next. The poor boy had his heart broken in that field."

She hadn't thought of it like that. Alistair had seemed so awkward, and she had been so confident all of a sudden. He'd been the one who wanted to leave. She'd watched him start to go through the wall, and that was why she had turned around. Asking her for a second meeting had seemed so much like an afterthought that her response had sounded right.

Pouting, she popped her hand onto her fist and sighed. "Well, I don't know when I want to meet him again. We can't keep meeting at Ceridwen's altar. At some point or another, there's going to be someone there getting their own familiar."

Both her sisters hummed under their breath and stared off into the distance. They all thought as hard as they could about the perfect opportunity and place to meet with young Alistair.

Their mother cleared her throat in the doorway. "Thea, if you like this boy that much, do you really want to keep meeting him in secret?"

"I don't think we necessarily met in secret?" Perhaps they had, though. They had snuck away from both of their own cities and then disappeared into the night to meet.

Was that how Alistair thought, as well? Was he hiding her?

She supposed he must be. His father had made it clear at the familiar ceremony that he thought Thea and her family were beneath them. She still remembered the cool gazes of both his brothers and how horribly they had smiled at her; how they had teased her about poor Browning.

They were not a good or kind family. She wouldn't blame Alistair for their foolishness.

Sniffing, she shook her head. "I don't want to hide him. No part of me is embarrassed that I know him, nor do I wish to hide our friendship from others. It's an honor to have him in my life."

Thea had expected her mother to argue with her. Máthair hadn't hidden how little she thought of the Orbweaver men either, and the hatred between their families went deep.

But Máthair smiled at her and nodded. "Your father's family had no love for me either, Thea. But we endured the hardship of convincing them I was worthy of him. It's not a simple path to walk, but it is one I am familiar with, and one I will help you through, no matter how difficult that becomes."

Thea stood up from the bed and launched at her mother. She wrapped the dear woman in her arms, holding her tight to her heart because even though her mother didn't agree with this entire mess, that didn't mean she would stop Thea from seeking a relationship with

Alistair.

She was the luckiest girl in the world to have a mother who loved her so much. Even to support her when she didn't agree with what Thea wanted to do.

Sighing, she leaned back and looked up into her mother's eyes. "Thank you."

Máthair smoothed her hair back from her face, smiling in that soft way that always said how much she loved Thea, no matter what happened. "Have you thought about inviting him to Beltane, my darling? I know it is not widely celebrated in Wildecliff. It would be difficult for him to get here, perhaps, but we'd treat him like family once he arrived."

Beltane.

She hadn't thought about the May festival, but it was a lovely time for people to gather. And if he'd never celebrated the festival before, it was quite the sight. She knew he would enjoy it.

Alistair had made it very clear that he followed the old ways. He'd found so many ancient texts in that school of his and said they made so much more sense than the way he'd been trained at the Academy. Maybe, if he came to the Beltane festival, he would see how much better it was in Waterdown. Maybe he'd even consider moving here, since it seemed to align with his beliefs better.

"You're far too intelligent for your own good," she told her mother, pointing at her with a shaking finger. "That's the perfect idea. I think he'd love it."

Marigold hugged her from behind, slamming into Thea so hard that she ended up back in her mother's arms. "Beltane! Does that mean we get to meet him as well?"

"I'd prefer it if you didn't," she said, mashed against her

mother's collarbone.

"Oh, come on. We won't scare him away! We couldn't even if we tried." Marigold followed her words with a hard squeeze that drew all the breath from Thea's lungs.

She didn't think they would necessarily scare him off, but she also didn't think they would encourage Alistair to seek a longer relationship with Thea. They were terrifying in their own way. And more than most people were used to dealing with.

"I'll write to him," she said. "I'll go now and have Browning take it to him. Beltane isn't much to ask, is it?"

Suddenly nervous, she untangled herself from her family's arms and made her way down the hall to her room. Browning hopped along behind her, having been underneath Marigold's bed for her conversation with her sisters. But he knew there was a long journey ahead for him. Hopefully, he didn't mind all that much.

Except, when she opened the door to her room, there was already a familiar in her window.

"Atlas!" she exclaimed. "You're here!"

He held out his clawed hand as though waiting for something. He hadn't arrived with a letter of his own, which meant...

Oh. Alistair hadn't wanted to wait for her to write him a letter. He'd sent his familiar, intending to get another date to see her, whether she was ready or not. Thea didn't know if she should blush bright red or if she should be angry with him for rushing her.

She settled for the former.

Finding her quill, she penned out a letter that she hoped he would find agreeable.

ALISTAIR,

WOULD YOU PLEASE JOIN ME IN WATERDOWN FOR THE BELTANE FESTIVAL? THERE ARE QUITE A FEW TRADITIONS I'D LIKE TO SEE IF YOU'RE FAMILIAR WITH THEM.

LOOKING FORWARD TO SEEING YOU AGAIN,

THEA

She hoped the last bit wasn't too telling, but she was nothing if not honest. Blowing on the ink until it dried, she rolled the letter up and handed it to Atlas.

As the raven took off into the air, she wondered if Alistair was thinking of her at the same time.

CHAPTER 16

He was breaking so many rules by being here. Alistair gulped one last time and looked back to the shores of Wildecliff. The boat he'd chartered to take him across was an old Waterdown ship that usually brought produce to his city. The man said he came daily with orders back and forth across the shore and was more than happy to take a person. For a price.

Alistair didn't worry about the coin. His family had plenty of that. What he did worry about was his father catching wind that an Orbweaver had gotten on a boat headed to Waterdown.

He adjusted the cloak around his head to make sure no part of his brightly colored hair was visible. People knew of him. They knew his family. All it would take was one person realizing that he'd snuck off, and then all of this would end. His father would torture him until he forgot how to breathe.

No one had seen him, though, and now he had to let these worries melt away.

Because today he got to see her again. After three weeks, he finally got to see her.

Alistair turned his face to the breeze and to Waterdown that revealed itself on the horizon. He reminded himself of their plan. She would meet him at the docks, alone. Her family had a lot to prepare for, apparently, and that meant that she was the only one who could spare some time away from the festivities. They would then, of course, meet her family while they headed up to the Beltane festival, which was in the northernmost part of Waterdown.

Most of this was foreign to him. He had no idea how to celebrate Beltane in the old ways. His family only celebrated in a very modern way, which was to say very little celebration at all.

He let the cloak fall away from his face at the very last moment and straightened the vest he wore underneath it. He didn't know how to dress for a Beltane festival, and he hoped that he wasn't overdressed. But the light brown tweed pants he wore had to be suitable, even down to the shiny black shoes on his feet. He wore a matching tweed vest over a pale white shirt and hoped that was enough not to make him stand out overly much.

The boat approached one of the nearest docs, and the man behind him shouted, "Here's the town, boy!"

Though he knew better than to trust a salty seaman who had been weathered and beaten down by the elements, he still left an additional coin on the barrel where he had placed his original payment. "For safe passage. And, I assume that you will be ready for the return trip tomorrow morning?"

The man worked his jaw and then grinned, revealing a few teeth were missing. "How early are we talking?"

"Sunrise."

He rolled his eyes, but the greed for coin was stronger than his desire for the festival. "That's fine, then. I don't mind coming a little early if there's more coin to be had. Off with you. Hopefully, you find yourself a May Queen."

Alistair didn't know what that meant, but he already knew in his soul that he'd found one. If there was to be a queen, Thea was the only one that sparkled in his eyes. Not for her beauty, although that was undeniable, and certainly not for her wit, for she was rather odd. But because looking at her made his soul feel full, and he had never felt that before.

For good measure, he placed another coin on the barrel. "Sunrise," he reminded the old man.

"Hard to forget."

Alistair walked up to the edge of the shallow barge and reached for a pole that braced the dock. There were bundles of rope splayed out all over the wooden surface as though no fisherman worried that someone would trip over the bundle and land in the sparkling waves. Perhaps they didn't care. There were four other boats docking at the same time, as well. All of those sailors were shouting orders and tossing crates of food, wine, and mead up into the arms of those who waited for the goods.

The air was filled with sound—shouts of men, the laughter of women, the creaking of ropes, and the slosh of waves against wooden surfaces. He'd never thought that a harbor could be so loud. But then again, he supposed it must be similar in Wildecliff when one wasn't sneaking off in the early morning light.

"Alistair!" His name echoed over the heads of the people in front of him.

He knew that voice. He'd know it anywhere. Stretching his considerable height from his normal hunch, he peered over the crowd, trying to find her. But there were too many people. It would have been easier to look through a telescope while he was in the boat than it was to stand here in the midst of the crowd.

A large man with a beard gave him a strange look, then gruffly told him to move.

A lady with her arms full of what looked like wheat snorted when he didn't move and then whispered how he wasn't from here.

And suddenly, all that noise and sound became a little more overwhelming than he'd expected. His palms slicked with sweat; his eyes turned left to right, but he couldn't find any familiar faces. Worst of all, he had the strange sensation of spinning, even though he was standing still.

Then, as though compelled by a spell, the crowd parted. She stood at the end of the dock, wearing a pretty lavender gown with a square neckline and a trim waist that made her look even smaller than she was. Her dark hair was pulled back from her face with a little bow that had tails flying behind her head as she frantically waved at him.

She was so pretty.

No, it was more than that. She wasn't just pretty, she was....

He touched a hand to his heart and realized that the feeling in his chest was something he had never felt with anyone else. Thea was his favorite feeling, even though he didn't have a name for it.

Alistair pulled the cloak free from his shoulders and laid it over his arm as he meandered through the crowd. He knew where she was now. Time would rush by them no matter how hard he tried to slow it down, and he wanted to savor each footstep that drew him to her side.

Carefully stepping over a bundle of rope, skirting around a bucket of fish that was still flopping inside, and then he was there. Right in front of her.

The wind toyed with her hair, smoothing it over the velvet soft curves of her cheeks. The smile on her face lit up his entire soul.

"You're here!" she exclaimed. "I didn't think you'd come."

"Why not?"

She shrugged. "It's a long way. And I didn't think your father would let you."

Considering his father had no idea he was here, she was correct about that. He rubbed the back of his neck and let out a little laugh. "Well, about that..."

Apparently, she didn't care to hear about his family's troubles, and for that, he was grateful. The last thing he wanted to talk about was how his father would skin him alive for being here or how he needed to find a way out of that house, or he feared he would end up dead.

Thea danced on her toes only two words into his reply, so he stopped himself and watched with an amused half smile as she wiggled in front of him. "Did you have something you wanted to say?"

She pulled her hand out from behind her and revealed the flower crowns she had hidden. Two of them. One made with the prettiest of yellow honeysuckle and another made with beautiful red tulips.

He could smell them without even leaning toward them. The bright, crisp scent of their petals filled the air with the promise of spring. The smell was directly from the earth and so vibrant it made something in his chest twist.

"What are these?" he asked.

"You have to wear flowers during the Beltane festival! It's a May celebration. We're celebrating the feminine wrapping around the masculine, and a time for the earth to turn over into something new." A blush spread across her cheeks as though roses had kissed her skin. "Here. Let me."

He leaned his head down and let her place the tulips on top of his head. He wouldn't mention that he knew the meaning of these flowers. Red tulips were a declaration of love, and though he knew she wouldn't say the words so soon, it still made his chest swell with pride.

He reached for the honeysuckle in her hands, taking it out of her grip so that he could place it on top of her head himself. Because honeysuckle meant devoted affection, and he wanted her to know he felt that way. He was entirely devoted to her, as mad as it sounded.

"There," he said with a smile. "Now we are both adorned. What next?"

She blinked at him, seemingly lost in her own thoughts, before she shook herself free from them. "Ah, well, Máthair and my sisters are a little ahead of the plans, surprisingly. Everyone is in the town square, so we can hurry there and start eating!"

"Eating?" He glanced up at the sky and saw the sun hadn't even reached its peak yet. "It's hardly even noon."

"Beltane festivals are about eating until you can't eat anymore. Then you take a small break for any of the festivities; the may pole, the may queen announcement, offerings to the fae, or the bonfires." She ticked off each of the options on her fingers. "But regardless, the food is the best part of the festival. My mother is an especially good cook, and I helped a lot this year as well."

He'd try anything she made. Although, he hoped it was tasty because he'd never managed to fake enjoying a food he didn't like.

Alistair let her drag him through the town and tried his best not to focus on how strange this place was compared to his home. Waterdown was... warm? Everything was warm. That was the only way he knew how to describe it.

Every house was a different color as they walked down the main street. Yellows, blues, even a couple of pink houses, which startled him so much he almost dragged Thea back to look at it. The cobblestone streets weren't even remotely orderly. Different sized stones, some even as small as his fist, all interwoven together to create a flat surface. And then there were the windows. Hundreds of windows all in different colors, so if the sun shone through them, they cast rainbows on the ground.

He'd never thought that Waterdown would look like this. Even his wildest dreams could not have conjured such a place.

Bright yellow bouquets hung from every doorway. He supposed that it must be in celebration for Beltane as well, although he didn't know why. And he didn't have the time to ask as Thea dragged him through the streets to the center of town, where countless tables were all set up around the central well.

Brightly colored banners and flowers hung above their heads, strung between the buildings. And the food! She hadn't said enough about the food because there were mounds of it on every table.

His eyes couldn't soak in enough of the bounty he saw in every direction. His father had made it sound as though the people in Waterdown were struggling. Suffering, even. But this was the town center of a city that had all it needed. This was a city with means.

Thea waved over her head again, jumping up and down for someone's attention. And as he followed the direction she looked in, he saw three women who looked almost exactly like Thea.

There were more of her?

He was in so much trouble.

Not that he minded meeting her family. It was an honor to be brought all this way. And yet, seeing them in person felt a lot more real. He had expected to court her in the same way he would in Wildecliff. Away from everyone's sight until they were ready to get married, and then they would tell their families their decision and hope that both sides agreed. Everyone in Wildecliff was secretive and hard-pressed to share their world or their thoughts. They weren't likely to introduce each other to their families too soon.

But here, he could see how close everyone was. The neighbors all pointed at each other and laughed. There were people visibly hugging, and so many smiles were all around. In Wildecliff, it was strange to see someone smiling. Sinister, almost.

Thea grabbed his hand again and dragged him toward the table where her mother and two sisters sat. "I know you haven't met them before, but don't be nervous."

"I'm not nervous." He lied. Of course, he was nervous. In fact, he thought if he swallowed wrong that he might throw up all over her.

"It's going to be fine, you'll see." She squeezed his fingers and dragged him over to the table.

He remembered her mother. The tall, graceful woman had stood up to his father in a way that only she could have done. Her bravery had made him melt even then. A year later, she didn't show a single change, as though the world knew how beautiful she was and how they would all be unlucky to see an ounce of her allure disappear.

Thea's two sisters were stunning as well. He nodded at them, trying very hard not to blush bright red because they were so remarkable, and he felt as though he were very much overdressed. Her sisters also wore different shades of purple, though their sundresses were comfortable, while he looked too formal. And of course, her mother wore a bright green sundress with hand-stitched yellow flowers embroidered along the hemline.

"Have a seat," Fenna said with a bright smile. "You're welcome at our table, Alistair Orbweaver."

He winced at his name. He wasn't embarrassed by his family name. There was nothing he could do to change that, but it still felt strange to have her call him by name when he knew she didn't like his family.

Sitting down on the bench with them, he held his hands in his lap and tried very hard not to look too suspicious. Or strange. Or awkward. Really, any of the things his brothers had called him for the entirety of his life.

Thea didn't seem to notice a change in him. She chattered on with her sisters, talking about how many boats were in the harbor and what they were bringing before she grabbed his plate in front of him.

"Are you hungry?" she asked, those big eyes reflecting the earth and warm chocolate upon him.

He blinked a few times, then nodded. "I suppose so."

"Good, because I think you'll like the quiche Máthair made. It's lamb and wild mushroom, one of my favorites!" She piled the quiche slices onto his plate, then added two sweet treats. "Belladonna and Marigold made the hot cross buns this year. They made enough for the entire village to eat."

"Oh hush," the eldest sister said. The one he assumed was Belladonna. "We made enough for us and the quill maker."

"You could just call him by name, given the situation."

"I refuse to do that." Belladonna sniffed but then pushed a small platter toward him. "You have to try the shortbread as well. Thea made it.”

Alistair looked at the shortbread with far more interest. He could take a slice, even though he'd never had shortbread before. He didn't think, at least.

Thea nudged it closer. "It's lavender and lemon. I'm going to leave half of it for Brighid, since she's our household deity. She'll like it, at least, I think."

Even though his plate was already quite full, he placed a slice of her shortbread in the middle of it all. "Thank you, Thea."

She smiled at him, and all his worries faded away. Her family might not like him, and he might be afraid of what would happen the rest of the day. But right now, they were eating together. Their first meal shared.

Nothing would ruin this moment for him.

CHAPTER 17

Thea had gone over a lot with her sisters. Beltane was the festival of light and happiness. There were so many opportunities for a couple to fall in love during this festival, and if she wanted to make sure that Alistair stayed with her for forever, then Beltane was the perfect time for it.

Forever seemed like an awfully long time. They were only eighteen. Planning that time until the end of the world seemed like a bit of a rush. But her sisters knew best, and if they wanted to help her, well, she would not turn away such a gift.

So they ate. They laughed. Her family welcomed him with open arms to prove how amazing they would be to have as in-laws. And though Alistair seemed uncomfortable for the first bit, he loosened up enough for her to see how pleased he was. He liked them.

He liked her.

Thea wasn't blind. She saw how many glances he stole in her direction and how his cheeks turned bright red whenever she caught him looking. He'd come all this way for her. Probably turning aside everything he knew about her town and her people just to see her.

That had to mean something, didn't it?

He even helped pick up the table. Alistair loaded his arms with plates so high she was certain he'd drop them, but he gave her a wink and then staggered off in the well's direction where the elders of Waterdown had gathered to clean the plates. They were all color coordinated so they'd return to the correct home. Although, their plates would simply disappear back to their cottage when the time was right.

"I like him," Belladonna said, crossing her arms as she stood beside Thea and watched Alistair make his way back to them. "He's a little too concerned about that suit of his, and I still think it's ridiculous that he dressed up for a Beltane festival. But he's trying hard, and I like that."

"Me too." Marigold paused and looked over at Alistair as well. "He's got kindness in his eyes. That's a good match for our Thea, if I do say so myself."

Her eldest sister snorted. "A match might be a little more credit than he deserves, but he seems like a nice enough boy. I'll allow that."

Thea didn't like that they were talking as though she wasn't there. "Excuse me? He's going to be here any second, and I'd prefer it if you two witches weren't talking about him as though he wasn't here at all."

Her sisters rolled their eyes in tandem before meandering away. But Belladonna tossed over her shoulder, "We're going to be at the bonfires! You should bring your friend."

She'd shouted loud enough that Alistair had heard her. And when he walked up to her side, he tucked his hands into his pockets and looked at her through his mop of hair. "Bonfires?"

Explaining all this to him felt as though she had a foreigner in her midst. "Do you not light fires for Beltane?"

"We do." He nudged his toe in the dirt. "But they're in the fireplace. We light them all at the same time in the house and let them burn throughout the night. Sometimes we eat good food, but most of the time my father considers the fires enough to honor Ostara. It's the one time a year we use the fireplaces."

Balthazar Orbweaver toyed with the gods. Just hearing the story made the hair on Thea's arms stand straight up. "You're lucky Ostara hasn't cursed your family."

"I wouldn't be so quick to say she hasn't." He chuckled, but the sound had no mirth in it. "Anyway, you said something about bonfires? Is that the right way to do it?"

"Oh yes!" She clasped her hands over her heart. "Ostara loves bonfires. First, of course, we'll crown the May Queen, and there's the may pole to dance around! You wouldn't do that, though. So I suppose I'll skip this year. And then the bonfires are the last bit of it. Couples will run and leap through the flames so their love burns bright, or you can jump through yourself for good luck."

She paused in her rambling. Would he want to jump through the flames with her? That seemed rather... forward. She shouldn't expect that.

He held out his hand for her to take. "We'll see where the night leads us, shall we?"

That was the best answer she could have hoped for. No pressure. No expectations. Just her and Alistair exploring the world together. As it should be.

She didn't know how she got so lucky as to meet him when she did or why he'd ever sent her that letter, but she was so pleased that he was here.

Together, they walked away from the town square, and she drew him to a larger open area outside Waterdown. The Beltane festival was always held in the same part of the fields that surrounded the town. There was a small platform, overgrown with grass now, but that was where they always set up the may pole. Already young women were dancing around it and a band playing a jaunty tune with four fiddles and a few drums. The rainbow-colored strips of fabric wrapped around the pole as the sky turned pink with streaks of the setting sun.

"May pole?" Alistair asked, nodding toward the young women dancing.

"They dance for many reasons." She still held his hand in hers, and she wondered how long it would take him to realize they were holding each other's hands. "Most of them dance for fertility, however. Spring is the perfect time for babies to be welcomed, and most of these young women have been struggling."

It was a bad year for it. She'd overheard her mother talking with the mayor of the town when the other woman had come to visit. Apparently, most of the women in the town were facing some strange fertility crisis, and no one could figure out why. The nearest witch who dealt with mothers and children lived in Wildecliff, and unfortunately, they hadn't convinced her to come over the river to see to their people.

She was glad she wasn't looking to have a child any time soon. Thea couldn't imagine the grief that came with waiting for a baby that never came.

Alistair squeezed her fingers. "And the colored fabric?"

"Ostara and Flora like colors," she explained. "The goddesses of spring hate anything bland."

Alistair looked down at his own clothes, and she had to cover her mouth with her free hand. He might be a little overdressed and bland, but that didn't mean he didn't look the part. He'd rolled his sleeves up his arms and done everything he could to be involved in the Beltane festival. For that, she thought it was rather lucky to have him here.

A shout echoed from further up the hill. "May Queen! May Queen!"

They were going to announce this year's May queen sooner than she thought. Thea grabbed his arm and yanked him toward the hill where they would crown the May queen. Though she'd never been one herself, she always had some small amount of hope in her chest that this would be her year.

Maybe having Alistair here would be the good luck charm she needed.

A large crowd gathered before the mayor, most of them young women like Thea. Some of them had their beaus with them, and of course, there were plenty of elders who were so excited to see who was crowned this year. Usually, it was someone younger, but rumor had it that the mayor had other plans this year.

She stood at the front of the crowd—her pressed blue suit with gold buttons clearly marking her as the Mayor of Waterdown. She was lovely, with her blonde hair coiffed and twisted at the base of her neck. And though the mayor had been casually thought of as perhaps a little too masculine, Thea had always thought it only enhanced the strange flavor of her beauty.

The mayor was more than the leader of their town. She was the first female mayor Waterdown had ever elected, and Thea thought she'd done a fine job of it thus far.

Hands on her hips, the mayor looked down at the ranks of young women standing around her. "The may queen this year is a young woman who has shown excellent kindness, remarkable standards in magic, and a love for this town that very few others could match. And while I know there are plenty of younger girls who were hoping to be May Queen this year; I have it on good authority from Ostara herself that this year she wishes to have a May Queen of marriageable age. A May Queen who will represent what this time is actually about. Fertility and the coming of spring."

So the rumors were true then. Ostara wanted someone older this year, although Thea couldn't guess why.

She hugged Alistair's arm so tightly that she feared she might cut off his circulation. But what if she was crowned? What would she do? What would she say?

The mayor looked throughout the crowd with her piercing blue eyes, and then her gaze settled upon Thea's sister.

"Belladonna," the mayor said, her voice booming throughout the clearing. "Ostara has called upon you to represent her in this time of summoning."

Belladonna's eyes nearly bulged out of her head at the announcement. And quite a few others murmured in the crowd. They understood an older May Queen, but one Belladonna's age? The murmuring died down as her sister walked through them, however.

She had that way about her. Sometimes her sister looked like an otherworldly creature who had stepped out of the forest to guide them into a time of magic and spells. Most times, her sister looked like the true meaning of hag. But today, as the sunset turned blood red, she walked toward the mayor with grace and virtue.

Even those who were angry about their own children not being picked sighed as Belladonna joined the mayor. "I accept this great honor, and my only hope is that I serve Ostara with pride."

That was it.

Usually, the May Queen gave a long speech, but her sister knew that this moment wasn't about her. It was about the goddess.

The crowd cheered, and Thea tugged Alistair's arm away from the crowd. He looked down at her with surprise, a question on his tongue before they had even stepped three feet away.

"Are we not going to watch your sister?" he asked, though he let her tug him through the crowd with no complaints. "I thought the May Queen position was rather important?"

"Oh, it is. But we'll see her speech again. They've got to cover her in flowers and get her into a white dress first." Thea had other plans than waiting for her sister to get ready. She'd already smelled the ash in the air and the way the wind had blown smoke toward them.

The bonfires were lit. This was her favorite part of the Beltane festival. She loved watching people leap through the flames in the hopes that their wishes would come true. So many couples would hold hands and leap as though nothing was stopping them from getting to the other side. They did not fear the flames. They did not fear the heat. For no matter what stood in their way, they would always be together.

They clambered up a larger hill and then stood at the top. Far below them were the fires. This year, Waterdown had decided they would have three large bonfires and that each of them would be for different people. Two for singular leapers and one for couples.

"This is a good view," she breathed and then sat down on the ground.

Alistair hesitated, and she wondered if he worried the mud would sully his pants. But then he sat down beside her with a heavy thud.

She tried not to look at him, even though her eyes kept seeking his. With the moon coming out on the horizon and darkness falling around them, it felt as though they were the only two people in the world. And maybe they were.

For the long moments of silence, it was just them and the moon. The warm light of the fires played across her skirts and burnished her fingers with outlines of gold. She could see every freckle on his face and how they dusted the backs of his hands. How his long legs stretched so much farther than her own, and it seemed even the grass clung to him.

She watched as her friend Clodagh walked through the crowd with her fingers intertwined with another young woman's. That must be the young woman she'd talked about, and then they were leaping through the fires together.

Her heart squeezed in her chest. Maybe someday she'd have someone to leap through the fires with. Just not yet.

Alistair reached for her hand and twined their fingers together until they'd almost made a kind of knot between them. "You're suddenly quiet."

"Is that a bad thing?"

"I'm unused to you being quiet."

Thea wasn't sure if that was a compliment. She supposed she talked quite a bit, but hopefully, that wasn't overwhelming for him. Or too much. Or... Or....

His fingers squeezed hers. "Do you know why I wrote you that letter?"

"Which one?" She looked down at their hands together, and she found that she quite liked what she saw. "You've written me many."

Alistair chuckled. "The first one."

"Ah. I've never really thought about it." That was a lie. Thea had thought about it a lot.

She'd first explained it away as guilt. His family had been so cruel, and she supposed that was why he'd wanted to apologize. And then she'd written him back, and maybe he had to keep writing to her, or else he'd be considered rude.

He cleared his throat and turned her hand over in his. Alistair traced the outlines on her palms, the life line, the love line, and even her fortune line before he continued. "When I saw you in that clearing, I thought you were the most lovely girl I'd ever seen in my life. Not just because of your hair or how your eyes remind me of hot chocolate on a winter's day. Not because of your clothes or how you stood up to my father, either. I thought you were beautiful because of the love in your eyes when you looked at Browning. A creature most people would have hated immediately."

"He's easy to love," she corrected.

"Oh, I know. I've met him many times now." Alistair laughed, then lifted her hand to his lips.

He pressed a kiss to her knuckles and then turned to face her. He moved his legs so that they were on either side of her body. Trapped, surrounded by him, she had never felt so at home.

Those deep green eyes stared into hers, and he whispered, "I'd very much like to kiss you, Thea."

She'd never been kissed before in her life. Never even thought about it. But as her gaze drifted down to his mouth, she realized she'd like to kiss him as well. So she nodded.

Alistair leaned forward, and his hand cupped the back of her neck.

He drew her close and kissed her lips as though she were made of glass. Delicate. Soft. She hadn't thought his mouth would be so soft.

His mouth moved against hers. Once, twice, three times. Gentle, chaste kisses, but they made her feel something bloom inside herself.

He drew back ever so slowly, his cheeks bright red and a genuine grin on his face. "There," he whispered. "Does that make up for not jumping through the bonfires with you?"

The words were so preposterous that a laugh escaped her, unbidden. She pressed a hand to her mouth as though she could hold his kisses there for good, then she nodded.

And when he turned back to watch the bonfires, he wrapped an arm around her shoulder. She leaned into his warmth and thought she would never forget this night. Never.

CHAPTER 18

Alistair felt like he hadn't breathed since they kissed. He'd come all the way back across the river from Danu and meandered home as though walking on clouds.

They'd kissed.

Even now, thinking those words made him feel a little silly. Of course, they had kissed. He'd desperately wanted to do that since the first moment she walked out of the fog like the witch from his dreams. He just hadn't thought it would happen so soon. So early. He hadn't realized that he even had it in him to ask.

And the next couple of days, he walked through his home as though he were a new man. Alistair held his shoulders a little straighter. He didn't fear what his brothers would say or do to him in the halls. Some might even say that he held his chin a little higher because he was so certain that he was valuable.

She'd given him a gift with that kiss. It somehow felt as though she'd handed him his soul back.

His father passed him in the hall and turned his nose up. "Why do you look like that?"

Alistair didn't know what his father meant. He wore the same clothes. He had done his hair the same as he always did. And yes, there was still dirt underneath his fingernails, but this time, he was rather proud of it. He would fit right in if he returned to Waterdown. Returned to her.

Clearing his throat, he lifted his chest and set his jaw. "I look the same as always, Father."

"You look..." Balthazar made another face as though he'd smelled something disgusting. "Happy."

Well, he was. For the first time in his life, he knew what happiness felt like and how that emotion could fill him up from the bottom of his soul to the top of his head.

What a magical thing to happen to him this late in his life.

He let out a little laugh and watched as his father recoiled from him in horror. He replied, "I suppose I am."

"Change it, and quickly," Balthazar snarled. "You know we have company coming over tonight and I won't have you ruining the dinner with your laughter and... glee." Again with that wrinkled expression.

Alistair wished he had enough confidence to refuse to change a thing about himself. He wished he could tell his father that there was nothing wrong with happiness, and this house might be a little more wholesome if there was more of it around. But he was not that man. Not yet.

Clearing his throat, he ducked his head as he saw his father's hand glow with magic. "Understood."

"Was it?" Balthazar looked down at him cruelly as though he intended to harm his youngest son even though the boy had agreed to do what he wanted. "You know who's coming to dinner tonight, don't you?"

He didn't. Alistair wasn't included in the plans, and if someone was coming to the house, most of the time, he was sent up to his room without an invitation at all.

"I do not, sir."

"The Sphecidae elder and his son are joining us for dinner. I have big plans for them and for their interactions with our family in the coming months. You will not ruin this opportunity for our family. Do you hear me, boy?"

"Loud and clear, sir."

His father flexed his hand and then let it loosen before walking away from Alistair. The tension that had built in his shoulders eased, and suddenly Alistair was leaning against the wall, breathing hard and unsure of what had happened.

Had his father cast some kind of spell while they were talking? Or was he so terrified of his father that he forgot to breathe in the man's presence?

Pushing himself off the wall, he staggered down to his room to change for dinner. While he recognized the name, he thought he had only heard it from school. Sphecidae. It was a pretentious last name for a family of wasps. Quite literally. The head of the Sphecidae family had gotten his magic from that Latin-named class of creatures, and they'd used it to their advantage ever since.

Alistair thought he remembered the son talking about poison in their classes. Something about learning how to effectively use each one to their advantage, but he couldn't quite remember the conversation.

It wasn't like he enjoyed himself at the Academy. Most of the time, Alistair kept his head down and looked for the faerie creatures who needed his help.

Sighing, he stripped out of the comfortable clothing he'd put on this morning. He enjoyed his matching vest and trousers with a pressed white linen shirt that he could roll up at the wrists. He'd caught Thea looking at the rolled sleeves quite a few times, and he wondered if she liked that on him as well.

He'd have to ask her the next time he wrote her a letter.

But tonight, he needed to look the part of an Orbweaver son. He took his time making sure every part of his suit was pressed, that the black tie he'd chosen wouldn't move in the slightest, and that the starched jacket lay perfectly in place with matching ruby cufflinks. His father would be proud of how he looked rich without trying all that hard. That was, after all, how his father wanted all his sons to look.

Rich.

Effortless.

Deadly.

Alistair snorted and then made his way out of his room. Deadly wasn't something Alistair would ever accomplish, but he'd never find it in himself to be disappointed about that. He didn't want to be someone others feared.

Wandering down the cold halls, making sure his cufflinks were latched, he mused that he wouldn't mind a life in Waterdown. His eldest brother would get this house, anyway. And the other would stick around or work at the Academy. Which left Alistair to do whatever he wanted whenever he wanted.

At least, that's what he hoped. The future without Balthazar Orbweaver in it looked rather bright.

He rounded a corner and headed into the dining room, where his family waited for him. It was a cold room, the same as the rest of the house. But a maid had lit the fire behind the table, throwing off waves of heat that were hard for even the magic of this house to suppress. Surprising. He'd never seen a flame in that fireplace.

The wooden table stretched too large and was covered with a black tablecloth. Food was already on the table, as though they were expecting their guests soon, and Alistair knew he was late. Especially as his father and two brothers stood, then rolled their eyes as they realized it was not their guests that had walked through the door.

"Alistair," Balthazar hissed. "Sit. Down."

Right. He had his spot, and it was the one farthest down the table. At the end of his family. They all sat on the same side, his father at the head and the three brothers to his left. Guests would sit to Balthazar's right when they arrived.

Alistair had only a few minutes after sitting to muse that someone must have put a spell on the food to keep it warm when the doorbell rang. His father instantly straightened, and Alistair saw both of his brothers twitch.

Nerves?

Why would any of them be nervous because they were entertaining? They'd done this far too many times before for anyone to be nervous. Hadn't they?

The head butler entered the room with two people walking behind him. The head of the Sphecidae family was much older than his father, or at least looked like it. His head was entirely white, with long white eyelashes that blinked like spider legs around his eyes. The man was all too pale and wore clothing in the faintest hint of yellow. Almost as though the suit had aged rather than been dyed. He stood with a straight spine, though, and confidence in his eyes that made Alistair twitch.

The young man behind him didn't look a thing like his father. Alistair remembered him now. He'd been in Lysander's year, so only one ahead of Alistair. Which meant the young man had graduated with his brother. Although neither of them were looking for work just yet, the hungry look in their eyes suggested that they both wanted to take their family's power from whoever stood in their way.

Alistair noted that the Sphecidae's son had darker hair, though still a hay-colored blonde. Not white, like his father. His suit was perfectly starched as well, though his was white as snow. Why did he have a better suit than his father? It didn't make any sense at all. Both of them were ungodly pale, though. Like their skin had never seen the touch of the sun.

"Balthazar," the Sphecidae elder said.

His father stood and extended his hand for the other man to take. "Corpious, it is good to see you, old friend."

Friend? Alistair should have heard the name before now if his father had considered this strange man a friend. He might not be privy to his father's innermost thoughts, but Alistair knew what was going on in this house. He snuck through the halls like a mouse, and no one ever knew he was listening. But no one had ever said this man's name before.

It was hard to forget a name so similar to a corpse.

They shook hands as Corpious's son sat down on the opposite side of Lysander. They nodded to each other, the recognition in their eyes less one of friendship and more of hatred.

"Shall we?" His father said, sweeping out his arm to gesture at the food. "As you can see, we have spared no expense."

Corpious's eyes cast over the food and clearly found it all lacking. Even though there was a roast peacock, three different kinds of fish, and more vegetables and fruit than any man could want. It was a feast fit for a king and the fact that this man was picking it apart with his eyes? The look made even Alistair's hackles rise. A man should be thankful for what he was offered. What he was freely given.

If he'd been a better son, he might have mentioned it. Maybe he would have stood up for his father's honor.

Such loyalty would require a better father, he mused. Alistair waited until their guests took their seats and reluctantly picked at the food before he allowed his own father and brothers to serve themselves as well. It made him even more hungry, waiting for everyone to have their own food at the ready. Even worse, to see Corpious's son tucking into the food without waiting for any of them at all.

Lysander sipped his wine before speaking across the table. "Well, Marren. I thought you were shipping off for the continent to learn more magic from the elders."

Their guest swallowed his food before brandishing a grin on his face. He'd eaten beets first, Alistair thought, because for some strange reason, it looked as though his teeth were covered in blood. "I decided to stay behind and help my father with the house."

"A house like that couldn't require much work." Again Lysander sipped his wine. "It's rather small, wouldn't you agree?"

The way Marren wrapped his fingers around the handle of the knife beside his plate said otherwise. But the young man didn't respond in the slightest. Instead, he turned his attention to their fathers, who were quietly speaking at the end of the table.

His father didn't waste any time getting down to business. Alistair couldn't hear a thing that was being said, but Cassius had leaned in whenever his father twitched his fingers. Was his eldest brother involved as well?

He kept his head down while they all ate dinner. Alistair didn't move a muscle when the butlers came in to clear their plates and then took the rest of the food away. But he kept his eyes on his father and the pale man who radiated dark energy. He didn't like it. Something was wrong. As though static electricity filled the air, and he couldn't escape from it.

Marren stared at Lysander over a particularly large cake cut into the shape of the Academy. "How long do you think you'll be riding on daddy's coattails?"

"Excuse me?" his brother asked.

"Well, we all knew at school that you aren't as talented as Cassius. You certainly aren't as deadly as your father. So I wanted to know if you were going to continue being a burden to your family or if you planned to do something about that." This time Marren sipped at his glass of red wine as though he had somehow won the chess game in front of them.

Cassius spun away from their father to defend his brother. Their argument didn't disturb the two older men, who were still very deeply in talk with each other.

The cake moved.

Alistair blinked a few times to clear his vision, but he was correct. Where the front door of the school was supposed to be, there was movement from deep inside the cake. As though something was inside of it, trying to burst out.

The frosting shifted again until the tiny mouse-like face of a brownie poked through. What was it doing? They might not be able to see her, but they could see the cake moving! They'd cast spells before they even realized there was a fae in there.

"Excuse me," Alistair muttered, then leapt forward with a knife in his hand.

Marren hissed, lifting his own knife as though Alistair were going to attack him. Everyone at the table stopped talking and looked at him as though he'd lost his mind.

Alistair tried a sheepish half smile and then pointed to the cake. "I thought it looked so delicious we might as well cut into it."

If looks could kill, then Balthazar would have murdered his son. "We have people to do that, boy."

He was going to be in so much trouble for doing this. "I know. I just didn't want to wait. Sweet tooth."

He carefully sliced around the brownie, ignoring the glares from all the members of his family as he lifted the slice onto his own plate and then sat back down. All it would take was a single wave of his father's hand, and he'd be on the floor in pain. But the business was more important than punishing his idiotic youngest son.

When everyone returned to their own conversations, he used his fork to lift the cake off the brownie. She was covered in frosting, dripping with it really. Then she sat up and scrubbed her face with her hands.

Alistair tried to gesture for her to move with his fork, but she refused to do so. Instead, she pointed to his father and squeaked.

"What is it?" he whispered, trying to hear what she was saying over the sound of other people's conversations.

But then he heard it.

"Poison."

Alistair lifted his eyebrows, but then he saw it. Corpious put his finger in his father's drink for a split second and then continued the conversation as though nothing had happened at all. Balthazar lifted the glass casually, still talking with the man while he lifted it to his lips.

He had a moment where he considered letting his father die. All the fear and terror in his life would disappear. It would be all right if his father was simply... gone.

But then he stood and growled, "That bastard."

Everyone paused again, looking at the youngest son, who had lost his mind.

Balthazar's face wrinkled with fury. "Son. Sit down."

"He poisoned your drink," Alistair said. "I saw him put his finger in it. And isn't his gift poison?"

His father looked down at the glass, then back to his son—only a few heartbeats. But Alistair felt as though his father had seen him for the first time before all hell broke loose in the dining room.

Corpious and Marren tried their best. The eldest son of the Sphecidae family could fling poison out of his mouth like he was spitting it upon the world. One such glob landed on Lysander's hand, who howled with rage.

But it was Balthazar who would have the last say. His father let out a roar, and the shadows in the room clung together, then stretched out like giant spider legs. They clamped around both the intruders to their home, twisting the darkness around them—squeezing tightly—until Corpious's pale face turned purple.

"Did you think you could kill me in my own home?" Balthazar hissed. "I long thought it was time for a new head of the Sphecidae family. It's a shame that means you must lose yours."

His father lifted his hand, then twisted it in the air. His movement brought along a sickening crack as Corpious's head turned and then snapped.

Blood leaked out of the pale man's nose, and then the shadows dropped him onto the floor.

Dead.

Alistair wheezed out a small breath. So much madness had happened in a split second. And it wouldn't have happened if he had said nothing.

He watched as his father approached young Marren, who still struggled in the bonds of shadows. His father touched a fingertip to Marren's chin and forced the young man to look at him. "You and I are going to have a talk about how our families will work together from now on. What do you think?"

There was no other option but for Marren to nod. The shadows carried him from the room while Alistair's brothers scurried after their father.

He held out his hand for the trembling brownie to sit in and lifted her to his cheek. He breathed with her, slowly, in and out, in and out.

What had he done?

CHAPTER 19

Well, I still think it's rude," Clodagh muttered, kicking the soil that Thea had just overturned. "The man kisses you and then disappears? It's just wrong. Wrong, I tell you."

"Clodagh," she said with a laugh. "I can't expect him to talk to me all the time. He's busy! He has... school and his family, and..."

"Excuses. Those all sound like excuses."

The sun beat down on their heads, and it was getting a little too warm for comfort. Her pale blue dress was already stuck to her back, and the hem was heavy with mud. Thea lifted her hand to the floppy hat on her head and pushed it back so she could properly glare at her friend. The gardens needed to be weeded, and this section of the earth was getting dug up for next year's garden. She should have had an earlier start, but Thea had been up all night worrying about the things her friend was making worse.

"You know," Thea started, then paused to think about what she wanted to say. "I think that he's just busy."

"You already said that." Clodagh grabbed the hoe out of her hands. "What if you're a bad kisser?"

"I'm not a bad kisser." She grabbed the hoe back as the words sank barbs into her soul. What if she was horrible at kissing?

She'd never done it before. The mere idea of pressing their mouths together made little sense, but it wasn't like she'd had any practice with the boys in the village. They were always panting after her mother or her sisters. Not a little wild Thea.

Thea looked down at the ground and told herself not to let those words wiggle like worms into her mind. He'd come here for a reason. He'd wanted to see her for a reason.

One bad kiss couldn't ruin all that, could it?

Clodagh sighed and planted her hands on her hips. "Either way, you should forget about him. If he can't write to you after all that happened? He doesn't deserve to be in your life. That's what I say."

But Thea wanted him to be in her life. She'd see him every day if she could. Alistair lived in her mind like a ghost. Haunting her every step with whispers of romance and a life that she couldn't live, no matter how hard she tried. Not here, at least.

A caw echoed over their heads. She looked up to see the silhouette of a crow gliding through the clouds.

No. A raven.

"Atlas!" she gasped, letting the hoe fall from her hand and promptly land on Clodagh's toe.

As her friend let out a pained, wordless shout, she rushed toward the small landing place her mother had left out for moments like this. If Atlas was going to make the flight regularly, her mother had said, then he needed somewhere more comfortable than a window sill to land upon.

The grace with which the familiar moved was a wondrous thing to see. The thorns in his feathers didn't bother him at all as he landed on the wooden perch and shook himself until his black plumes billowed out around him.

"I didn't think I'd see you again," she said quietly as she reached out to pat his head.

Atlas gave her an unimpressed look. Apparently, she'd said something that either offended him or his master. She knew that expression well.

"I'm sorry." Thea took the letter off his leg and gave him another gentle stroke down his back. "People talk and put things into my head. I never should have questioned him. He's been busy?"

The raven squawked again, although this time she swore it sounded... sad.

Browning hopped up next to her and let out a very loud ribbit. Thea glanced down to realize her own familiar wanted to be lifted, his arms held out to her like a child. Without hesitating, she swung him up into her arms.

His strange, croaking voice broke through the horrible sound he made, and she heard him in her head. "Atlas says sad."

"Sad?" She looked at the bird as though it should tell her more immediately. "What do you mean, he's sad?"

The raven looked at the letter in her hand and then took off into flight. He must not have time to entertain her when she held the answer in her hands. She supposed she didn't blame him.

Thea ripped open the letter as Clodagh limped over to join her.

"What's that?" her friend asked.

"A letter," she replied impatiently.

"I'm not blind. I can see it's a letter, Thea, but what's it say?"

She scanned her eyes over the looping swirls and graceful lettering.

Thea,

I'm sorry I haven't written to you sooner. A situation happened at the manor, and I haven't been able to get away from my family in a... while.

You have no reason to trust that these words are the truth. You may not trust me at all, considering how long I've made you wait. But if you have any feelings for me left, I'm by the altar now. I'll stay here all day waiting for you.

Just... come? Let me explain.

Alistair.

Her heart tumbled in her chest. It flipped and rolled and then landed in a puddle at her feet because he hadn't thought she was a terrible kisser. He hadn't thought he'd gotten what he wanted from her and then forgot about the little muddy girl from Waterdown.

Alistair wanted to see her. He was waiting for her right now, and she had so many chores to do.

She looked up and met Clodagh's gaze.

"Oh no," her friend muttered. "I know that look. What? What do you want?"

"I have to go." Thea already backed away from Clodagh, trying not to give her friend an opportunity to escape. "You can finish my chores, can't you? All you have to do is finish hoeing the garden, and I know you've done that before, so you can't mess it up."

"I have places to be as well. I'm supposed to be meeting with—"

"Thank you!" Thea sprinted up the hill and away from the little cottage. Hopefully, Clodagh would do her work, or she'd be in so much trouble. But Browning was with her; maybe she could blame it all on the toad.

Besides, it was time for her to see about a boy who made her heart flutter and her stomach twist and turn in her belly.

The old boat would have to do at this time of day. Browning stood at the helm, watching the water with a keen eye. Plenty of ships were moving through the deep waters of the river Danu, but they'd see her long before they needed to turn. She paddled the boat past them, riding the waves they left behind and grinning from ear to ear. A few of the sailors waved to her with wide smiles on their own faces. They must have understood that she was heading off to follow her heart.

After all, wasn't that a sailor's life? They all followed a heart that called for the depths of the ocean and a life of adventure. She might not mind that when she was older, either.

In the hour it took to paddle, her arms grew heavy and aching. Sweat slicked down her back, but she didn't care. The pretty blue dress would have to do, no matter how horrid she smelled or how disheveled she was.

Maybe she should have dunked herself in the river before she made it to him, but Thea didn't have time for that. She wanted to see him. He wanted to see her. They'd be all right with a little mud and sweat.

Her boat hit the shore, and she breathed a sigh of relief. Soon she would see him. Soon, all of this would make sense even if it hadn't this morning.

Thea nearly tripped getting out of the boat and almost dunked herself into the river, regardless. But she caught herself on the edge and only soaked a small portion of her skirts. Grabbing Browning in her arms, she raced through the wood with its overgrown bushes and trees until she careened into the clearing where the altar stood.

And there he was.

Alistair turned with a half smile on his face, all those freckles standing out too stark on his pale face. The boy needed to see the sun more, she resolved. Mostly because she wondered what a burnished tan would look like on his skin.

Her arms trembled, and she let Browning slide to the ground. "You're here," she said.

"I promised I would be." He lifted his arms up by his sides in an awkward kind of shrug. "I had to apologize in person. The idea that you were... worried about how I felt or why I didn't write? It was eating me up."

Tears burned in her eyes because she had known he wouldn't go silent on her without good reason. Her gut had said there was nothing wrong in the slightest, at least between them. But Clodagh had gotten under her skin, and now she felt horrible that she'd questioned this for even a minute.

Thea launched herself through the void of discomfort and silence between them. She ran so fast into him that he made an "oof" sound before he wrapped his arms around her as well. She didn't care that she probably stank to the high heavens after a day of working in the garden. Nothing mattered other than her arms around his trim waist and the feeling of his breath on the top of her head.

"I'm sorry," she said into his shoulder.

"What do you have to be sorry about?" His hand lifted behind her and then cupped the back of her head. He held her so gently as though he feared she'd disappear from his arms. "I'm the one who didn't write to you after... after..."

Oh no. There was that awkwardness again. There was the feeling that something had happened between them that changed everything. Thea found that she hated a single kiss could make them feel so terrible.

Something had to be done. And in her opinion, the best thing to do was the exact problem which had brought them here.

Besides, she wanted to prove Clodagh wrong. Thea wasn't a horrible kisser.

She leaned back in his arms and held onto his shoulders. She breathed in the summer scent of his breath, like mint and basil and sweet summer wine. His exhale fanned over her face even as she drew him down to touch his lips to hers once more.

This time was so much different from the first. He'd originally kissed her with the hesitation of a young man who wasn't quite certain why she'd let him do this. And Thea hadn't known how to react, not really. But this? This was something else.

His hand flexed in her hair, his other hand curled into a fist in her dress at the base of her spine. They discovered a new rhythm, slow and languid, as they discovered what it meant to enjoy a kiss. Or perhaps, considering the way butterflies had awoken into flight in her belly, how a kiss was endured.

It was wonderful. And horrible. And exciting. And life changing as he seemed to sink into her skin, inch by inch, until she didn't know where she ended and where he began. When he drew away for breath, his lips were red as wine.

Thea traced a finger over the thin line of red and smiled. "I don't know why you were gone," she whispered. "But I'm glad you're back."

His brows drew down as though her words made him very sad. Saying nothing, he linked their fingers and drew her away from the altar. They walked through the woods into a small clearing she'd never seen before. The trees were sparse. Grass grew so deep and thick it was like moss around them. And tiny flowers sprinkled the ground with every color.

"Here," he finally said, drawing her to the thickest part of the grass. "Would you spend an afternoon with me? Just you and I?"

How could she say no? Thea let him draw her down into the grass and spent the afternoon listening to him.

Alistair explained everything that had happened to his family. How another powerful visitor had nearly killed his father and then how their guest had remained and been tortured in their basement for days until the young man relented. He explained his house grew so cold after so much of his father's magic that he'd not slept for two days. Every word seemed wrenched out of him as though he were pulling the story out like nails that had been hammered into his soul.

She listened because she was good at that. But also because it sounded like he needed to purge himself of the story. And when he was done, Thea found herself with her head on his chest while he'd stretched his arms behind his head to stare up at the sky.

It was strange to lie with a person like this. She'd snuggled with her sisters in bed but never a young man. Never someone so... so...

His heart beat steadily under her head, and the warmth of his skin heated her from head to toe. It felt so natural to rest her head on him, and it shouldn't.

But it did.

She pressed her hand against the drum of his heart and sighed.

"It's hard to imagine you as part of that family when you tell me stories like this. Your magic seems nothing like your father's or your brother's."

"Oh, but it is." He lifted a hand and gestured with his fingers above them.

The slightest wiggle of his finger and she could see the magic above them. The web that sparkled with diamonds and hid the faerie world from their gaze. She tried to touch it but couldn't.

"If you had your whistle I made you, then you'd be able to touch it," he said.

But she always had it with her. Thea reached underneath her bodice and drew out the whistle. Lifting it to her lips, she blew as she reached out her hand and touched the glistening web.

She could feel him smile. Alistair grabbed her hand with his and guided her fingers to pluck certain glistening strings. "This is how I see the world. So you have to know, it's all spider magic. The veil I can draw back at will is like a web that separates our world from theirs. And when I wish, I can manipulate that web so that myself or others can see the fae as they are."

"My mother says that your power is dangerous in the wrong hands." She let the whistle slip from her lips. "She says that you should keep it secret."

"I do." Alistair swallowed hard. "My father knows what I can do, but not to the extent of it. He calls it a small gift, just as he called yours. But they never know how powerful our gifts are until we're tested. If I wanted to, I could rip open this web and let out a thousand faerie creatures into our world. It would be an unstoppable army, by my guess. The last time that happened was when the Wild Hunt devoured half of all humanity."

She'd heard the story before but had never believed it was real.

Shivering, she tucked herself closer against him. "My magic is a small gift. I cannot affect the lives of others with my power. All I can do is eat plants. Some of them are poisonous, some of them aren't. Most give me a little boost of magic or power, but not for long. Chewing lavender to scare away my fears isn't exactly powerful."

He squeezed her shoulders with an arm. "I think you haven't found the right plants to experiment with yet, then. You're as powerful as I am, Thea, even though you question that every day. Until you realize your worth, I'll believe it for you."

Tucking her face into his chest, she hid herself from the world and all those scary thoughts. And he let her. She discovered that Alistair was a wonderful shield against all the things she didn't want to think about.

Their afternoon passed slowly like they were taking their time flipping through the pages of a book. They let go of all the dark thoughts and terrifying explanations. Instead, they experienced life in a meadow together. Quietly.

CHAPTER 20

He thought he might love her.

Alistair had this thought a few months after they'd been meeting at least twice a week. Sometimes it was at the altar; other times, he could make an excuse to run away to Waterdown. No one had caught them yet, and the secret burned inside his chest with exhilarating adventure at all times.

She sometimes sent him home with a bundle of flowers. Each one she claimed to have plucked when she thought about him. The basket was always difficult to carry because it was so large.

And he knew it was early to be thinking words so strong as love. Thea had barely even talked to her family about their meetings other than the first time they'd met him. But he still dreamt about eating dinner with them and laughing at their jokes but understanding them this time. He wondered what it was like to have a family like theirs. One so close to each other that they teased and laughed and never threatened each other's lives.

Alistair wouldn't mind living with her or her family. Even though all those women might be a little overwhelming, he often thought about how soft it had all felt. And then he remembered he was in the Orbweaver Manor, and his life was full of sharp edges.

A knock pounded against his door. Alistair hadn't the faintest idea who would want to speak with him. He'd been alone for the better part of three days. His father was busy doing something in the basement, Alistair didn't want to know, and his brothers were out helping the Academy get ready for their next year.

He hated to think about what those poor new students would endure under the not-so-watchful eyes of his brothers. Alistair, however, would be safely tucked away from them in his last year at the Academy. Which was coming all too soon now that he thought about it.

How many more weeks did he even have with her? How many weeks until they would be parted for an entire year?

Alistair hadn't considered it yet but found he didn't enjoy the thought. They could write, of course. They were good at that now; after all, it had been two years. But they were older, too. And she was a beautiful young woman who could catch the eye of many men in Waterdown.

He'd seen those men now. They were all tall and broad—either farmers or sailors with big shoulders and heavy arms. As he walked towards the door, he paused in front of the mirror. He was tall. Taller than most of those men, if he was being honest. But Alistair had always been lean. Stringy, his brothers like to say. Fragile, his father called him.

How did one fix that? He could offer to work on one of the ships for a season, but his father wouldn't let him get past the door if he tried. Maybe he'd ask around school. Someone at the Academy had to know why those men looked like that and how he could turn himself into one.

Resolving himself to becoming handsome and brawny, he swung open his door, expecting a servant.

Balthazar stood in the hallway, waiting for Alistair. The sight of his father was so startling he forgot to look down at his feet. Instead, he stared right at the wrinkles winging from the corners of Balthazar's eyes, the quiet slope of his shoulders, and the hard jump of muscles at his jaw.

His father was angry. But Alistair had no idea what he'd done this time.

"Uh," Alistair stuttered, then swallowed. "Father."

Where was the intent to be a strong, brawny man? All of a sudden, Alistair felt all that bravery drain out of him as though he had been smashed beneath his father's shoe. He was the beaten son of a man with so much anger in him that he could have powered a city with it. And that didn't go away because some girl had given him a reason for being.

Still, he wished he could funnel all the excitement of knowing Thea was in his life and change that into a power of his own.

"You're coming with me to the town square," Balthazar snarled as though even he couldn't believe the words coming out of his mouth. "Get your things and meet me at the carriage."

"Now?"

His father raised an eyebrow. "Now, boy."

Alistair only had a few moments to stare at his father's back as the old man walked away from him. What nonsense was this? He never went to the town square with his father. Cassius or Lysander did, depending on how busy one of his older brothers was. No one invited Alistair.

Ever.

He knew very well that change in this house was something to be terrified of. Pausing only for a moment to lock eyes with Atlas, he gathered up his coat and tossed it over his shoulders. Things? What did his father mean by things?

Frantically, he grabbed something that resembled a wallet so he wouldn't look like a penniless fool walking around the town beside his father and then raced down the hall. Nerves churned in his stomach until he feared he might throw up the moment he stepped into the carriage. If his father was bringing him to the town square, then that meant something was wrong. Terribly wrong.

At least it was the same footman as always at the top of the carriage. The man touched his fingers to his hat, but the expression on his face was troubled. So much for reassurance.

He opened the door to the carriage, and the darkness inside seemed to swallow his father. Darkness clung to Balthazar's shoulders like literal hands that tugged his clothing back into place every time he moved. Those long spider legs of darkness then would retreat behind him, ready at any point to either defend or attack.

Shivering, Alistair got into the carriage and sat down on the cushions far from his father. The icy air surrounded him, digging underneath his coat and dragging out all the heat. Without thought, he reached into the pockets of his jacket, pulled out the knit hat he so adored, and plopped it onto his head.

His father eyed him with disgust. "You will not wear that once we reach the town square."

"I wouldn't dream of it." Although Alistair would try. It was too cold around his father not to wear something on his head. His ears might fall off.

Balthazar leaned back in the cushions and watched the windows as they started away from their home. The neat rows of identical houses never changed, no matter where they went in Wildecliff. Although their dark manor had the perfect view of Sunspell Academy, that certainly set them apart.

"You're in your last year, aren't you, boy?"

Alistair wasn't certain what his father was talking about until his mind caught up with the conversation. "I am, sir."

"And what are your plans for afterwards?"

He had no plans. Wildecliff wasn't the place for him, Alistair had decided. And if he had his way, his father would forget he'd ever had a third son, so Alistair could sneak off to Waterdown one last time and never return.

Of course, he couldn't tell his father that. Balthazar would murder him right here in the carriage and have his shadows clean up the body before anyone even knew Alistair was missing.

Swallowing hard, he opened his mouth to figure out some lie to tell his father. He didn't have to.

Balthazar lifted a hand for silence. "Did you think I wouldn't notice you sneaking off? I know you've been leaving the house a lot more lately and returning far more pleased with yourself than you have any right to do. You've got some lady somewhere that you've fallen in love with. Is that it?"

All the blood in his body went ice cold. Alistair felt as though one of the shadows had him by the throat. He refused to let his father know about Thea. He didn't dare to even whisper her name in front of the old man who would tarnish her memory with fear.

So he nodded. That was all he could do. Lying to his father had worse repercussions than not telling him the entire truth.

Balthazar hummed and touched a thin finger to his lips. "I don't disagree with you having a dalliance with a girl foolish enough to do so. We all sow our wild oats, and for one, I'm pleased to know you're not inept at everything. However, you will recognize that this girl is a passing fancy, and you will marry the woman I choose. Just as your brothers will."

The silence pounded against his ears afterward. Was that it? Was that all his father would say to him?

Alistair had no intention of marrying anyone that his father picked. The young woman would be just as cruel as his family, and everyone else in Wildecliff could be. She would be a horrible wife, a terrible mother, a partner that would drag him down into the abyss of despair and madness.

He had to get out of here. He had to leave this life before his father ruined any future Alistair might have dreamt of.

"Don't think about running," his father murmured, turning his attention back to the window. "All you boys want to run, but you forget that you're tied to me. I can always find my blood, and that sings in you louder than you know."

And if it were possible, Alistair would drain that blood from his body drop by drop to get away.

A shadow curled over his shoulder and placed a talon against his belly. The long spider leg didn't feel like a shadow. It felt real and solid and sharp against the unprotected flesh it could rip into.

Alistair swallowed hard. "I won't run, father. I know my place is with this family, in our house, upholding the good nature of your name."

He said the words to appease his father's desire. Maybe if he said what Balthazar wanted to hear, then his father would forget about his youngest son again.

But this time, the long leg of the spider coiled around his neck. All the breath wheezed out of his lungs, and he couldn't inhale. His fingers clawed at the carapace, but he couldn't remove the powerful magic that slowly sank into his skin. Coughing, Alistair took a long time trying to fill his chest with air once more.

"Words are binding," his father said. "You went to the same school as your brothers and yet you all forget that."

The carriage rattled to the side as they hit a particularly large hole in the cobblestone streets. The rocking movement gave Alistair one more moment to look at the floor in horror before he had to school his expression into something placid. Something calm.

He straightened and looked his father in the eyes. Cold. With no expression on either of their faces. "What was that?"

"Just an assurance that you'll do what you say you'll do." Balthazar had tricked him, and his father was quite pleased with himself. "My boys have always wanted to stray, but there is more to our family than you know. I need to know that there will be someone here to take care of our name and our home when I am gone."

"I have two older brothers who are more interested in that fate than I am."

"And they are not immortal. Besides, there are plans for them in place which will take more of their attention than the family home."

A spike of anger through Alistair's chest made him reckless. "Then you should have one of them marry so that their wife might take that role."

His father scoffed. "As though I would ever entrust our family home to a woman. The magic inside that house must be fed, son. I'll show you it someday. But for now, you will learn what magic really is. We're buying the ingredients for my spells. Keep close to me while we're here."

The carriage rolled to a stop in the town square, where many shops were already setting up an outdoor space for buyers to peruse. It was market day, and Alistair had lost track of time.

He'd closed his hand on the handle of the door when his father grabbed onto his wrist and prevented him from leaving. "One more thing."

What else could he endure? He already had a spell cast on him, and one whose rules he did not know. Alistair blinked and realized he hadn't been this close to Balthazar in a while.

His father had gotten old. Older than he should be at his age. The wrinkles around his eyes made the orbs look sunken and pale. His skin had lost any illusion of luster and cracked around the edges of his lips. He looked as though he were ill.

Or dying.

And a man who looked his mortality in the face had every reason to go mad.

"You're going to work at the school after you graduate," his father said. "There's a role that will be offered to you this year. You're going to take it."

"I have no interest in working at Sunspell or staying there for longer than my schooling. Besides, Cassius is already working there. And Lysander—"

His father released his hold on Alistair's hand. "Your brothers have had too many complaints about them, and they will be dismissed from the school this year. They'll be looking for work elsewhere. Cassius will become the head of the household under my supervision, as the plan always was. Lysander will go out on a ship to seek out new magic. And you will work at the Academy intending to become a professor."

"Why?" Alistair couldn't imagine why his father had planned all this to happen. This wasn't the way it was supposed to go.

The eldest brother worked at the Academy, which was arguably the most esteemed position. The middle brother remained with the household in case something happened during the dangerous job at the Academy. And the youngest—the one who should have been forgotten about—was supposed to go off and adventure with nothing to his name.

His father leaned forward, and the gleam in his eye made Alistair's heart stop in his chest. "Everyone has underestimated the use of your power, my boy. I know you've been enjoying that. You want to keep the fae world a secret from everyone else and safe from all those who might use it. Noble of you. But that has to stop."

The kick of his heart in his chest made him gasp. "Why? Why would I do any of that when they don't want to be found?"

"Because this family already has a god trapped in its basement. And when our enemies see the form of that god and know that our family cannot be beaten, then we will remain the strongest family in Wildecliff for centuries to come. Who better to control a god than the only person who can see him, even when he's invisible?"

As though he hadn't ended Alistair's life as he knew it, Balthazar stepped out of the carriage and straightened the shoulders of his jacket. He walked away from Alistair without ever looking back. As though he knew his son couldn't follow him.

If he did, Alistair feared he might start screaming.

He wasn't safe here.

He wasn't safe anywhere but in Thea's arms, and now he feared that bringing her even close to this life might risk her very life.

CHAPTER 21

Thea mused on how her life had taken such a turn. One moment she was a little girl with little girl dreams, and then suddenly, she'd become a woman. She had a young man in her life who made her heart beat wildly in her chest. She dreamt of a future she'd never once thought she'd have in her life.

Of course, there were ups and downs. Alistair had been strange the past couple of weeks, but he also had been visiting her in Waterdown, and that wasn't easy. Getting across the river without his father finding him was taking a toll on the poor man's nerves. Which was why she'd agreed to see him herself today.

She raced down the magical halls toward the front door. The house teased her, making the hallway longer and longer until she burst into wild laughter. "House!" she shouted.

The hallway shortened and spilled her out into the kitchen, where her mother waited. Máthair leaned against the cold stove, an apple in her hand which wasn't quite in season yet, with her head tilted.

"Are you going to see that boy again?"

Thea grabbed the apple out of her mother's hand and took a big bite. "Oh Máthair, you know I don't have a boy in my life."

"Do you not?" Her mother tilted her head even more as though she were trying to see right through her soul. "And here I was thinking your head has been in the clouds all summer because of a young Wildecliff boy. Orbweaver, I do believe. You know we met."

Thea shrugged and tried to look as though she had forgotten. "Oh, did you? And did you like him?"

With a bubble of laughter, her mother grabbed her around the waist and tucked Thea into her arms. She squeezed too hard, wiggling her daughter around until Thea squealed to be let go. "You know I liked him, you silly girl! He was a perfect gentleman, and you proved me wrong about Orbweaver men. How many times do you want to hear it?"

"A thousand times!" Giggling, she wrenched herself out of her mother's arms and took the apple with her. "He's a good person, mother. I like him a lot."

"I know you do. You've been happier this summer than I've ever seen you. I just wish you weren't growing up so fast." Máthair's smile turned into one of bittersweet happiness. "But I suppose that summer is ending, and he'll soon be returning to school. One last year for him, I assume?"

"He's older than the others. At eighteen here, he'd already be going into work." Thea bit her lip because at eighteen herself; she now had more responsibilities. Soon, she'd have to think about who she might want to marry and what job she wanted to have. Obviously, she couldn't do what her mother and her sisters did, but...

Today she didn't have to think about that. Today, all she had to think about was Alistair and how he waited for her in a grove of trees behind a magical altar.

"Don't forget to take Browning," her mother said. "He's been annoyed with you leaving him behind this summer."

Said toad hopped out of her room with a scowl on his face. Clearly, he'd thought he was going to be left and then would be sullen the rest of the week. Her mother had ruined his grumpy plans.

But Thea already had his sling wrapped around her shoulders. "I had planned on bringing him this time."

Her heart needed more time with her familiar. Besides, he deserved more adventure in his life, not just bringing letters when dear Atlas needed a break. She picked up Browning underneath the arms and lifted him high into the air before settling him in his sling. One of his back feet stuck dramatically straight up until he wiggled into a comfortable position.

"Be safe!" her mother called after her.

When was she not? Thea might sneak away to meet with an Orbweaver boy, but she was never risky with any of her choices in her life. Alistair was as safe as cuddling with a kitten.

She paddled across the river until her arms burned and her eyes watered with the wind. But she didn't stop until the sun was high on the horizon and the tip of the boat hit the shore.

Splashing through the waves, she tucked her pale blue skirts into her waistband. Alistair had said he liked it when she wore the color because it made her look like a painting by a great artist. Her skirts were the waves of the sea as they met her pale skin, the sand he claimed, and then disappeared into the dark forests of her hair. He'd become quite the poet as they aged. And every time he said things like that, her face burned bright red. But she loved it.

Maybe she loved him; she mused as she brushed branches out of her way. Would that be mad? They'd only known each other for a summer, but she'd never felt more like herself than in the moments she spent with him.

He waited for her beside the altar, and that half smile broke her heart. She hadn't gotten a real smile out of him in a while, that made her wonder what was happening in his home.

There were new stress lines on his forehead and around his eyes this week. Ones she hadn't seen before and could only mean that there were horrible things happening that he hadn't told her about. But he was here. Right in front of her. She had the chance to fix those awful thoughts if he gave it to her.

As she staggered to a halt on the other side of the altar, her hair slid over her face in a billow of waves that obscured her vision. Before she could even shove it out of her way, he was there.

Alistair slid each individual curl away from her face, smoothing her hair back on her head and taking his time to make sure every strand was in place. His half smile bloomed into a full grin, and he plucked a twig from her hair. He held it up to the sun, his thin fingers spinning it in the golden light.

"How do you always show up with these in your hair?"

She shrugged. "There are a lot of branches on my way to get here."

"You could cut them."

"But where's the fun in that?" She placed a hand on his chest, feeling his heart beat beneath her palm. "I don't mind if the forest wants to have its way with my hair."

A spark burned in his eyes. A passion that she'd never seen before, mixed with a desperation that almost frightened her. Alistair slid his hand behind her neck, trapping her where she was. Between the forest and his body, like a deer trapped in front of a wolf. "And what if I wanted to have my way with your hair?"

The breath wheezed from her lungs. "I'd let you."

His lips descended to her cheek, brushing like velvet against her skin. "And if I wanted to have my way with your lips?"

Oh, why was she so dizzy? Thea's hand curled in his shirt, holding herself steady with the brace of his body. "I think you've already done that before."

When had he gotten so forward? Thea didn't remember him being like this. Alistair had always been so unsure of himself. Not quite capable of taking that next leap into what she had always hoped would be passionate and kind.

She knew next to nothing about what they should do past kissing. It wasn't like her mother had given her any talk about what happened between men and women. A few wives in the village talked about it, and Clodagh. But she didn't trust Clodagh to tell her the actual truth about it all. Besides, Clodagh only knew how to woo women. Her relationships with men had always failed disastrously.

Loosening the strap that held poor Browning between them, she let her familiar drop to the ground, where he hopped away from them lest he be caught between them. He hated it when they did this. She loved it.

Thea wrapped her arms around his neck and drew him down until their lips touched. She sighed against his mouth. So soft. So gentle. Even when he had this false bravado of being a man who told her what he wanted and took it when he wanted, he still touched her with such gentleness and such understanding. He made her feel like she was in control, no matter how he felt or what happened between them.

His arms wrapped around her waist, tugging her against him until they were pressed flush against each other. They had laid in the grass together, but this was different. Something had changed in his movements, perhaps more intent. His hands flexed against her sides but then smoothed up her ribs.

She let out a little gasp as his long fingers brushed the undersides of her breasts. And though he paused, she had the passing thought that she'd quite liked that.

Thea parted her lips and lost all sense of where they were as his tongue plunged into her mouth. Their kiss changed again. This time it became more intense, hotter. He tasted like earl gray tea and some dark magic that she'd never once considered. But then he lifted a hand and palmed her breast and... and...

A sound escaped her lips. A moan, she thought, although it was a horribly embarrassing sound to make. They both stiffened for a moment, breaking away as though the noise had put them both back in the present.

His lips were bright red. Hers probably were too. They stared at each other, wide-eyed and shocked that they had gone so far.

She knew the taste of desperation, though. And she didn't think that kiss was because he wanted to rush her or that he had grown tired of waiting. That kiss had almost felt like a goodbye.

"What happened?" she asked.

Alistair's cheeks paled. "I'm sorry, I shouldn't have—"

"I'm not talking about that, Alistair. I also know you well enough to know something is wrong. So what happened?"

A little of his color returned, but not enough to make her feel better. He reached for the altar and braced himself against it. Then he muttered some curse, an apology to Ceredwin, and then he hopped up to sit on top of it. Alistair's back curved over his knees, and he braced his arms there to cushion his head in his hands.

"My father..." The rest was too muffled by his palms against his mouth.

So something was wrong. She'd been right, and even that couldn't make her feel better about having guessed that something had changed.

Kneeling in front of him, Thea shifted so she could look through his hands, where she sat between his legs. "Alistair? I know this might not be easy to talk about, but you do have to talk about it with me. It looks like it's eating you up inside and that's breaking my heart."

He peeled his thumbs off his face so he could clearly say, "My father cursed me."

"Cursed you?"

"He tricked me into dedicating my life to the family and the Orbweaver name."

Well, that didn't sound too bad. She'd heard worse curses out there, and having to be true to your family wasn't the worst of them. He could have been cursed to lose all his limbs or have rabbit ears for the rest of his life. Curses were tricky things.

"That doesn't sound too bad," she said. "Why are you acting like this is the last time we'll see each other?"

Finally, he looked at her, and she saw the answer in his eyes. He feared exactly what she said. He really did. The sorrow on his features was as though he'd already lost her.

Thea slid her fingers along his jaw, stroking the faint stubble that had grown there. "Alistair. It's honorable to be dedicated to your family and their name. Why would I ever want to leave you because of that?"

"The Orbweaver name requires that I stay in that house. That I remain in Wildecliff my entire life." He held her hand against his face. "I cannot tell you all the dark things that happen in that manor, but I will say that I can't subject you to that. You deserve better, Thea."

"Alistair Orbweaver, are you trying to tell me what to do with my life?" Thea tried to tug her hand away from him, but he held it with rather surprising strength. "I make my own decisions about where I want to be and who I want to be with. Neither you nor your family can order me around."

That half smile had returned as he held her hand with an iron grip. "I'm telling you, it would be dangerous to keep meeting with me. My family is not one that you want to tie yourself to."

"Well, what if I want to?"

"Do you?"

She pretended to think about it, all while trying to wrestle her wrist out of his grasp. "I think I might. You're the best person I've ever met, Alistair, and I don't want to let that go to waste. Not when we've only just discovered each other."

"We've been writing for two years."

"And two years is not enough to satisfy me!" Finally, she managed to jerk her hand free and stood up. Thea planted her hands on her hips, glaring at him as he smiled up at her. "Alistair Orbweaver, I think I might be convinced to love you, if you'd let me."

Well, she hadn't meant to say that much. But now that she had, it felt like a weight was lifted off her chest. She'd wanted to say something like that for a while now, and he needed to know it.

He stood, his eyes wide and his hands already reaching for her again. Alistair tugged her until she had both her hands planted against his chest, and their bodies were so close she could feel his breath on his cheeks.

"You could love me?" he murmured.

"I could."

He leaned a little closer again, all the passion returning to his eyes. "Do you mean to say that you aren't already in love with me, Miss Thea?"

Oh, she couldn't tell him that. She couldn't admit to all of her feelings before he'd admitted to his. So, instead of telling the truth, she sniffed imperiously and said, "You'll have to convince me first, Alistair."

"Then I suppose first I should show you what you're getting into." That passion disappeared, and a hard glint appeared in his eyes. "Come with me to Wildecliff. We'll go together through the wall, and you can decide after you see the manor whether or not you want to love me."

Her head was spinning. What did he want from her? Did he want her to be in love with him or not?

"I—"

But he was already tugging her toward the opening in the forest where his family had disappeared. And she thought maybe it wouldn't be so bad to put his fears at rest. Nothing in his family history could scare her so much that she'd deny him.

"Browning!" she called out and then held the sling open for her toad to hop in.

Apparently, she was going to Wildecliff. What an adventure.

CHAPTER 22

She knew this generally wasn't done. Most people from her city never entered Wildecliff, nor any other visitors. They were madly protective of their walled city, and everyone had to enter through the port. There were then interview questions to answer and a strict screening process. If the only reason to visit their city was to shop, then the people were turned away. That's how it had always worked, at least.

Now, she was sneaking through a crack in the wall with a young man who lived here, but she knew this was more than against the rules. They were breaking every iota of how the cities were run, all so that she could see the house where he had grown up.

But there was a stiffness in him she'd never seen before. He held himself too rigid, with his spine stick straight. The Alistair she knew and adored always had a slight curve to his spine, as though he didn't want to be as tall as he was. His height could make him intimidating, and he never wanted to make others uncomfortable. She'd always liked that about him. He was the unassuming son of a man who took up too much space.

The moment they reached the wall, all of that changed. He dropped the persona of the young man she knew and became someone else entirely. Someone who held himself with the presence of an Orbweaver, and Thea wasn't sure she liked it all that much.

The crack in the wall was just large enough for them to slip through. He held her hand, dragging her further into the darkness as stones scraped against her chest and caught at her clothing. Browning let out a little croak of fear as a particularly jagged rock got a little too close to his head.

How thick was this wall?

It felt as though it were miles thick, capable of withstanding an army that could blast it with cannon fire for years and never get to the heart of the city. But when they slipped free onto the streets beyond, she looked back and realized it wasn't that thick at all. Perhaps six feet, but nowhere near the hours it felt to slip through.

Alistair picked up a loose brick they'd knocked free and tossed it through the opening to the other side. "If someone finds that, then they'll brick up the exit again. The city watch doesn't want people to know this exists. It's the only weak point on the entire wall."

She didn't care. Thea couldn't focus on what he was saying when all she could see was the massive expanse of the city that unfolded around them with crisp, clean edges. If Waterdown was a many-colored quilt, then Wildecliff was the starched edges of a very expensive shirt. The cobblestone streets were perfectly clean, without a single dust mote that dared to disgrace the city. Every house was the same. She could see down the street that they might change to a different shade of gray now and then, but they all lacked color.

In fact, if it hadn't been for the manicured hedges that bordered people's property, she'd have thought she had lost all her ability to see color at all.

Thea glanced over to look at Alistair and realized he fit in here so much better than he did in Waterdown. Though his crop of colorful reddish blonde hair didn't quite seem right, his black and white clothing was out of the same book. She looked down at her colorful blue skirts and the checkered vivid green sling around her neck and wondered how they wouldn't get caught.

Anyone would look at her and know she wasn't supposed to be there. She was an anomaly in a place like this.

Alistair held out his hand for her to take and gave her that little half smile that she now thought might be fake. "Shall we?"

"Where are we going?" She put her hand in his, though, hoping that she could trust him.

"My family home is still the plan, but I thought I could show you the rest of Wildecliff as well. If you have time, of course."

Something ugly twisted in her stomach. She didn't have time for this, in fact. Thea feared this dreary place might sink its claws into her, and she'd never be able to see color again. The rainbows of the world kept her going in the darkest of times. How was she supposed to survive here?

"Thea?" Alistair asked, his voice shuddering with hesitation. "Do you not want to do this anymore?"

"Of course I do!" The bright way she replied should convince him that she wasn't having second guesses, but... she was. She really was.

Thea allowed him to draw her into the city. She counted every single house they passed but eventually thought they'd gone in a circle and stopped counting. Even the windows were the same. She saw curtains, but they were all the same drab colors. Why would anyone live without color? Everyone must be so sad here, knowing that the only brightness they ever got was in the flowers outside their homes.

She let her finger trail over a bloom when they crossed the street. The rose even felt sad. Its petals burst into dust at her touch, and Thea had the distinct feeling that she shouldn't place any of these plants on her tongue. They were poison, not anything like what they actually stood for.

"This is my favorite spot in the city," Alistair said as they climbed a small stairwell in a back alley.

"Here?"

"Yes. This back alley is one of my favorites."

She thought he was joking because surely there were better places for him to enjoy than an alleyway behind two buildings. But he didn't laugh. He didn't even add anything else, so she had to imagine he was...telling the truth.

How horrid.

She looked around them and surmised that the alley had more character than the rest of the city. There were footsteps worn into the stone stairs from years of people walking this same street. And the dampness that was trapped in the small space gave the air a bit more of a scent rather than stale air.

If she made herself think about it, then this alleyway felt like the most real part of Wildecliff so far.

"I can understand why. It's not like the rest of Wildecliff, is it?" She peered up at the small sliver of the sun above them and slipped her hand into the sling.

Browning wrapped a webbed hand around her finger. That was the only support she'd get from her friend because she absolutely would not let him hop about beside her. Someone in Wildecliff might kick him. She'd never forgotten the way his siblings had reacted when they saw her familiar the first time.

"We're going to step out onto a crowded street," Alistair murmured, then squeezed her fingers. "Just walk next to me. Keep your head held high and don't look anyone in the eyes. You're going to do fine."

Fine? That didn't sound fine?

She nodded firmly as though she were well prepared for such a thing to happen, and then they reached the top of the stairs.

While the back streets they had previously crossed were empty and devoid of life, she now knew that was because everyone had come to the center of the city. Hundreds of people were here, and each one looked as though they had spent hours getting ready in the morning.

A woman walked past her with a pressed pencil skirt on and a billowing white shirt. Her coiffed hair was wrapped so tightly to her skull that it lifted the skin on either side of her eyes and gave her a rather pinched expression. The moment the woman looked at Thea, however, that look tightened even more. She surveyed Thea as though she'd never seen such a creature in her life.

Thea was reminded that her skirts had dipped into the water as she got out of the boat and there was likely mud on her hem. Not to mention that her wild hair still hung around her face without a tie, and Alistair might very well have missed a few twigs in the dark locks.

She tucked a strand behind her ear and then noticed another man staring at her in shock. The businessman wore a suit that probably cost more than Thea's house was worth, and he leaned over to whisper to a lady beside him in a gown that would have befitted an opera. The emerald dress was dusted in a fine coating of expensive jewels. Immediately upon hearing him, the woman craned her neck to see where Thea was standing and then laughed.

Laughed.

The sound carried even through the murmurings of the crowd to Thea's ears. Her cheeks burned. She never should have come here, and damn it, Alistair should never have brought her to this place. She wasn't prepared to be in Wildecliff.

Or maybe she just wasn't like him. Being here reminded her that they were very different people from very different places. Even though he was quite happy to walk through the throngs of people, this wasn't the place for her.

"Is that a toad?" someone hissed as they passed through a particularly thick grouping of people.

She lost her grip on Alistair's hand, and suddenly, she was swallowed up by the crowd. Someone touched her hair, tugging at a curl or maybe a stray leaf that had been caught in it. Another person tapped her shoulder where the sling started.

They were all talking at the same time, so she couldn't quite make out what they were saying—only snippets of the conversation that continued as though she weren't there.

"What a wild little creature."

"A toad? You saw it correctly!"

"Monstrous, isn't she?"

"I didn't think we were still taking in the poor? Shouldn't we direct her to the poorhouse next to the harbor?"

Thea lost control of her breath and started heaving air in and out of her lungs. She couldn't breathe, couldn't see straight. This was all too much, and she wanted to go home to her warm little hearth and to the family that would hold her in their arms.

She wasn't some monstrous, poor person who had wandered into their city by accident. She was happy and well off with her family. Colors existed in her world, and they didn't care about the latest fashion trend or what earrings another person was wearing.

But she couldn't move. Her knees locked in place, and trembles vibrated through her entire body because she didn't know where she was. She didn't even know how to get back to the small crack in the wall so she could escape.

The crowd parted around a tall young man who shoved his way through them. Alistair threw elbows into ribs and hissed out words that sounded like curses, convincing enough that people gave him a wide berth. And then he stopped in front of her with his hands on his hips.

For a moment, looking up into his angry green eyes, she thought he might go the route his brothers had gone. He would seem weak if he helped her, so he could easily offer to take her to that poorhouse, so no one told his father what had happened here.

He offered her his hand, though, with a slight bow following. "Please, allow me to escort you away from this immoral crowd."

A few gasps erupted all around them.

"Immoral?" the woman in green hissed. "I've never been called such by an Orbweaver."

"Actually you have."

"I have not!"

Thea knew that he'd wanted to startle them. He wanted them to see that they'd been rude and that no one should forgive them for this. Even though it would come at a cost to himself, his father would never let him live this one down. She knew it, and he knew it too; Alistair had still chosen to be her hero in the most Wildecliff way possible. He'd offered to help her while insulting those that wouldn't.

She slipped her hand into his and let him draw her away from all those people who didn't know her. Alistair moved her down the streets with more purpose until only a few people were wandering the streets.

Then he drew her close to his heart and placed his chin on top of her head. "I'm sorry," he said. "I had your hand and then it just slipped out of my grasp. It took me too long to figure out where you were."

"It's all right," she replied. "You couldn't have known."

But he should have, some part of her screamed. He should have known where she was, and he shouldn't have ever let her go.

"Do you still want to see my home?"

"Yes." No.

Alistair gripped her hand in his again. Together, they skirted past crowds and eased through corridors until finally, they stood before a house that she hadn't thought possible with all the pale buildings around them.

"This is Orbweaver manor," he breathed, staring up at the dark building with her. "The house where all my nightmares came true."

Understandably so. The house was too dark and too crooked. Everything about it was sharp angles and terrifying features. Even the windows were dark. And though it was warm outside today, the faintest edge of frost was on the bottoms of the windows on the first floor. This was not a welcoming home. It was not a home meant for children to play in or for visitors to linger.

The grounds were barely maintained. There were only a few hedges that had seen better days, and frozen in time, rose bushes she could feel were no longer growing. This building looked nothing like the rest of the houses that they'd passed. The sheer terror she felt in looking at it made her question why she'd come here.

She watched as the front door opened and a butler stepped outside. He threw what looked like black liquid outside. The moment that liquid struck the stones leading up to the house, it burst into a shower of sparks and then sank into the stones themselves. A curse, she could only imagine—more black magic to fill his family home with more cold and pain.

Alistair's hand smoothed down her back. "You don't have to come inside if you don't want."

What kind of person would she be if she didn't go inside? She'd come all this way because he wanted to prove to her that she couldn't be with him. Even after all that, Thea still had a small ember of hope in her chest that they could figure this out.

But the house...this was no place for people to live.

Browning poked his head out of her sling and let out a loud ribbit. When she glanced down at him, he shook his head in a vigorous no. He didn't want to go in there right now either, and that was strange, considering he'd gone inside the home before.

She'd take his warning for what it was. Straightening her shoulders, she looked up at Alistair and politely replied, "I don't think I'd like to go inside right now, if I'm being honest. Perhaps another time."

The defeated expression on his face threatened to rip her soul out of her body. But it seemed as though he understood.

Alistair wrapped his arm around her waist and tugged her to his side. "We'll follow the back roads back to the crack in the wall. How's that sound?"

"That was an option?"

"Only if you didn't want to get home before dark. But we've got some time now that I'm not giving you a tour of the haunted manor." Though he jested, she didn't hear any mirth in his voice. "We'll make sure no one sees you."

Though she didn't respond, Thea was grateful she wouldn't have to see those terrifying people again. She had hoped this trip into Wildecliff would make her want to live here. That maybe it would convince her life with him was possible.

Instead, all it had done was widen the gap between them.

CHAPTER 23

Three weeks. Then four. Then six weeks had passed, and he hadn't heard anything from her. Not a single letter nor even a flower flew over the river.

Alistair knew how she'd felt in the middle of that crowd. He knew how awful it was to have so many people questioning every inch of who you were. They did it to him every day when he walked through the town. But he hadn't thought they would descend upon her like the vultures they were.

At first, he had thought he would send a letter to her through Atlas. He'd have the bird take it with an apology and had even written the letter so many times that he could have bound all the pages into a book.

But it didn't seem right to push her. Not when she'd had such a horrible experience, and he'd been the one to tell her that she had to live here with him. It was the truth, but that didn't mean it was easy to process.

Then he'd been so caught up with returning to Sunspell Academy, especially with the understanding that he would have to take a position here when it was offered. The first two weeks back at school had swallowed him up with work that felt as though he were being targeted.

Of course, until they offered him the position of Professor. They didn't know what he would teach yet, but surely the title would be enough to convince a young man such as himself to allow them to partake in his specialized brand of magic.

That's when he figured out what his father's actual plan was. Solidify the family by any means necessary. If that meant exposing the faerie world? Then so be it. Alistair would take the curses that were hurled upon him by all the fae, but his family name would live on forever.

He had his hands full trying to distract the professors who wanted to poke into his magic, and instead, hid in the Academy while trying to complete his own studies. All of this, compiled with no small amount of self-loathing for his continued involvement in Thea's life, paralyzed him.

Which led to him standing in the middle of the school halls, shocked as he overheard a few students talking about Waterdown. He'd expected their conversation to be the usual issues of how people in that city were so dirty and how they were all so poor. The propaganda had been getting a little out of hand as of late. No doubt, because his father had spread rumors that there was a desperate need for Wildecliff to take care of its neighbor, that would only cause them more issues. No one wanted to trade with a city who abutted such a disgusting town.

But the students weren't saying that at all. In fact, they were talking about what time of year it was.

"Did you know they have a ceremony soon? I heard that all the eligible ladies gather up with all the bachelors and choose who they're going to marry. It's quite barbaric, allowing all the youngsters of the city to pick who they want to spend the rest of their lives with." The first year was a young girl with a crop of bright blonde hair cut a little too short to be fashionable.

"At eighteen, no less!" The other girl was in her second year, and though they looked fairly similar to each other, Alistair wasn't all that certain that the girls were sisters. "But apparently they don't mind ending a marriage over there. Can you imagine? Marrying a man for ten years and then deciding it wasn't what you wanted? Barbaric indeed."

"Our parents know who is best for us and why they are best. That's why they pick who we marry." The first girl shuddered and then started down the adjacent hall, which led toward the first-year classes.

Her friend, or sister, stood there for a few moments before shaking her head. "I wouldn't want to pick. I'd choose someone entirely wrong for me. I'm certain of it."

He watched them walk away as riotous thoughts plagued him. They were only eighteen, and the mere thought of marriage right now made him break out into a cold sweat. Why would she be thinking of it? Was she?

Thea hadn't told him about some festival to pick out a partner. She should have mentioned something if there was a chance of her having to choose a husband. Right? She should have told him. Otherwise, what were they doing?

She'd kissed him. She'd told him that she could fall in love with him if he let her. That didn't add up to what those girls had been saying.

He tried to shake it off. Alistair started down the halls toward his own classes, ones that he might teach next year. He needed to focus on what he could do for the school and for his own future. She hadn't talked to him for six weeks, and he refused to let that get to him.

Except...

What if she hadn't written because she'd already chosen someone else for a husband? He'd never thought of himself as a jealous man, but his chest burned at the thought. He wanted to punch a hole through the wall or maybe grab onto his brothers and get into a fight. They'd let him. They wouldn't care if he wanted them to pummel him into the ground, and Alistair feared that might be the only way to make himself feel better.

"What are you thinking?" he hissed at himself. "She's going to be fine. She always is. Thea doesn't need you to look out for her, and if she doesn't want to marry you, then she doesn't want to marry you. There's nothing you can do to change her mind."

But maybe there was.

He changed course. The class would continue without him, and his position wasn't going anywhere. His father had already paid a large sum to make sure Alistair had a job waiting for him. Right now, he had to make sure Thea hadn't forgotten about him because she'd found some farmer boy to satisfy her better.

Every step that brought him closer to his room made him angrier. How dare she? After everything they'd gone through together, everything they had done, she wanted to marry someone else? He had put all of his heart and soul into loving her! Sure he hadn't told her that yet. But that didn't mean she could forget him this easily!

Stomping into his room, he wrote a hastily worded letter that might have been a little angry and then thrust it at Atlas. "Make sure she meets me at the altar," he snarled.

The familiar seemed to understand his tone. His raven smoothed out its feathers, thorns poking out in all directions as he nodded. Then Atlas took off into the sky, like an eagle who had caught its prey.

He wasted no time. Three brownies waved their arms at him, likely trying to remind him that he shouldn't go to see her when he was angry, but damn it. He was.

The last time he'd seen her, he was prepared to say goodbye. He'd told himself it was okay to let her go, and he had readied himself for it. Not now! There was a chance he could keep her forever, and he would not let her go now.

Because he loved her, too. He loved her so much it felt like he'd ripped a part of his soul off and handed it to her. He was more himself when he was with her than without.

Alistair grabbed his coat and headed out of the school. A voice called out behind him, one of the professors most likely to warn him that he couldn't leave just yet. They could expel him, then. Maybe that would make all of this go away if he was lucky.

Ignoring the shouts behind him, he marched right out of the school and down the streets. He didn't need a carriage. Walking all the way to the hole in the wall might cool him down by the time he saw her.

It didn't.

All the walk did was remind him how tired, hungry, and angry he was. And that he was so scared he might have lost her without fighting at all. Then he had to wait. She couldn't get over the river quickly, just as he couldn't, and that meant the moon had already risen by the time the leaves rustled to alert him of her approach.

He'd counted to a hundred what felt like a million times until his anger was under control. The sound of her made it all surge to life again, and then the sight of her blew out the candle of his rage like a cool breeze.

She looked so beautiful standing there with twigs in her hair and a white nightgown blowing in the slight wind. Her hair was unbound, as always, and he wanted to bury his fingers into those strands while dragging her to him.

He couldn't, though. Not until he knew she was still unattached. He refused to ruin someone else's life by holding her to his heart and promising he would never let her go. And that broke him. In that moment, he felt his heart shatter in his chest and stop beating.

Six weeks felt like six months. Six years. He hadn't seen her in a lifetime, and knowing that she was still alive and well made his soul take flight.

"Hello," she said, breathless and alone. She hadn't brought Browning with her this time. "Your letter made it seem like it was urgent."

"It is." He stepped forward, his hands clenched at his sides so that he didn't grab onto her and pull her into his arms. "I had to know... I heard some students..."

This wasn't how it was supposed to go. He wasn't supposed to be incapable of talking to her. He'd wanted to be angry. Upset that she would ever put herself in a situation where she might choose someone else. But he couldn't be that jealous person when she was right here in front of him.

"Are you all right?" she asked.

"There were students in my school who said that at eighteen

people in Waterdown choose who they're going to marry, and I was afraid you had done that, and that's why you hadn't written to me in six weeks." He blurted it all out to purge the fear from his chest. But he didn't feel much better after saying it.

Tiny wrinkles appeared between her eyes. "You think I chose another man to be my husband?"

"Well, I..." He should have known she'd be so direct. "That was my fear, yes. I thought perhaps you had not written because of that."

She tilted her head back and laughed so loudly that the birds erupted from their nests in the trees. The sound was not without mirth, although he thought maybe there was a hint of anger in it.

"Alistair," she said once she stopped laughing long enough to look at him. "Why would I be interested in anyone other than you? I'd like to think it's rather obvious that I wouldn't want to marry anyone other than the ridiculous boy from across the river."

"Then why didn't you write to me?"

"I just... I suppose I was afraid. Your home is very different from mine, and I know that it's difficult to think about bringing someone like me into your world." She tucked a strand of hair behind her ear and took a step closer. "You saw how they teased me, Alistair. You shouldn't want a wife that will make you the laughingstock of the city."

"You wouldn't be." He wouldn't let them. Alistair could hold himself back no longer and leapt for her. He grabbed her hands in his, holding them so tightly he saw her fingers turn white. "Are you saying that you'd marry me?"

"Well, not right now. But when we're older."

"Oh, thank the gods." To both details. He wasn't ready to get married, but he wanted to marry her—more than anything.

Before he could second guess himself, Alistair leaned down and plucked two long strands of grass from the base of Ceredwin's altar. He bent one into a perfect circle and muttered an old spell. He felt a bit of himself rip away, as it always did with magic like this, and then the strand of grass wove into a circle.

She gasped. "How did you do that? I thought it was impossible for people to perform magic outside of their gift."

"Little magic we can all do. And when we can be together without fear, I will show you." And then Alistair bent down onto one knee, holding up the makeshift ring for her. "Thea Earthshaker of Waterdown, I cannot propose to you with a proper ring, but I can make you a promise that someday, I will give you a real one."

He watched as she pressed her hands to her mouth, and he hoped that meant something good. He hoped she would say yes.

Come to find out, she said nothing. Instead, Thea nodded her head so quickly that her hair flew in front of her face like a dark shawl. Alistair gently pushed the tiny circle onto her finger and then made one for himself.

"So you never forget that you weren't the only one to make the promise." He put the ring on himself and then whispered a spell a faerie had taught him once. A spell that would make nature one with him.

The grass flattened, darkened, and then dyed his skin permanently where the ring had been. The black line would never fade. He'd have to skin the finger if he wanted it off, but he knew he never would.

"How—" Thea whispered.

"Faerie magic. I don't want to ever forget this night or this conversation. I will bring you with me everywhere, Thea. No matter where I go." Already, he rubbed a finger over the new tattoo as though it were a worry stone. And he felt all his anxiety drift away with the slight touch. As though she had taken his hand and told him everything would be all right.

Thea bit her lip, worrying the soft cushion with a flash of bright teeth. "Then I'd like to do that, too."

"You would?"

"I would." She held out her hand and looked away.

"It won't hurt," he said with a chuckle. Then he whispered the spell and watched as the greenery sank into her skin forever.

Thea peeked out at him and then realized it was over. With a soft squeak, she held their hands up to the moonlight so they could look at the tattooed skin together.

"I think we're going to be together forever," she said quietly.

"Then would you come visit me? There's a break in my school, and I know my father and brothers will be traveling. I want you to see my home, Thea. I know it's terrifying and the people of Wildecliff are not what you expected, but... Give me a chance to show you that a life with me wouldn't be so terrible."

He felt his heart crack around the edges at her tremulous smile.

But then she whispered, "I'll visit you, Alistair. I missed you."

CHAPTER 24

Moonlight played with the ends of her hair, and Browning let out a little grumble in her sling. They both didn't want to be standing in the middle of Wildecliff during the nighttime. It had been hard enough finding the place, even with Alistair's detailed instructions.

He'd given her every detail necessary to find her way through the city on her own. So detailed, in fact, that he had even mentioned certain colors of draperies inside of windows. Thea could imagine him walking this same path, counting his steps and noting every tiny thing she might see to make sure she safely got to his home.

But standing in front of the terrifying building made her want to turn right back around and retrace all those steps.

She'd thought this dark building was terrifying during the

day, but it turned into its own beast during the night. The windows glared at her with bright yellow eyes. A churning noise echoed into the street from the belly of the home, likely from the kitchens, but her mind turned it into the growl of a beast. Waves of mist billowed away from the home as though the building had created its own weather phenomenon.

And yet, she had promised that she would try harder. Thea had promised to try again, if only because they could meet without the fear of running into his brothers or father.

She touched the tiny black line on her ring finger and whispered a prayer to the ancestors.

Browning held up a sprig of lavender, but she didn't want to chew on it. She wanted to get through this without needing something or someone to help her. The house was terrifying, but that didn't mean it wasn't possible for her to do it on her own.

Sighing, she scrubbed a hand over her face and gently pushed the wart-covered hand back into the sling. "Stay hidden, Browning. I don't want you getting hurt in there."

He snuggled deeper into the sling as she opened the iron gate and walked up to the front door. All she had to do was knock. That was it. Alistair would be there on the other side, and he would make everything better.

They'd promised to marry each other, after all. They'd promised, and she wouldn't go back on those words.

Swallowing hard, Thea struck her knuckles to the door once, and it swung open on its own. Did they not lock the door? As though they knew no one would dare enter the famed Orbweaver home without an invitation? And here she was. Standing there like an idiot without an address in her hand or anyone to announce her.

The interior of the home was worse than she'd imagined. The fog seemed to fill the house too. White mist reached up for her with bony hands, as though even the building wanted to shove her out. If it were like her own home, then she wouldn't be surprised if the building could. Glimmering chandeliers hung from the ceiling, two of them leading to a giant stairwell that had seen better days. In her mind, the entire room smelled and felt like a crypt. Ancient, beautiful objects that never saw the light of day or eyes that appreciated them.

But then the mist parted, and Alistair walked around the corner. The half smile on his face was so sweet and so genuinely excited that she forgot how to breathe. He wanted her here. Even if the house didn't.

He wore his usual dark pants and a white shirt. But this time, he also had on a long navy coat that came down to his knees. The collar stood straight around his neck, giving him a rather regal look even though his hair flopped in front of his eyes.

Opening his arms wide for her, he grinned as she ran to him. Thea struck him a little too hard, and they stumbled back a few steps together until he had fully wrapped her up. She felt his lips press against her hair in a kiss, and some of her fear eased. She took a deep breath of his woody scent, knowing he wouldn't let anything happen to her in his terrifying house.

"You're here," he murmured against her. "I didn't think you'd come."

"I wasn't sure I would." Already she imagined the mist of the house coiling up her legs, wrapping around her ankles, and dragging her back outside. "I don't think the house wants me here."

"The house doesn't have an opinion. You're feeling the dark magic in the basement. My father's experiments have gotten rather... explosive, lately."

Alistair drew back and smoothed his hand over the top of her head. He wrapped a strand of her hair around his finger, then set to work putting everything back in place as he seemed to so enjoy. And while he did that, Thea took her time counting the freckles on his cheeks. She had thought last time there were about four hundred, but she'd never had enough time to count all of them. Maybe he'd let her take a pen to them someday to mark all the ones she'd counted.

"Would you like a tour?"

"I think I'd like to get somewhere safe for a little while." Thea had tried to put a brave face on for him, but this building…there was something wrong with it.

He looked like she'd asked him to stick a pin underneath his fingernail. "Uh, well. I suppose I could show you my bedroom, then?"

Oh, no. That was too forward. She flushed, her cheeks flaring so hot that it made even the tips of her ears hurt. "Is there anywhere else we could go first?"

He bit his lip, then offered, "The library, perhaps?"

Libraries were safe. The walls were always havens to so many ideas that they were usually easy enough for her to step into. She'd never been in a library that didn't feel like it was a warm hug.

Thea nodded. "The library sounds good."

She followed him down the hall, but the energy inside this house didn't want her here. The darkness seemed to stretch for her, reaching out its long tendrils and sticking to her shoes. Slowing her down. Holding her still. Alistair held one of her hands carefully in his own. The other she stuck down into the sling so Browning could hold onto her finger.

They traveled down long hallways with rugs so thick she couldn't hear her own footsteps. The black wallpaper sometimes changed into patterns that were barely there. Sometimes they were geometric; sometimes they looked like vines growing up and down the walls. The chandeliers, however, were always the same. Glowing orange orbs that flickered above her head when she walked underneath them.

There were no windows in the interior portion of the house. It seemed like the house was built for darkness to reign.

"The library," Alistair said, gesturing with a wide sweep of his arm to an open doorway. "My father has the greatest collection in all of Wildecliff. Many scholars from the Academy come here because he has grimoires that are original copies. I've read some myself, but many of them are beyond me in skills of magic and curses."

She stepped inside, expecting to be enveloped with the warmth of potential knowledge and years of people coming to this room for sanctuary. She'd expected a warm nook to tuck herself into with a cup of tea and a soft cushion where she could lose herself for hours.

That was not this room.

The library here was like a dead thing that still wheezed in breath through rattling ribs. All the books were bound with chains. And if they weren't, they fluttered on the floor like butterflies dying on the cold stone. There was a large window, but it was covered in frost. She could only see the fragmented image of reality outside these icy walls.

Her breath fogged before her. "Why is it so cold?"

"Oh." Alistair stumbled in front of her, frantically reaching into his pockets. "That's the magic. My father's spells either put off a lot of heat or a lot of freezing air. He's chosen the latter because it's easier to stay warm than it is to cool down. I had the brownies of the house make you something when you said you'd try coming here... Hold on. Where did I put it?"

She watched him pat down his long coat until he found the item in the inner pocket. Then he pulled out a bright blue hat, knitted by faerie hands, with splashes of colors all through it. It would be a little big for her, she thought, but it was the thought that counts.

"To keep your ears warm," he said, then pulled it down over her hair. He took his time making sure he didn't move a single lock into the wrong place.

It wasn't wool. She didn't know what kind of yarn the brownies had used because it was so soft against her ears. Like she was leaning against a rabbit. She ran her fingers over the woven edges, a simple design but one that would keep her very warm indeed.

She smiled, chewing on the corner of her lip. "I didn't bring them anything! I should thank them for such a lovely gift."

"Next time." He grinned, so certain there would even be a next time when all Thea could think was that she never wanted to return to this horrible place. "The library, I take it, is not a safe place?"

She swallowed hard and shook her head. "I'm sorry."

"We'll try the kitchens." He held out his hand for her to take, and she decided she'd let him take her through the entire house until she found a room where she could breathe.

The kitchens weren't any better. The belching fireplaces made her head spin with fear. So he took her to the dining room, which felt as though she were about to be sacrificed at any moment. The drawing room where his father had his wine every night wasn't any better. She imagined how many people had sat in each of those chairs, shaking in fear, and she couldn't focus on anything but the whispering ghosts of their screams.

Finally, they ended up in front of his bedroom door, as he'd wanted her to see from the beginning. "Are you sure this is all right?" he asked.

She nodded and focused hard on the door as he swung it open.

Cold air whipped around her head again, and she was certain this would be another problem, and yet...

"The window is nice," she whispered as she walked into the room.

It was the only window in the house without a single touch of frost on it. And there was a fire crackling in the hearth. The faint pops of wood were merry rather than aggressive like the rest of the house. And there was Atlas. Sitting on a small stand with puffed-up feathers as though he wanted to look his best for her.

She tried very hard not to look over at the plush bed in the corner that could have easily fit three people. Her little cot at home seemed meager and small compared to that monstrosity. But it looked very comfortable, and after all the fear that had tightened every muscle in her body, she wondered if she could snuggle up in it and feel a little better. At least for a while.

She shouldn't. Sure, they'd had their moments in the woods, but that felt as though they were wild and free. This was his home. A bed. It was so much more serious than what they had done before. At least, that's how she felt about it.

Clearing her throat, she stepped up to the fire and pulled Browning out of his sling. "Warm up," she said quietly as he hopped toward the fire.

The faint hush of fabric made her flinch, and she turned toward Alistair. He'd sat down on the bed, looking rather dejected.

They stared at each other, neither wanting to say what they were thinking. Finally, Alistair broke the silence. "You don't like it here."

"It's just... just..." She struggled to find the right word but then blurted out, "Sad."

He stiffened. "Sad?

"Well... Yes. This entire building feels like no one should live in it.

Every corner of this house is so uninviting. I couldn't be comfortable here if I tried, and even if I lived here with you, I'd be so terrified every time I walked around the corner."

Thea wrapped her arms around her waist. She knew it was insulting to tell him all that. This was his childhood home, after all, and he'd said his father had trapped him in this horrible place. Her heart broke for him.

But there was no chance that she'd be able to live here. No matter how hard she tried to force herself to find a sense of ease within these walls.

He leaned forward, bracing his forearms on his knees as he stared at the floor. "This has been my family's home for generations. You would want for nothing while you live here. The servants would cater to your every need—"

"Servants?" She repeated the word as though it was poisonous. "This house isn't so giant. I'd think the rest of you would know how to take care of it."

"How do you think people in Wildecliff live?" He glared at her, and there was a spark in his eyes that looked more like his brothers' than she'd ever seen before. "We aren't living out in the wilds like simple farmers here. We have people to hire and do the work that we don't have time for."

"Everyone has time to clean," she hissed. "You just don't want to do it and you have enough money to pay someone else to do it for you."

"Or perhaps there are greater aspirations in life than to till the earth until your hands bleed. Don't think I haven't noticed the calluses on your palms or the way your arms are far too defined for a woman. These are things that could change, though. I don't judge you for them."

"It sounds like you do."

She didn't know how to respond to this sudden anger. She hadn't insulted him by calling his house sad. It was. No one could argue with that. And now it felt as though he wanted her to live with him because he wanted to change her.

She wouldn't change living in this house. Thea knew that even if she moved to Wildecliff, she wouldn't become one of those fine ladies with clean fingernails and hair pulled too tightly away from her face. Location didn't change a person. Not when they already knew who they wanted to be.

Alistair sighed and scrubbed his hands down his face. "I didn't want you to come here so we could argue."

"Then why did you want me to come here?"

"So you could see how much better it is here! And yes, the house is not very kind, but we have working plumbing, servants to cook for us, electric lights, and you'd never have to work another day in your life. That has to be better than what your future in Waterdown is."

There it was.

The truth.

She narrowed her eyes at him and laid it all out before them. "Do you think I'm lesser than you because I live in Waterdown?"

"No."

"Do you think I am at the same level as your servants because I work on a farm to keep people fed?"

His ears turned red. "No. You know I don't think that."

"Then why do you want to change me?"

"I think the life I'm offering you here, no matter how different, would be better than what you currently have." His words trailed off into a whisper at the end. Perhaps he knew that he'd toed a line he could never draw back from.

"I see," she breathed. The anger in her chest hurt. It was like a dragon had burst to life inside her and then seized hold of her tongue. If he could say something he couldn't take back, then so could she. "I think you've made it very clear that our differences might be too hard to overcome, Alistair. You're the son of the richest family in Wildecliff, and I'm just the girl from over the wall."

His jaw dropped open as he leapt up. "That's not how I feel, and you know it."

She shook her head and backed away from him before he caught hold of her. Because if he touched her, then she'd crumble. She deserved to be angry right now. She deserved to be mad at him.

"I'm going," she whispered.

"You just got here."

"And I don't think I want to be here." Thea scooped Browning up into her arms and refused to look Alistair in the eye. "I'm sorry."

But she wasn't. Not really.

Thea fled his house and felt every time a tendril of darkness shook off her shoulders. That haunted building would remain in her nightmares for the rest of her life, she feared.

And perhaps the loss of him as well.

CHAPTER 25

Why did it feel like they were always arguing? He didn't know what to say or how to fix this. Alistair had practically asked her to marry him! She had to know how strongly he felt about her?

The night passed without a single moment of sleep from him. And because they were on a small break in the school schedule, he could remain in his own room all night without having to worry about when he would get back to the Academy.

Staggering down to the kitchens the next morning, he sat down at the giant table, put his head on the worn wood, and tried to talk his body into functioning. Even when it didn't want to.

A warm hand touched his back. "Coffee?"

"Please, Nora. If you don't mind."

The maid who had been with him since he was a child set to

action. She put the teapot so quietly onto the fireplace he almost didn't hear it at all. Then the water started bubbling, and the gentle sounds lulled him into a sense of false peace.

Was that… peppermint he smelled? Did she think he was hungover? That would be more likely if he were one of his brothers. Alistair was heart sick.

He sighed and lifted his head from the table. "I didn't get into my father's brandy last night. You can make noise."

Nora glanced over at him with a grin that dropped instantly from her face. "Goodness, look at you, little master. You look like you walked hand in hand with death last night."

"In a way." Alistair groaned and put his head back on the table. "I lost her, Nora. I definitely lost her this time."

"One of the fae?"

"Thea."

Just saying her name made him want to pound his head against the table. Why had he been such an ass to her? She'd been nothing but honest, and he was the one who kept pushing her to come here when he knew how horrible this house was. This was his fault, surely.

Although she had been cruel in her own way. Calling his home and life sad? She should know that he had nothing else. There was no other option with this curse around his neck. He had to uphold his family's name and keep the house alive.

Damn it, he was stuck. His father hadn't just cursed him to remain here but to remain alone.

The screeching sound of a mug slid across the table and bumped against his hand. "So this is all about a girl, then?"

"Not just any girl." He sat up and reached for the coffee that might make him feel more like a person today. "The only girl. She's the only one for me, Nora. I can't think without her in my life."

"Well, that sounds a little dramatic. I've yet to meet a woman who could kill a man just by leaving." She perched on the edge of the table and waved her hand. "Why don't you tell me about her?"

So he did.

He might have waxed poetic about how the stars sparkled in her eyes and how the sound of her laugh was better than any symphony he'd ever heard. Alistair knew without a doubt that he lingered a little too long in describing every detail of her expression when she took care of the familiars. He knew she would do the same to the fae if given the chance, and they would love her for it.

And when he was finished, he looked at Nora's pleased grin and groaned. "Stop looking at me like that. She's never coming back. I told you, I already lost her."

"I'm just so happy to see you in love. Here I was, thinking it wasn't possible for an Orbweaver to feel that emotion and here you are. Yet again, proving everyone wrong about your family." She shook her head. "There has to be something we can do about it. This couldn't have been your first fight?"

"It was." As much as he hated to admit it. All their earlier disagreements had been much easier to figure out. Most of them were him being a little idiotic, though. Maybe that gave this situation hope?

The more he thought about it, the less he believed himself. Thea was a discerning young woman with a heart of gold. She wouldn't suffer a fool in her life.

He'd been too hard on her. He'd been fueled by anger and incapable of keeping his own mouth shut. The last thing he wanted to admit was that he'd made a mistake, but he could here.

Shaking his head, he pressed his lips together. "I don't think there's anything I can do to fix it this time, Nora."

"Well, you can't just give up." She twitched her skirts and stepped down onto the floor. "If there's anything I've learned in this life, it's that love is the only thing worth fighting for. And you are very much in love, little master. Your heart is as much hers as it is your own, if I'm reading the situation right. Fight for her. Tell her you are so sorry for the insensitive words that came out of your mouth when you felt like she was attacking you. Apologize. Grovel. Do whatever it takes until she listens to you. And then do better in the future, Alistair. If you want to keep her in your life, then you need to learn how to grow yourself."

She was right. She was always right.

He stood with his mug of coffee in his hands and gave her a little nod. Then he staggered out of the kitchens toward his room, where he resolved himself to figure out the best way to word this apology. After all, it would not be an easy one.

Thea had to believe that he meant every word he said. He should do it in person, but Alistair had never been particularly brave. He feared what she would say if he walked up to her front door.

Or what her sisters would do to him if they found him where Thea didn't want him.

A shout echoed through the halls as though someone was fighting. Alistair winced, but he knew his place in this house. At the very least, he had to go see what was happening. Perhaps his father had decided that his elder sons weren't as wonderful as he thought. That might cheer Alistair up a little.

Instead, as he walked into his father's drawing room, he found a sight he'd never seen before.

His father was smiling.

A gleeful smile spread across his face with a wide-mouthed grin. It wrinkled around the edges of his eyes as he stared down at a piece of paper in his hand.

"You see?" he waved it at Cassius, who stood solemnly to his side. "I told you this would all happen sooner than we expected. Now is the time, my sons! Now I will need you more than ever."

Sons?

Alistair stepped into the room and realized Lysander was standing right in the doorway as well. Both of his brothers were curved in on themselves as though they were afraid. He had never seen them look like this before.

Balthazar spun, so his back was to Alistair, holding the letter up to the dim light that broke through the windows. "I've been waiting for this letter for years!"

What was his father talking about? A letter? Things moving forward? He hadn't told Alistair about anything when they were in that carriage together, but that didn't mean that his father hadn't put things in motion.

Were they going to attack a few families in Wildecliff? There were some who had more children than Balthazar and therefore were getting dangerously close to the same amount of power their family had.

Lysander wrapped his hand around Alistair's arm and jerked him out of the drawing room. With a hiss, he slammed Alistair's back against the wall next to the drawing room so no one would know they were out there.

"What are you doing, whelp?" he asked.

"I heard father shouting. I thought I should—"

"You thought nothing. Do you hear me? Nothing. You will not tell father you were here, or that you heard anything of what he said. You should not be here."

Anger, just like he'd felt when Thea called him a sad being living in a sad home, burst into flames within his chest. "Why? Why should I not be here? Because I'm not as much his son as you?"

"No, you little idiot. I'm trying to keep you out of all this." Lysander shoved his shoulder hard one more time, slamming him back into the wall. "It's too late for Cassius and I. We're stuck in this as much as father is, but you can still get out. Call it a change of heart or whatever you want to say. I just want you to get out of the way."

Those words stopped Alistair in his tracks. Why would Lysander want to warn him after all the horrible things his brothers had done to him? They didn't have any love lost between them.

"What is going on?" Alistair asked. He slipped out from underneath Lysander's arm and stood in the hallway. Facing his brother for the first time in their lives. "You sound scared."

"We all should be." He took a step closer to Alistair and then lowered his voice. "Father and the ministers who run Wildecliff have been listening to poison. They claim no one will deliver goods to us for much longer because of how poor Waterdown is making us look. They're attacking Waterdown and Strongmeadow. They intend to wipe them out."

His world ground to a halt. Alistair felt as though the entire house shifted to the side, and he would have fallen if Lysander hadn't grabbed onto his arm. "They're what?"

"We're looking at a war, brother. And if Father and those men have their way, then the river will run red with blood for years to come. Stay out of it, whelp." Another shove, this time half-hearted, and he didn't let go for a few moments. His fingers lingered on Alistair's arm, but then he let go and turned his attention back to the study. "I'll be missed."

"Be safe," Alistair replied, but he knew it was far too late for that.

They weren't close, he or his brothers. But he had the sudden realization that he wished they were. Life might have been a little easier if they could have overcome their differences. At least for him and Lysander.

He waited until he was alone once again in the corridor before he bolted. There had to be another ship. One last ship out to Waterdown, and then he could at least warn them. He could tell them all to prepare and to get their children out of bed before fire rained down upon them.

He didn't know what his father's plan was, but he knew Balthazar. If the old man wanted a war, then he wanted to make sure no one lived to talk about it. There would only be his father's victory—nothing else.

Alistair sprinted through the house and grabbed his blue coat by the door. He looked over his shoulder one last time, half expecting his father's shadowy spiders to follow him. But the house was quiet. As if it were holding its breath, waiting for the next moment.

He fled from that house of nightmares and darkness. He raced through the streets where people were already leaving their homes. Shouts of encouragement followed him, but he couldn't guess why they yelled. Surely they didn't know he was trying to warn Waterdown that his own people were attacking them?

Finally, he made it through the front gates that closed off the port from the rest of the city. There were still people milling about, although they seemed to move aimlessly. Entirely without purpose, where this was a bustling port full of people racing to and from.

Breathless, he stopped the first person who looked like a sailor. "Sir, excuse me. Excuse me!"

The man's face was so tanned it looked like leather stretched over a skull. He wore a dark black outfit with moth-eaten holes at the hems and a scowl on his face as he placed a bundle of fish on the docks.

"What do you want boy," the sailor grumbled. His voice was raspy with misuse.

"Is there... Is there a boat headed for Waterdown?"

"Now?"

"Yes, now. As soon as possible."

The man hooked a thumb over his shoulder and gestured at the docks. "There was one more ship headed out, but that's the last one. I thought you'd have heard by now?"

Alistair wanted to sprint to the boat, but he had to know. "Heard what?"

"They're going to cast a spell upon Waterdown at any moment. That's why that's the last boat. No more trade with those people. No more trade across the river at all." The sailor ran a hand through his hair and shrugged. "I guess that means I'm out of a job."

No more boats? They were attacking this soon? They couldn't! Waterdown needed time to address the fact that their neighbor wanted to fight with them. It was common courtesy in such situations that the attacking city would at least allow the other to know that they were thinking about it.

"What about the children?" he wheezed.

The sailor shrugged. "I guess they didn't think about that. Or if they did, they didn't care all that much."

His heart broke. So many families would be ripped apart in such a short amount of time. He had to stop them.

He couldn't.

He sprinted over the fallen ropes and all the items that had been pulled out of ships that would otherwise be in the waters of the river. He leapt wildly over a large chest that had most likely contained some captain's goods and then noticed that the only boat with its sails still out was already moving off the dock.

"Wait!" he screamed, sprinting faster than he ever had before. "I'm coming! Wait!"

Someone on the ship noticed him. They pointed and waved to a sailor, gesturing that someone still needed to get onto the ship.

Hope bloomed in his chest and then died a slow death as he reached the end of the dock and barely missed the ship. It was just outside of reach; otherwise, he would have jumped onto it. Perhaps he could have swum to reach it, but the wind caught the sails.

The last ship to Waterdown sailed out of his reach. Just as she had.

He bent and braced himself on his knees as he tried to catch his breath, and the first spell soared over his head. Fire illuminated the sky.

CHAPTER 26

Thea woke to the scent of smoke and the faint sound of screaming outside her window. She thought for a moment she was dreaming. The house wouldn't let a fire start. But then she heard the screams again. She'd never heard anyone yell like that, not unless they were being chased by a sibling.

Then the door to her bedroom burst open, and her mother rushed in. Máthair had a scrap of fabric tied over her face, and an arm raised up high. "We have to go," she shouted. "Thea! Thea, are you all right?"

Thea rolled out of bed onto her hands and knees, suddenly coughing. The smoke filled her room from the door her mother had opened, and the house groaned. Like it was in pain.

"What happened?" she whispered, her fingers scrabbling for

Browning's sling. "Is the house on fire?"

Browning's webbed hand touched hers and grabbed on as her mother swung her up to standing. "Everything's on fire, sweet girl. We have to run."

Everything?

They bolted out of her room, and a burst of heat struck her face. All those beloved portraits on the wall, the comfy rugs that had cushioned her feet for years, were burning. Her sister's rooms. She let out a horrified sound as they ran past Belladonna's room, but she could see from the swinging door that it was empty. Her sisters, at least, must have made it out alive.

The front door slammed open, and the house seemed to roll. Thea and her mother tumbled out onto the grass in front of their home as the entirety of their magical house lit on fire. Thea swore she heard it scream, and then all the magic rushed out in a great gust of wind.

"No," her mother wheezed, holding out a hand for the magic that disappeared into the sky. "Henry."

Had her father's magic been what made their home what it was? Thea's heart squeezed as she felt the last of the house magic disappear, and her soul felt as though she had lost someone very dear.

Two other people fell to their knees beside them. Belladonna wrapped an arm around their mother while Marigold hugged Thea tight to her chest.

She looked up into her sister's bright blue eyes and saw ash had smudged her cheeks. "What happened?" Thea asked. "Did the fireplace get out of control? I thought..."

"No." Marigold licked her thumb and rubbed at the spot on Marigold's cheek. "Everything is burning, Thea. I don't know what we're going to do."

Why did her mother keep saying that? Then her gaze focused beyond her sister, and her stomach dropped out of her chest.

The fields were on fire. All the wheat and every garden, all burning to a crisp as smoke rose into the darkness, lit by the flames themselves. The flames chased the smoke up into the air. She could only see a few houses from theirs, but that was on fire, too.

"Waterdown?" she asked.

Their mother staggered to her feet, tears leaving streaks of pale down her cheeks. "We don't have time to check on anyone. We have to go to the Pillars of Lugh. The god will protect us as he always has."

But the warrior king didn't get involved with mortal affairs. They could pray for hours at the pillar before he heard them. They were more likely to see his house, Failinis, than they were to see the god himself.

And the town. If the houses on the outskirts were burning like this, then surely the entirety of Waterdown was on first. They were supposed to sit in safety and do nothing?

"Clodagh," Thea whispered.

Her friend lived in the city with her father. But if Waterdown was burning, then there was no way for any of them to know if she got out.

"Don't even think about it," Máthair scolded.

Thea was thinking about it. No one else would help her friend if the others all sought shelter. Already she could see many of her people running toward the forest, which hid the Pillars from sight. Her heart hurt, knowing that the flames might reach the woods, and they would all be at Lugh's mercy. He could decide to save the trees that were in his namesake, or he could let them all burn.

She took a step away from her family, clinging to Marigold's hands for a few more moments. "I have to go."

"You will not!" her mother shouted.

"Take care of him." She placed Browning in Marigold's arms, even though Marigold likely had her own familiar to look after. If all the familiars had even made it out of the house. But she couldn't think of that right now.

Thea raced away from the most important women in her life and sprinted toward the town. She ran through burning fields and smoke that filled the air so thickly she coughed until she couldn't inhale any longer. Thea stopped to rip at the bottom of her nightgown until she had enough fabric to cover her face and mouth. She needed every inch of that fabric to get through the sections of fields that were burning.

She was so close now. The city was over the next rise, but that hill was on fire. All of it. There wasn't even a blade of grass not affected by the flames that ravaged the land she loved.

If she'd been one of her sisters, maybe she could have used magic to clear a path for herself. But she didn't know of any herb or medicine that would let her control the elements. There weren't plants for that.

A hard thud on her chest reminded Thea that she wasn't entirely alone. Even though they'd fought, at least Alistair had given her a gift she could use when she needed it.

Thea fished out the small whistle necklace, lifted it to her lips, and blew.

There were fire faeries everywhere. Ones she'd never even heard of before. Without a name, she couldn't convince them to help her, but she could still beg.

"Fae of the flames," she called out, letting the whistle drop from her lips. "I beg of you to help me."

She blew into the tiny whistle again and saw that the little creatures had frozen where they were. The fire was their clothing, she noticed.

Tiny flame skirts and bodices that rippled in the wind. Their hair was like tiny torches that lit up the night, and their skin was deep as the darkest of coals.

"I need to get to the city to make sure my dearest friend is still alive." Thea didn't know if they listened or if they even cared for her plight. "I am afraid I have lost her."

She had thought there would be no pity from the fae. They cared little for the mortals who ruined their lands and constantly encroached on what had always been their home. Thea couldn't say she would blame them for letting the entirety of Waterdown turn to ash.

But as she lifted the whistle to her mouth again and blew, she saw that they were doing the exact opposite. The tiny fire fae were herding the flames away. And the flames reacted like their pets—little dogs who were all too happy to do the bidding of these terrifying faerie creatures. A path formed in front of her that would lead her safely into the town.

Although, she would guess that safety ended the moment she stepped foot into Waterdown.

Letting the whistle thud back against her chest, she tried to bow low before the smoke filled her lungs again. "Thank you," she whispered. "Thank you so much."

Thea knew this would not come without a price. She'd have to leave something out for the fae, or they would return even greater than before. Still, the image wouldn't leave her mind that the fae seemed to be corralling the fire, not controlling it. They didn't appear to be the ones who had set the flames, which could only mean that someone else had set fire to Waterdown.

Someone who wanted to see everyone dead.

She reached the top of the hill and then pressed her hands to her mouth in horror. Every building was on fire in Waterdown. Every single one. Sparks still rained down from the sky as a giant orb hung above the city. The bright glowing light spread fire and destruction wherever it hovered above. A curse, she realized—a curse, unlike anything they'd ever seen before.

People still ran out of their homes, holding wet towels and blankets over their heads. There were only a few, though. A much larger crowd had gathered far enough from the city to be relatively safe. And they all stood there watching their homes burn.

"Clodagh!" Thea screamed, cupping her hands around her mouth, hoping her friend would hear her yell. "Clodagh!"

No one replied. There were so many people screaming, though. How would she hear her friend? No one could pick out individual voices.

Except... Then she heard her.

"Thea? Thea!"

Someone split away from the crowd and darted toward her. Clodagh was covered in ash and grime. Her pretty face was smeared with black marks and streaks of tears that had tried to cut through the ash. But she was alive.

Thea ran toward her, and they both struck each other hard. Wrapping her arms frantically around her friend, she patted Clodagh down as she tried to find any injuries. "Are you hurt? Your family? Are they here?"

"We're all fine," Clodagh said against her neck, squeezing tighter. "No one was hurt. We're all alive."

Oh, thank all the gods and goddesses. Thea didn't know what she would do without Clodagh telling her what an idiot she was or how stupid she was being. She squeezed tighter as the thought flickered through her mind that she might never have hugged Clodagh again. They could have lost each other.

Clodagh's father came up behind them and gathered up both girls in his massive arms. "Thea," he rumbled in her ear. "We'd thought the outer reaches were not attacked…"

She tried to wrap her mind around what he said, but it didn't settle well with her. "Attacked?" She looked up at him. "We were attacked?"

He nodded up at the glowing red curse above their heads. "That's Orbweaver magic. An old curse, for sure. No one has seen a spell like that in a very long time. But I know Balthazar's work when I see it."

No. It wasn't possible. She would have known because Alistair would have told her. And he would have known because he knew everything that happened in that house, even if this father didn't want him to.

Right?

"It can't be," she whispered.

"There have been rumors," he hissed. "A few of the dock workers suggested Wildecliff has been waiting for a moment to strike us for a very long time, but no one ever thought they'd go to war with their neighbor. Why would they? We've done nothing to them and they've done nothing to us."

Clodagh squeezed Thea in her arms a little tighter. "War?"

"It is, child. Unfortunately. Now, you two stay right here while I go get some water with the others. Thankfully, we still have a few amongst us who have a talent with the waves. Perhaps we can find some sailor who doesn't mind helping out."

They sat on the hill after he left, and Thea watched in a numb state as half the people of her town got to work fixing everything that had happened. The people of Waterdown staggered through the streets, some of them with their hands lifted as they guided water to the homes that needed it most.

"Thea?" Clodagh asked. "Are you all right?"

"I should have known," she whispered. "He should have told me."

And he would have. She knew he would. Even though they were arguing and he might not have wanted to make it worse. Wouldn't he? Or was he afraid that telling her would be the end of them?

Maybe he would have said something if she hadn't been so pushy. So rude. Maybe he would have told her that the entire reason he'd wanted her to come to his home hadn't been to selfishly learn if she could stay there, but because something terrible was about to happen, and he wanted to stop it.

Clodagh wrapped an arm around her shoulders, and they remained silent as the town tried to control the curse that died above their heads. It took all night. The sun rose on the horizon and cast its light upon the damage that Thea couldn't imagine ever being fixed.

The houses were gone. The ash that covered the streets would remain for years as they tried to clean everything up. Only three of their many docks remained standing, and even then, they were nothing more than crumbling pieces of ruin. And still the fire burned.

She shook as a house collapsed in on itself.

"Thea," Clodagh finally said, her voice hoarse from the smoke. "Where is your family?"

"The Pillars," she said, startled at how awful she sounded. "They prayed for someone to save us."

"I don't think anyone is coming to help."

No. They weren't. And there should have been one person who would help them after all she'd been through with him. Someone who had promised that he would love her. Support her. Wanted to make her his wife someday.

The anger that came with that thought nearly spun her head around on her shoulders. Thea stood, shaking Clodagh off of her and wobbling as her legs groaned from being seated for so long.

"That bastard," she hissed.

"What bastard?"

She didn't stop to answer Clodagh. Instead, she stomped down the hill toward the streets. Her feet left prints in the ash. She didn't care that other people were waving to her or that they were asking for her help. Thea had one purpose in her movements and one purpose alone.

The sturdiest dock was the longest one as well. It was meant for larger ships, and many of the planks had burned through in the magic that had destroyed her home. She didn't care. Thea hardly even noticed her feet made the entire thing creak.

She marched all the way to the end of the dock, hands curled into fists at her side, and then she stood at the end. The wind blew smoke across the water toward the city that had already closed its doors. Someday those doors would open again. They would swing open to let out all the decay and rot that would eat them from the inside out.

Hands shaking at her sides, she screamed across the waters, hoping that a young man would hear her. "I hate you! I will never forgive you for this. All Orbweaver men are foul villains, and I will never forget!"

CHAPTER 27

10 years later

Dust motes floated in the air throughout the study. Alistair had tried everything he possibly could to get rid of them. Every spell that he knew from the damned Academy. Every maid that he could hire. None of it changed.

It was like the spirit of his father had hung around in the form of dust just to make him angry.

Blowing a breath across the paperwork in front of him, he cleared a few spots of ink that had gotten too messy to see. Leaning back, he lifted the paper to the meager silver light coming through the window and realized that he'd somehow dragged his hand across the wet ink. The words were not legible. The whole thing needed to be rewritten, and he already had a stack the size of his arm in front of him that needed the same treatment.

He could break down and use the magical quill that wouldn't allow him to make mistakes. But the spell had been wearing out for a while on that and… well…he only used it for special occasions.

Letting out a groan, he dropped his head onto the table with a thud. The papers rattled beside him, shifting as though they were going to tumble onto the floor. Maybe that would be an excuse for him to leave this room for the day and come back to it all tomorrow.

When had his life taken this horrible turn? He wanted to live a life full of mystery and wild adventures. Now, he sat at his father's desk every day and signed papers until his vision swam.

The door creaked open, and he let his mind wander in guessing whether it was the maid or if it was an errant fae who had wandered into his home. The faerie creatures had been particularly pushy the past few months. Red deer kept showing up outside of his house while leaving scratch marks on the ground.

Reminders that he was supposed to do his job in protecting them. So far, he'd kept that promise, but the Academy was pushing him more and more lately. The Headmistress wanted to see into the faerie realm. She wanted him to make something that would let them peer through the veil.

They had no idea he'd already made something exactly like that.

A warm hand smoothed between his shoulder blades. "Alistair, have you eaten today?"

"No," he muttered into the table. "I have too much work to do."

"You never have too much work for food." Something clinked against the table and then scraped over the edge. "Make sure you get something in your belly, or you'll keel over. And I'm sure your father would love to know that you passed out trying to do all the work he did on a regular basis."

"Why does it feel like you're making fun of me?" Alistair finally lifted his head and leaned back in the chair.

Nora, not one of the fae, had brought him a small tray with a tiny brass teapot, two cups, and a plate full of breakfast food. Eggs, bacon, freshly buttered bread. It all smelled delicious, but his stomach turned at the sight of it.

She no longer wore the maid's outfit he'd gotten so used to. Instead, Nora had been promoted and therefore wore whatever she wanted. She'd taken to wearing men's trousers in a deep blue, with a lovely blouse that had tiny blue flowers all over it. The matching blue vest with silver buttons didn't make her look masculine in the slightest, nor did she look like a butler. But maybe that was aided by the face-framing curls she let hang out of her bun.

He still had his father's voice in his head, muttering that men didn't get to eat until the work was done, and if he was so weak, then one of his brothers should have this job. He had to shake off the memory before his body would let him even consider taking a bite without vomiting.

Nora sat down on the edge of his desk, not caring at all that she crinkled a few of those very important documents.

What were they again?

She leaned forward and ran her thumb over his forehead. "You've ink on your head again."

He mumbled through the mouthful of food, "Probably because I laid it on wet ink."

With pursed lips and a scowl that should have been blistering, Nora eyed him as she always did when she was disappointed. She had every reason to be. Alistair had thrown himself into the work as only a man possessed could do. And that was years ago.

She'd changed in that time. The creases around her eyes were deeper. Her forehead now had permanent wrinkles that came with running an entire household full of maids, while her counterpart, the head butler, pretended he still ran the other side of it. Though he was so ancient, he frequently forgot their names. She'd done a good job stepping into the role, though.

Alistair didn't know what he'd do without her.

Sighing, he put his bread back down onto the plate and pulled a handkerchief out of his front pocket. "I understand you think I'm going to work myself into an early grave if I keep this up."

"Not think. Know." She crossed her arms over her chest. "Look at your father. He died all too early, and that was because of this work."

One might think that was the cause of his father's death. But Alistair had a feeling it was more likely the ancient god he kept in their basement. The one that Alistair was still ignoring because he didn't want to deal with the creature's wrath once it was let out.

Rubbing the back of his neck, he stared at all the papers and relented. "I know it's too much work for one man to do. That's why father always had Cassius to help him. Paperwork doesn't move if someone isn't doing it."

"It only grows bigger the more you ignore it." Nora nodded. "So why haven't you thought about finding someone to help you?"

He had. But the documents here... Surely there were family secrets in them? "I don't know anyone in Wildecliff that I would hire on. After father's death, you know how the vultures swarmed. They all wanted a job here, or to marry one of my brothers. All the gossip started when they were turned away. I want to avoid that tragedy again."

It wasn't that he cared so much if people were talking about his family. That never bothered Alistair. What bothered him was that they were talking about family secrets. Things even he hadn't known about. When the crowds of Wildecliff had smelled blood in the water, everyone arrived early for the feast.

"Then don't hire someone from Wildecliff." Nora lifted an eyebrow. "The gates are open again. The war is over."

So it was. A year ago now, in fact, although very few people would admit it had been that long.

He reached up to pinch the bridge of his nose as a headache bloomed behind his eyes, but his glasses got in the way. Ripping them off, he slumped in his chair with a little too much angst.

Alistair hated that he had to wear glasses now. He hated how chained he was to this desk and if someone could help him, then...

"Fine," he muttered. "What do I have to do?"

"Oh good. I'm glad you agreed." Nora stood and left the room for a few moments.

He stared after his head housekeeper as though she had lost her mind. Why had she walked out after he asked a question? Was she not at least required to answer it?

Then she bustled back in with a stack of papers in her hands. "I thought you needed help, and that you wouldn't admit it easily. I already submitted the position through a job agency. There is a business set up in Waterdown Commons that is working on creating relationships between the two river cities."

She set the stack down in front of him with a thud. Dust billowed from underneath it and made Alistair sneeze a few times before he pressed the handkerchief back against his mouth.

"And this is?" he asked.

"All the applications. There were quite a few qualified people who wished to work with you, and some that were... less qualified." She tapped her finger against the stack. "I already took the liberty of looking through the applications, although I'll admit, I don't know exactly what you'll want this person to do. All I need is for you to review them and—"

He picked the top application off the stack and handed it to her.

Nora blinked at him owlishly. "What are you doing?"

"I trust your opinion more than anyone else's, Nora. If you think this person was the best of the bunch, then hire them."

"Well, I..." Nora took the paper hesitantly. "I didn't place them in any particular order. There were at least twelve applicants who had remarkable references and..."

He interrupted her again. "Hire them. I don't care who they are or where they come from. If they can even do half a stack in a month, that's better than I'm doing now."

"Regardless, I think it would be wise for you to at least read which applicant you've handed me."

She tried to return the piece of paper to him, but honestly, he didn't care. Whatever man or woman wanted to leave the haven of their home in Waterdown and come to this dying city... They could come here. He'd give them a roof over their head, food, and whatever amount of work they wanted to do. At this point, he was so beyond caring that he didn't think it mattered who the person was.

He'd have very little to do with them, anyway, considering his work at the Academy kept him rather busy. Being a professor wasn't the job he'd ever wanted, but the children kept him on his toes.

Sighing, he stood and tried not to wince at the crick in his back that had tightened up after sitting for such a long time. "Just send them a letter, Nora. The sooner they can get in here, the better. I'd prefer not to be sitting at that desk for so long."

"Do you want them to have any other responsibilities in the home?" She stood with him, her eyes a little too wide. "You're hiring a secretary, but I don't know if you have enough work to keep them busy the entire time."

Again, he didn't care about any of that. "Put them in for a half-time secretary and if you need someone else to work in the house with you, then use them as you see fit."

Nora scanned over the document in her hand. "I think this person would be qualified for a lot of jobs in the household, but I want to warn you—"

He wanted no more warnings. He didn't want to talk either. The headache seemed to get worse now that he wasn't so engrossed in signing paperwork, and that meant he couldn't think through the pain that tightened around his skull like someone had tied a band around his head. "Nora."

Apparently, he'd said the word with a bit more of a tone than he should have. She straightened and eyed him with a nervous glance. "Master."

"Please don't call me that." He put his chilly hand against his forehead, which seemed to help a bit. "I have a headache that feels like it's going to split my skull in two. Can you please have one of the maids bring up one of your famous teas?"

"For the headache or for sleep?"

"Can you mix the two?"

She nodded. "I can. And I'll take care of this for you as well. It shouldn't take much longer than a couple of weeks to get someone on a ship and bring them over."

"Good." He hoped it would be sooner than that, but school was starting soon, anyway. If someone came in two weeks, he likely wouldn't see them for a while.

Maybe, if he were particularly lucky, the next time he saw that desk, there would be half the amount of papers on it. Nora would figure out how to get the new secretary notarized so they could sign everything for him.

Slowly walking down the hallway, he remembered what this house had once been. The cold mist remained in certain sections of the house, but a lot of the old finery had been sold off after he had to deal with his father's debt. The floors were even colder these days without the fine rugs. Though faint shadows of where they once were remained on the floors, as though the house wanted to remind him it had once been great.

No more chandeliers swung over his head. Instead, there were merely bare bulbs illuminating the corridors. They flickered as he walked underneath them through the undecorated halls. No statues. No artwork. It was a house that felt like the skeleton of what had once been a home. But he knew that it had never been a home—only a prison for those who lived here.

Alistair paused at the base of the stairwell. Behind him was the locked door to the basement where all the mist erupted from. The cold, white tendrils clung to his ankles as though they wanted him to open that door and disappear into the depths that had consumed his father.

He would never. Could never.

Alistair knew what awaited him in those lonely shadows, and he knew it would not be kind. Nor did it care to see another Orbweaver whispering promises they never would keep.

He wrapped his hand around the banister and pulled himself away from that door. Each step up the stairwell felt as though he were trying to run through deep water. But he made it to the landing where his father's portrait had once hung. Now, there was only a blank wall with a large rectangle of darkness.

Trailing his fingers over the shadow, he crept up the stairwell toward his own room.

"I know," he muttered to the ghost of his father, who walked with him every step of the way. "You hate what this house has become. But it's all your fault, you know. You bound me to this house, father, and I will take care of it best I can. Still, all you did was chain me to a corpse and tell me not to eat it to survive."

Shuffling down the long hall, he tried not to look at the locked doors to his brother's rooms as he made it to his own.

CHAPTER 28

A job?" Clodagh howled the words as though they were the funniest thing she'd ever heard. "You want a job in Wildecliff?"

Thea winced and put down the small bundle of herbs she'd brought into town. "What's so funny about that?"

"It's just..." Clodagh waved a hand up and down Thea's body as though that explained everything.

It did, in a way. Compared to her friend, who wore the latest in fashions, Thea looked a little... worn down. Clodagh's dress was smooth and thin. It hugged her curves, where there were curves at least, with a sweeping square neckline. Slits up the sides of her dress showed off her long, freckled legs. Thea still wore the old style of clothing. Her skirts swayed around her waist in a giant circle whenever she moved, and her blouse tucked into the skirts to give her a tinier waist. But even her blouse had seen better days.

Thea's family needed money. Sure, there were many ways they could help the town, and had in the times since the war. They'd made sure that food was available to the hungry masses while the town was rebuilt by all the people who desperately needed homes. But no one in Waterdown had money, and her mother was a bleeding heart when it came to starving mouths.

Some people could afford to order wood from other cities. They'd smuggled it in during the early stages of the war and then more often later on. Wood could burn, though, and Wildecliff had done everything they could to ensure that the wood was cursed when it had arrived on Waterdown's shores. Whether it was wood-eating beetles or tragic rot that turned homes into mush, they'd eventually had to build stone homes.

Waterdown didn't look like it used to. Everything here was rock and earth. None of the buildings were painted bright colors, and there were very few stores. Only those who hadn't been able to leave were still here, and that meant money had gotten even more scarce.

"We need money," she muttered, balancing the basket on her hip as she peered down the well in the center of town.

"You've got all the food and water you can want. What do you need a job for?"

"To rebuild the house. To get clothes on my mother's back that aren't ancient or moth eaten. To have something other than a curse that lingers no matter how long we try to fight against it." She could continue, but Clodagh wouldn't understand. Her father had done well after the war.

Clodagh sighed and seemed to understand that maybe, just maybe, this was something she couldn't understand. And Thea needed her support for this.

A job was a job. It was money. And she didn't care who was paying her.

Thea shrugged and added, "I just have to go sign the paperwork today and we'll see where I'm headed. Someone will need a secretary or a maid or… something else."

"You shouldn't be focusing on getting paid, and instead, you should focus on getting married." Clodagh crossed her arms over her chest and glared at her. "That's what I did, and I think it was rather successful."

"Of course. I should find an old man who's going to die at any point. Then, when he does die under very suspicious circumstances, I will take his money and ride off into the sunset with my true beloved, who somehow did not conspire to do all this with me. Is that right?"

"Precisely."

Thea rolled her eyes. Clodagh didn't really believe she'd gotten away with all that, and no one assumed it was her? She was even madder than Thea had ever thought.

"Not all of us can get away with murder, Clodagh."

"Not murder. He died of natural causes. That was proven time and time again." Her friend brushed a billow of red hair away from her face and grinned. "All I'm saying is that I got the life I wanted. Money, the woman that makes me smile, and a house in Strongmeadow that didn't get hit so hard in the war. You could try it."

"I couldn't stomach being with a man like that." Thea made a face as though that wasn't the real reason why she wouldn't do it.

Clodagh saw right through her. With a soft, sad smile, Clodagh put her hand on Thea's shoulder. "You know it's been long enough, right? Ten years is more than enough time to forget him."

Him.

The word that her entire world always revolved around. Everyone always seemed to think she could just let the memory go, as though she were blowing seeds from a dandelion puff. She should let all those memories float away in the wind, and then everything would be fine.

How was she supposed to do that when he had practically branded himself into her skin? Into her soul? Thea had lived and breathed for him. And now people wanted her just to let him go?

She was happier like this. Living without him was like living without a limb. But it was better than not living at all.

Clodagh sighed and shook her head. "I don't know how you still even think about him. It's not love, you've told me that enough times. But how can you let him live within you even as a memory?"

Thea shrugged. "I can't imagine a time when I wouldn't remember him."

And that was enough of this conversation. Thea didn't want to talk about Alistair anymore because… Damn it. Now she'd thought his name. She'd have to reset the calendar she kept in her house, and she'd been so good about not thinking the word Alistair.

Now she wouldn't be able to stop. It had taken her months the last time to train her mind back to thinking about him and not giving damned Alistair Orbweaver even more space in her mind.

She shoved the herbs into Clodagh's arms. "Would you give this to Miss Breathnach, please? She asked mother to help with her baby, apparently colic has been going around."

The shock on her friend's face was worth the risky move. Hopefully, Clodagh would deliver those herbs to the correct place and not just leave them on the well for someone else to snag. Either way, Thea needed to get out of this conversation before more dangerous memories popped up.

She marched down the street like a woman on a mission. And she supposed she was. A job waited for her; she was certain of it. Thea had woken up with a feeling that her life was going to change today. Of course, with a feeling like that, she'd gotten up to drink her tea and check the leaves for any messages.

Today she'd seen a spade for good fortune through industry over a straight line, which remarked on her careful planning. She'd done everything right, and now even the tea leaves thought she'd get a job.

She paused in front of the agency door. They'd gotten a sign, she realized with a little happiness. The quill and ink looked freshly painted and were lovely to look at. Although, they'd forgotten to name the agency.

But, then again, she didn't know the name of the agency either. Maybe they didn't have one yet.

She opened the door, and a bell chimed. There was only a long desk at the back of the room where a bespectacled woman stood waiting for any customers or job seekers to enter. The rest of the room was still blank, but the windows looked out onto the river. Mrs. O'Connor didn't suffer fools being in her shop, and that's why she said there were no decorations. No colors, no distractions.

But Thea's eyes still strayed to the large windows. Boats had returned to their harbor. After so many years of still waters and an empty river, there were more boats than ever before. Each ship contained cargo, people seeking labor, and those who wanted to make a home in either Wildecliff or Waterdown. So many people who would return home or make a place for themselves here.

It gave her hope.

"Miss Thea," the woman behind the counter said. "I'm glad you came in today! I was about to send one of the runners off to find you."

They both knew very well that the agency didn't have the money yet to hire any of the runners to find people. But Thea was pleased enough to think that someday, her job might give the agency enough coin to hire one of those boys. "Is that so?"

"There is a job for you. In Wildecliff." Mrs. O'Connor slid a file over to her. "Secretarial work, mostly, although they did make an addition to the packet that you may help out the maids in the household as well. It sounds like there's a lot of work to be done."

"You know I'm no stranger to hard work." Thea glanced over the document, trying to read through the fine print without looking like she didn't trust Mrs. O'Connor.

Gods and Goddesses knew that the job agency had gone above and beyond trying to find a job for a young woman who hadn't been formally trained. That had made it very difficult to get Thea a job.

But this was the first person who'd offered to hire her. She had to wonder why.

The document looked straightforward, however. Half of her time would be spent doing secretarial work that would be taught once she arrived in Wildecliff, and then she would need to spend the rest of her time with the maid staff.

She would have taken the maid's job full time, so this was better than expected. Then her eyes strayed to how much they were going to pay her, and her jaw dropped open in shock.

She met Mrs. O'Connor's laughing gaze. "Is that number right?"

"Which one?" The mad woman had the audacity to take the paper back and wiggle her glasses back in place. "I'm afraid I don't know what number you're looking at, my dear."

"This one!" Thea leaned across the desk to jab at the paper. "That ridiculously high monthly allotment! They can't be serious? Seven gold pieces for a month of work?"

For most jobs, that was the entire year's worth of pay. She would have been lucky here to get a job that paid a silver a month, let alone gold.

"Yes, that looks to be the accurate number." Mrs. O'Connor looked up at her through the glasses. "They were quite adamant that they wouldn't pay less. And that someone of your arithmancy skills, with mathematical capabilities, and, of course, your glowing recommendations, was worth this amount of pay."

Thea let out a shriek that rattled the rafters. "I have a job!"

"You have to accept the job first," Mrs. O'Connor chuckled, then slid the paper back over to her with a quill and inkwell. "Sign here, date it, and make sure that you're back here in a week to catch the first ship out to Wildecliff. There is a lot for us to do to prepare you for the work, but I think you're qualified."

Thea had never signed something so fast in her life. She left her mark as it felt like her soul took flight out of her body and soared into the heavens. "I can't believe this is happening."

"You'll have to tell your mother."

Thea waved her hand in the air. "That's fine. Marigold and her family are moving back into the house. Her husband has unfortunately discovered nothing in that mine of his, other than rock and dirt. Belladonna needs help more than ever with her three children. They'll hardly even notice that I'm gone."

"If you say so." Mrs. O'Connor took the paperwork back and put it into a folder. "Just remember, your first paycheck goes directly to our agency and then it changes to ten percent every month for one year."

"I'm more than happy to do so. Thank you for not giving up on me."

"How could I? You and your family have done more for this town than anyone else has. I'm very pleased to have worked with you, Thea, and I hope this job is everything that you're looking for." Mrs.

O'Connor handed her back a secondary folder and smiled at her. "All the details are in here. The ship has already been chartered. I'm afraid you don't have any seating underneath, but it should only take the day to get over to Wildecliff. Make sure none of your things get wet. And I believe it goes without saying, but this is a higher class household than most. You'll have to be prepared to look the part."

Thea would figure that out later. She ignored the flash of old fear and a memory of laughter as she walked down the street. Ten years had passed since that fateful day when she had decided she wouldn't stay. Ten years was a long time for a child to grow into a woman and a city to grow up in general.

Straightening her shoulders, she nodded. "I won't let you down. I'll look the part, talk the part, and stay out of the way of whoever owns this house."

The address made little sense to her, but most addresses were dodgy. She'd find a map or ask someone the moment she was off the ship. Hopefully, there were still bleeding hearts in Wildecliff who could send her on her way.

If not, she would figure it out. That's what Thea did these days, anyway. She made do with what she had.

"Thank you," she said one more time before rushing out of the job agency and back onto the street.

Pressing the sheets of paper to her chest, she looked up at the sky and mouthed another thank you to the gods that must be looking down at her with glee. Finally, after all her years of worship and being the perfect daughter, the gods had seen fit to bless her.

"So you got the job?" Clodagh's voice burst through her bubble of happiness.

Thea whirled to find her best friend leaning against the wall of the agency, her skirts stirring in the breeze. "I did. I got the job, and it's a damned good one. I can make sure mama has clothes. The house can get fixed. Maybe we can even hire a curse maker to bring it back to life! The same way Papa did."

Clodagh rolled her eyes. "You know, I could have helped with any of that. You don't have to move to Wildecliff to get money. The gods know I have more money than I know what to do with."

"But now this money will be mine." She slapped the folder against her chest. "And it even says I can bring Browning. What employer allows a witch to bring her familiar?"

"Someone who doesn't care what spells you're casting in their house. Must be someone who thinks they're powerful." Clodagh lifted a brow and shoved herself off the wall. She added, "Are you prepared to handle Wildecliff again? You hate Wildecliff."

She did. More than anything else.

But she loved her mother more than she hated Wildecliff. So Thea nodded. "Can you show me how to fit in?"

"In Wildecliff? Not a chance." But then Clodagh grinned. "I can make you more beautiful and confident, though. Who would dare say a single word against you when you glow like the moon?"

CHAPTER 29

Alistair stood in front of his house, hands on his hips, trying his best not to give up. Yesterday it was the roof. Two days ago, the stairs had given out. Today? Apparently, today the windows were going to break on three different levels.

The house was bleeding money. No. Hemorrhaging money to such an extent that he didn't know how his father had kept up with all of it.

"No," he grumbled. "I know exactly how you kept up with it, you old bat."

Debts. Mountains and mountains of debt that his father hadn't been able to crawl out of. Thus, the debts landed on his damned lap. But he supposed the old saying of shit rolls downhill really was true, and he should have been more careful when he was younger.

Or more reckless, and he should have run away.

Squeezing the bridge of his nose, he tried his best to push the headache away. At least, until Nora opened the front door and shouted, "If you keep doing that, you're going to make the headache worse!"

"I didn't hire you as head housekeeper to turn you into a harpy!"

"No, you hired me to take care of the house!" She pointed up at the windows. "Those need to be fixed before Thea gets here!"

The word sent him into a spiral of nausea, heartbreak, and outright fear. A cold sweat broke out over his entire body, and he had to grab onto the sharp iron fence to balance himself. Alistair was quite certain that he had gone white as a sheet and likely looked as though he were going to pass out.

He felt like it. The mere mention of her name turned him into an angry young man again. He'd run down the docks to salvage what little he could of their relationship, and then all the fires had happened.

He'd stood on the dock for hours, certain that he was watching her die. And though no Orbweaver man would be caught dead crying, he had forced himself to stay frozen on that dock. Watching. Waiting. Hoping.

And at the first light of day, he thought he'd heard her scream that she would never forgive him for this. That she hated him.

And he'd deserved that. Alistair had taken those words, and he had become them. Absorbed them. Used them to become a different man. A better one, he hoped, at least as much as he could be in a place like this.

He'd thought after ten years that hearing the sound of her name wouldn't make him flinch, but it still did. All the guilt that had only grown in the years that had passed since the last time he'd seen the love of his life suddenly welled over his head and awakened something inside him.

His heart.

His soul.

His Thea.

He shook his head and staggered to the front door. Bracing himself on the door frame, he asked, "What did you just say?"

"Oh my," Nora said, her own face paler than normal. "I told you to look at the paperwork! I thought you at least saw the name, you foolish man."

"I didn't."

"Well, maybe it's a different Thea? There could be countless of them in Waterdown. Neither of us knows."

He knew. In his gut, he knew there was only one Thea, and she was now coming to his home. "It's her. I know it's her."

"Why would she take a job from you if it was her? You two have a history." Nora shook her head. "It's not. I'm quite certain it's not."

He might have once sided with her just so that he didn't have to feel this anxiety building in his chest, but he knew. He could tell. Thea was returning to Wildecliff, and he had been the one to bring her here.

He'd have to relive all of those horrible memories. She'd be afraid of his home once again, but this time, she worked for him. He could never let her do that. The absolute fear that had taken over her the first time she'd stepped foot in this house was not something he could expect anyone to suffer through—especially not one of his staff.

Damn it. He was going to be her employer. That added a whole new layer of depravity to how he felt about her.

Sinking down onto the front step, he cupped his head in his hands. "Nora, what am I going to do?"

"Oh, it can't be that bad." Although she most assuredly knew it was that bad and that he would lose his mind if they weren't careful.

She sat down beside him, and they stayed like that for a while.

Quietly sitting in each other's company as they had for many years before this. She always knew when to talk and when not to, thankfully. Like the older sibling, he'd never had.

Finally, she let out a brief hum of breath. "Well, there are two things I know. First is that she must have seen who was hiring her, and thus, she chose to come here and work for you. That has to mean something. And second, we've got a little work to do before she gets here. But if you cannot see her, then we will have you at the Academy when she first arrives. You can take some time and then decide from there when to meet her. It's not usual for a new maid to not meet the master of the house for some time."

"She's not just a maid," he muttered into his palms. "She's the love of my life and the only person who has ever made me feel as though I wasn't Alistair Orbweaver."

"But you are."

"Sometimes I don't want to be."

Nora grunted. "Well, that's just ridiculous. You are who you are and there's nothing wrong with that. You shouldn't be ashamed of being a good man. Besides, you've been on your own for this long. Maybe it'll be good for you to see her again. She can't be the paragon you remember."

Thea wasn't a paragon of a woman, though. Not even in his memory. She'd been gritty and strange—a wild creature trapped in the skin of a tame-looking woman. But that had been part of the allure. Thea was a girl made of moonbeams and wrapped in spider silk. A beauty he would never be able to catch in a jar who still could light up his entire world like a firefly.

And here he was. Thinking about her again. He'd promised himself he would stop doing that, and ten years had dulled the feeling. Or at least, that's what he thought.

But now, the mere idea of seeing her in the flesh made his entire body sweat like he'd run ten miles. "I will be her employer, Nora. I can't be in love with one of my staff."

"You aren't in love with her. You've just been existing in a state of loneliness for so long that you don't know how to see another person as a person." Nora rolled her eyes at the expression he gave her. "Fine. Fine! I don't know why you've wrapped yourself up in this girl, but I understand even saying that was foolish. You know how you feel."

He took a deep breath and let one of his deepest thoughts take flight. "It's been years since I've seen her. A lifetime since I've spoken to her. So long that the letters I wrote her have curled, and the ink has faded. But sometimes I think of her, and it still gets harder to breathe."

Nora's expression changed from her teasing look to one of complete and utter tragedy. "Alistair. You have to let her go."

Did he, though? It had been ten years, and he still wanted to hold her against his heart. He still wanted to apologize and tell her he'd been an idiot for ever letting go and not seeing what his father had planned. His heart beat for her, and it only continued beating on the off chance that he might see her again.

Now she would work for him. In his house. Living under the same roof. Breathing the same air.

Even though he knew those thoughts were foolish, yet he couldn't stop thinking about the first time she'd come into this home.

He glanced over his shoulder down the dark, empty hall that led to the stairs. "She's afraid of this house. I don't know why she'd ever agree to work here."

"From what I've heard, times are rather desperate in Waterdown still."

"And here. Times aren't easy for any of us." He nodded up at the windows. "I haven't the faintest idea how we're going to pay for that. But I know she can't see the house like a ruin when she arrives, or I'll never live it down."

"Because she'll be angry at you? Or because we're paying our staff so well that they could leave at any point and buy their own house?"

Perhaps that. But he wouldn't be his father. Alistair could take some money away from the staff and pay for all the fixes in a heartbeat. But these people deserved to have their own lives as well, and he refused to be the reason they had to choose between fresh bread or day old.

Nora grabbed onto his hand and squeezed it. "You've given them all a good chance at having a good life. But we've got a new staff member coming on to work, and she has enough skills to take on the role of a maid. It might not be the easiest transition for her, but if you think Miss Thea can be spared from paperwork for a while..."

He already knew where she was going with it. Letting go of one of the staff members would hurt, but it would save them seven gold a month. Alistair hated the solution, but he knew a dead end when he saw one.

"I'll let you choose who, then." He stood and dusted off his pants. "And send one of the boys out to talk with a glass maker. Those windows need fixing before the winter hits."

"I'll do that promptly." Nora stood as well, although she did so a little slower than he did. Years of hard work hadn't been kind on her back, as she liked to remind him. "And what are you planning on doing while I get all this figured out?"

His mind raced.

Thea was coming here. To his home. The place she hated. There was still a trapped fae or god in his basement that made the entire building freezing cold. He had no idea what he was going to have her do, but it didn't feel right to make her work. Thea had every reason to hate him, and that meant she would have no safe place and no one to lean on while she was here.

Sighing, he put his hands on his hips and narrowed his gaze on the stairwell. "Send up four of the butlers to the second floor for me, would you? To my room."

"Why?"

He didn't answer. There was work to be done, and unfortunately, it was work that needed to be done sooner rather than later. Alistair marched up the stairwell with his father's voice whispering in his ear.

"How dare you let one of them into my house? A Waterdown woman! I told you we all have our dalliances, but the moment you let a woman like that into my house—"

Alistair waved his hand through the faint outline of his father's spirit and continued toward his room. Opening the door, he motioned for Atlas to fly over to him. His beloved familiar hadn't aged a day. But, he supposed, that was the gift of familiars.

"What do you think about a new view, my friend?" He stroked his finger down Atlas's chest and the soft downy feathers there. "We've been looking out the same window for ages, and I think it's time that we move to one of the better rooms. Shall we?"

Heading out of his bedroom, he left the doors open and waited for the butlers to meet him at the head of the stairs. They had all been with the family for some time. If they had opinions on how Alistair ran the house in comparison to his father, they kept those opinions to themselves.

"Move my things to the eastern wing," he said. "I would like to set up my old bedroom into a guest room, of sorts. Do we have any extra furniture that we haven't sold?"

The oldest butler in his neatly pressed black suit nodded. "There are a few in the attic, sir. Enough to furnish a room, albeit plainly."

"Good, that will do." Atlas walked up to his shoulder and clacked his beak in Alistair's ear. "Don't worry about cleaning. I have a few favors that I'm going to call in. Just make sure that the furniture is there and that the old furniture ends up in the new room."

"New room?" The youngest butler appeared confused by all this. "Where are you moving, Master?"

"To my father's old room," he replied. "It's pastime I take the master bedroom as my own."

All the butlers looked surprised at that, and he couldn't blame them. Alistair had declared that no one was to go into the eastern wing. Not because of some memory of his father or anything he wanted to keep sacred there. But because there were plenty of spells lingering that he didn't want anyone to get caught up in.

Which reminded him....

Alistair left the butlers where they were and meandered toward the eastern wing. He reached into his pocket for a handful of caramels that he always kept with him in case he needed to summon the fae.

"Brownies?" he called when he was out of earshot of the others. "I need to ask a favor of you all."

Like little balls of lint, three tumbled down from the top of a serving table. Two brownies opened up tiny doors that looked like mouse holes near the trim of the hall. Four more peeked out at him from underneath the rug nearby. Not quite as many as he hoped, but household spirits were scarce when there weren't as many people to help.

He drew out the gold foiled wrapped caramels and held them out for all the fae to see. "I need help curse hunting in the eastern wing. I hoped you might be interested in a little fun?"

The brownies all raced toward him, their hands outstretched and their mouselike whiskers twitching frantically.

"Thank you," he said. "My father was rather adept at casting curses and if I'm moving into his bedroom, I'd like to not get trapped in the dreaming world."

The nearest brownie had on a tiny red dress. She took her caramel with very gentle hands, holding it with both hers, and then looked him in the eye. "We'll keep you safe, little Alistair. Just as you've kept us safe all these years."

Sometimes he thought they meant allowing them to live in the house and providing them with fresh milk and cream. But sometimes, he wondered if it was much more than that.

CHAPTER 30

The wind blew through her hair and tangled the locks into knots at the back of her neck. But it didn't matter. Thea was on the boat to freedom.

Sure, she was headed to a place she hated above all others. A place filled with memories she'd rather forget. But Wildecliff was a large city, and she could avoid the people she didn't want to see. All she had to do was get to her job, and then she'd be so busy she wouldn't have time to think about anything other than the work that needed to be done.

"This is a new start for us, Browning," she said with her face turned toward the sun.

She'd get freckles if she kept this up, and that knowledge made Thea want to look at the sun even more. Freckles were beautiful. They were different. And she'd need to cling to whatever was different as long as she stayed here.

"It's not like I'm abandoning them." Her familiar likely didn't know who she was talking about, but Thea did. She wasn't leaving her family behind.

Máthair would have her hands full, and their tiny house would soon echo with the shrieks of children who had never had to live with their cousins. Belladonna and Marigold would take up more space than her mother was prepared for, and five children in a house that small would drive anyone mad. Not to mention the husbands. Máthair liked her son-in-laws well enough, but they were men, and her mother had not had to deal with men for a very long time.

Thea would have been one more mouth to feed. One more person to take care of when everyone was already screeching at Máthair to do something. Besides, now Thea would be the only child consistently bringing money back to the family, and no small amount of money at that.

"This was the right choice." She nodded firmly and then blinked down at her sling. "Right, Browning?"

There was no answering rustle or croak.

"Browning?"

Where had that blasted toad gotten off to?

She peered through the nearest bundle of ropes, but there was no toad in sight. As they approached the docks to Wildecliff, Thea knew she only had a few moments to find her wayward familiar before someone stepped on him.

"Browning!" she hissed as she moved past a large group of individuals.

A few of them glared at her, and she couldn't blame them. Everyone was excited to start their new life in Wildecliff, and no one wanted to walk into the city with a crazy person raving behind them.

"Sorry," Thea muttered as she moved past them. "Sorry, I'm just looking for my familiar."

"She should have better control over the beast," someone said. The person was lost in the crowd of others, or Thea might have turned around to strike them.

She had plenty of control over her familiar, but Browning wasn't some trained pet. When he wanted to wander, she wouldn't tell him otherwise. Who was she to tell a magical creature that he couldn't do what he wanted?

Finally, she spotted the dastardly little fellow. Browning had somehow climbed on top of a barrel. She could only assume he'd convinced someone to put him up there and now stood on his thin back legs to look over the railing at Wildecliff. His webbed fingers gripped the wooden support and his belly squeezed between the rungs.

"Browning!" she scolded before scooping him up in her arms. "What did I tell you about wandering off?"

He looked up at her with those wide yellow eyes, blew up his throat, and croaked, "Wildecliff."

"Yes, yes I know." She laid him into the sling and then made sure it was comfortably hung over her neck. "I didn't think we'd ever be coming back here, either."

She hadn't forgotten the valor of her little familiar, who had traveled here far more often than she had. Browning had gone through more hardship than she could imagine delivering messages back and forth across the river. And he rarely got to ride on a ship like this.

She squeezed him to her side and then moved to stand with the others at the front of the ship. They'd already been advised that once the planks were down, they were to stand to the right on the docks because their items would be piled opposite. One of the sailors had told her to be quick about it. If the pile got too high, some of the luggage would fall into the sea, and no one would help her get her things.

The planks thudded against the wooden docks, and everyone else seemed to know that they needed to move forward. Thea found herself caught in the wave of people until they were all standing and waiting. Yet again, she had no idea how she'd gotten here. Although she supposed, it was rather nice not to have to think.

The sailors all started shouting, and then luggage was slung off the boat and landed on the dock. The crowd was quick, as the sailors had suggested they be. But Thea didn't see her bag. Over and over again, people gathered up their items and made their way into the city. While Thea and Browning stood there, still waiting for her bag.

Then she saw it. The large patchwork tote had taken forever to make. Máthair had insisted they imbue as much goodwill into the bag as they could, and the wooden handles had been carved out of a beam from their old home. No matter where she went, her mother claimed, Thea would always know she was loved and looked after.

As if she would ever forget that. Darting in between two sailors who had gotten off the ship as well, she grabbed onto the handles of her bag and hauled it into her arms. It was heavy. Probably too heavy for her to be carrying on her own. But there were certain things she'd refused to leave behind. No matter how silly it was for her to bring them.

"Gods above, girl," one sailor said with a laugh. "What do you have in that bag? Bricks?"

"Books, actually!" And a handful of other spell crafting items, but they didn't need to know any of that.

The less the Wildecliff people knew about her bringing what they might consider contraband items into their city, the better. Unfortunately, the bag was bulkier than she'd expected. Thea's entire weight shifted backward until she was carrying the heavy object with the small of her back rather than her arms. But still, she made it on her own all the way to the front gates of Wildecliff.

It was still so strange to see the giant stone doors open. They were simple doors. Nothing like the interior of the city, but then again, the wall wasn't spectacular either. Wildecliff had made sure the wall and the entrance were usable, safe, and that they wouldn't fall apart over the centuries. Apparently, that was the one thing they would sacrifice aesthetics for.

Many guards stood in front of the gates. They wore the traditional dark black uniform of the Wildecliff guardians—golden buckles and buttons gleamed in the sun. Though, the last time she'd come here, she didn't remember them carrying muskets. And they certainly hadn't carried swords as they did now.

"Stop." One of the guards meandered over to her, and she immediately didn't trust him. Anyone who wore a greasy mustache like that wasn't a good person. "Papers, please."

"Papers?" Thea gaped at him, her arms full of her things and a little overladen with the toad slung around her waist. "What do you mean, papers?"

"Everyone has papers if they're coming into Wildecliff, Miss. No visitors allowed otherwise."

"Oh, I'm not visiting." She tried to smile at him over the patchwork bag in her arms. Thea wasn't so sure he saw her smile. "I was hired as a secretary here. So thank you very much for being so thoughtful and looking out over your city, but I'm going to be moving here for the foreseeable future."

The kindly look in his eyes fell away. That mustache twitched as though he'd smelled something disgusting. "Papers, Miss."

She'd heard him the first time. Why was he repeating himself?

A second guard joined him. This one was a much larger man with a stomach that stretched his suit a little too tightly around his midriff. "Is this one causing you trouble, Jenkins?"

"She refuses to provide her papers."

Thea cleared her throat. "I'm not refusing to provide anything. I'm just not sure what you're talking about. No one gave me papers."

The paunchy guard laughed and lifted his arms as though she'd told him something impossible. "Well, then there's nothing we can do for you. No papers. No entrance. Those are the rules, little lady."

"But I was hired to work here. Someone is expecting me."

What was she going to do if they didn't let her in? Thea turned to look back at the ship, hoping one of the sailors could bring her back home. But the ship was already in the harbor, meandering back toward Waterdown as the sun set.

What would she do? They were going to make her sleep on the docks until her employer started asking questions.

Drawing her brows down into a dark frown, she lowered her bag so they could see her face. "Gentlemen. I need you to explain what these papers are. No one told me that I was required to have them, and no one on that ship was holding them as they disembarked. So why am I the only person you're asking for papers?"

The two guards looked at each other, and she swore they smiled before their angry expressions returned.

The mustached man stepped forward a little too aggressively. "Ma'am, I'm going to give you one more chance."

Thea's mouth ran away without her. "One more chance for me to tell you, yet again, that I do not have the papers you're asking for?"

The men moved with surprising speed, considering their sizes.

Thea barely had time to blink before the bag was slapped out of her hands and landed hard in a puddle. Then the larger man put both his hands on her shoulders and shoved. She stumbled over a small box containing hooks and fishing equipment, then fell next to her bag.

She hit her palms hard on the stones, and she hissed out an angry breath. Her ribs ached. She'd barely twisted in time to not squish Browning as she fell, but the poor toad had tumbled out of his sling and was at least five feet away from her. He rolled onto his stomach and wheezed out a long breath as though he'd had the wind knocked out of him.

What had just happened? Her head reeled, and her mind whirled with the realization that they'd just accosted her. They'd tossed her onto her back, and no one had even tried to stop them. As she looked up, she realized no one was even looking at her. They all stayed out of the way.

She heard the sound of tearing. Thea wasn't quick enough to react. Instead, all she could do was sit up as the guards tore the handle off her bag and threw the wood out of reach.

The mustached man rifled through her things, tossing her bloomers into the mud until he found the folder for her employment. Thumbing through it, he tossed a few of the pages in the direction of her bloomers before pulling out the official document she'd signed.

He lifted a brow, waved the document at her, and then said, "Papers. That's all I asked for. We didn't have to do all this, Miss."

But it seemed like they'd wanted to. They'd enjoyed throwing her things around and making her day horrible.

The man set the folder on top of her ripped-up bag, patted it twice, and then sighed. "You're allowed through. Documents like that are more than enough to prove you've got a right to be here. Gather up your things quick, Miss. The doors close at sundown."

She watched as they walked away, whistling as though they hadn't assaulted a woman. And then she shakily looked down at her arms and skirts soaked with water and mud. No one would want to hire her. Her employer would take one look at the mud-covered woman who had arrived from Waterdown, and he'd send her right back home.

Tears stung her eyes. She'd wanted this so badly. She'd been so excited.

A wart-covered head nudged underneath her hand. Browning croaked, the deep rumble one of anger as he watched the men walk away from her. Then reached between them and handed her a single gladiolus bloom. She didn't know where he'd gotten it from, but she knew what he wanted.

Gladiolus were the flowers of the sword. If she placed it on her tongue, she'd have the strength of ten men. She could throw those idiots into the river all night until her anger was satisfied.

But she couldn't. She wasn't the villain of any story, no matter how much she desired to be.

Sighing, she shook her head and dashed away the tears. "Come on, Browning. We need to get to the correct address before it's dark."

Thea gathered up her things as quickly as she could. The handle had been ripped out of the fabric, so it took a bit for her to tie everything up into a knot that wouldn't unravel the moment she lifted the bag. But she made sure the handle from her childhood home was safely tucked into the mess. She had to bring her father with her, after all.

The damned thing was even heavier to carry now, suddenly more burdensome as she realized she wasn't going to a fairytale job. She had to live in Wildecliff. A city she hated—filled with people she hated.

The faint color of roses that had helped her be so excited fell away from her eyes as she staggered through the front gates and searched for the correct street name to meander down.

"At least it can't get any worse than this," she huffed to Browning.

People stared at her. She must have made quite the spectacle, huffing and puffing down the road with her patchwork bag. Red-faced. Breathing like she'd run from Waterdown all the way here and covered in mud. Thea was a terrifying beast to these clean, perfectly coiffed people.

The city of Wildecliff was a well-oiled clock, moving with gears that were polished to perfection. And Thea? She was a speck of dirt on otherwise pristine glass.

"Hanover street," she wheezed. Then she looked at the other directional signs. "Ah, perfect. Obscurum. That's the right street."

She had found the correct street on her own, and that was a win. But the moment she rounded the corner and saw those black spires, the wrought-iron fence, and the sudden wave of cold, Thea realized she'd made a mistake.

A horrible. Terrible. Irredeemable mistake.

She marched up to the iron gates, dropped her bag in front of it, and then pawed through her things. "This is the wrong address," she muttered. "It's the wrong one. I took the wrong street, I just need to find the right one. I'll be a little late, but that's quite all right. I'm sure they won't mind, considering I just moved from my own city."

Then she ripped out the folder, flipped it open, and ran her finger across the lines. "Employer. Academia Araneidae. Main duties will be secretarial in nature, half time providing maid services as needed by the head maid. Address. 36 Obscurum."

She looked up and noted the number next to the gate.

36.

Damn it. She was at the right address. But that didn't make any sense because if she were supposed to be working for the Orbweavers, then it would say Orbweaver on the document. Maybe someone else had bought the house. Of course, if someone had, then she could only assume something had happened to Alistair and his family. Which shouldn't make her heart twist the way it did, but...

Browning put his webbed hand on the paper and looked up at her.

"It's not him," she said. "It can't be. See? Employer is Academia Araneidae."

Browning nodded, then croaked, "Araneidae. Latin for spider."

Damn. Well.

She looked up at the house and swallowed hard. The windows seemed to loom, and the house appeared to stretch higher as though it were ready to swallow her up. She couldn't do it. She couldn't go in there.

So Thea did the only thing she could do. She paced in front of the iron fence, muttering about the pros and cons of working here until she felt a lick of bravery.

CHAPTER 31

Alistair stood before the front door, his fist pressed against his lips. He'd watched her through the glass for quite some time now, assuming that Thea would eventually give up and make her way toward the building.

She didn't.

She paced back and forth like a madwoman. He could see her lips moving, so he could only assume she was muttering to herself or to Browning while she walked by a patchwork bag of her things that had clearly ripped in her journey. If anyone walked by the house, they would think he was about to be robbed. Or cursed. Or worse.

At this point, he didn't care what anyone else thought. All he cared about was that the woman of his dreams stood outside his door again, and he couldn't say a word to her.

What would he say? "Welcome back to this house. I'm sure you never thought you'd come back here. I'm sorry you had to?"

That was a horrible way to greet her after so many years. How long had it been? Alistair counted on his fingers as she started her next round of pacing. He thought it had been ten, but the years had wandered past him so quickly he couldn't be sure.

Who was he kidding? He knew it had been exactly ten years, three months, and seven days since he'd seen her last. That was why they were back in the school year, that was why the winds were already growing a little chilly, and the leaves had turned into a deep red surrounding his house.

And damn it, after all this time, he had missed her more than he wanted to admit.

"She's still out there pacing, is she?" Nora stopped beside him and put her hands on her hips.

"She is."

"I guess that means she didn't know she was going to be working here, then."

"The addresses are a little confusing." He couldn't remember there being any addresses in Waterdown. Everyone knew where everyone lived, and if they didn't, then they knew the neighbor. She probably hadn't thought it would be so difficult to find his home, and she'd not expected to come here again, anyway. "Maybe she got the words mixed up?"

"Are you trying to convince yourself that she's working for a neighbor and that another young woman from Waterdown will turn the corner at any minute?" Nora snorted. "No one in this house is that lucky."

He bristled at her tone. "We'll be lucky to have her working for us. Thea is a hard worker, I remember that much. Something so integral to her personality wouldn't have changed, even in so many years. If anyone in this house is unlucky, it's me. But I will manage just fine."

Nora's brows lifted higher with every word that he said. Finally, she dropped her hands from her hips and held them up. "I wasn't meaning to imply that the new mistress wouldn't be able to do the job, Alistair. Only that we're all in a rather unlucky situation, considering she won't even walk up to the front door."

All the anger in his chest deflated like she'd poked him with a hairpin. Of course, she hadn't meant any insult. Nora didn't have an unkind bone in her body.

"Wait," he said. "Mistress?"

With a saucy wink, Nora turned down the hall and called over her shoulder, "I'll let her in the servant's entrance and get one of the boys to help with that bag of hers. We'll get her all settled in the kitchen and then you can meet with her if you want. Or not. Up to you."

"She's not the new mistress of this house!" he shouted after her, but some part of him enjoyed thinking that she was. Mistress of the Orbweaver Manor. He'd never thought he'd hear such words, but they felt right even if the house grumbled almost immediately.

If the house didn't like the idea, then maybe that was something he needed to consider.

Alistair tried to stay out of sight. He didn't need to lurk in the windows to see if she came into his house, but... Well, his feet were stuck to the floor, and all he wanted to do was make sure she got into the house safely. That's all.

At least, that's what he told himself. But as the door to the servant's entrance opened below the stairs leading into his house, he realized Thea would be less than six feet away from him. He could have opened the door at any point and looked into those lovely, dark eyes.

His breathing turned ragged. Alistair struggled to focus as she picked up her bag on her own and marched toward the hidden stairwell. Her jaw was set, and her brows furrowed. He only had a few seconds to glance over those features and realized that she'd changed in ten years.

He didn't know how. Alistair didn't have enough time to really look at her face before she rounded the stairs and disappeared. The tail of her skirts drifted around the corner like mist moving amongst the undergrowth, and he had the same flashing vision in his mind. A witch stepping out of the moors, will-o'-the-wisps tangled in her skirts and around her hair. A witch who called to him more than any other ever had.

Sighing, he rubbed his forehead and told himself to return to his office. There would be time to meet her—time to see her again.

And yet...

The front door clicked open as though the building itself knew what he wanted. The faint hint of her perfume blew toward him, and he inhaled the scent of pine and wild places that he'd not been able to indulge in for years.

How could she do this to him? How had he done this to himself?

Alistair would never survive with her under his roof. He'd constantly be wondering where she was, what she was doing, and if she was comfortable. How was he supposed to manage this on his own?

He turned around, ready to head back to his office when he realized he hadn't told Nora where to put her. Thea couldn't stay with the other servants. She wasn't... she wasn't a servant, and he refused to think of her like that.

He rounded the corner that he hated to walk by. The basement door was right next to the door that circled down into the kitchens, and the chilly air that blew out of that room coiled around his ankles. If he let it, he knew the god in their basement would drag him down into the depths of that darkness and drown him.

Shivering, Alistair made his way down to the kitchens. He knew that's where they would be. Nora always told him that people were more comfortable in warm kitchens than anywhere else in the house. Even in this one.

The sound of voices made him slow.

"You're the new secretary, then?" Nora said, along with the sound of a pot banging down on the stove. "There's a lot for you to do here, but I think you'll fit in just fine. Would you like a tour of the house?"

So that was his head maid's plan. She would pretend not to know that Thea had been here and walked these halls before.

A long pause was Nora's answer before he heard her voice. Her lovely voice that always sounded as though she were about to burst into song. "No, thank you. I know my way around."

"Oh! So you've been here before?"

Another long pause. "In another lifetime, I suppose. I'll work hard here, though. You don't have to worry about that. The job agency said I'll only be part time as a secretary. What else needs to be done around the house?"

They chattered on for a while about the work that Nora usually did on her own. Alistair leaned against the wall, letting their soft voices wash over him. The sounds were not something that he was used to hearing in this house. A quiet, immediate camaraderie of two women who had worked their entire lives for what they wanted.

Nora had always been kind, but hearing her together with Thea made his heart squeeze in his chest. This was what he had dreamt about all those years ago. He'd sneak down into the kitchens in the middle of the night, wondering where his wayward wife had gotten off to. Only to find her in the kitchens like he always used to sneak off to when he was a boy. For a few moments, he imagined he was in that life. That none of the nightmares had happened, and they'd gotten married. Started a family. Breathed new life into the Orbweaver name.

"Oh!"

His eyes snapped open in horror, only to find Nora standing in the doorway to the kitchens, her hand pressed against her heart.

Thea's voice echoed from the room beyond. "Are you all right?"

Frantically he shook his head, eyes wide, heart thudding in his chest. He didn't want to see her. Couldn't see her. What would happen if Thea realized he'd been lurking in the shadows like some monster out of a story? He'd never live down the embarrassment.

Gesturing wildly, he tried to convey that he didn't want Nora to tell Thea that he was standing right here. Although his flailing arms likely meant nothing to Nora, whose eyes were tracking his movements with confusion.

"Uh," Nora stuttered before clearing her throat. "I forgot I have to bring tea up to the master of the house. My apologies, dear. Are you all right in the kitchen alone?"

The stove gave a rather large belch and clank, and Alistair winced in sympathy for the poor woman beyond, who had been so terrified of those stoves. They were old then, and now they were ancient. The sounds they made appeared to be that of a living creature.

Thea let out a little chuckle that he swore filled the room with a bright light. "I'll be fine. Do you mind if I make myself some tea?"

"Just be careful of the stove, darling. It tends to bite."

"Bite?"

Nora pinched her lips together, unimpressed that he was still standing in front of her. "The flames, I mean! It can get a little out of hand, sometimes. Those old stoves, you know how they can get."

"Ah." He heard Thea shuffle through the room and then the clink of what he assumed was a canister of tea leaves. "I'm not afraid of fire, Miss Nora."

He squeezed his eyes shut, knowing he was at fault for that. Sure, he hadn't taken part in cursing Waterdown. He hadn't even known his father was going to attack, but he could have. If he were more active in his father's life, then he might have known what Balthazar had planned. He might have saved them all.

"Good for you," Nora said as she swept toward him and angrily yanked his arm.

He allowed himself to be dragged up the stairwell without looking behind him to see if Thea had noticed the commotion. But he didn't appreciate how Nora tossed him away from the stairwell and then glared at him.

"What?" he asked.

"You're going to lurk like that? No wonder the poor girl was terrified to walk in here. This house is enough to rattle the best of us, Alistair Orbweaver. You cannot make it worse by scaring her at every chance you get!"

"I wasn't trying to scare her! I came down to let you know that she will not be sleeping in the servants' quarters." He crossed his arms over his chest and tried to stare down his nose at her. "Does that cool your anger?"

She blinked at him. "No, it doesn't. She should be with the people she's going to work with. Although, there are few of them left. And the servants' quarters are by far the least terrifying place in this house."

He disagreed. Those rooms were safe, but they shared a wall with the basement. He'd hear the maids talking about hearing groans at night and how it sometimes felt as though they were being watched in their sleep.

Thea didn't deserve that. He wouldn't allow her to go through it.

"The last time she came here, I gave her a tour of the entire house," he said. "The only place she felt safe was my room."

"Because you were there."

"No." He shook his head. "No, because there was something about that room that specifically made her feel safe. I don't know if it's the years of the protection spells I cast, or what. Something about that room made her feel secure, and that is where she is going to stay."

Nora blinked at him, and then her jaw fell open. "You moved out of your bedroom? You've always had that bedroom."

He sighed and rubbed the back of his neck. "It's my house now, Nora. I suppose it was only a matter of time before I took the master bedroom."

"I just... How will you feel safe?"

Now that was a question. He wouldn't, most likely. His father's ghost would haunt him until the wee hours of the morning. But... he'd endure.

It would all be worth it if he knew for certain that she didn't live in fear here especially while she worked for him.

Alistair forced a smile and shook his head. "I'll be fine, Nora. Just see that she settles in well enough. I had some butlers bring old furniture in the room, so there's at least a comfortable bed and a wardrobe for her to use. The rest... Well, she brought enough to make it feel somewhat like home."

The way Nora watched him made his skin crawl. As though she peered underneath his skin to the soul beneath that wanted to hide how strong he felt for her. That he would give up anything to know Thea was happy here.

Nora bit her lip and hesitantly said, "It's been ten years, Alistair."

"I know."

"It's been ten years," she emphasized. "I don't know what happened between the two of you, but I can guess what happened right after. You are the most important person in this house. You are the only one who can keep this house running, and I know how important that is to you."

"I fail to follow."

"Keep your wits about you. It's been a long time since you two have seen each other, and a lot can change in ten years." Nora fisted her hands in her skirts and dropped into a curtsey as though that might make her words easier to swallow. "Don't give too much of yourself to a woman who might have already moved on."

He watched Nora walk away from him while his stomach rose into his throat. Had she? Moved on, that was.

He didn't know what he'd do if he found out that she had a family back in Waterdown and was only here for the money. It was entirely possible.

Alistair tugged at the neckline of his shirt, which felt far too tight. Then he decided to go to his study, where there was plenty of work to dive into. Not to distract himself from the worrisome thought, of course. Just to work.

CHAPTER 32

Thea stood alone in the middle of the kitchen and tried not to jump every time the stove rattled. She was a grown woman now, damn it, and she should be able to wait for the housekeeper to come back. She'd survived far worse than a kitchen like this.

Still, Thea suddenly was a little girl again. Standing in the doorway and watching this kitchen run like clockwork while she feared what brewed inside the rattling monstrosities. At least now she could see they were just stoves. And the haunted feeling of this house came from the people within it, not the house itself.

Still, it was hard not to compare any building to the one she'd grown up in. Houses seemed to have their own personalities, spelled or not.

Thea sprinkled chamomile tea into her cup, then added a generous fistful of her own lavender, lemon balm, and valerian for good measure. She needed all the steadying herbs she could get.

Browning let out a loud croak, so she pulled him out of the sling and popped him onto the table. He appeared to know right where to go. The toad maneuvered himself over to a stool, hopped onto the floor, and headed for one of the many shelves close to the floor.

There used to be more maids here if she remembered correctly. When she'd first come to visit, it had seemed like all the staff moved in an intricate dance. They never bumped into each other, even though there was a teeming swell of people all moving about their daily jobs.

No one stood in the kitchen with her. And that struck Thea as rather odd.

She sipped at her tea and read over all the bottles and balms on the shelves until the housekeeper came back. Nora looked a little disheveled, as one might after dealing with Balthazar. Thea could only imagine what the old man had said to the poor woman.

"I assume the master has been placated?" she asked, taking another sip of the boiling liquid.

Nora's wide eyes met hers before she snapped herself out of whatever state she'd found herself. "Ah. The master is easy. Sorry, my dear, I forgot what we were talking about."

Their master was easy? She'd never heard someone call Balthazar that before. "Expectations."

"Right. As you can see, we're a little short staffed." A few frizzy strands had popped out of Nora's braided hair. "There are many young people who would work here, but with all the changes, I'm afraid we haven't been able to keep people on. There are two other maids, one lives here, but her mother is ill, so she's away. The other lives with her children and comes during the day to help with cooking. Of course, we still have three butlers, and they all live down here with us."

It was all rather a lot to keep track of, but Thea supposed it would come naturally with practice. "And where will I be staying? I assume the maids' quarters are around here somewhere."

Yet again, Nora appeared to flounder. The other woman struggled for words in a surprising turn of events.

Thea had thought that was a rather simple question. They'd known she was coming, and that surely meant there was a place for her to stay.

She arched an eyebrow and waited until the other woman found her voice.

"Uh, right. Well. I'm afraid the maid's quarters are currently undergoing some construction, so there's another room we've prepared for you in the meantime." Nora gestured toward the kitchen door. "If you'll follow me, I'm happy to show you to the room you'll be staying in."

Why did that sound like a lie?

Thea wasn't talented at scenting out a lie. Not like her mother. Máthair knew a lie even before someone thought to say it. But that didn't sound truthful to her in the slightest.

"I thought you said one of the maids stays in those quarters?"

"She does." Nora paused in the doorway and straightened her shoulders. "But since she's helping her mother, we thought this was the perfect chance to make a few changes. It shouldn't take too long, but you should feel free to make yourself at home in the bedroom provided. Follow me, dear."

Thea looked from the cup in her hand to the bag on the floor. She'd have to set down her calming tea, and that made her nervous.

That was until Nora shouted, "Leave the bag! That's what the butlers are for. You'll hurt yourself carrying that thing up and down the stairs."

Stairs? Oh, no. That wouldn't do. She didn't want to be any closer to Alistair than she needed to be. The further away from him, the better, considering she hadn't the faintest idea how either of them would react to seeing each other again after all this time.

"Browning," she hissed. "Come with us."

The toad looked up from his perusing of what appeared to be a selection of jams and then waved her on without him. The toad wouldn't even be of help.

Clutching the tiny teacup, she took the saucer with her to have something to do with her hands as she meandered up the dark stairwell. Everything in this house lacked light, and that broke her heart. A building like this deserved to be flooded with sunbeams.

The stairs were covered with a fine layer of dust as though no one cleaned the servants' quarters at all. Then they stepped into the entrance of the home, and she looked around, expecting to see all the terrifying pieces of art and skulls that had startled her so many years ago.

The Orbweaver Manor was empty. No rugs. No artwork. Just a few lingering pieces of furniture with white sheets laid over them.

"What's all this?" she asked, walking over to one of the covered pieces and dragging her finger over the pale dust.

"Ah, the master has been selling many of the old pieces of furniture. He says it reminds him of times he has no interest in recalling." Nora cleared her throat and then held out her arm toward the stairwell. "You'll be staying on the second floor."

"Why?" That was where Alistair's room had been, and she was certain it would be the easiest place for him to find her. Besides, hadn't there only been the boys' rooms up there?

Thea watched Nora climb the stairs and then looked behind them. There was a second door next to the one they'd just left. Mist erupted from underneath the door, and she swore a sound came from underneath it. Like the breath of a person hiding out of reach.

"Thea?" Nora's voice broke through the strange noise, and it disappeared. "Keep up, please. I don't have all day to show you around."

She wrenched her gaze away from the strange door and forced herself to follow Nora up the stairwell. At the top, she took another sip of the tea that was taking the edge off of her nerves. "Is, um... Are the master's sons in?"

Nora gave her a strange look. "The master has no children."

What?

As her mind struggled to catch up with what Nora had said, she was forced to trail after the other woman while trying to piece together her thoughts. If the master had no children, then that meant Balthazar no longer lived in this house. Or maybe he'd died if the world was lucky.

Then whose house was this? Cassius? She'd only heard nightmares about that man, so it made little sense that Nora would call him easy.

Thea almost walked right into Nora's back as the other woman stopped in front of a very familiar door. "This will be your room while you're here. I think you'll find it satisfactory, but if you need anything else, please don't hesitate to ask me."

Her jaw dropped open. "But this is... This is..."

Was that a smile? She thought Nora hid a grin before she started walking away. "The boys will bring your bag up later, unless you need something now?"

"No, I think I'll be all right."

"Good. Get a bath, dear. It looks like you fell into a mud puddle. I know better than to ask questions about that, especially since you came over on the ferry service. But I imagine it would be nice for you to be clean before dinner."

Nora started back down the stairs, and Thea frantically sipped at her cup of tea. She needed whatever anxiety-healing properties the plants could give her, or she felt like she might explode.

This wasn't just a room. It was his room.

Alistair's bedroom had been the only room in the house that hadn't made her feel like her skin would peel off at any minute. But how was it that this room was the only one available for her to sleep in?

She eyed the other two doors, both suspiciously locked from the outside. What had happened in this house? Ten years was a long time for many things to break. And yet, she still felt that inner throb of evil that never left this home.

Placing her hand on the door, she shoved it open. She half expected to see him there. Sitting on the edge of his bed, looking for all the world like he'd given up on life itself. Nothing was the same inside these walls either. The bed was smaller and covered with a plain green coverlet. There was a modest wardrobe in the corner and a desk in front of the window. But nothing was even faintly familiar.

She walked into the middle of the room and popped her fists onto her hips. So many questions. And she'd gotten no answers so far other than she'd need to do two jobs while she was here. At the very least, she could help her family. This time, she would not give up so easily.

"You don't scare me," she said, her voice sharp and hard in the empty room. "You can't run me off this time."

The house let out a creaking moan as it shifted on its foundations.

"Grumpy," she muttered as she walked over to the door that she assumed was a closet. "And here I was thinking you were more terrifying than the last time I walked these halls. I think you've gotten old. And tired."

She shoved this door open as well, albeit with a brief hesitation. The bravery that had spurred her into provoking the house didn't stay with her while she explored the room. Sure, this was Alistair's bedroom. That didn't mean she didn't have a spike of fear while staring into the darkness of the connecting room.

"What?" she whispered, sliding her hand along the wall until she felt the light switch. Because, of course, the Orbweaver Manor ran on electricity and light bulbs. Not candles like the rest of them.

The bulb overhead flickered to life, and Thea let out a little gasp as she looked over the quaint bathroom. Modern plumbing was a wonderful invention. She couldn't stop staring at the giant clawfoot tub at the back of the room. It was deep, and the porcelain had chipped with age. But she could sit in that and soak for hours on end.

Maybe this job was worth it after all.

She opened up the medicine cabinet behind the mirror and peered through it. Nothing overly interesting, although there was an unmarked bottle with what looked like soap. Popping the top open, she sniffed it and suddenly was thrown back ten years.

Warm woods, mossy glens, a boy with a thousand freckles that she never got to count. He told her he feared she'd never love him because of where he came from, and she promised she'd love him every day of her life if he let her.

Tears pricked her eyes as she put the bottle back on the shelf. Thea tried to distract herself by running a bath. The pipes complained and clanked, but hot water came out of the faucets. She had trouble focusing until she stopped in front of the mirror again and stared into her own watery eyes. The steam eventually fogged up the mirror, and only then did she turn back to the water.

"Clean," she muttered as though she were talking to someone else.

"Getting clean is the first priority. Then the butlers will bring up a change of clothes for me."

Thea unbuttoned her blouse and let her skirts drop to the floor. Her skin prickled with the strangeness of being naked in a house that wasn't her own. She'd lived in the same house for such a long time. Being here, alone... It felt odd.

Her fingers danced over the edge of the mirror. Comfort lay just out of her reach. She didn't have to give in to the urge but... but...

Tomorrow. She'd be stronger tomorrow after a good night's sleep.

Thea took the soap off the shelf in the mirror and poured four drops into the steaming water. Then she turned off the faucet and got into the tub, where the heat of the water could ease the muscles in her back and thighs.

The room filled with the scent of him. And she hated how comforting that was, even after all these years.

She hissed as she sank underneath the heat. She must have bruises on her back or it wouldn't hurt that badly. The damned men at the dock were the stuff of nightmares. If only she were like her sisters. She could have coaxed a plant to grow in their beds overnight and strangled them in their sleep.

She'd only just relaxed into the tub when the door creaked open. Thea froze, unsure of what to do. If a butler was coming in to ask her a question, she was indecent. And if the unknown master of the house had arrived to make his demands, then she now knew the real request of this job. But no one came through the door. It stayed slightly open, and the darkness peered back at her.

Eyes wide, breathing ragged, she watched the shadows as they seemed to move behind the door. Shadows with a life of their own. Shadows that shouldn't move like that.

"Ribbit." Browning shoved his way through the small opening and then kicked the door closed behind him. With a snort that echoed through the room, he hopped over to the tub.

Determination glowed in his eyes, and she knew all too well what the toad wanted.

"No," she scolded, pointing a finger at him and flicking hot water. "Don't even think about it."

But when had her familiar ever listened to her? He rolled his eyes before he scrunched up his fat body and wiggled his back end.

"No. Browning!"

The toad launched himself up into the air in a graceful arc. He twisted mid-leap and landed in a gentle swan dive in the center of her tub. Unlike any other of his kind, Browning very much enjoyed the hot water. The moss on his back soaked up a lot of it, and she always swore he was brighter green after a hot bath.

She watched him paddle around a bit before he came to a halt at the opposite end of the tub, floating on his back and splashing water over his belly with his front legs.

"You're the worst familiar I've ever met," she grumbled. "If I get warts from this, I'm throwing you out the window."

He let out a little hum of pleasure, ignoring his witch.

And in a way, she was happy he'd come in. At least she wasn't alone in this cold, dark house.

CHAPTER 33

Alistair tried to avoid her in the house, and at first, that appeared to go quite well. He had so much work for the upcoming school year anyway, and the house was big enough for the two of them.

And then came the first fateful day when he saw her. He was at the top of the stairwell, heading down to the dining room for breakfast, as he always did. She was on the second landing, thankfully not looking at him. But he could see her, and his heart stopped beating in his chest.

From this distance, it didn't look like she'd changed a single day since he saw her. All that dark hair tumbled down her back, almost to her waist now. She wore the same bright colors that he so rarely saw in Wildecliff. That day she'd worn a vivid green, like the color of leaves with the sun filtering through them.

He'd watched as she smoothed her hands down the bodice of her dress, took a deep breath, and then marched down the stairs as though she felt no fear at all. And his chest had swelled with pride in knowing that he'd assisted that in some way. She had a safe place to rest her head at night. He'd done that.

Of course, at the time, she didn't know he was even in the building.

Until the second time he saw her, which was a little harder to avoid. He'd been leaving the kitchens after talking with Nora about the finances and what they could order to stock the kitchens. It wasn't much, unfortunately. They both had to give up a few of their favorite things, but that didn't matter. They could run a household on porridge if they needed to.

He had made it to the top of the stairs when he heard the whispered word.

"Alistair?"

Without looking, he had walked away from her and rushed to his father's study. He couldn't see her this close. He wasn't ready to look Thea in the eyes when she had come so far, and he had been the dolt who hired the woman he was still very much in love with.

Remembering all the times he'd seen her and then run away like a coward made his head hurt. Groaning, Alistair laid his head down on his desk and sighed. He couldn't even stay in his own study because he swore he'd heard her approach a few mornings ago, and he refused to have her meet him for the first time while he was working. She could continue helping Nora. The gods knew that poor woman needed all the help she could get running this place.

So he'd found refuge in the library because he remembered Thea had been particularly nervous in this room, and she was very unlikely to seek him out here. Trudging down the stairs with all the papers while balancing a quill and ink on the top hadn't been the smartest of choices, but he'd made it down here without too much of an issue.

The library whispered around him. The grimoires liked to make their opinions known, and right now, they were disappointed in the head of their household. He ran through the shadows of the house as though trying to avoid the young woman who had joined them. The grimoires thought it would be smarter just to get rid of her. Send her off from the home if it was going to disturb their peace so much.

But they also didn't like it when anyone was in the library. He ignored them and pulled another sheet to sign in front of him.

The words swam before his eyes. Something about desiring to document the history of the Orbweaver men and wanting permission to put his father's name and his own likeness in a book that would be published next year.

Why? So they could idolize the man who had caused a war between two sides of the river? He refused to even consider why people would want to worship his father as a hero. Balthazar Orbweaver had been a monster.

Pulling a blank sheet of paper in front of himself, he started to write his letter in response. First, he would thank the author for reaching out and asking for permission. Second, he would compliment them in their endeavor, as recording history was an honorable struggle. However, he would not allow anyone to use the history of his family in documentation other than what he himself had written.

It wasn't a great excuse, but it should keep the man off his front step at the very least.

Alistair signed his name with a flourish and then rubbed his forehead. Why had his headache returned already?

He adjusted his fingers and realized he wasn't wearing his glasses. That was why he'd had a headache the entire day. The problem now was, where had he placed his glasses? He was constantly putting them where they didn't need to go, and if he asked the fae...

Someone cleared their throat in the doorway to the library.

Hopefully, Nora, since she remembered that he always forgot his glasses in certain places. But when he looked up, Alistair's eyes widened, and his stomach dropped to his feet.

Thea leaned against the door frame. The long, tangled waves of her hair blanketed her arm. She'd pulled the mass over her shoulder, and it obscured her bright yellow bodice that fell into a full circle skirt. His eyes trailed down the swooshing fabric to note that it stopped just below her knees. Rainbow striped socks covered her calves, and she wore bright yellow boots with the slightest heel.

She was so far from any woman he'd ever seen in Wildecliff, and it made him breathless to look at her.

"So you are still here," she said. "I thought Nora was joking when she kept talking about the master of the house not having children and being kinder than the previous one. I should have guessed that person was you."

She'd been asking about him?

Alistair found he couldn't think of what to say. Or how to speak. She was standing right in front of him, as he'd always seen her in his dreams, but that didn't mean... Well, she might not want to see him. She worked for him now, and that was a rather difficult relationship to manage between two people.

Let alone two people who had once been very close to each other. How was he supposed to navigate this conversation when his tongue was stuck to the roof of his mouth?

She reached into the pocket of her dress—he took a moment to marvel that there were pockets in those skirts—and pulled out his glasses. "Nora said you get headaches if you work for too long without these. I thought you might need them."

"Ah." He cleared his throat and held out his hand. "I do need those, thank you. I was just wondering where I'd left them."

"On the banister, actually. I found them when I was coming down the stairs this morning for breakfast." She twirled them on her finger but made no move to walk toward his desk. "Can I ask you a question, Alistair?"

The sound of his name coming out of her lovely lips would have sent him to his knees if he were standing. But he wasn't, and frankly, he wasn't sure he could stand right now. "I don't see why not."

What if she asked about what had happened between them? What if she wanted to know why his family had been behind the death and destruction of so many people in her city?

Sweat slicked his palms, and he tried to wipe them on his pants below the desk, but that didn't help. His heart thudded hard in his chest, and electricity shuddered through his fingers as though he was holding onto the end of an electrical cable.

"You hired me to work for you, right?"

He nodded. "I'm afraid I didn't look at the name on the application. I should have been more detail oriented when hiring someone."

"So you wouldn't have hired me if you had known who was applying for the job?" She lifted a single dark eyebrow, and he realized there were more wrinkles on her forehead. As if she had somehow learned how to frown in the time since he'd last seen her.

He supposed she had plenty of reasons to frown, thanks to his family. Alistair shook his head to clear his mind of the thoughts. "I suppose if you were the most qualified for the role, then I still would have hired you."

"For what job?"

"Secretarial work." What was she on about? She knew why she

was here.

"Ah ha." She pushed herself off the doorframe and waltzed into the room. Her heels clacked against the floor so loudly that even some grimoires quieted down. "I have to admit, I don't mind living here while getting paid for doing so. But it does feel rather unfair to everyone else who is working hard while I'm doing undemanding jobs and waiting for my employer to give me something to do. Especially related to the job I was hired for."

She held out his glasses for him to take, but he couldn't focus on anything other than that she was leaning over his desk. His Thea. And she hadn't changed a bit, other than perhaps becoming a little more angular. He remembered the curve of her jaw being a little smoother, perhaps not quite so sharp. But those eyes.... Oh, those midnight eyes still saw straight into his soul.

"Pardon?" he stuttered.

"I'm supposed to be your secretary, Alistair. I think that job is a little more difficult if you don't talk to me." She lifted her hand so that his glasses were right in front of his eyes. "So, are you going to use me as a secretary or not?"

Use her?

He could think of a million ways he wanted to use her, and none of them were befitting thoughts for a gentleman. Clearing his throat, he reached up for his glasses. "I can have Nora instruct you on the finer details. She should have already sent out your signature so people know you may sign documents on my behalf."

The frame of the glasses slid into his grip while Thea shifted her fingers. Suddenly, his hand was in her grasp, and he couldn't think because he was touching her again. After all these years.

Her hands were more calloused than he remembered, although

maybe they always had been. But she held onto his hand with a surprisingly firm grip, tilting it back and forth as she stared down at his fingers.

He could feel his pulse racing in his throat and wasn't certain how much more of this stress he could take. "What are you doing?"

"I remember you always had dirt underneath your fingernails," she muttered, still peering down at his hands as though they offended her. "I guess some things do change after all."

What did she mean by that?

What things changed? And more importantly, what things stayed the same?

Completely thrown off and incapable of thinking about anything else, Alistair put his glasses on and then curled his hands into fists on the desk. "I have too much work to do here, as you can see, to be outside with my hands in the dirt."

"That's a shame. I always thought you enjoyed having your hands in the dirt." Thea put her hands back on her hips and tilted her chin up. "Regardless, I think it is best if we pretend our history didn't happen. We are adults, and we can be around each other in a professional setting without making it awkward."

Could they?

Alistair wasn't so sure he could wake up with her in his house every day and not think about all the things they'd been through together. Or the life that had been stolen from them by cruel people who only saw the world in black and white.

"I..." he hesitated. How could he say yes to something like that? "I'm glad you're here."

No, that wasn't what he meant to say at all. Why had that come out of his mouth when there were a million other things he could have said?

His cheeks burned, and the sweat on his palms kicked up a notch. If he could have run out of the room, he would have. But that would require him to walk past her, and he feared what he'd do if he were closer to her.

Thea's eyes widened, but she didn't look quite as affected as him. Alistair didn't know if he should be offended by that or not.

She shifted on her feet, shuffling back and forth before sighing. "Alistair, I'm still very unsure why you hired me, or if it was a mistake. Whatever the reason for me being here, whether that is your desire to see me or fate, I came here to do a job. And that job requires you to train me, not Nora. She said she doesn't know how to do the work you're doing, or what it is you do. I'd appreciate not going into this blind."

"Of course." He needed to pull himself together. He wasn't the young man she'd fallen in love with, and she wasn't the same young woman he'd been so fond of. They were adults now. Completely different people.

Pulling himself together, he stood up and braced his hands on the desk as well. "I'll teach you how to go through these documents and respond in a timely manner. There are an unending amount of them, as my father had set up an expectation that people only write to us. I have yet to convince anyone to do otherwise."

"And should I be expecting a visit from your father any time soon?" she asked.

"No. He's dead. Although you may see his spirit around here. The old man refuses to stay in the grave. This house hasn't run the way he thought it would after putting me in charge. That makes it rather hard for him to rest."

Her eyes had widened again. "Ah. And your brothers? I've heard enough stories about them to make me not wish to meet either of them."

"Also dead."

The silence stretched between them, taut and ready to snap at any moment. He knew how startling it was for him to so callously mention their demise, but they hadn't been all that close. Especially in the later years of Cassius and Lysander's foolish existences.

"I'm so sorry to hear that," Thea whispered. She placed her hand on top of his on the desk, only to snatch her fingers away again a moment after. "Losing family is one of the hardest things a person can suffer."

"If only." Losing his family had been nothing short of a blessing, but he couldn't say that to her. She'd think he was a monster.

Alistair stepped away from her so he didn't get lost in the stars of her eyes. He pointed to a stack of paper beside him and cleared his throat. "This is the first of many stacks. Nora sent out your signature, correct?"

"Yes."

"Then for today, if you can organize the stack into different categories, that way I can go through them more efficiently, that will suffice." He needed to get out of this room. Away from the kindness in her eyes and the pity in her voice. He had to pull himself together and become her employer rather than the man he was.

Perhaps she was feeling the same way. Thea nodded and rounded the desk as he vacated it. "I can do that. What time would you like it finished?"

Tomorrow. Three days from now. A week. The further away from him, the better.

But he couldn't say any of that because then he wasn't being the employer she expected. That he expected himself to be.

Who would have thought having a secretary would make everything this much harder?

"By tomorrow morning, if you think that's possible."

She eyed the stack of pages and then set her jaw. "I think that'll be acceptable. And tomorrow, when we reconvene, I imagine you have more papers for me to go through?"

"For the time being. Eventually, I'd prefer it if I never saw the papers again." But that was letting her know too much. Did employers speak with their employees about how they felt?

He'd need to talk with a butler to understand what might be too far. Then maybe he could create his own ground rules in his head.

With a sharp nod, Alistair left the library on wobbly legs while his heart screamed for him to stay.

CHAPTER 34

Thea tried to settle into the house in the best way she could. She helped Alistair with paperwork every day, organizing everything into stacks that made sense to her mind. Some days he thought she did a good job, other days he was so preoccupied with something else that he waved her out of his office before looking.

It wasn't... terrible?

She still woke up every night with nightmares, and she hated living in the house. But for the most part, the job kept her so busy that her mind couldn't wander. If she didn't think about the darkness and the lingering shadows, then it was easier to go about her day.

And that seemed like what the others in the house did. Nora ignored the tendrils that looked like spider legs. They reached out from underneath the stove and touched her shoes as she walked by. Thea had only met a couple of other people who worked here, certainly less than Nora had led her to believe, and they all swore they didn't see the shadows move at all.

She paused in the kitchen, staring intently at the darkness underneath the stove. And there they were again. Like dark spiders waiting for their prey.

"What are you looking at, dear?" Nora asked as she walked into the kitchen. Her arms were full of fresh vegetables from the market. Clods of dirt still hung on the roots.

"You don't see them?" Thea asked. "The spiders."

"Oh, yes. Those are leftovers from Balthazar. We see so much less of them now that Alistair's taken over the household." Nora dropped her armful on the table and sighed. "It's so hard to put good energy into food when one is afraid, you know. That's why I ignore them."

Thea had been wondering about Nora's gift. And though Balthazar would have considered it a small gift, Thea thought it was rather lovely to put feeling into what others were about to eat.

"And they don't bother you?" Thea had to ask the question. They'd been bothering her.

"Not usually. The more you get to know them, the easier they are to be around. They don't like the light. That makes it easiest in the kitchens because the stove pretty much always keeps them trapped there. Just don't let your feet get too close."

Nora said it all as though it were normal to live with shadow monsters who wanted to grab onto your toes. Thea thought it was all rather horrifying, but then a thought caught in her mind.

"You said they're afraid of light?" she asked.

"All of Balthazar's creations do poorly in well-lit areas. His brand of spider magic relied entirely on the darkness. Thus a dark house." Nora grabbed a knife from a drawer and pulled the vegetables toward her. "Aren't you supposed to be working with Alistair today?"

"He had to go to the school, so he said I could help out in the kitchens." Something chewed inside her. A thought that wanted to be let out.

Apparently, the housekeeper could already see that. "What is going on in that head of yours?"

Thea wasn't sure. But that tug in her stomach told her to spend her day in the library and, well... why not? "Do you mind if I work in the library today? I noticed there's a particularly large amount of dust and I had hoped to clean that."

"Really?" Nora lifted a brow. "And what do you need to clean the space?"

"Everything?"

"You do what you want, girl. Just make sure it won't anger the master when he returns." Nora pointed with the knife to a closet behind Thea. "Go ahead and get what you want. I need to prepare dinner, and lunch, and then breakfast for the week for all the butlers since they're moving more of the furniture from the attic and selling it at the market."

"I'll stay out of your hair." Thea flashed her a grin and then spent most of her morning hauling buckets of water, a large amount of soap, three mops, two brooms, and an armful of different bins and buckets to the library.

Once she had all her goodies piled up on one side of the room, she turned around to survey the damage. Even Browning had joined her. He sat on top of a pile of buckets, looking rather stoic as he eyed the mess.

There were seven giant bookshelves, each one matching like dominos throughout the room. To the right, a larger space had been cleared next to a fireplace full of soot and the desk that Alistair preferred for work. Books were strewn about the room, pages littering the floor, and grimoires fought each other for space on the shelves that they had already cleared most of the books off of.

"We've got our work cut out for us," she muttered.

Browning croaked in response.

"Do you think you could tame a few of those grimoires on the floor? I want to look at that fireplace."

And so they set off. Browning took off to the left, Thea to the right. She peered up into the fireplace and saw so much soot that no one would have safely been able to light a fire in there. The whole building would burn to the ground. Thankfully, she could get some of it away from the areas in the room. They'd need a chimney sweep to do the rest.

She tied her skirts into a knot at her waist, tucked her hair into a bright pink scarf, and set to work. It took her at least an hour to clean out the fireplace. But when she was finished and covered in soot, she could see that the fireplace had actually been made of bronze. It would glow with a fire and bounce the light around the room. Which was exactly what she wanted.

"Perfect." She clapped her hands together one last time and then looked up the chimney. "I don't think we'll have to hire a chimney sweep after all, Browning! The soot was almost entirely at the bottom here."

No ribbit replied to her.

Thea turned to find her toad in a fierce battle with a grimoire on the floor. The book kept snapping at Browning and throwing pages at the toad until he couldn't see where it was. Although, now that she looked at it, it appeared as though the grimoire was attempting to clamp onto her familiar and swallow him.

How dare it?

Stomping over, she muttered the entire way. "Get off of my familiar, you dusty, decrepit, no good... out of print novel!"

With the last insult, she stomped down hard on the book cover and flattened it before it got another bite out of Browning. The grimoire let out a little wheeze. Dust fluttered over the floor, but then it fell silent.

Stooping, she picked it up and brandished the leather volume at the other grimoires. "You will all stay put from now on, do you hear me?"

The sudden silence that came after her words startled her. She hadn't realized how loud the library had been until this moment. No more shuffling pages. No more angry sounds of grimoires grunting in the corner.

She glanced down at Browning and grinned triumphantly. "You see? All they needed was someone to tell them to behave."

Then the bookshelves creaked, and all the grimoires fell off their shelves. A wave of books rushed toward them, all their pages flying through the air with razor-sharp edges and the books themselves chomping along the floor with single-minded intent.

Thea dropped the grimoire in her hand, grabbed Browning, and sprinted out of the room. She could hear the buckets she'd neatly stacked all falling behind her. Sliding across the hall, she pin-wheeled her arms for balance, then promptly grabbed onto the doors and slammed them shut.

She threw her entire weight into holding the doors closed. Bracing her feet against the wall, she shouted over the sound of the grimoires, "Browning! Maybe try to get some help?"

"What in the world did you do to my library?"

Thea tilted her head backward to look behind her. And there he was. Upside down, of course, but Alistair stared at her with that half smile that made all her insides mushy.

"Ah, I had a theory that I wanted to put into practice. As you can see, it's not going well."

"A theory?"

"I'd rather not share until I see if it's going to work or not." The door jerked in her arms.

Alistair sighed. "I suppose I should know better than to ask questions about your plans. I'm going to open the door now."

"I wouldn't advise it."

"They are my books, Thea."

It was his funeral. She shrugged, let go of the door, and launched herself to safety behind him. Grimoires spilled out of the room and then skidded to a silent halt in front of Alistair's feet.

"Back to the shelves," he scolded. "You all know better."

The grimoires grumbled, but they all went back to their assigned sections on the bookshelves. Quite a few floated back to where they should be, and they picked up their missing pages along the way.

Alistair followed them into the room and then turned to look at her. "So far, all I'm seeing is that you cleaned the fireplace."

"Well, I had to bring all that up here as well." She gestured to the stack of cleaning objects that were now haphazardly tossed around the room. "You are interrupting me in the middle of this project."

"Which entails?"

She blinked. "Cleaning."

"Ah." He bit his lips and looked around them while nodding. "I see."

She understood how that might be a little confusing. Pointing at a bucket of water, she said, "So I'll just... get to it then."

"Right." He looked at his desk, then back at her. The awkwardness deepened. "I have paperwork to do. So I'll just..."

"I thought you were going to the school?" She watched him settle behind the desk and grab a handful of documents.

"I was."

And that was it. That was all Alistair said before diving into his work and not paying a single attention to what she was doing. Or at least making it appear as though he wasn't looking at her. She had a feeling he might be.

She'd do just fine with an audience. Cleaning was cleaning.

She dragged the water bucket over to the massive window that took up the entire back wall and then pulled both mops over for good measure. The problem wasn't cleaning the bottom windows, it was the top ones that were easily two stories up.

Right. Library. There were plenty of ladders around.

Thea grabbed the closest ladder and waved away Browning's worried croak. She'd be fine. She had climbed ladders before, and besides, the windows wouldn't wash themselves. Manhandling the bucket up the ladder to the top felt a little dangerous, but she made it with the mop in her hand. Prepared to clean what she could only assume were the dirtiest windows she'd ever seen.

Slopping the mop into the bucket, she slapped it hard against the window. She half hoped it would break the glass and Alistair would have to replace them. No luck there, though. The glass remained sturdy as ever. Shockingly, the water mingled with some black substance that looked like oil. It wasn't smoke residue. Leaning closer, she realized it was the sticky remains of a dark spell gone awry.

Obviously, his father had been fond of the library while he was doing his spider shadow work.

"You're going to wash off," she snarled at the window. "I'll be here all day if that's what is required to fix you."

And that was what she did. Another hour of dunking the mop, slapping at the windows, and angrily snarling at them while she tried her best to clean them. The top ones were the most stubborn. Water ran down them, though, and at least that took care of the bottom ones.

She'd had to change out the bucket five times in the hour, and her arms were aching by the end of it. Had she made any progress at all? They still looked blurry to her. If only she could get rid of the thin film that prevented the sun from entering the room.

Leaning precariously forward, she used a rag she'd brought up to put some elbow grease into the cleaning. And there, there it was. The glass looked like glass on this pane, and a bright beam of light speared into the library.

At the same time, she heard a hiss in her ear. Like a wild cat had lunged at her. Except it wasn't a cat at all.

The shadows had all coiled up at the base of the ladder between herself and the glass. They launched at her face, all tendrils and spider legs that twisted together as they reached for her face.

Thea didn't think. She reacted. She flinched away from the darkness that wanted to attach itself to her, and the entire ladder tilted backward. A small shriek echoed from her lips before she curled up her body to shield herself from the hard floor that would strike her any second.

Until warm arms caught her underneath her shoulders and legs. She landed neatly in Alistair's arms as the spidery shadow creatures struck the light beam and sizzled out of existence. She looked up at Alistair while he stared in shock as his father's creations melted in the sunlight.

"So that's what you were up to," he murmured.

She'd forgotten how to breathe as he held her. The boy she remembered had been wiry. Alistair had a certain strength to him back then, but she would never have called him strong. Now there were actual biceps holding onto her. A hard chest that she leaned against. Perhaps not the body of a working man, but still a man nonetheless.

Oh goodness, was she trembling? She needed to stop doing that, or he would wonder what was wrong with her. She was already wondering that.

Thea had every reason in the world to hate the man who had just saved her life. Possibly. She might have been fine if she had hit the floor.

But he still had all those freckles. And she'd never finished counting them.

Shaking her head to clear it of those mad thoughts, Thea cleared her throat and looked at the window with him. "Yes. Nora said something about how the spiders were afraid of light, and I thought... Why not bring more of it into the room?"

"Light. Of course they're afraid of that," he muttered while letting her legs slide down to the floor. "What a marvel idea, Thea. May I help?"

She blinked up at him owlishly. "Do you know how to help?"

He gave her that crooked half smile. "It's been ten years, Thea, not forty. I know how to clean if I have to."

"You could have fooled me. Everything needs to be cleaned in this house." She tried not to sound too surly, but she was rather uncomfortable and startled at the way her heart beat faster because he smiled at her.

"Well, I've been rather busy keeping the house from being

condemned." He rolled his sleeves up his forearms, and she was entranced by the veins there that stood out.

He wasn't a boy anymore, and that was regretfully distracting.

She bit her lip hard and nodded. "Right, then. Back to the windows?"

"Shall I get another bucket?"

Nodding, she started her way back up the ladder and tried not to look at him as he left the room. What had she gotten herself into now? Thea knew better than to fall for her employer.

CHAPTER 35

He had known things might change once she moved into the house, but he hadn't realized how much Thea would turn his life around. She'd gotten used to him being there now. They didn't hide from each other, at the very least. But that meant they saw each other all the time now.

He swore she waited for him on the stairs in the morning. Otherwise, how was it possible for her to walk out to the stairwell from the second story at the same exact time he did?

And he was ashamed to admit that he looked forward to it every morning now. Her bright smile started his day off with a happiness that he hadn't felt before. Certainly not in this house.

Perhaps he should ask her to have breakfast with him in the mornings. Alistair straightened his tie and looked in the mirror one last time to make sure that his suit for the Academy had nothing out of place. Unfortunately, today he had to go to that cursed building, and he couldn't avoid it any longer.

Students, after all, needed a professor to be taught.

He didn't recognize the man in the mirror, but that was the point. Alistair's unruly hair was tamed with gel away from his face. The pressed suit had once been his father's, and it always made him uncomfortable to see how well it fit him. His blue jacket was the same, however. Always. He'd decided a long time ago it didn't matter if he wore it in since he took it off, anyway.

Sighing, he picked up the black leather briefcase containing his lesson for the day. He was technically the Professor of Ancient World Studies, but the Headmistress always pushed him to teach more about the fae than other creatures. Every year she pushed for what he'd created that would give their students the ability to see what he saw.

Now that he was older, he knew what the red stag had warned him about. Sooner rather than later, the Academy wouldn't give him an easy choice. They would try to force him to make a magical artifact that would let them control the fae. Or worse, rip between the realms so the Academy and their investors could pull whatever they wanted out of the Otherworld.

He was the only person standing in their way. Because he was the only one who could do it.

Alistair had never told them he'd already created an artifact that could do what they wanted. He'd already shown one person how to peer between the worlds, and he'd caught her three days ago with that whistle to her mouth as she watched the household brownies run from room to room.

If that knowledge ever got out, he wouldn't be able to lie any longer. The Academy was willing to go to great lengths to get what they wanted.

Pinching the bridge of his nose, he stroked a finger down Atlas's chest one last time. "When are you going to be ready to meet her, old friend?"

The raven croaked, a worried expression on his worn features.

"Hm," Alistair muttered. "I felt the same."

But he couldn't hide from her much longer. He wasn't as lucky as his raven.

Marching down the stairs, he paused and waited for a few heartbeats at the second level. She was late. Or maybe he was. But when he didn't see her walk out of her room, Alistair reminded himself that it was all right if she didn't greet him every single morning. She owed him nothing.

"Looking for me?" Her bright voice floated from the bottom of the stairwell.

He bit his lip and told himself not to be too obvious. Alistair turned slowly, looking as nonchalant as he thought possible. She stood at the bottom of the stairs, his glasses dangling off her fingers.

"Ah." Alistair cleared his throat. "No. I was wondering if I needed to bring anything from Cassius's old room."

"Of course." She nodded as though she believed him. Kind woman that she was. "Will you be needing these?"

"Always." He made his way down the rest of the stairs, worried he might trip at any moment. "Where were they this time?"

"Surprisingly, they were on top of the glass case where we keep the mugs. I don't think I'm going to ask how they got up there." Thea grinned as she handed over the glasses, her fingers brushing against his. "You need to look after them better, Alistair. You're blind without them."

Oh, now that wasn't true. He was blind without her. Darkness and grief had blinded the entire house until she walked into this empty building and made it sparkle again.

Blinking the thoughts out of his head, he placed the glasses on his nose and nodded. "It will be a mystery that none shall ever solve, I fear. There's a stack of documents on my desk that I'd like you to go over. I assume you know which ones to throw out at this point?"

"All of them?"

"Precisely." And because he quite enjoyed this banter, Alistair gave her a wink. "Do you have any other plans for the day?"

Thea held out her arm for him to take, like the gentlewoman she was, and guided him toward the door. "Well, the library is finished. So I thought I might tackle the dining room today."

"That was one of my father's most cursed rooms. I don't think the shadows will be easy to banish in that one." He paused at the front door and grabbed onto her hand. "May I suggest a different room? At least until I can get back and help you."

He'd surprised himself by holding onto her, but the thought of those shadows attacking her with no one to assist made his entire body ache. He wanted her to be free to explore the house, absolutely. But that didn't mean risking her life.

A strange expression crossed her face, and Thea looked down at their hands. Without a word, she traced her thumb over his ring finger and the faint, dark outline of their promise rings. A tattoo that he would never, could never, remove.

His breath caught in his throat. The soft touch felt as though it meant something. Something important.

"I'll wait until you return, then." She looked back at him, her dark eyes wide and reflecting the entire universe within them. "Be safe today."

He wanted to kiss her. Alistair would have cut off his right hand to kiss her before he left. As if she'd chosen to live with him and see him out the door every morning. But he couldn't. They weren't the children they once were, and she only lived in this house because he paid her to do so.

The need was hard to push away, but somehow he managed. Alistair gave her a little nod and walked out of the front door. As always, it felt as though he had left a small piece of himself behind.

She'd wiggled underneath his skin, and how dare she do that? The ghost of his father laughed maniacally, and Alistair knew it was because the old man saw the writing on the wall. Alistair would never press her to reclaim what they'd left behind in their past. If she found another more suitable man here in Wildecliff, then Alistair would watch her happiness from afar. At least then, he'd know she was happy.

He opened the door to his carriage and absentmindedly nodded at his pooka disguised as a carriage man. "The Academy today."

The pooka gave him a wicked grin and pulled the overly large hat a little lower over its face. It knew how to be discreet when they rolled through town. But he'd never found someone who could drive better than the pooka, and it had returned to his life the moment his father died. Quite a talent, this creature. He'd employed it, and in return, they rarely had fresh milk in the Orbweaver Manor. It drove Nora mad.

He tried not to think of the lovely woman waiting for him back in his home. But Alistair's mind always seemed to wander back to her, no matter how often he directed his thoughts to the day at hand. Before he knew it, they'd made it up the edge of the cliff, and the massive architecture loomed in front of him.

The Academy hadn't changed a bit since he'd come here as a boy. The windows still gleamed a little too bright in the sun, and the building still seemed to stretch overhead.

Except now he was the professor, and the children looked at him in fear. Though few of them did, he was the only kind professor in the building, so he supposed he couldn't blame them.

Which was precisely why Alistair arrived earlier than most. He could take his time getting out of his carriage, wandering up the steps while he tried to pretend he wasn't here. And then the doors would open for him, as they did for professors, and he'd make his way to his own classroom.

His room was filled with skeletons of massive creatures long dead. Deep sea monsters and winged snakes that once covered their lands. But now they were dead. Long dead, if he taught the children correctly. Wooden desks filled the room, about thirty of them in total, and they all pointed toward the front of the classroom, which was an entire wall painted with blackboard paint. He'd done that work himself and hired a few local artists to fill the edges with illustrations.

If he had learned anything from his own time here, it was that sometimes students wanted something to look at while he was prattling on about history they didn't care about.

A porcelain teapot and matching cup sat on his desk already. Tiny tendrils of steam coiled out of the pot, and if he looked, he knew there would already be two of his favorite tea bags sitting in the cup next to two white cubes of sugar.

"Thank you," he called out while placing his jacket on the hook by the door. "You really didn't have to."

Answering squeaks rustled through the room. A few bwbachs had joined the other faeries at the school recently, and they'd taken quite a liking to Alistair. Like most of the household faeries he'd met, they too enjoyed a good cup of cream, and they were delighted when he started leaving them out around his office and classroom before he left. Now, he always found himself with a hot morning drink and a clean classroom.

Passing through a few of the desks, he sat down at his own and started pouring the hot water into his cup. "You have no idea how much I needed this."

A couple more chirps were his answer to that. Apparently, they'd suspected that he'd be a little tired. Except then, they all stopped talking as if the room was holding its breath.

He knew better than to be at ease in this school. Alistair sighed and set his cup down with a harsh tap.

Thus, he was looking at the door when it opened, and Marren Sphecidae entered. The man was only a few years older than Alistair, but he appeared so much older. He looked like his father, and that brought about dark memories neither of them wished to think about.

The gleam in Marren's eye made Alistair nervous. Though the poisonous man was bound to the Orbweaver family, that didn't mean that he didn't want to kill Alistair at the first chance.

"Good morning," Alistair said, standing up from his desk. "Can I help you?"

"Yes, my students were asking yesterday about the veil. I told them you were the professor to ask, but they all said you weren't teaching them about the fae this semester." Marren leaned against an empty desk and crossed his arms over his chest. "I thought the Headmistress might have something to say about that."

"They don't need to learn about the fae just yet. They need to learn about the history of many other creatures before we can get to the ones that are still alive." He gestured to the giant skeleton over Marren's head, which had once been a sea monster. "It is a class about Ancient History, after all."

"You can justify it all you want. The students need to know about what's out there now, not what used to be there." Marren shrugged. "But that's not my decision. If the Headmistress is happy with your work, then who am I to judge?"

They both knew very well that the Headmistress wanted Alistair to be teaching the students a lot more about the fae. Everyone in the Academy thought he was holding off to reveal some massive, expansive, terrifying creation that would reveal a brand new world to the rest of them. Alistair was not. He was biding his time until he could figure out a better plan than what he currently had.

Grinding his teeth, he tried his best to remain calm. "Thank you for your concern, Marren. I understand you have spent a long time in this school and amongst its staff. Your warning is something I should be grateful for."

And yet, he wasn't.

Marren lifted a pale brow. "Don't thank me just yet. You might want to wait until the Headmistress has a chat with you."

Ah. So the other professor had already informed their employer, and now he had to wait all day to see when she would walk through his door. Alistair had thought this would be a horrible day from the moment he woke up, and he'd been correct.

He wanted to slump into the chair at his desk and talk with the faeries. Maybe he could get them to put a rotting fish in Marren's desk.

But, as the other man started to leave, he watched the Sphecidae pause in his doorway. "Oh, and another thing."

Alistair didn't have time for this. He still needed to prepare for class. "What is it?"

"I heard you have a new staff member in your home. A lovely young woman from Waterdown with hair like the deepest of nights." Marren grinned, though the expression was terrifying. "And considering how our families are old friends, I thought perhaps it might be pastime for you to hold a dinner party at your home. You can introduce us."

"I have no interest in visitors."

"You haven't had visitors since your father died. Your brothers would have upheld the tradition, and yet, you insist on being different. I gave you a friendly reminder today, Alistair. Now this one is an actual warning." Marren slapped his hand against the doorframe. "If you don't invite old friends over, you'll find yourself lacking any at all. And in a place like this, in times like these, you need all the friends you can get."

Marren left the room but Alistair swore it grew colder the moment that foolish man left.

Friends. Even the word made him want to laugh. No one in the Academy was friends with each other, and few in Wildecliff knew the meaning of the word.

None of them cared for anyone other than themselves. They only wanted to be closer to see when the other would slip up. They waited for a displacement of power that someone else might fill. And if Alistair weren't careful, then that next displacement would be him. A shame to lose the last Orbweaver, but he wasn't all that impressive. Now was he?

A shiver trailed between his shoulder blades, and he coughed to clear it.

"Bwbach," he muttered, turning toward his desk where his tea had already gone cold. "Keep an eye on that one for me, will you? If he makes any threats toward my family, please let me know."

A quiet chirp echoed through his room, followed by the

scuttling of claws. He watched his door open and closed again, and then the room was empty. Though Alistair had grown used to being alone, he suddenly wished he were back home.

With her.

The woman with hair like the deepest of nights.

Again, a shudder traveled through him. He wasn't only protecting himself anymore, and Alistair feared he'd be a lackluster hero.

CHAPTER 36

No, I'm absolutely not going to try that." Thea shoved the plate back toward Nora. "You know how I feel about anything coming out of the sea."

"You grew up next to the sea. You should be able to eat anything that comes out of it." Nora pushed the plate back toward her. "It's rice, salmon, and seaweed. You shouldn't mind eating any of that!"

"It's the seaweed." Thea tried very hard not to gag at the thought. "It's unnatural. We shouldn't be eating something that smells like it's rotten."

"It doesn't smell at all!" The way the housekeeper laughed should have been a warning that the other woman was teasing her. But Thea couldn't tear her eyes away from the horrifying mixture of all the things she didn't like.

Well, she didn't mind rice. But she wanted nothing to do with the horrible seaweed that she was certain had been plucked out of a puddle and thrown into a basket.

Nora shook her head, still laughing. "Well, it's what we're having for dinner. It's one of Alistair's favorite dishes."

She'd have to speak with him about that. He needed to stop eating rotten food if he wanted to live longer than a few more years. The damned man had no idea what danger he was putting himself in.

She opened her mouth to tell Nora exactly that, only for both of them to freeze as the temperature inside the house dropped. Thea blew out a warm breath and watched as it fogged in front of her face. Rolling fog tumbled down the stairwell and spilled into the kitchen.

"What's all this?" she asked.

Though the housekeeper should have been able to respond, it appeared that even Nora didn't know what to say. Her gaze was locked on the rolling vapor while she whispered, "This used to happen when the old master was angry. The whole house would frost over, inside and out. It would take us days to fix once it thawed. But it's never done this while Alistair was master of the house."

Was Alistair that angry? She couldn't imagine what might have angered him but then remembered their last conversation when they were teenagers. She'd seen him angry then and decided maybe it was possible for him to be a little unreasonable.

Sighing, she leveraged herself away from the table and started toward the mist. "Someone has to go talk to him, then."

"I'd leave him alone if the house is reacting like this, Thea. Give him time."

She could. And maybe if he had aged like his father, then she would have let Alistair steep in his sadness and anger. But he wasn't Balthazar, and he wasn't like the rest of the Orbweavers either.

"I have been gone a very long time," she mumbled, her eyes on the fog. "But I know the young man I met all those years ago is still very much inside of him. I know Alistair, as I know the young woman inside myself that has never really grown up. Not without him."

The last bit slipped off her tongue unbidden. She hadn't meant to reveal so much, especially to Nora. The housekeeper was kind, but she was loyal to Alistair first and foremost.

Nora sighed. "As I told him when we first realized who you were, people change, my dear. You don't know the man upstairs, just like he doesn't know you."

She brought her brows down in determination and curled her hands into fists at her sides. "Then perhaps it's time for us to have a conversation about how different the both of us have become."

To start, she'd show him she wasn't afraid of magic anymore. Well, she might be a little afraid. But Thea didn't run. She would fight whatever dark magic had sunk its claws into him and this house because that was the right thing to do. Even if it terrified her.

The mist felt like frozen shards of ice against her ankles and knees as she stalked through it and up the stairs. The magic dug underneath her skirts, clawing at her legs as though it didn't want her to find Alistair.

"Well, I'm going to," she snapped at the mist. "Now, where is your master?"

Perhaps she was startled by the magic that lived in this house, or maybe she had given herself enough courage to walk through it, but it seemed as though the mist had flattened a bit. Thea stomped toward the stairs, ready to barge into his bedroom if need be. But when she paused at the base of them, she heard a noise from the library.

The faint rustling might have been anything in this house, but then there was a thud that was a little too loud to be anyone other than the master of the house. A furious one, at the sounds of it.

Thea changed course, and she knew she'd gone in the right direction by a certain familiar waiting outside the door.

"Atlas," she said with a soft smile. "How lovely to see you. And here I was, wondering if you had disappeared."

The raven gave her a glare and then snapped at her fingers when she reached out to pet him.

"Well, it's not my fault I've been gone." She frowned at him. "Your master could have reached out just as easily."

The raven puffed up, all his thorns on display.

She might have stayed to argue with him if she hadn't heard another sound from inside the library. Let the bird argue if he wanted, but she refused to hesitate any longer.

Thea opened the door to the library in time to see Alistair with his hands braced against his desk. He'd rolled up his sleeves and unbuttoned his shirt at least three buttons. His back moved with deep breaths as though he were trying to get a hold of himself.

Then he let out a sound that she could only describe as a roar, picked up a weight from the table, and launched it at the windows. The desk ornament was rather heavy, and the glass shattered as it struck the window. Tiny shards rained down on the bushes outside, and some splintered back into the house. She'd have to take care of that, considering there were no other maids.

"Well, that was quite dramatic," she said.

Thea didn't know what else to say. Alistair spun on her, and she'd never seen him quite so angry. Rage had turned his cheeks red, and his slicked-back hair had been tousled. Now, the locks were all over the place in every direction, as though he'd been struck by lightning.

Still breathing hard, he shook his head at her. "Not now, Thea."

"If not now, then when?"

"When I'm not quite so angry and less likely to say something I'll regret." He scrubbed a hand over his face and turned away from her. "Time, Thea. That's all I'm asking for."

"More time to throw things?"

"More time to figure out what the fuck I'm going to do." He spat out the words as though he were shooting arrows at her. "This is not something you can help with."

Wasn't it, though? He thought she couldn't help, and maybe the situation was so dire that throwing paperweights through windows was the only sensible thing to do. Thea simply refused to believe that. She could leave and let him deal with this on his own, but she could see how tired he was in the curve of his shoulders.

Alistair had been alone long enough, she decided.

She took the risk that he didn't want her to take. Thea crossed the room and grabbed onto his hand.

Alistair tried to pull it away, but he paused when he looked into her eyes and saw her holding onto him with a white-knuckled grip. He had to see what was in her eyes. Surely he knew it tore her apart to see him so angry and not know how to help.

"Sit down," she said. "Let me make you a pot of tea. Nothing is so broken that it cannot be fixed with peppermint tea and a healthy spoonful of honey."

He opened his mouth, clearly preparing to yell at her, but then she saw the anger filter out of him in one slow exhale. He nodded. With a quiet acceptance that she was here with him, Alistair leaned against his desk and waved an imperious hand in the air. "Go on, then."

"You will not leave or throw more things while I get tea?"

"No."

She rushed out of the room for a steaming pot. Nora usually had one at the ready, just in case anyone wanted a sip. She gathered all that up without a word on a tray with two teacups, plenty of sugar, and a small box of tea that had been left on the counter.

By the time she made it back to the library and makeshift office, she was startled to find Browning sitting on the table beside Alistair. The two appeared deep in conversation, one-sided as it might be, but both looked over at her as she walked in.

Thea kicked the door shut behind her and set the tray on the desk. "I grabbed whatever tea was on the table, to be honest. And I couldn't find the honey."

She hadn't even tried to look. However, Browning opened up his mouth, tilted his head all the way back, and froze in that position while the two of them looked at him.

"What's he doing?" Alistair asked.

"Tea," she answered honestly.

"Ah. Right, he did this to me once before." Alistair grimaced but still reached into the toad's mouth and pulled out a small can of peppermint tea with bright lilies painted on the sides, followed by a honey pot in the shape of an egg. "Perfect, Browning. Thank you."

Her familiar looked all too impressed with himself. He hopped off the table and made his way to the broken window, which he then leapt out of with all the grace of a swan. Why? She had absolutely no idea.

"Where's he off to, I wonder," she muttered before turning back to the steaming teapot and cups.

She made quick work of cleaning the slime away from their newly acquired tea and honey while Alistair moved behind the desk and started lighting a fire in the now clean fireplace. His hands moved as though he'd done it a thousand times before. They both finished at about the same time, then turned to look at each other with more awkwardness than she deemed appropriate.

Thea had to fix it, and quickly. The only way she knew how to do that was by making everything feel a little ridiculous.

She lifted the tray, set it down on the floor in front of the fire, and sat down with a flop. Then she pointed at the desk chair and said, "Bring that over for yourself. You seem like you've had a trying day and should be more comfortable than you would be seated on the floor."

"I can sit with you."

"I insist."

He gave her a look but dragged the chair screeching over the mahogany floors to a halt in front of her. Then he sat and lifted his brows.

"That'll do." She handed him over the teacup and blew on her own. "So, what was it that upset you?"

The long sigh that wheezed out of him was enough dramatics for her. She thought he'd try to brush it away, and yet, Alistair didn't.

He sighed and relented. "There is a man at the Academy, another professor, and he made some threats today. Not just against myself, but against you. I am trying to figure out the best way to address those threats."

"Oh." Well, that was surprising. "I'm just a maid."

"He knows that, but he also knows that you are a direct way of harming me. If he made any threat toward you, that is not something I can or will ignore."

Her heart fluttered in her chest. "I don't know why he'd think that. You and I haven't seen each other in ten years, and no one knew that we ever talked. To him, I must be nothing more than a new staff member. And to you, I am an unfortunate employee whose resume you did not read."

At least, that's what they had both told each other she was.

Alistair let out a little noise that came from the back of his throat, not quite a grunt, but something similar. He sipped his tea and muttered into the cup, "That's the story we cling to, yes."

Oh, he couldn't change it now. He couldn't give her that hope when she had only begun to let it go. She curled her fingers around the teacup in her hands. "Alistair, why would he think otherwise?"

He didn't answer that question. Instead, he only gave her more questions. "You have every reason to hate me, Thea. Every reason. My family was the one who started the fires. The ones who came up with the spell that destroyed your city. My father was the villain behind all of this and more. So much more."

"I don't hate you." She had said so in a moment of passion, but Thea had never been able to force herself to feel that hate. He was part of her. Hating him would be like hating herself. "I never did."

Something drained out of him like she'd drilled a hole into the bucket that held all his anger. Alistair drained the tea that must have been boiling hot and curved forward over his knees. He let the cup hang from his fingertips by the handle, dangling over the floor as the remaining drops dripped out.

He looked like a man defeated. But she knew in her heart that he didn't feel that way. Not when her own chest pounded with hope.

Finally, he looked up at her through the floppy locks of his hair. "I thought of you," he said. "Every day."

Breath caught in her chest, and tears pricked her eyes. Thea hadn't realized how badly she wanted to hear him say that. He hadn't forgotten her. Yes, this job had been a mistake to hire her, but... He hadn't forgotten.

She set her teacup on the floor, set his beside hers, and reached for his hands again. Thea held onto him with a strength she hoped belayed her emotions even as she met his gaze. "I never forgot you, Alistair Orbweaver. But that doesn't mean I should be your weakness. Not to this man or any other."

He didn't respond. Alistair looked down at their hands and freed one of his. He then flipped her left hand over and gently traced the shadow of a ring on her finger. Every feather light stroke warmed her chest. His touch spread through her belly until she swore a fire waited to consume her.

Carefully he traced the lines of her palm, each symbol there that marked a long life, good health, and a love that remained fractured for many years.

"I told myself if I ever saw you again, that I would show you everything. I would face my fears, my father, the family that dragged me down. And that if you would step foot in this home again, that I would never let you go." He smoothed his thumb over their ring, their promise, one more time. "In the long years since seeing you, in losing them all, I thought I had forgotten what it felt like to be happy. Now, I catch myself smiling and I realize it's because I'm thinking of you again. I cannot deny you anymore, Thea, not when you are so entangled in what I believe is happiness."

She leaned forward with every word until she could feel his breath on her lips. The heat from his body flooded into hers, and oh, how she'd longed for this moment. A moment when they could both let go of the weight of old chains. Again, after all these years, a moment like this made the world fall away.

It was just Thea.

Just Alistair.

No families, no threats, no world other than the two of them and the feeling of her heart thudding in her chest.

He swallowed hard. "I have to show you something, Thea. Something I myself have been frightened to look at while knowing that it might mean I am not worthy of you."

"What could possibly make you unworthy of me?" A shiver trailed down her spine, however.

Alistair stood, drawing her up to her feet as well, while he still held onto her hands. "My father trapped a spirit in the basement, and I fear it could very well be a god. He certainly thought it was. That is where all the dark magic comes from. The mist. The shadow spiders. All of it. He trapped a god in the basement and tortured it for more power. And I have been too afraid to face it since the house was turned over to me."

Thea's heart stuttered again for a very different reason. But she would not allow fear to stop them for one more moment. Not even a second.

She squeezed his hands, then drew herself up straight and tall. "Shall we meet the god of this house then, Alistair? I believe a few apologies are in order."

CHAPTER 37

Guilt and shame dogged his steps as Alistair brought her to the basement. Namely, because he should have done this years ago. Now that she stood by him, it seemed absurd that he hadn't faced his fears earlier.

His father had tortured whatever poor creature lived down there, and he had no idea how long the beast had suffered. Alistair was the head of the household now, and he should have released it long ago. Of course, he hadn't entertained asking it for more power as his father always had, but that didn't make him any better than the old man.

He'd left it there. Suffering. And now, ten years later, it wanted to kill him.

Thea squeezed his hand in hers as he paused in front of the door. "What are you afraid of?"

"It wants my death," he replied hoarsely. "It has begged for me to walk down those stairs so many times, I cannot even tell you a number. But every time I felt its magic reaching for me, it was always with the sharp edge of rage and hate."

"A creature who has been trapped for years can only know hate." She blinked up at him, those big eyes seeing far too much. "Now is our chance to teach it something other than rage or fear. You know it's the right thing to do."

And why was the right thing to do always so difficult?

Alistair squared his shoulders and gazed into her starry eyes. He'd promised himself years ago that if she ever came back into his life, he would be a better man. For her. For their future. For everything that they had seen in the clouds as they gazed up at them from the fields full of blue flowers.

This was the first chain to free himself. The house would fully be his once he faced this creature and made his apologies. If only he could apologize on behalf of his father.

The ghost of the old man stood behind him. He could feel the cold air pressed against his back as Balthazar hissed angry words into his ear.

"You will never be as powerful as I was. This woman will leave you. If you go into that basement, you will fail to bring about anything that you desire."

But then Thea reached her arms around him, and he felt her wrists move as she dashed them through the air.

"What are you doing?" he asked, awkwardly holding his arms at his sides. He wanted to wrap her in his arms and never let go. If only she would let him press her to his heart, he thought maybe they would both be happier.

"I'm getting rid of your father." Thea flapped her hands one last time through the air, and then he felt all the cold air drift away. "The man is a menace. You're dead, sir! Go toward the light."

The absolute ridiculousness of what she said punched him in the gut. Thea, the girl who had been so afraid to come into this house that she had never actually met his father while the man was alive, had no problem now ushering him away from his son. Balthazar likely thought he should be more feared now that he was a ghost.

And yet, this woman walked into all of their lives and turned everything upside down.

He tilted his head back and laughed. The sound erupted from his chest, though rusty with misuse, and seemed to banish the ill feelings from deep within the basement. As though even the creature locked up in there was surprised that Alistair could still feel joy.

And it was joy. He was certain of it. The emotion was rare to feel in this house, even now, but she had brought that into his life.

Alistair hooked an arm around her hips and gently shifted her to face the basement door again. "Shall we?"

"If your father doesn't mind leaving us alone for a bit, then yes." She grinned up at him, and he felt an answering half-smile cross his own face.

Alistair lifted a hand and muttered the spell that would open the door. His father had used the old ways to lock it—curses made of blood and hair and vials of slime that came from faerie creatures themselves. He'd spent a foolish amount of money on it, making sure that no one would ever get inside. Not unless he had deemed it appropriate.

Locks slid into place from behind the door. The clicking and creaking was a sound Alistair had heard many times in the middle of the night, but he'd never thought it was this. He'd always assumed the rattling was merely his father walking around or his brothers teasing him. Now he knew.

The door swung open, and a wave of white mist rolled up the stairs toward them. The strangely thick magic sparkled in the light and then disappeared into the gloom of the darkness.

He heard a voice from deep inside the very heart of his home.

"Alistair."

"It's there," he said quietly.

"I know." Thea squeezed his hand. "I heard it, too."

Together, they walked toward the stairs and descended into the dark. He should have brought a torch, he thought, and then the passing thought made him shake his head. This was his house. He knew there were light switches down here for people to see.

Except, he froze when he heard chains clanking. A deep grumble started up, the noise straight out of a nightmare. Then he heard the monster's breath. The beast in the manor who had haunted so many of his family for years. His father had found this god and brought him into the home. Tricked him. Made him perform like he was nothing more than an animal.

It had every right to want to kill Alistair. It should for all that his father had done.

He knew he'd thought the same thing a hundred times over by now, and yet, he still couldn't stop the words from running through his mind. He deserved this. And some part of that thought felt as though something had cast a spell over him.

Alistair had never questioned if he had a right to be alive. No time in his life had ever driven him to such dark musings, yet the closer he was to the basement, the more likely he was to think those thoughts. As though the creature wanted him to accept what it was going to do before it did it.

Thea's hand slipped out of his, and he heard her hand scraping along the wall. The faintest click of a switch being flipped and then a line of bulbs flickered to life. Bare bulbs cast harsh shadows throughout the room, but his eyes didn't linger on those lights for very long.

The basement was long. It went the length of the house, like a too wide hallway. All the way at the end, with no windows to give it light, was a strange creature chained to the wall. The beast was covered in fur from head to toe. However it had a flat face, like a human. Its hair was so long that it dragged on the ground even as the beast lumbered to standing.

Upright, it was easily eight feet tall, though lean. Too lean. Years of mistreatment had created a skeletal mass out of what had once been an impressive creature.

Thea sucked in a hesitant breath. "That's not a god."

"No, it's not."

"Then what is it?"

He lifted a brow in question. "You can see it?"

Though she had her eyes on the standing creature, Thea must have felt his gaze. She nodded, then swallowed hard. "I can. Should I not be able to?"

Because he couldn't stop himself, Alistair ran his finger along the back of her neck. He drew his touch down past the edge of her bodice and into the hollow between her shoulders. His fingers bumped against a gold chain, just as he thought she might still wear.

Carefully, Alistair drew out her whistle and let it thud against her breastbone. "You should only be able to see it with that."

The creature let out a roar that shook the rafters above their head. Dust rained down upon them, but Alistair wouldn't allow the creature to make him fear it. Not anymore. Not now that he knew it wasn't a god, but a fae creature who had been locked up for far too long.

He started down the distance that held the beast at bay, only to pause as Thea grabbed onto his arm.

"Where are you going?" she asked.

"To talk with it. It's been here for ten years with no one but itself. The spells my father put on the door kept out any of the fae as well."

"So it is one of the fae, then?"

"Yes." He kept his eyes on the creature who watched him with no small amount of hate. "It's a domovoy."

He'd never seen one before and had thought they were myths. No one spoke of these creatures anymore. The people in Wildecliff had long forgotten many of the fae, and he'd only read about the domovoy in books.

"And what kind of fae is it then?" Thea asked, walking beside him until they were a mere six feet away from it.

"A household deity," he murmured. Alistair lifted his hand and watched as the creature followed it with only its eyes. "They were long thought to be dead, but they are lesser gods. Gods of the household, if you will. People often left meals in the kitchen at night to make sure a domovoy would bless the home."

"Lesser gods," Thea repeated. "So he's quite powerful?"

"Indeed. How my father trapped him is a mystery to me."

"Might it have something to do with that?" Thea pointed to the side of the creature's neck.

And there it was. A rune burned into its skin. His father must have fought long and hard to pin this creature to the ground long enough to brand him, and yet, there was the proof that his father was even more cruel than he imagined.

"I do not recognize that rune," he murmured.

"Oh." Thea clapped her hands together. "I do!"

And then she took off for the stairs, disappearing into the spear of light from the upper levels of his home.

That left him and the beast in the room alone. The domovoy smelled the air, tilting his head back and inhaling so deeply that Alistair could see his ribs even through the thick matts of his fur. The single bulb above its head revealed all the scars along the creature's body. So many scars.

He could only imagine what the beast had endured. This poor faerie had suffered so much at the hands of his family.

"I am sorry," he said, pitching his voice low and quiet. "I know you've been calling to me for a very long time."

The domovoy chuffed out a low breat, like an angry bull.

"I know," Alistair replied. "You have been begging for me to help you and I have ignored you. That was a terrible thing to do to one so honorable. It is a mistake I will never forgive myself for, although I'm sure that apology does not matter to one such as you."

Again the beast chuffed, this time though he was certain there might be a word in there. A word that sounded familiar and yet unknown to him.

"I have no right to beg for my life. I have no right to even ask for your forgiveness after what my father did." He held his hands up as the creature glared. "All I can ask is that you leave me alive to continue to make amends for what happened. You may go. Find yourself a better house with a better family who will not drain you dry for magic."

The domovoy lunged at him. The chains held it back, snapping with a harsh crack even after all these years. But the creature was but a hand's length away from his face now. Alistair stared into golden eyes filled with so much sadness it made his own soul scream.

Footsteps stomped down the stairwell as Thea came rushing back into the basement.

"I found it!" she shouted. "I knew I'd seen that mark before!"

Alistair didn't look behind him. All he could do was watch in awe as the domovoy seemed to soften in front of his eyes. The creature looked at Thea as though she were a priceless artifact in a room full of sand.

He knew that feeling. It was the same one he felt every time he looked at her.

"Alistair," she said, her voice much closer than before. "Can you get this grimoire off of me? It latched on when I grabbed the other."

He turned away from the beast to see that she had a grimoire quite literally latched onto her shoulder. The book had a decent grip on her and grumbled as he yanked it off. She held another one that fluttered in her grip like it thought it had wings and could fly away.

"Oh stop," she scolded as she flipped through its pages. "It doesn't tickle that much."

Bemused, he realized both he and the domovoy were watching her with rapt attention as she flipped through the grimoire and then shouted with glee.

"See?"

He grabbed the book she thrust at him and peered at the notation on the rune that was burned into the domovoy. "A rune of binding that can only be removed with the blood of the caster. This rune was specifically designed to capture fae and similar creatures who will then have to do the bidding of the caster." He looked up from the book. "How did you remember this?"

"Cleaning rooms full of books is rather boring and requires reading breaks for entertainment purposes." She looked all too pleased with herself. "The blood of the binder. You just have to put your blood on the rune, Alistair. You can free the domovoy right now."

Both of them looked at him with far different expressions—hers of happiness, the domovoy's of complete and utter mistrust.

He couldn't stop now, however, and he'd told himself that he would stop living in fear of what might happen next.

Alistair sighed and handed the book back to her. His words were for the domovoy. "If I release you, then I know there is a chance you will kill me. You've wanted revenge on my father for years now, but you must know that he's dead. His ghost remains here and killing me will only satisfy him further. You may leave, domovoy. Start your life anew."

The creature glared at him as though it had no intent on doing so, but what else could Alistair do? He had to let it go.

"Here." Thea handed him a small pin she unclipped from her bodice. A tear opened up that he hadn't noticed before. "Use this."

He'd ask her about the state of her clothing tomorrow. But today, he used the pin to poke a small hole in his thumb and reached forward to press it against the creature's burned neck.

Instantly, a hundred things happened all at once. A blast of magic shoved Alistair and Thea away from the domovoy. The chains snapped free and struck the dirt floor with hard thuds. Thea gasped. The domovoy lunged forward and pressed Alistair against the wall with a scream of rage that made the entire building shake.

He turned his head away from the slathering jaws, not quite brave enough to look death in the eyes.

But that death never came. And when Alistair opened his eyes again, he was shocked to see Thea standing beside the domovoy with her hand on its arm. The beast was frozen, staring at the gentle touch it likely hadn't felt in years.

"Come," she whispered, her wide eyes staring up into the beast's. "Come with me."

The domovoy staggered away from Alistair, completely under her spell.

"Would you like some tea?" she asked. "I think you've earned it."

Alistair remained pressed against the wall, frozen, as the woman he loved helped the domovoy up the stairs and into the light for the first time in likely fifty years. And she did it without fear.

He hadn't ever fallen out of love with her, he realized. She'd always had his heart.

CHAPTER 38

T hank you, dear. I'm so sorry to even ask you to help with this,"
Nora said as she bustled through the kitchen. "It's just that the
other maid, you see, her mother still isn't doing well and she's
the only one who knows how to run the kitchen with me. Without
her, I can't serve like I usually do."

"Isn't that a butler's job?" Thea asked as she tied the pretty
white apron around her waist. The laced edges were rather lovely,
if outdated.

"It would be if the boys weren't off to school." Nora placed
a large tray down on the table and started loading it with food.
"Unfortunately, that just leaves little ol' me to take care of
everything. Normally that's fine! I don't mean to complain. Feeding
one man isn't all that hard, even with you added into the lot. I don't
mind cooking for a few people, but when the meal has to be fancy
because Alistair invited important people from the school, well, it's
just a little overwhelming. Is it hot in here?"

Thea watched as Nora fanned her face. The housekeeper was

bright red and perhaps a little concerningly pale at the same time. The poor woman had met her match with this plan and she was too overwhelmed to even think straight.

Grabbing a few additional plates, Thea loaded up the tray with a bright smile and then placed it on the dumbwaiter to yank upstairs. "I think the food looks marvelous, Nora. In fact, I would believe it if you said you had cooked this for a king before."

Though the words were ridiculous, they made Nora feel a little better. Her red face cleared up a little, and the splotches smoothed out. "Do you think?"

"I know." Thea marched back and dropped a kiss to the other woman's cheek. "Now stop worrying so much, or you're going to make the food taste off because everyone will get anxious."

Nora pressed her hands against her cheeks. "Oh no. Do you think I already did that?"

With a shrug, Thea started up the stairs. "At the very least, they'll leave a little earlier that way!"

And she knew that was what Alistair hoped. The poor man had been beside himself for the past week, trying to plan all this. He kept muttering about pig headed men who tried to force him into doing things he didn't want to do. Which, considering the fact that they'd just freed the domovoy from the basement, she could only imagine meant he was feeling what the creature had felt.

She'd set the domovoy up in one of the spare bedrooms. After all that, the beast refused to leave the house. It had made a nest in the corner out of Lysander's old clothes and seemed quite content to stay there for a while. She brought it tea and biscuits every now and then, but Alistair kept telling her to leave it milk.

Unfortunately, they had no milk because that liquid curdled the moment Alistair's carriage man walked by. She'd have to ask about that later.

For now, Thea had to learn how to pretend to be a good little maid who wanted nothing more than to serve food to these esteemed guests. She had a feeling she'd break the moment one of these Wildecliff professors thought they could talk down to her, but she'd do her best. Alistair needed her to help.

She was quite sure he'd be angry to see her helping. He'd explicitly told her to spend her evening in her own bedroom, and if anyone asked about her, he would say she went back to Waterdown for the night. As though that was easy.

Even getting letters home was hard enough. Her mother had to pull a few favors to get the last one to Thea, and even that had been shorter than either of them would have liked.

Sighing, she walked over to the dumbwaiter and yanked on the chain. The food came up rather easily, although it clanked and groaned. She suspected it needed to be oiled but didn't know who would do that now that the butlers were back in school.

"Is it just Nora and I left?" she mused as she carried the tray toward the dining room door.

Using her hip, she bumped the door open and walked into what clearly was meant to be a masterpiece. They'd found a chandelier in the basement, which now gleamed and cast rainbow lights all over the room. And though it was still gloomy—the house would never be anything else—the table was at least pristine and there were three other tables on each wall filled to the brim with fountains, drinks, and glasses ready for anyone to use. She'd never seen such opulence. Not to mention the giant table with green velvet chairs and all the food already piled there.

Why did they need more food if they already had enough to feed an army in front of them?

Each chair was filled with people from the Academy. Thea had tried to pull details out of Alistair about who was getting invited, but he refused to give her even a hint about the event. Thus, she walked in blind.

Hopefully, they would all appreciate a polite young maid and not want her to be rude or snobby as the rest of them were. Otherwise, she'd be rather embarrassing.

Trying to stay as quiet as a mouse, she skirted around a group of people who had yet to sit down and placed the tray in the center of the last table. Tea cakes, cucumber sandwiches, and plenty of other meats must have been the last item to top off what was quite the spread.

"There," she muttered. "That should last them for a while."

"I wouldn't count on that." The oily voice was a little too smooth, a little too high pitched, and strangely musical. She hated it immediately.

Thea turned to eye the man who stood beside her. He lacked all color, she observed. White hair. Pale blue eyes. Alabaster, paper thin skin. He looked like a ghost.

She dipped into a low curtsey, hoping that would be enough to turn the man's attention away from her. "Ah, well, I will go get more food, then. I'm afraid I'm new to the job. You'll have to forgive me, sir."

"I don't have to do any such thing." He looked her up and down like she was a beetle he'd stepped on. "That's the first thing you need to learn, girl. If you're one of the help, then you have to satisfy me. Not the other way around."

She felt all the blood drain out of her face. This wasn't what she had expected in coming here. Of course, she had known that people in Wildecliff weren't the same as the people she'd grown up with, but she hadn't expected someone like... well. This.

Standing from her curtsey, she prepared herself to give this man the tongue lashing he'd never had before. Someone had to put him in his place, and if that had to be one of the "help," she'd be happy to oblige.

But she saw Alistair out of the corner of her eyes. He stood behind the crowd and had clearly been talking with an older woman. She stood tall and straight with silver hair that was coiled around the top of her head. Alistair had seen Thea, though, and stopped talking. He stared at her with horror, and then his gaze turned to anger.

He'd do something foolish if she let him. A small part of her wanted to see what that would look like.

But this was an evening for him and his coworkers. She refused to let it turn into a fight.

She watched as Alistair excused himself from his conversation and stalked toward her. It was now or never. He'd make it across the room in no time on those long legs, and then she wasn't all that certain she could hold him back.

"Hold that thought," she muttered.

"Excuse me?" the pale man asked.

Thea grabbed a glass half full of wine and met Alistair in the middle of the room. She thrust it at him, standing in his way so he couldn't go any further.

"Stop it," she hissed as she tried to force him to take the glass. "Everyone will look, and then what will you do?"

"You're not supposed to be here." His attention zeroed in on her, and suddenly she wished she'd let him yell at the other man. "You were to stay in your room, away from everyone here."

"Nora and I are the only ones left to help. I didn't have a choice unless you wanted to serve these people yourself." Which was a conversation she needed to have with him. How was this esteemed house bleeding money? "Take the glass so people don't think we're arguing."

"We are arguing. Get upstairs, now, and do not come back until I tell you to do so." He pinched the bridge of his nose and waved the glass of wine away. "I already have a headache."

"I'm going to continue serving because that's what the house needs right now." Louder, she added, "I'll go get you a tea for that headache. Do you need anything else while I'm down there?"

"A maid wouldn't say that," he grumbled.

"This one does." Thea hoped no one saw her reach out and touch his elbow. "Let me do this for you, Alistair. Nora can't cook and serve at the same time."

He looked at her, and she saw hopelessness in his eyes. He feared one of these people would hurt her, but surely he knew that wouldn't happen? She could take care of herself, after all.

"Don't talk with any of them," Alistair muttered. "Especially not that one."

She already knew he meant the pale man. He didn't have to warn her away from that one twice.

Thea kept her head down for the rest of the evening, and it seemed to go a little smoother. Most of the people at the table were polite enough. They'd snap their fingers and point to whatever they wanted refilled at least, and that kept her on her toes. For the most part, she was quite pleased with her performance.

Alistair had worried for nothing, she decided. They were all focused on each other and him. As if he had some grand announcement, and that was the meaning of the dinner.

The longer it went, the more she was quite certain they were all waiting for something. They kept looking at Alistair every time he moved, and then they would all seem rather disappointed when he did nothing but look back at them. And by the end of the dinner, everyone seemed slow to leave.

Thea stood at the front door, handing everyone back their jackets. Thankfully, Nora had organized them, so it was rather easy to get them to their owners. They all wanted to leave anyway. Not a single, well dressed person remained long enough to even say goodbye to Alistair.

At least he remained in the dining room. He couldn't see how quickly they all wanted to get away from him.

The last jacket in her hands, she held it out to the owner. The black suede wouldn't keep the person warm, but she had a feeling that it was more about a show of wealth than comfort.

"Have a nice evening," she said with a bright smile.

That smile shook when she met the eyes of the pale man again. He reached for his jacket, took it out of her grip, and then caught her hand in one of his.

"The evening was an utmost pleasure," he murmured. "If only because you were here to brighten it."

Thea tried hard not to rip her hand out of his grip. He leaned down and pressed a kiss to the back of her fingers, lingering a little too long. His lips were hot against her skin, and she'd thought he would be ice cold. Like a corpse.

"Thank you," she said when he released her hand. "Master Alistair goes to great lengths to ensure that his guests feel welcome."

"Oh, I don't think that was Master Alistair in the slightest." The man tried to smile at her, but it looked more like he was baring his teeth. "I think that was all you."

She pressed her back against the wall when he leaned forward. He pretended not to notice and instead grabbed a lock of her hair and twined it around his finger.

"I am needed in the kitchen," she said.

"You have midnight hair," he murmured. "Has anyone ever told you that? I half expect to see stars if I look hard enough."

She wanted to tell him the only stars he would find would be a horrible case of dandruff. And, in fact, if he wanted to look that hard, she'd make sure she dried her scalp out. Thea would endure the itch to disgust him.

But she felt the ice cold touch of the house growing angry again. She'd thought the reaction was the domovoy in the basement, but apparently, the house itself was still very connected to the man who owned it. And now there was no one left to see what Alistair did.

A shadowy tendril curled around the pale man's shoulder. The shadow looked like the leg of a spider, but it was... different now. A little less sharp around the edges, and perhaps even more deadly for it.

One moment the pale man had her pinned to the wall; the next, he had been thrown in the opposite direction. He hit the adjacent wall with a hard thud that made his breath wheeze out of his lungs. Sliding down the wallpaper, the man didn't even try to protect himself as Alistair grabbed a fist full of his shirt and hauled him upright.

"What did I tell you about her?" Alistair hissed into his face. "Say it. I want to know if you heard me."

"Stay away from her."

"That's right. And you didn't listen, did you?" Alistair's magic billowed around him. Shadows crawled along the floor to join in on the magic that had been gifted to him by his father. "Remember what my father said to you all those years ago? After days of hearing you scream in the basement?"

The pale man didn't shake in Alistair's hands as Thea might have expected. Instead, he tilted his head back and laughed. "Oh, I remember, Alistair. But you are not your father."

A darkness shifted inside Alistair. He leaned closer to the other man and snarled, "I can be, if I wish."

Thea shivered at the tones in Alistair's voice. He released the other man with a harsh shake, and she watched as the pale man straightened his shirt and put his jacket on.

But then, as he started out the door, he paused in front of her. "Alistair will not be around much longer, and you'll need a new master. One who is able to actually use your talents. Call me when you're ready."

A snarl ripped out of Alistair, and he grabbed the back of the other man's neck. With a harsh shove, he threw the visitor out the front door and slammed it behind him. Shoulders moving up and down in great heaving breaths, he braced himself against the frame.

"Alistair?" she asked, watching him with wide eyes. "Are you all right?"

To be honest, she wasn't sure if he was. But the tingly feeling up and down her arms was rather... thrilling.

CHAPTER 39

Alistair couldn't think. Couldn't breathe.

All he could see was that Marren had trapped Thea against the wall, and that horrible monster of a man planned to do whatever he wanted. And then to hear him try to convince her to go to his home rather than the Orbweaver manor? What woman would be so mad as to go with that man?

A little voice in his head whispered that maybe that would be easier for her, though. Maybe, after all the terrifying shadows and the fae creature chained up in the basement, she'd prefer the pale man's home. Sure, it wouldn't be as lavish. But she'd be safer. Happier.

She was better off without Alistair.

And that mere thought in his head made him want to break things. He'd never been a violent man. He knew that answering frustration with his fists was the most foolish thing to do, especially since he'd seen his family do just that for years.

He should talk about this. Talk with her. Nor should he have forced Marren out of his house as though he were kicking a child out onto the streets, and yet... Breath still sawed from his lungs. He still saw the danger she was in and how little he could do to save her from it.

"Alistair?" she asked. "Are you all right?"

It was the worst thing she could have said to him.

He whirled upon her, anger making his face and chest feel hot while his hands were ice cold with fear. "No, I'm not all right. You were supposed to stay in your room so none of those vultures saw you. And yet, where were you?"

Thea blinked up at him. "I helped where I was needed."

"No, you—" He caught himself before he said something stupid. Pressing his lips into a thin line, he pointed at her and snarled through his teeth, "You took a risk."

"A risk that needed to be taken. Nora couldn't have done it on her own and you certainly weren't going to serve them. I fail to see what the argument is here, Alistair. You're angry at me for what?"

"For not listening!" he blustered. The shout echoed down the hall, startling even Alistair with its ferocity. Quieting his voice, he hissed, "You have caught the attention of the most dangerous man at that school. Make no mistakes. Marren will hunt you down if he desires to do so. He's the only family in Wildecliff that is even close to a similar power to mine."

"And that should scare me, why?"

He had to make a point. She needed to understand why this made him want to vomit and why she couldn't do whatever she wanted in a place like this. Wildecliff wasn't safe like Waterdown. She couldn't just... just...

The worry and fear in his chest changed into an anger he couldn't control. It blew through his entire body until he couldn't stop himself from moving.

He cornered her against the same wall, pressing her back against it as she stared up at him with wide eyes.

"He had you pinned," he growled. "There was nowhere for you to go or to escape. If he wanted to, he could have spat any manner of venom on you. That poison would sink beneath your skin and cause you unimaginable pain. Or perhaps he could have forced you to do his bidding, even when you didn't want to. He could make you a puppet or a plaything for himself or his friends. And don't think for a second that he wouldn't. Marren is no fool. He may play the part well, but he'd been trying to harm my family for years."

"Because your father tortured him?"

"Because my father killed his. They tried to poison Balthazar at his own table and, as such, they were punished."

She drew her hands up and pressed them against his chest. "You don't have to walk that path any longer. Look at what you did for the domovoy. You could do the same for his family."

Oh, she was so innocent. It broke his heart.

Some of the anger floated away as he lifted his hand and slid his fingers behind her neck. "Don't think me that far from my father, Thea. If he had harmed a single hair on your head, I would have ripped his chest open and served you his bleeding heart on a platter."

"I don't have any use for his heart." Her fingers curled in the fabric of his shirt, drawing him closer. "I'm going to put myself in danger sometimes, Alistair. Wildecliff is not the safest place to live, but I won't stop living simply because I am here."

"How am I meant to endure this worry, then?" He didn't know the answer to that question. "My heart will stop, and then where will you be?"

"Oh, I don't think it'll stop." She smiled up at him, and he felt like the rays of the sun played across his face. "Are you going to keep talking or are you going to kiss me?"

Kiss her?

Oh, of course. He'd moved without realizing. His hand behind her neck drew her even closer, and somehow he'd placed his other hand on her hip. Thea was locked in place, incapable of movement unless he allowed it. And the only movement he wanted from her was to be closer to him.

A hundred reasons why he shouldn't kiss her played in his mind. They were not ready for this step. He was rushing her, or perhaps it was only adrenaline that convinced both of them to take this leap. He was a fool if he thought she wanted him and wasn't just grateful that he'd saved her.

Alistair dashed all those thoughts aside. Because when they were alone, then it was just the two of them. No thoughts. No memories. Just Alistair and Thea.

He drew her closer until he could feel her breath puff against his lips. And suddenly, he was an eighteen-year-old boy again, waiting to kiss the first girl he'd ever cared about. Wanting her to see him for who he was and not as an Orbweaver.

She had then, and she would again.

Sighing into the kiss, he leaned down and devoured her lips with his own. He could taste the forest on her tongue. Wildness burned through her as powerfully as her magic, and he adored every second of it. She tasted like sin and witchcraft, a combination he'd never forget.

Nipping at her lip, he sighed into her mouth again before drawing back. "We can't," he whispered. "We can't after everything that we've...

That I've..."

Her fingers curled tighter in his shirt, and she glared up at him. "Alistair Orbweaver, if I can forgive you for what your family did, then you can forgive yourself for it."

"I've never apologized for it," he whispered. He brought their foreheads together so he could at least touch her more. So he knew she wouldn't pull away from him. "You shouldn't forgive me without that."

"Then apologize," she scolded. "Get it over with, Alistair, because I cannot suffer through this any longer. You are the only one in this house that blames yourself for what happened. Even if I did when I was a child, I know better now."

"I'm sorry."

She pulled back enough to stare up into his eyes as though she knew he needed her to be present in this moment.

"I'm so sorry for what my family did. For what I did to you. If I had known the plan, or been more involved in their lives, then I would have been able to help you. I ran to the dock that day. The moment I found out, I thought I could make it to Waterdown and warn everyone. I missed the last boat by a few seconds, and then they were gone." He took a long, deep breath. "If I had been a braver young man, I would have leapt into the river and swam to your side. I would have been there in Waterdown when the spell hit so that I could get you and your family to safety."

She slid her hands up his chest and framed his face with her palms. "You were a child, Alistair. Just like I was a child. There was nothing we could have done to stop what evil, bitter men did to our families and our lives. Nothing. You do not hold the weight of their sins on your shoulders simply because you are related to them."

And just like that, as though he'd been waiting for her forgiveness for far too long, the horrible pressing feeling on his shoulders abated. Perhaps it would come back eventually, but for now, he felt as though he could breathe again.

Alistair took another deep breath and felt his ribs expand fully. It was the first time he'd felt... like himself. The first time in a very long time.

When he kissed her again—and how could he not kiss her again—he allowed himself to ease into the kiss. There was no rush, no necessary need to force anything to happen. He could enjoy exploring the taste of her, knowing that she wouldn't run this time.

Neither of them wanted to avoid what had happened between them. What was happening between them.

He let go of her head and flattened his hand against the wall, focusing entirely on her. How she had pressed herself to his chest so he could feel her from shoulder to knee. How she let out a little gasp of surprise and then a long sigh of pleasure as he squeezed her waist, perhaps a little too tightly.

He wanted her, he realized. More than he'd ever wanted anything.

Not because of her beauty or rarity in Wildecliff. But for the soul that glowed in her chest and made his entire body ache to look at her.

He had missed her. Even while she lived under his roof, he missed her. As though not seeing her every second of the day was detrimental to his well-being. And now that she was here, he couldn't get enough of her.

If he didn't stop himself now, he wouldn't stop. Couldn't. Alistair knew damned well that this was more than a few years in the making, but he couldn't woo her like this. She deserved so much more than a passion filled night because he was afraid of what monsters she'd awoken at that dinner. And he intended to give that to her.

Just not quite yet.

He withdrew from her and smiled at the soft sound of disappointment she made. She clearly hadn't wanted this to end either, and that was good. He'd take that as a sign that someday soon, he should continue.

"We can't," he whispered, touching a thumb to her swollen bottom lip. "Not right now."

"Why is that?"

Alistair chuckled. "You are not a woman to fall under my spell because another man almost had you. That will not do for the story we remember for the rest of our lives."

"As if he could ever sway me," she muttered, but then her eyes caught upon his lips. She lifted her hand and traced the outline of his mouth, then the soft lines around them. "I haven't seen you smile like this since I came back."

"What do you mean?"

She pushed one side of his mouth down a little. "You have a half smile when you aren't feeling particularly cheerful but still want to smile. It's not the same as this one. This is a real smile."

"I guess I'm feeling particularly happy." He kissed the tips of her fingers as she skated them across his lips. "I told you. You make me happy."

Her cheeks turned a dusty pink, and he thought that was the prettiest color he'd ever seen. It was the perfect shade to match those lovely berry lips that even now tempted him. Even when he'd said they both had to be good because he had plans.

And oh, those plans would make sure she never wanted to go home. Never wanted to leave him.

As much as they both wished to ignore the world they were in, he always had the thought in his mind that he was trapped here. His father had made certain of that.

The house was Alistair's, and that meant that he would never leave this place until the day he died. He wasn't even certain if he could have a vacation or a holiday where they took off for the Sapphire Isles, even for a week or two. Life here would be different for her, and he would forever fear that a life with him had trapped her adventurous spirit.

Thea tapped her fingers against his collarbone, bringing him back to reality. "Don't go down that path."

"What path?"

"Whatever path made your face turn like that." She crossed her eyes and stuck out her tongue. "You get all mopey and that's not what I want. You are not allowed to be mopey ever again, and if you are, then I will give you a reason to be so."

"And how are you going to do that?"

He watched, bemused, as she tried her best to think up a way that she would make him unhappy. But the longer she thought, the more he knew she wouldn't be able to come up with anything. His Thea was rather predictable like that. And he already knew what she was going to say before she ever said it.

"Well, I'm not quite sure. If you're unhappy, then I'm unhappy. I don't enjoy the thought of being unhappy, so you must then endeavor to be blissful whenever I am around."

"That should not be difficult."

"Good, then it's settled. You'll be happier from now on. I will help where I am needed. And the house will make a turn for the better." And though she clearly wanted to kiss him again, Thea remained where she was. "But perhaps we shouldn't wait much longer? I've heard waiting on such things can make a person's blood pressure too high."

"For health reasons, we should not wait," he agreed.

"Then when?"

A bubble of laughter escaped him. Alistair pressed a small kiss to her nose and then forced himself to take two large steps away from her. Even if it felt a little like trying to rip velcro off of velvet. "Patience, Thea."

"I've never had an abundance of that."

"Indeed, you have not." He gave her an awkward little bow. "Until the next time we see each other, then."

"I'll see you at dinner. We live in the same house."

Right, well, that would not be when he made his romantic gesture. But hopefully, she wouldn't expect him to sweep the table free from food and toss her atop it. Considering the look in her eyes, she might just think that.

Clearing his throat, he took another step back. "I have some work to do in the study."

"Ah, yes. I have to help Nora clean everything up."

Why couldn't he stop looking at her? Turn around, he told himself. But he couldn't. Pursing his lips, he added, "Have a good evening then."

"Alistair, if you don't walk back to your study, then I'm going to assume you've changed your mind and take matters into my own hands."

He grinned at her. A real grin, one last time, before whirling around. He did have some complicated plans to make.

CHAPTER 40

Thea spent a long time waiting for him to make the next move. She'd been waiting for him because she knew how important this was for Alistair. Clearly, showing his feelings had taken a toll on him, and then having to pull himself away from her had been even more difficult. She didn't need to push him.

But the damn man had been waiting for a week now, and she wanted to get this over with. No more longing stares as they walked past each other. No more tantalizing moments where she wondered if he was finally going to make his move.

Instead, all she'd gotten was a week of frustration and angst. She wanted him to touch her, damn it! She wanted to kiss him, to linger together where they had never been given that opportunity as children.

Didn't he feel the same?

Most likely, only honor and all that ridiculous nonsense went on in his head.

"If you bang those pots any harder, I think you'll shatter the metal," Nora called out with a laugh.

"Maybe if they were broken, I would get a little attention from the master of the house," she muttered under her breath before calling out, "Sorry!"

Nora walked over to her and put her hands on her hips. "Dear girl. You are distracted today."

"There's a lot on my mind, Nora. I apologize, it's just…" Thea blew a hair away from her face and mirrored Nora's pose. "Well, if I could focus on something other than what's going on, then that would be better for everyone involved."

"Why don't you head into the garden? There's plenty there for you to do and I don't need you denting all the pots when I have to use them tonight."

The garden?

There was a garden?

Thea couldn't stop her jaw from dropping open. "There's a garden here? Why didn't anyone tell me?"

"Well, we didn't know you'd be interested? Besides, no one has taken care of it for years. The whole thing is just weeds and dead plants." Nora shrugged. "If I had more time, I might have spent some afternoons getting the gardens in tiptop shape, but as you can see…"

"You're busy."

"Very." Nora flapped a towel at her. "And you're too angry to be in my kitchen. Go on with you. You'll spoil the meat!"

She didn't need to be told twice. Thea threw off her apron and fled from the heat of the kitchens and the shadows that still lingered there. Instead, she rushed up the stairs to find this mystery garden that Nora had spoken of.

"Garden," she muttered. "If I were a garden, where would I be?"

Outside, obviously. But the house was on a very small plot. The entire building took up most of that plot, which meant the garden had to be attached to the house in some way except...

There were markings on the floor. At first, she thought they were dirt smudges, but then she realized they were painted there. Gold dust clung to the edges, and an arrow pointed down a section of the house she'd rarely visited. Those were Balthazar's old quarters, so she'd never even thought to poke around in there.

"So the old man had a garden," she said as she followed the glittering arrows. "Leave it to him to need his own personal stock of poisonous plants."

And she had no question that the place was full of poison. Why wouldn't it be? There was so much here that it would be easier to put into a spell if he had access to it always. Balthazar was a rich man, not a foolish one.

The golden arrows led to a single door down the hallway full of darkness. The door was the oldest she'd seen in the building, with peeling paint and old runes that had been scratched off with a knife. Likely to protect the rest of the house.

Thea rested her hand on the wood and took a deep breath. This felt important. Like something wonderful and magical was about to be revealed. She pushed the door open and felt her soul take flight.

The garden had been hidden inside the interior of the home. A glass greenhouse stood before her with green vines hanging from every joint that held the panes in place. Sunlight beamed through the glass and cast tiny rainbows all over the ground. And there, in the center, stood Alistair.

He wore a simple pair of black slacks and a white shirt that he'd rolled up at the sleeves. Black suspenders were loose at his shoulders, one halfway off his arm already. He'd unbuttoned his shirt and revealed for the very first time that his freckles actually trailed down his neck and onto his chest.

He held a glass of wine in one hand and stood on top of a lovely blanket that had been sewn in patches. There wasn't a picnic or food, just a bottle of wine, an extra glass, and the man she loved waiting for her.

"What's all this?" she asked with a slight laugh.

"I promised you a better way of proving that I'm worth your attention." He gestured with the wine and gave her a crooked half smile. "This was the best I could come up with."

"It's a good start."

Thea stepped toward him, only to have him meet her halfway. He reached for her hands and gathered them up to his chest. "I have something to show you."

"Oh?"

Alistair reached into his pocket and pulled out a thin, green ribbon. It seemed quite old and strangely familiar. Although, she wouldn't quite place where she knew it from.

"This was the ribbon attached to the first letter you sent me," he murmured. "I've had it for years now, and it's always brought me good luck."

"You kept it?"

"Of course, I did. Just like I kept every letter you sent me, every gift you gave me, and every memory of you close to my heart." He looked up through that floppy hair of his and smiled. A real smile. "I love you, Thea. More than I ever thought possible to love anything. I know there are plenty of reasons for us not to love each other. But no matter how far my heart wandered, I've always found myself coming back to you."

Her heart squeezed in her chest. She'd always felt the same but hadn't dared to dream that he would as well. Some part of her, the part that had held back from this and them, snapped.

Thea reached for him and drew him to her lips. She kissed him like she'd dreamt ever since she was a child. With every ounce of who she was and every bit of her love pouring into him in a hungry meeting of lips, teeth, and tongue.

"I love you," she whispered against him. "I have loved you since before we met and for lifetimes beyond that. I will love you until the stars tumble from the sky and the last god dies. You are part of me, Alistair. I won't ever let you go again."

As though those were magic words, he surged up to meet her. He wrapped one arm around her waist and the other behind her back, binding her to him in one great lunge. He swallowed the sounds of her whimpers until she lost herself in the feeling of him.

They sank onto the blanket together, although she couldn't guess which one of them had moved first. All she knew was that he drew her into his arms and the warmth of his body. Alistair raked his hands through her hair, the billowing darkness shrouding her shoulders with his movements.

"Do you remember all those times we met in the meadows?" he whispered as he broke away from her kiss. He pressed a kiss to her throat, right over her rapidly beating pulse. "Those were the most precious memories to me. Being outside with you, in your element, with all of nature to see us. That's why I wanted to bring you here."

She was delirious. Surely he wasn't saying such sweet things?

But then she felt his fingers at the ties of her dress and realized, yes, he was saying that. They were here, and she wasn't dreaming.

Fingers tangling in his shirt, she unbuttoned the rest of the buttons. The chest she revealed made her gasp. She'd known he was a thin man, but she hadn't expected him to be muscular as well. The flat planes of his pecs were dotted with freckles, and a fine dusting of nearly blonde hair disappeared into the waistband of his pants. She could see his ribs, a little more than she wished, but he was so lovely. So perfectly built for her.

He caught the back of her neck with another searing kiss that melted her against that chest. The warmth of his skin startled her. He heated the icy tips of her fingers, spreading heat to the very core of her.

"Move up for me," he whispered against her lips.

She shifted so he could draw off her bodice, revealing nothing but a shift underneath. However, she was tired of waiting. Thea decided all of this had been a long time coming, and she refused to be satisfied with a slow pace.

Standing quickly, she stepped out of her skirts and sank back onto their blanket in their semblance of wildness in this cursed city. She pushed him onto his back, following him down until she was stretched out on top of him, perched with her elbows on his chest.

When he moved, she stopped with a slight touch on the tip of his nose. Thea took her time, letting her eyes feast on his form. She touched him as she'd wanted to for years. Skating her hands down his chest, letting her fingers trail over the ridges of his abs. She felt the power of his ribs rising and falling with each breath. Even that bulge in his pants simultaneously terrified her and excited her at the same time.

They had waited years for this. She refused to be some fainting woman who turned her head to the side and endured. Not today.

His fingers trailed up her thighs, drawing the skirt of her shift up higher and higher. His eyes watched hers the entire time as though gauging to see if she wanted this.

Thea refused to let him doubt himself for a minute. She leaned down and pressed a kiss right over his heart. "I've been wanting this for a very long time, Alistair. Don't stop now."

Apparently, that's what he needed to hear. His hands fisted at her sides, then loosened to guide her onto her back. He moved on top of her, naturally fitting between her legs with a slight groan so wonderful to hear out of his mouth. "Thea," he whispered.

"I know," she said, smoothing her hands up his back even as she lifted her hips for him. "I know."

His lips trailed down her throat, down to her chest. She gasped as his mouth closed over the tips of her breasts, and spikes of pleasure flooded through her body, even through the fabric. She had no idea what he was doing to her, but.. but... Oh, how was a woman supposed to think through this?

Thea arched into his touch as he subjected her to the same treatment that she had given him, although his hands were much bolder. She shivered as he cupped her breasts. Quaked when he palmed the globes of her bottom, kneading the flesh there until she let out a little sigh. And then she had to hold in a groan as his fingers found that spot between her legs that she'd only touched herself.

"Thea," he whispered. "You're perfect."

And then he sank a finger into her and she saw stars. Alistair played her body with the talent of a violinist on stage. He watched her with rapt attention, noticing all the tiny movements she made when she enjoyed what he was doing.

A deep thrum started in her belly, a tensing coil she couldn't quite catch no matter how hard she tried. She gripped the blanket fabric in tight fists, dangerously on the edge of a miraculous burst of stars. No other person had gotten her there before, and she'd been quite certain it wasn't possible. Until him.

"Thea." His voice was a siren calling her to a night of her own demise. She couldn't care less.

Thea opened her eyes and looked up at him, panting and half mad with desire.

He knelt between her legs, his shirt already off and the light playing over the muscular caps of his shoulders. His hands were at the belt of his pants, and she almost couldn't stand it.

"I want it to be together," he said, his voice deeper than she'd ever heard it. "Can you handle that?"

She bit her lip and nodded. The image of him, the knowledge of what was going to come... her mind whirled with the possibilities, but none of those imagined moments could ever compare to him pressing against the notch between her legs. Simultaneously too big and perfect for everything that she had in mind. His breaths puffed against her collarbone, and then he kissed her.

His tongue surged into her mouth at the same time as he pressed forward and sank deep. A quiet sound escaped her lips, her stomach clenching. Perhaps around him as well, because he let out a groan that rocked through her.

"Thea," he said. "By the gods, you're perfect."

She cupped the back of his neck and held on as he eased deeper and deeper into her until she had no idea where he began, and she ended. Their lips pressed in a never-ending kiss as he found a pace that satisfied them both. He built that coiling pressure inside her again, but this time it was new. Different. So powerful she thought it might explode out of her at any moment.

Alistair wrenched himself free from their kiss, breathing hard and eyes shut, as though the feeling of her was too much. He touched their foreheads together and groaned, "I love you."

Somehow he changed the angle, and it was too much. Not enough. Wait, no, it was definitely enough.

Thea arched into him with a soft sound of surprise, her eyes snapping open, although she wasn't really looking at anything. She came with him, together, as it always should have been. And in the glimmering rainbows cast through glass, she realized that life had never had enough color until he had come into her life.

She'd seen a thousand flowers, made hundreds of bouquets, and never once realized there was a color to this feeling.

It was him. He was her hidden color, her rainbow, her love.

Their breathing slowed, and Alistair pressed his lips to her shoulder, neck, cheek, and over each eyelid. "Stay with me," he said. "Please."

"I have a better idea." She smoothed that unruly hair back from his face and smiled. "Why don't you move back into your old bedroom with me? I don't want to sleep in the master. I want to sleep with you. In comfort."

He grinned, a real, whole smile that seemed so frequent these days. "I'd like that."

CHAPTER 41

Alistair whistled as he walked into his office. Everyone in the Academy gave each other a strange look as he meandered over to his desk with a rather impressive jaunt to his step. He knew he was walking around like there were clouds beneath his feet. And in truth, there were.

He'd had a week of bliss at home. A week back in his own room, with the woman of his dreams in his arms. And they had finally dropped all pretense of the past. They were together. He didn't care what anyone said about that.

His father was gone. No one could scold him about how he deserved someone better than her in his bed. No one was better than her. Particularly in his bed.

Setting his things down in his chair, he looked out through the windows of his room with a wide grin on his face. She had filled his life with so much bliss. He hadn't been joking when he told her that for him; she was happiness to him. Every time she walked into his office door, he smiled. Sometimes she'd come out of the bathroom after a bath, her wet hair in a tangle over her shoulder and already soaking her nightgown on one side, and he'd realize how lucky he was.

She wasn't perfect. She broke things on a regular basis. The grimoires wanted to eat her every time she came into the library, and most of the time, the tea she brought him was burnt. But there was something about her that made him smile. He couldn't stop himself from doing it now.

Rubbing a hand down his face, he let out a little chuckle. "I have to get a hold of myself," he muttered. "The students will think I've lost my mind."

He'd been speaking for the fae, but another voice interrupted his thoughts. "Yes, what are you going to do about that intriguing young woman in your care?"

The Headmistress.

He hadn't seen her in a very long time. She'd kept in her own office, for the most part, only coming out for official gatherings, and even then, he rarely saw her.

Clearing his throat, Alistair turned around to greet her. "Ma'am. I was unaware you knew about Thea. Or even that you'd met."

The Headmistress closed the door behind her, a poor sign for how this conversation was going to go. A deep amethyst gown hugged tight to her waist and billowed out from her hips. Tiny gold runes were inscribed throughout the velvet, shimmering whenever the light hit them. She held a cane in her hand, although she had no reason to use one. No matter how old the woman got, she always seemed to stand with a straight back and powerful demeanor. The cane was merely for show. Or perhaps as a weapon in case she needed it.

He swallowed hard. The glare on her face was a bad sign. Extremely bad sign if he were being honest with himself.

"I know everything, Orbweaver. Haven't you learned that after ten years of working for me?" She tapped the cane against the ground. "No, I was led to believe that you were going to give me what I wanted. And come to find out, you were playing with my staff's hopes."

He blinked. "Excuse me?"

"You are well aware that I hired you for a reason. I gave you all the resources this school has, and I have been very patient with you." She eyed him with no small amount of disgust. "You are a disappointment, Alistair Orbweaver. Your father would never have taken so long."

He refused to let the words wiggle under his skin. He'd done everything he could as a teacher here. The students were unruly, and he knew he wasn't changing their minds about how the world worked. Their parents did that. But he taught them well, and they retained more information about what he'd taught them than the other professors. Surely that should count for something.

Unless…

The memory of the fiadh rudh flashed in his mind. Tiny faeries hung off the deer's antlers as the red stag told him to protect the fae. That beast had known something he didn't, and apparently, now was the time the Academy would finally play their card.

"I'm afraid I don't know what you're talking about," he said quietly. "I've done my job better than most in this school. I never call in sick. The students who leave my classroom have an adequate understanding of history and where we came from. If you're asking more of me, Headmistress, then I must admit I can't imagine what it is you seek."

She slammed her cane on the ground again, and a blanket of darkness covered the windows. Shadows moved at her beck and call. He'd known that before. She summoned light and devoured it. At least, that's what the rumors claimed.

As darkness closed in on him and Alistair realized the truth of her power. She didn't devour the light. She snuffed it out entirely.

"Alistair Orbweaver, I hired you because you are the first and only person to have a gift that sees between the worlds. When you were hired, it was under the expressed understanding that you would share that gift with the Academy. You were tasked with creating a way for myself and the others in this school to break through the veil and use the fae to our whims. You were meant to be the reason we discovered the way to control our gods rather than the other way around."

"Even saying such a thing is blasphemy," he muttered, taking a few heavy steps away from her. "The gods have always ruled our lands. I will not be caught in some web meant to change that."

"You don't have a choice," she hissed. "I will fire you, Alistair. More than that? Every powerful person who lives in Wildecliff will hunt you down and strip away everything you love. We allowed you to have this time because we believe in you. If you are not going to do what we want, then that is fine. But it's not just your life at risk."

Would they ever stop threatening his life?

"I can leave," he tried. "I have no reason to stay here. Not now."

"Do you not? And here it was my understanding that your father bound you to that house." She rolled her eyes. "Alistair, I'm no fool. Neither was your father. He knew you wouldn't want to complete this task because of some foolish desire to maintain that you are a good man and no one else in your family was. Now, take care of that family you so adore. Bring us something that can see through the veil at the next gathering. Or that young maid in your house is the first person I will take."

Desperation set in. His vision skewed, and his lungs heaved in great gulps, but it still felt like he couldn't breathe. "I could kill myself. That would take care of all this."

"Would it?" She lifted a brow, then turned to leave. "Alistair, I know many ways to keep a person alive. You will give me what I want, no matter how long I have to torture you to get it."

He refused to believe there wasn't a way out of this. Not after how happy he'd been when he walked into work today. There had to be an option. A way to fight back. Something…

The Headmistress stopped at the door of his classroom. "I've taken the liberty of canceling your classes for the day. I assume you have more important work to be doing rather than teaching young minds who don't care about history."

And then the door slammed shut behind her.

He groped for a chair and sank into it. "What am I going to do?" he whispered. "I can't risk her life. I won't."

A tiny faerie crawled up his pant leg. The same kind of faerie that had hung off the red stag's antlers. It gave him a sharp look and then scolded, "You're making decisions for her."

"Excuse me?"

"We wouldn't have sent you a witch for a bride if we didn't know how strong she was." It crossed its tiny arms over its chest, dragonfly wings fluttering with anger. "Talk to Thea. See what she thinks."

The fae knew about Thea?

Of course they did, he scolded himself. He'd known all along that he was being watched by the fae. It shouldn't surprise him that they had a hand in finding Thea for him. Or the two of them finding each other.

"I wanted a little more time with her to myself," he muttered. "She's a gift to my life and… I didn't want anyone else to muddle that up."

"Then talk to her about it." The faerie stomped its foot on his thigh, hard. "You're not a fool, Alistair Orbweaver. We chose you for a reason."

As it took off toward the window he always left open for their kind, he had to wonder how much they knew about him. If the fae had already picked out Thea because they believed in her, then did they know what would happen?

Either way, the little creature had been right. He needed to talk with her. He needed her to understand the dangers that were coming for them and to see if maybe she had any ideas that might help them continue forward.

Sighing, he rubbed the back of his neck and gathered up his things. It was a bit of a trek back to the house, and the carriage had already left without him. But he'd use the walk to figure out what he was going to say to her.

Of course, by the time he made it back home, he hadn't the faintest idea what to say. Slipping into the manor was easy enough. He hung up his jacket and set his case down by the door. The house was quiet, but it had been for quite some time.

Now that the domovoy wasn't in the basement, there wasn't so much of an icy chill when he walked into the entryway. The windows were spotless, and the sun shone on the giant stairway in front of him—beams of light caught in the dust motes merrily spun through the air. Thea would hate those, but he thought them rather charming.

Feeling heavier than he had since his father died, Alistair made his way to the stairs and sat down hard on them. He thudded down, but it didn't feel like he had eased any of the tormented weight that made him so darn tired. Leaning back on his arms, he stared up three levels to the ceiling. There was a skylight up there, he thought. Maybe. It was hard to tell from this angle.

He didn't know how long he sat there, staring up the stairs, until a pale face leaned over the railing on the second floor and looked back at him. Her dark hair slid like ink over her shoulder and trailed into the air. He almost expected a wet plop to hit him on the forehead.

"Alistair?" she asked.

"It's me."

"You're home early."

"Something happened."

"Ah." Thea's brows wrinkled. "I'm coming down. Stay where you are."

Well, he wasn't planning on going anywhere. He didn't move and listened to the sound of her footsteps as she marched down the stairs and then plopped down next to him. Tilting her own head back, Thea looked up at the ceiling.

"What are we looking at?"

He shook his head. "I'm not sure. I think there used to be a skylight up there."

"Ah." She nodded as though that made sense to be staring at. "I could get a very tall ladder and then we could try to clean it?"

"Sounds dangerous."

"All the best things are."

They stayed quiet for a little while as she reached out and held his hand. Just sitting on the stairs, leaning back on their elbows, looking up at the same stupid thing on the ceiling that didn't matter in the slightest.

Finally, he sighed and said, "They invited me to the next gathering."

"What's that?"

"A place where all the staff go to mingle. The best and the brightest of all Wildecliff are there in what I would argue is a complete and utter waste of money." Really, it was a giant party for everyone to pat each other on the back and talk about how great they were. He hated going with his father back in the day, and once Balthazar had died, no one ever invited Alistair again.

She squeezed his hand. "That sounds like a good thing?"

"The Headmistress tasked me with bringing a way to rip through the veil of the world so they can control the fae and the gods. If I fail to do so, then the Academy and those powerful people will attack people I love."

Thea nodded and made a long sound in the back of her throat. "So you're worried about me again, I take it?"

"Very much so." He couldn't even look at her because the mere thought of those bastards hunting her down, intending to harm her, made him shake. He wanted to hit something, and he never wanted to do that.

But he'd gotten a taste by shoving Marren out the door and watching him roll to the sidewalk. Now he wanted to snarl at everyone who threatened him. He wanted to flatten the city into dust at her feet and then offer her their hearts forever, daring to threaten her wellbeing. He wanted...

Thea pressed her lips to the back of his hand, kissing his knuckles as though she wasn't worried about what was going through his head. "You know you can't let them see the gods."

Finally, he looked at her and his heart twisted in his chest. "But I can't lose you, either."

"You won't. We'll find a way to beat them. Shutting me out only means you have one head to plan with, and together, I believe we're unstoppable." She held his head to her heart, and his knuckles brushed the warm metal of the necklace he had made her. "I'm scared, Alistair. I'm always scared. But that doesn't mean I choose myself over countless others. Fear is a warning, yes. But it should fuel us as well."

His brave, foolish, ridiculous woman would let no one stop her. Alistair drew her closer and pressed their foreheads together. "You always say the right thing."

"That's because I'm smarter than you."

"Of course it is," he replied with a chuckle. "Do you have any plans on how to stop them?"

"Not yet. But I know a few grimoires that might have some ideas." She lifted their hands between them and kissed his hand again. "Have faith, my Alistair. Nothing will ever come between us again."

CHAPTER 42

Thea tried her best to cheer Alistair up, but she knew it was a losing battle. He always worried for her safety, and now they were threatening more than just Thea.

So when she entered their now shared bedroom, she knew she had to come up with a plan. Something that would encourage him to see that there was a future for all of them, even if it hadn't felt like it.

The only problem was that she was very much out of her element. Thea knew nothing about the people in Wildecliff other than those who lived in this house. And running to the market for more vegetables didn't count as meeting people. She'd always been the shy one in her family. It didn't matter to her if she saw a few people. She was perfectly happy with Nora, Alistair, and Browning.

Sighing, she looked over at their bed to see Alistair already laying on top of the covers. He stared up at the ceiling, as he tended to do when he was thinking, with her green ribbon tied around his thumb. He kept tying it, untying it and then rotating the threads around his fingers as he thought. No wonder it was so tattered.

Perhaps she'd let him think. Two minds, that's what she had told him. Two minds were better than one.

But, when she walked into the bathroom, she found Browning standing in the middle of the floor with an expectant look on his face. He threw his head back and opened his mouth with a dramatic flourish.

Thea cleared her throat and blinked her confusion away. "Right. I would imagine that means you have something for me?"

He tried to nod, but that was rather difficult with his mouth open so wide.

Sighing, she reached into his mouth and pulled out a letter on green parchment paper. And a small box that didn't look all that familiar. This must all be from her family, but she couldn't imagine what they were sending her, considering she hadn't written a letter in a while.

Unwrinkling the letter, she scanned her eyes over the words.

DEAREST DAUGHTER,

WE HAVEN'T HEARD FROM YOU IN A LONG TIME. I CAN ONLY IMAGINE THAT THINGS HAVE WORKED OUT FOR THE BETTER. IF I REMEMBER ALISTAIR CORRECTLY, EVEN THOUGH I ONLY MET HIM ONCE, THAT BOY WAS MORE THAN HIS FATHER EVER GAVE HIM CREDIT FOR.

DON'T GIVE UP ON HIM, SWEETHEART. ESPECIALLY NOT IN A TIME WHEN HE NEEDS YOU MOST. YOUR FATHER NEVER GAVE UP ON ME, AND THAT WAS THE GREATEST GIFT HE EVER GAVE ME.

I SENT ALONG SOMETHING THAT MIGHT GIVE YOU BOTH A LITTLE HOPE. IT'S A SMALL GIFT, LIKE YOURS, BUT I THINK YOU'LL ENJOY IT.

MARIGOLD AND BELLADONNA HELPED, OF COURSE.
KEEP YOUR CHIN UP,
MATHAIR

Why did that bring tears to her eyes?

Thea sniffed back the emotion with a shake of her head. She couldn't walk out of the bathroom all teary-eyed, or Alistair would lose his head.

Still. The fact that her family supported her even now was a wonderful touch.

As she brushed her teeth, she tilted the box back and forth. What had her mother sent? Thea had taken everything with her when she'd left. There was a lot to pack, obviously. And if Marigold and Belladonna had helped, then she could only imagine it was some kind of plant.

But what plant would they send to Wildecliff?

Her curiosity would get the better of her if she didn't hurry. She brushed her teeth only about half the time she needed, threw her pale nightgown over her head, and padded back into the bedroom.

"My mother sent a gift," she said, still turning the box over in her hands. "She said it was something to cheer us up."

Maybe not quite that, but Alistair didn't need to know her mother was pitying them and sending them a gift for hope. He still needed some of his pride, after all.

He sat up in the bed and frowned. "Your mother?"

"Mhmm." Thea perched on the edge of the mattress and held the box out to him. "I have no idea what it is. Maybe you should open it."

Though he frowned at the box, Alistair took it from her and

lifted the top. "I don't know why your mother would send us a gift. She should be angry at me. I stole you away from your family and moved you to Wildecliff."

"Well, we both were unaware that it was you who hired me. You could have been anyone." Thea waved her hand in the air. "My mother didn't mind, anyway. There's plenty for her to do with the grand babies and my sisters' husbands. She's busy all the time."

Alistair paused in unwrapping and blinked at her. "You have nieces and nephews now?"

"I do." She should have talked to him about her family by now, but there hadn't been a lot of time. "Both Marigold and Belladonna are married with children. Their husbands are quite kind. Mother is still on her own, of course, but she helps out with the children while my sisters have taken over most of the food production for Waterdown."

"Ah. And I suppose that became quite important once the food crop had been destroyed by my father."

She bit her lip. This wasn't the conversation she'd wanted to have over a gift. "That still isn't your fault, Alistair."

He reached for her hand and gave it a little squeeze. "I am working on accepting that, but it's rather hard when you know your family caused destruction and death for so many. Your family has always helped others, Thea. It will take time for me to not feel some manner of guilt. Perhaps I always will."

And maybe that was how he had to deal with his family's history. Feeling sorry wasn't a bad thing, she mused. Then she nudged the gift in his hands. "Open it."

He reached into the box and pulled out a small plant and pot wrapped up with fabric. It looked like a tiny ivy, although there were already buds on it, so Thea imagined it must bloom. A small square of paper had been tied to the tallest part of the ivy.

She reached for the note and read it out loud. "Plant me in the corner of a room and I will guard your dreams."

What? What in the world had her sisters thought up?

"Plants don't guard dreams," Alistair murmured.

"Sometimes they do." She set the paper down and reached for the plant. "Marigold can make new species, remember? This must be something she thought up and then enchanted into life. And if it looks after dreams, then obviously it should be in a bedroom."

"Plant in the corner of a room, though?"

She'd admit that was a strange requirement. Marigold had made stranger plants, though. And if this one didn't need natural sunlight or... dirt, then she supposed that was the way it had been designed.

Holding the tiny plant up higher, she frowned at it as she walked over to the corner of their bedroom. "I don't know. Marigold has quite the imagination."

Her sister could and would do anything with plants that she wanted. Thea put the ivy in the corner of the room and took a couple of steps back. She wasn't sure how to "plant" it, considering there was no earth to move or any way for her to set it into the ground. She hoped that putting it near the wall would suffice.

Thankfully, she knew her sister well enough. The ivy shivered as though it had woken up after a very long nap. Stretching its little leaves higher, it suddenly grew at a pace that shouldn't have been possible. It stretched up to the ceiling, over the bed, and then let some tendrils hang over their bed as little buds opened up to reveal lovely white flowers.

Tiny petals rained down on the bed, and Thea knew what that meant. Marigold had designed this flower to bloom in such a way that there was a meaning for Thea.

She picked up a single petal from the bed and popped it into her mouth.

"Thea," Alistair said in shock. "You have no idea what that'll do to you."

"That's part of the fun."

As the petal melted on her tongue, a sense of hope and calm filled her. An inner strength surged forward within her, and she knew without a doubt that they could handle this situation. She didn't fear. Didn't worry. None of those emotions could stand when this calm confidence reigned throughout her body.

She gave Alistair a little smile and a nod. "It's a good feeling."

He heaved out a long, dramatic sigh. "I wish you wouldn't do that so often. What if that was poisonous?"

"Plants can't poison me."

"You don't know that. You haven't eaten every kind of poison."

Walking toward him, Thea ticked off all the poisonous plants she'd eaten on her fingers. "Poison ivy, poison oak, belladonna, oleander—"

He grabbed onto her hips and jerked her into his arms. With a little squeal, she fell on top of him on the bed as more petals rained down on top of them. "Stop talking about all the poisons you've willfully ingested, you mad woman. Why would you eat all of that?"

"Because I wanted to know what would happen if I did."

"You wanted to kill yourself? Is that it?"

She burst into laughter as she stared down into his beloved face. "No, darling. I don't ever want to die. Not while you're still here."

Did he think she'd leave him that easily? The man would have to pry her cold dead hands off him at this point. She'd waited far too long for him.

Alistair wrapped his arms around her waist and tucked her a little more firmly into him. "Good. I don't think I could lose you after getting you back."

It felt so right to lie draped over him with her head on his chest. She listened to his heartbeat as she had all those years ago in a meadow with nothing but the birds and the fae to see them. "Tell me about this gathering. Then I might have a better idea how to beat them."

"It's different every year. This one we'll be going to a ceremony to see a titan arum bloom for the first time in fifty years." He traced circles on her back. "Apparently, everyone in the Academy is quite excited about it. The flower has magical qualities, although I don't think they approved anyone to gather components from the plant this year."

"A corpse flower?" She'd always wanted to see one of those bloom.

"Indeed. The problem is that they still expect me to show up with some object or spell so that everyone can see the fae and the gods when they wish."

She could see how that was the key problem. Unfortunately, so many of those people from the Academy wanted power they had not been given. Such greed would lead them down a path of destruction and ruin if they weren't careful. "They seem to lump the fae and gods into the same group. I know you can see both, but are they really the same?"

The question felt blasphemous to even ask. Of course, the fae differed from the gods. Otherwise, shouldn't they all worship the fae as well?

Alistair shifted uncomfortably beneath her. "In a way, they are the same. Some of the fae are less powerful, and thus they aren't considered to be worthy of worship by many. But we worship them in our own ways. Leaving out cream or sugar for them, thanking the household spirits for their assistance. We haven't forgotten how to worship the fae, we just do it in different ways than we do the gods."

Thea planted her hands on his chest and sat up so she could stare down at him. "Are the gods just... faeries?"

He swallowed hard, and she already knew the answer before he said it. "You can't go around claiming that gods are faeries. Someone will walk into this room and take your head off for that."

No, she would not flinch at the threat. "So they are faeries, then?"

"They're Tuatha de Danaan, and that is very diff—" he hesitated before sighing. "It's technically just a different faerie, but they're more powerful than a brownie or a pooka. You can't go around expecting gods to be treated like the fae and be accepting of that."

"But if the gods are faeries, then they should be able to be reasoned with. Just like the fae."

Her mind whirled with the possibilities, even though Alistair was already shaking his head.

"Oh, no," he muttered, reaching up to frame her face with his hands. "You will not plan on asking the fae for help. We cannot get them involved."

"Why not? This affects them too."

"Because they tasked me to take care of them. It's my job to prevent them from getting involved with this, not make them further invested." He squeezed her face in his hands one more time before leaning up and kissing her. "We have to keep them safe, Thea. The people in the Academy would wring them dry of their magic. All their abilities to help us would be gone. We have to protect them at all costs."

"I know that," she whispered against his lips. "I know that there is nothing more important than the gods and the creatures who normal people cannot see. But I also don't want to see you hurt because we protected them."

"This is not an us against them situation," he replied. "We are the ones who have to save them. And I know that frightens you. It scares me too."

She'd been so certain that her mother's gift would be the answer to all their problems. Sure, she didn't feel the anxiety right now. But that didn't mean they had figured out the situation.

All she wanted was for them to go about their normal lives. She wanted to wake up every morning without fear of threats or what some idiot would do to them. Their lives should be private and with no one else interfering with how they wanted to live.

"One day soon," she whispered, pressing their foreheads together. "I dream we will have a regular morning routine. I'll get up a little later than you, and you'll have a cup of tea ready for me at the dining table. Brewed correctly and without burnt leaves."

"And I like to imagine walking into the kitchen and listening to you reading silly stories from the newspaper." He kissed the tip of her nose. "We'll figure this out, Thea. I promise."

But as she rested her head against his chest, her stomach turned with the sick feeling that they might not figure it out in time.

CHAPTER 43

listair stared up at the house where the gathering took place. It was made to look like a large greenhouse, but he knew there were living quarters hidden inside. Sometimes magic astounded him; other times, it reminded him just how terrible things could get.

Thea's hand clenched on his arm for a moment before she smiled and pulled his attention to a man approaching them. "Ah, lovely. You're here."

Her words were so sarcastic he could only imagine who it was. And yes, of course. Marren.

Narrowing his eyes at the pale man who walked toward them, he bared his teeth in what he hoped looked like a feral smile. "Marren. Interesting to see you here."

"I do work for the Academy as well." He reached for Thea's free hand and forced her to lift it. Then he pressed a kiss to the back of her knuckles, lingering a little too long for comfort. "Besides, I heard you were bringing such a lovely young woman with you."

He wasn't wrong. Thea looked splendent tonight. He'd dressed her in one of his mother's best gowns, though the style was a little outdated. The blue fabric clung to her chest and stomach like sea foam, so light it was almost white. Then it burst into color around her hips in a beautiful sky blue that made her hair seem to shimmer with colors. Her bare arms were always delicately raised as though she were about to dance. And a tiny diamond necklace circled her neck—a gift from Alistair to remind the other men that she was already taken.

Alistair could feel the tension spreading through Thea's body. She wanted to rip her hand out of this man's grip, and likely slap him. Of course, she wouldn't. This was too important for both of them, and making a scene as soon as they got here would only make more eyes follow them throughout the night.

She endured for him, and Alistair didn't know how to repay her for that.

With a slight smile on his face, Marren let her hand drop and then turned to Alistair. "I hope you brought what the Headmistress asked for. She's very excited to see what you might have planned."

He had nothing planned. That was the problem. After a full week of talking it over, mulling through the possibilities of the lies they could tell, all they had come up with was telling the truth. And he knew that was a foolish plan. He knew that there were no good people in Wildecliff who would remark on the honorable way he handled this situation. Only bad would come of this.

But, as Thea had said when they were home, only good could fight evil. And if he wanted to beat them, they at least had to try to make it seem like they were on the better side.

He could attempt to reason with the Headmistress and would. She was not a foolish woman, and if he told her why it was a bad idea to see through the veil, then maybe she would listen. If none of that worked, he had promised Thea they would seek out the old gods and use them on their side. He didn't want to. He didn't even know the rules about dealing with such monsters, but... If they had to get the gods on their side, then they would.

"Are you ready?" he asked Thea, ignoring Marren.

"I've never been more ready in my life." She gazed up at him as though he hung the stars from the sky. Thea placed her hand delicately on top of his arm, and he drew her into the greenhouse.

Alistair let his senses be filled with colors and light. So many rare plants grew here, most of them bought from far-off places and lands well outside their knowledge. The greenhouse itself must have cost a fortune to build, with all the glass structures and green-tinged copper framing. Paths meandered through the garden, and he steered them to the right, where many bright yellow roses grew.

They were familiar plants, and that would be less overwhelming to a woman whose whole life was blooms.

"I'm all right, you know," she said with a slight laugh. "There are people here we need to speak with."

"And people I want to avoid for a while." A servant walked down the path toward them. The young man with fiery red hair held a drink tray with goblets of wine.

Just what Alistair needed.

He grabbed one as the servant passed and made sure that Thea didn't want one. She shook her head with a wry grin. "I'd rather have my wits about me tonight."

"To each their own," he muttered, and he took a hefty swallow of the wine. "I'll need a little liquid courage."

"Why's that?" A voice interrupted them.

Another couple had merged onto their path. The woman was stunning in a vivid ochre gown that offset the lovely gems in her curly hair. She'd coiled it up at the top of her head while a few tendrils framed her dark face. She taught astrology, he thought. The man beside her was a spell-casting professor, and he wore a red suit with gold edges. So many spells were sewn into his clothes that it would have been impossible for another person to even think about attacking him.

"Alistair," Claudette said with a smile. "I've heard you have quite the spectacle to show all of us tonight."

"I'm afraid you've been misinformed." Damn it; the words made his entire body shiver. "The Headmistress has asked for something that is frankly impossible. We're here to see the corpse flower. Nothing more and nothing less."

Her partner frowned and eyed Thea with distaste. "Isn't she your maid?"

He'd forgotten the two of them had been at the dinner party. They would have seen Thea then, and of course, that would confuse them as to why she was here. None of the others in Wildecliff seemed to understand that he could fall in love with someone who performed manual labor for a living.

Although he had forgotten, he was still paying her a wage. They needed to figure all of that out sooner rather than later. She didn't deserve to be an employee of his when she was so much more. She could have all his money if she wanted it. He didn't care.

"Alistair?" Claudette asked, breaking him out of his thoughts.

He realized everyone was staring at him with rather curious expressions on their faces. Even Thea looked at him with wide eyes, waiting to see what he would say.

"She was employed in my house, yes," he stammered over the

words before gaining confidence. "But she's much more than a maid. I've known her my entire life. I'd appreciate it if you called her by her name."

"Which is?" Claudette asked though she didn't sound snippy about it. Instead, she sounded rather... kind?

Thea stepped forward, holding out her hand. "My name is Thea. I'm from Waterdown and have known Alistair since we were children, like he said. It's a rather long and complicated story to explain how I ended up here."

"And one I hope to hear someday." Claudette shook her hand, even though she looked at the dirt underneath Thea's nails for a little too long. "You are a very curious woman, Thea. I rarely say that."

"Then it's an honor to be so named." The grin on Thea's face lit up the entire greenhouse with so much happiness. Alistair felt it like a punch to the gut, and it seemed the other two people were unaffected.

Did they not see how much she could bring happiness into this dark world? She smiled, and it was like all his worries floated away. Surely they could sense the same thing?

They must not have because their demeanor didn't change at all. But Claudette looked over at him with a surprised expression before clearing the emotion from her usually glass-like face. "She's good for you, Alistair. Take care of this one, would you?"

Goodbyes bidden, the other couple drifted away from them to wander through the flowers a little longer before the great spectacle of the night.

"See?" Thea said, nudging him with her elbow. "Not everyone in Wildecliff is like your family. I think we could be friends with them."

"Her husband is a boring fool who only talks about spell casting and what the students aren't doing right."

"And you're being a little judgmental." She never once let that smile budge. "I think there's more to this place than you give it credit for, Alistair."

They'd have to agree to disagree on that one. But maybe he could be convinced otherwise.

Wrapping an arm around her waist, he tugged her into his arms. "You make me see things differently, I'll admit."

"Oh, do I?" She looped her arms around him as well. "You know, it's inappropriate for you to touch me like this in public. What will all the esteemed people in the Academy think of their history professor?"

"They'll think he's madly in love with his maid," he muttered. Alistair leaned closer, wanting nothing more than to kiss her. "And I will tell them they are correct. I have fallen in love with a woman from Waterdown, and I would never want another in my life. Not for a single second of the day."

"How sweet."

He kissed her once, softly, just enough to satisfy the urge in him that said he had to tell her how much she meant to him. That she needed to understand how she had changed his life for the better.

"Alistair." The sound of the Headmistress's voice shattered any good feelings he had.

He pulled back from Thea, almost throwing her into the bushes to keep her away from the horrible woman that strode toward them. Four other people followed her, one being Marren and the other two taking up spots on the board of education that ran the Academy.

"Ma'am," he said, casting his eyes down onto the floor as he prepared himself to disappoint her. She would soon realize that he would not do anything that she wanted. And he needed to prepare himself for the inevitability of her wrath.

"You were tasked with bringing something to this party," she said. "And have you?"

"I have not." He would be strong. Alistair squared his shoulders and met her angry gaze head on. "The fae are not to be played with. Their world remains hidden from ours for a reason, and I will not give you a way to see through the veil. My gift was a mistake, and should never have been given to any of our kind. We all know that."

The silence and shock that radiated through the air felt like electricity. No one seemed to know what to say. He wasn't certain that anyone had ever told the Headmistress "no" to an order before. Even she seemed a little thrown off by his declaration.

She let out a little snort. "You are a bigger fool than I thought. Your father was right about you, Alistair. You are no good for the school or this city if you won't do what it takes to protect it."

"My father never wanted to protect this city. He wanted to protect his own assets, his greed, and his pride. The thought of protecting the people here or our way of life never crossed his mind, and I think you know that very well. You suffer from the same faults he did." Alistair took a deep breath, steeling himself. "I have no interest in playing your games, Headmistress. I will not be gifting you any magical object or spell that will satisfy your curiosity."

"Curiosity?" she chuckled. "That's what you think this is? You think I want to toy with the gods because I want more power? Dear boy. As long as the gods have us in a chokehold, how will anyone in this city ever truly flourish? The gods rule over us and as long as they do, that means we cannot rule over our own city."

Thea curled her hand around his arm, holding onto him as she replied, "The gods have a right to that worship. All you will do is make them angry, and I can only imagine that angry gods would flatten this city to the ground."

The Headmistress blinked at Thea a few times as though surprised the other woman would even open her mouth. "Who are you?"

"Thea." She dipped into a slight curtsey. "And I agree with him, ma'am. There is so much we don't know or understand about their world. We cannot afford to anger them when we need them to protect us."

"You both know so little about this world." The Headmistress sniffed and looked Thea up and down. "You have a small gift, girl. What right do you have to tell me how I should think?"

"It's not small," Thea said. "My gift is powerful for myself, and for no one else."

"And therefore useless." The Headmistress turned her disappointed attention to Alistair. "I already warned you about what would happen if you refused me. I'm sorry to see that our lives will turn in this direction, Orbweaver."

A small bit of his nerves eased. At least she wouldn't insist on punishing him in front of everyone. He had time to prepare. Time to figure out how to unbind himself from the damned house and maybe leave with Thea. They could go to Waterdown. They could hop onto a ship in the harbor and disappear from everyone's lives.

He nodded. "I knew the risks when I came to deny you."

"Then drink and enjoy your last night." Her lip curled, and she shook her head again. "You fool."

They walked away, and he sagged against Thea. "We did it," he whispered. "And she didn't try to kill us. That's a good thing, isn't it?"

"I think so." Then Thea pinched her nose. "I think the corpse flower is blooming. As disgusting as it smells, I would like to see it."

Ah, the aptly named corpse flower. Of course. At the very least, they should see the spectacle that only happened once every fifty years with this bloom. She'd wanted to see it so much, anyway. And he felt.... well. A bit like he had triumphed over an adversary that had dogged his steps for years.

If anything, he had been brave in front of Thea.

He tucked her hand into the crook of his elbow, and together, they walked toward the flower. He grabbed another glass of wine from a nearby servant who walked past them, and he let the anxiety ease from his shoulders. They were safe tonight.

The crowd of people standing around the corpse flower was impressive. He hadn't seen this many people from the Academy together in a very long time. Sipping at his wine, he tried not to let the smell overpower the taste in his mouth.

The flower was nearly six feet tall. And though the outside was a rather startling shade of vomit green, he'd heard the inside was a deep purple, like the inner muscles of a person's body. The stench was horrendous, but somehow he didn't mind it as much as he thought he would.

The petals shuddered. Everyone gasped at the slight movement from the flower. It seemed to open just slightly, then close again. Then another movement as the petals finally drew down.

"Look!" Thea whispered in awe. "It's blooming!"

A few people around them were whispering the same thing. Alistair tucked his arm around her and tried to contain his grin. Yes, the flower was impressive. But what he was most excited about was standing amongst his people with Thea at his side. None of them gave her another look as they all watched the flower.

This was what he had dreamt of for so long. This was all he had wanted.

His vision skewed to the side, and he shifted his weight a little more into her. Shaking his head, he tried to gather his wits again.

Except... Why was the world spinning?

He had a moment to look at the glass in his hand before he realized what a fool he was. The Headmistress wouldn't give him the night to prepare. She'd put something in his drink, although he didn't know how. He'd walked past the servant who had... only one glass left.

"Thea," he whispered, although the word came out garbled.

"Alistair?" she asked, and her voice sounded so far away. "Alistair, are you all right?"

He feared he wasn't. His stomach twisted in pain, and he dropped to his knees. All he could see were the spinning faces of the Academy, all watching with disinterest, as it felt like he had died in front of them. And the smell of a corpse. His?

No.

The flower.

"Alistair!" her scream echoed in his ears, but he could not drag himself back to her. No matter how hard he tried.

CHAPTER 44

A scream caught in her throat as Alistair withered in front of her. The poison in his drink was strong. As he slumped onto the ground, she could already see foam bubbling out of his mouth. Black veins spread out from his lips, eyes, and down his neck.

She had no idea what they'd poisoned him with. Though panic pressed against her chest, she knew she could help him. Thea could figure it out if only she could find his drink.

Frantically she grabbed his glass, but it had already fallen to the floor. Empty.

"Alistair," she said as she rolled him onto his back. "Alistair, wake up. Please."

His eyes rolled back in his head, and he shuddered one last time. Then his body went still. That foam trickled down his cheek and his skin turned paler than she could imagine. His freckles stood out so stark against the suddenly gray color, and she had the sudden thought she hadn't ever gotten the chance to count all of them. Not in their entirety.

"No," she whispered. "No, no. Alistair, you have to wake up."

Thea shoved his shoulders, but he didn't react. The limp weight of his body was too heavy for her to move on her own.

A choked sound echoed in her throat as tears burned in her eyes. "Alistair. Please, don't do this."

She hovered her shaking fingers over the buttons at his throat. She fumbled to give him more room to breathe. More air so that he didn't have to fight to breathe. That was why his chest wasn't rising and falling. He wasn't dead.

He couldn't be.

Keening cries reached her ears, but she was too busy untying the tie around his neck. The buttons were undone, but he still couldn't breathe. She needed to give him more ways to breathe easier so that he wasn't struggling so hard.

Shaking now, she realized the horrible cries were her. Those awful sounds wrenched out of her mouth as she grabbed his hands.

"You're so cold," she said, bringing his hands up to her lips and blowing on them to warm them. "We need to get you inside. A fire might... might help."

Maybe if she could warm up his skin, then the poison would loosen its hold on him. All she had to do was warm him up, and he'd open his eyes again. He'd be all right. He'd wake and smile at her with that half smile she loved so dearly.

"Can someone..." She cleared her throat and wiped her nose on the back of her forearm. "Can someone please help me get him up?"

But when she looked up from his body, there were no kind faces looking back at her. There were only smiles and grins. Some people had even returned to their conversations as though Alistair hadn't fallen in front of them. A group to her right didn't even notice her. They just kept talking about the corpse flower and how lucky they were to see it bloom.

And then everyone turned away. They all went back to living their lives as though a man hadn't died in front of them. They didn't care.

"Why isn't anyone looking at us?" she asked, her voice shaking with emotion. "Why can't any of you care about what is happening?"

No one responded to her. A couple of people started walking away through the greenery, disappearing into the gardens and likely to some meeting house beyond.

"Someone," she cried out. "Help us!"

She'd never felt more alone in her life. All these people walked away from her, knowing that they could help. They just chose not to.

Squeezing his limp hand tighter in hers, she steeled herself for what would be a very long walk. If they thought she wouldn't pick him up and haul his body out to the carriage where his pooka awaited them, then they were about to see the real spectacle of a lifetime.

She turned back toward Alistair, then stood up to wrench her damned skirts out of the way.

Except an oily voice interrupted her. "I warned you, didn't I? Soon you would need a new employer and now you are alone in Wildecliff. Such a pity."

That pale man had better stop talking, or she was going to punch him in the throat. Nostrils flaring with anger, she whirled on him. "If you're so invested in his life, and you seem to be around every corner, then perhaps you should help me get him back to the carriage."

"Now, why would I do that?" Marren stopped in front of her and crossed his arms over his chest. "It seems fitting that a dead body should remain next to the corpse flower. Maybe the bloom will consume him."

"That's not how an arum feeds," she hissed, dashing away tears that kept falling down her cheeks. "Are you going to help me or not?"

"Not." She shrugged. "I've been waiting to see the last Orbweaver die for a very long time. I wanted to savor the moment before I left for the night."

Anger burned in her chest until she felt like she couldn't breathe. "All of you monsters keep talking about him as though he is the reason for his father's evil. For his brother's nightmarish tendencies. He was the only good one in the family."

Apparently, that was the wrong thing to say. Marren rushed toward her so quickly that she tried to escape. Her foot caught on the edge of her skirt, and she fell backward. Thea landed hard beside Alistair on the ground once more.

He leaned down to hiss in her face, "You speak of great men who changed how Wildecliff works. Balthazar was evil, yes, but he was everything that a Wildecliff man aspires to be. His sons were dangerous, and they left this realm in a whirlwind of violence and blood. Alistair Orbweaver was the last, because he was the weakest and the easiest to pick off."

Lower lip trembling, she stared up at him with what she hoped was all the hatred in her heart. "None of you will ever be so great as this man. You are nothing more than a bully. You will die alone and unloved, and I pity you for that."

He laughed at her. "How quaint. You think I care about love? No, I care little for those paltry emotions that have no place here. You are the weakest amongst us, even lesser than Alistair. And now you will die beside him."

She didn't see a weapon on him. No one had drawn a sword or a dagger. She tilted her head up and glared. "I'd like to see you try to kill me."

He turned away, surveying the flower that had brought so many people to this room. There were few left now. Only two couples who stood so close to the flower they could have touched it if they wanted. And Marren, who curled up his lip at the smell but still stood close to it.

"Do you know there are many poisons in the world that can kill a man?" he asked.

"Of course I do. My family is full of farmers."

"Then you understand that there are very few poisons in this world that can kill someone like Alistair. His father took many precautions. He used to poison his sons with microdoses every single night for months on end. The boys were always very sickly when they were little." Marren smoothed his white hair back from his face. "Alistair didn't take to any of those poisons as well as his brothers did. One of those elixirs almost destroyed the blood vessels in his body. That's why he was always cold."

The horrific parenting technique startled her. Her heart ached for Alistair, but they were wasting time. She stood up and girded her skirts at her waistband, ignoring the startled sounds from the ladies nearby. Stockings were sure to ruin their sensibilities, but she'd be damned if she tripped again. "What a story."

"It is. So imagine my surprise when a young woman arrives in Wildecliff who can devour any flower, any poison from the land." He watched as she wedged her arms underneath Alistair's and grunted with effort. "You were an enigma and a problem in my plan. You'd taste any poison I gave him and not die from it."

Thea's heart thundered in her chest as she heaved Alistair upright. He was sort of in a seated position now, though limp in her arms. For such a thin man, he was surprisingly heavy. She wouldn't be able to lift him up like this, but she could drag him down the dirt pathway. That would have to do.

"Thea, are you listening to me?" Marren called out.

She let out a little grunt. "Not in the slightest."

"I'm trying to tell you that the poison in Alistair's cup had nothing to do with any poison you might think of. Although I'm very surprised it's taking so much longer to affect you."

What?

She blinked and realized that the vision in her right eye had gone blurry. She let Alistair lean against her legs as she rubbed at it, but nothing she did would clear her vision.

"What do you mean, affecting me?" she asked. "I drank nothing."

Marren stepped closer with his hands raised. "No, you didn't. And maybe that's the difference which I find so unusual. You see, he drank the poison only I can create. But you? You just had it on your hand."

He'd kissed her hand.

His gift was that he secreted poison, and he'd spit it onto her hand when he kissed the back of her knuckles. She should have guessed. She should have seen something on her skin that wasn't supposed to be there. Why hadn't either of them noticed?

The world seemed to tilt to the side, and she fell down onto her knees behind Alistair. Gasping for breath, Thea wrapped her arms around his body and held him to her chest.

"Even now, you are so unwilling to let him go." Marren walked by her and spat into his hand.

She could see now the poison he'd chosen for them was clear. No wonder it was so hard to see. He walked up next to her and patted her bare shoulder with that tainted hand. She didn't feel its wetness, but the sensation of icy cold spread down her arm.

"You're going to die here with him, Thea, and that's an awful thing to happen to you both. If you'd been more willing to work with me, I might have spared your life. Or at least argued to spare it with the Headmistress." He shrugged. "It's a shame to waste a pretty face, but that is sometimes how life goes. Now, I'm going to go inside and get myself a drink that doesn't have poison in it."

His laughter trailed away behind her. She struggled to breathe, mouth open against Alistair's shoulder as the remaining people left the area.

Soon, it was just her and Alistair. As it had always been. As it should have been. Forever and always. She loved him, and he loved her, and this wasn't supposed to be how it ended.

They were supposed to wake up with each other every single morning with a smile and a cup of tea. Their story should have been softer, as it was when they were children. Just two teenagers trying to figure out who they were and who they wanted to be. She should have had all the time in the world with him.

And these horrible people had taken that away from them both. The Headmistress. Marren. The Academy. No one wanted to see anyone else happy, and that was what was wrong with this place. With these people.

They were rotting from the inside out. Like a pumpkin left outside too long after Beltane.

"I'm sorry," she whispered against his skin. "I'm so sorry, Alistair. If I could save you, I would, but I have a small gift and it's not... It's not enough to bring someone back from the dead."

She heard a faint chirp beside them but could see nothing. For a moment, she let herself believe it was a chipmunk or a bird that lived in the greenhouse, but she knew better. With cold, numb fingers, she pulled out the tiny whistle and blew into it.

There they were.

Ten faerie creatures were all standing around them. Three of them looked like pixies with dragonfly wings. Three others were brownies with their adorable, mouse-like faces. The last was the pooka who had been waiting in the car, except this time he looked like some horrible mashup of a cat with a snake for a tail and human eyes.

They faded as she lost her breath, but Thea didn't want to be alone as she died. She struggled in one last breath and blew into the whistle.

The pooka had walked over to an aloe plant nearby and ripped a piece off. He held it out for her, bowing low.

Aloe. For healing.

Letting the whistle drop from her lips, she reached out for it and squeezed the goo into her mouth. The cool innards of the aloe plant helped a little, but not enough to curb the poison running through her veins.

Shakily lifting the whistle, she blew into it again. The brownies had gathered together and held out an iris for her to consume. For valor and faith.

She let the flower dissolve on her tongue and then looked at the pixies while exhaling. They held out a single white dogwood flower she hadn't even realized grew in this greenhouse.

"Love undiminished by adversity," she whispered, then swallowed the petals.

It was enough to keep her alive for a little while longer, but not enough to spare her life. Or Alistair's. And she shook with a great sense of rage that filled her from the bottom of her feet to the top of her head.

Reaching into her pocket with a steadier hand, she pulled out the flower her mother and sisters had created for her. "Courage," she said. "I need all of it."

Thea placed the flower on her tongue, and, as the words she had said rang through her mind, she realized all of it was exactly what she needed. She wanted revenge. She wanted to destroy these people who dared to take from her the one man she loved. The person she adored more than life itself.

They thought her weak.

She would prove them wrong.

Thea walked along the garden path, grabbing fistfuls of flowers as she passed. She didn't care what they were; she consumed them anyway. Joy. Glory. Magic. Wisdom. Over and over, the flowers of this greenhouse gave her power until she felt as though she walked without her feet ever touching the ground.

And then she turned toward the corpse flower as the poison in her veins thickened, and her limbs grew heavy.

"It's not enough," she growled as she stalked toward the one plant she certainly had never tasted.

Thea climbed onto the edge of the flower, lifted her hands, and ripped into it. The scent of a corpse grew so strong it stuck to her nose and flooded her lungs. She feared she would smell nothing else for the rest of her life, just rotting corpses and horrific nightmares as she tore into the flesh of the flower. Sticky ooze clung to her fingers as she lifted the shredded piece to her lips.

"I am not weak," she snarled as she looked up at the glistening red flesh of the flower. "And I will consume them all."

CHAPTER 45

He was... floating? No, that wasn't quite it. But there was no weight to his form, and Alistair was so certain there should be weight. He should feel heavy and grounded, no matter where he went.

Blinking his eyes open, he expected to look up at a glass ceiling with stars overhead. That's where he had been, at least. But there was no glass, no smell of plants, no sounds of other people. Just a distant skyline of stars that appeared a little too large and a little too close.

This wasn't right.

He'd been standing in front of Thea, and so sure that he... he... Had he been dying? Alistair remembered a wrenching pain twisting through his stomach and then a gurgle of breath fluttering out of his throat. He couldn't have died, though. Even in his worst moments, he'd never thought he would leave her first.

An uneasy tension settled onto him like a second skin. Wherever he was, he had to find Thea. He had to tell her he was all right because he didn't feel like he was dead.

Sitting up, he put a hand to his forehead as a headache bloomed behind his eyes. The pounding lance of pain distracted him for a few moments, but then his surroundings made the pain melt away.

He was sitting in a puddle of water, but the water extended as far as his eyes could see. It was just a flat, shallow... something? Not a lake by any means. And not a river because the water didn't move. It reflected the too-large stars above him and made it appear that he was sitting in the middle of a galaxy.

Definitely not where he had passed out. And not where he'd expected to wake up.

"Uh," he said through a dry mouth. "Hello?"

His words echoed, bouncing around him until he couldn't tell if someone else was returning his call or if he only heard himself. But his soul screamed that he wasn't alone. The eerie feeling of being watched lifted the hairs on his arms.

He stuck his hands in the water to push himself upright, only to find that he couldn't move once he did that. His entire body froze as though waiting for some miraculous moment, and then... then...

The world parted in front of him.

A woman's hand moved through the strange veil of starlight and pushed it aside as though she were a performer entering a stage. The curtain even wrinkled at her touch, warping the light of the stars, and then she slipped into this realm without giving him even a slight glimpse of what was hidden behind the fabric of the world.

His first impression was that she was tall. Taller than any woman he'd ever seen before. Eight feet, perhaps, with hair like fire. She wore a simple white gown tied at her waist with a small plaid tartan. The colors looked familiar, although he couldn't pinpoint why. Her bare feet sent no ripples over the water, although he could see her touching the water. She moved with a purpose and intent.

Then he looked at her face and couldn't look anywhere else. Her features seemed to shift between three different beings: one kind, one confident, and one stern. And, as she knelt in front of him, all that shifted to the face of kindness.

"Alistair," she said, her voice deep and raspy. "You've awakened."

"Where am I?" he asked, but it wasn't the first question he wanted to ask.

She chuckled, and the sound made ripples around them. And here he had thought the environment didn't react to her presence. Her billowing red hair shifted as though there was a breeze, but he couldn't feel any movement on his skin at all.

"Do you want to know where you are?" she asked. "Or do you want to know who I am?"

"Both."

"You can only ask for one." Her voice had deepened with humor. "But, because you've had a trying day, I will say that I believe you already know who I am."

His mind whirled with the possibilities. He'd been dead, hadn't he? An angel then? No, he didn't believe that someone like him would have an angel visiting him upon death, which meant she had to be... to be...

"Brighid," he whispered in awe. "Daughter of Dagda. Goddess of Spring."

She nodded, and suddenly, he knew where they were as well. This was the realm in between. Not quite in her realm of the fae and not quite in his, either. Looking around, he noted that a few scholars had claimed to be here, and they had all described the same phenomenon.

It was a place but not a place, with a sea that was not a sea.

"Are we in the Between?" he asked. "That must be where we are."

"Astute and quick, even while dying." She leaned back on her haunches. "You're impressive, Alistair Orbweaver."

"But why am I here?"

"I brought you here after the poison stopped your heart. There are fae waiting in your realm to bring you back to life if you so choose. They are keeping you here before your soul can move on to whatever afterlife awaits you mortals." She looked at him expectantly.

She must have known he'd have more questions. One, in particular, that meant so much.

He wanted to ask a thousand of them. Surely there had to be a reason for the fae to have stopped him from dying. Thea must be worried sick about him, and he'd left her alone with those monstrous fools from the Academy. How long had he been dying? Was his body already in a hospital, and she was... where was she?

He corralled his thoughts into one section of questions. "Why are you keeping me alive?"

"Because you kept your promise. All those years ago, when you spoke with a fae I sent you, you said you would keep us safe." She touched a finger to his jaw and tilted his head, so he had to stare into her eyes. "You were given every opportunity to create an object or spell that would let them see us. You didn't. Even at the cost of your own life."

"I am a man of my word," he said, although that wasn't the reason why he'd done it. Finally, he relented. "The fae have done so much for me. I wouldn't give you up to the Academy for anything."

She smiled at him. "Because you have a soft spot for those of us who are different."

"It's more than that. The fae are my family. When my father and brothers were cruel, I always found solace with the creatures who lived in my house. You and your kind are not gods or even fae to me. You're home."

"That is why this is your choice. Do you wish to live, or would you like to rest?"

It wasn't a question. "I want to be with her."

The softness in her gaze turned to something like warmth, and her face shifted to that sage expression that he knew was the form of her that was a goddess. The wisdom in her eyes burned through him. "As a reward for your loyalty and honesty, Alistair Orbweaver, I spare your life. You will be sent back to the mortal realm and to the woman you love. May you continue to honor the bond between our kinds."

It was all he'd ever wanted and more. She was so kind as to do this, but... there was still more to say.

As Brighid stood and walked toward the curtain once more, he called out, "Wait!"

She paused, still standing before him but not turning around. "What is it?"

"How do I help the domovoy who lives in my house?" He had to know if there was a way to save the poor creature. "My father tortured him and so far, nothing I have done has helped it. My gut says that creature is at the heart of why I am bound to the house. If I could leave it and this city, then I could help more fae creatures. Please."

She turned with an arched brow at his words. "Even now, when you are dying, you ask to help the fae?"

"I have dedicated my life to you and your people. Why would I not ask now how to help him?" His cheeks burned. "Besides, if I can help him, then I suppose I might help myself."

"You are more intelligent than I thought," she said with a laugh. "Child of Balthazar Orbweaver, you can heal the domovoy with his wife."

"His wife?"

"You haven't noticed her?" Brighid shrugged. "She's been under your stove for years. Household spirits sometimes find their other half as well, little mortal. The kikimora who hides beneath your stove and nips at the toes of your housekeeper is the domovoy's bride. She won't come out until she's certain it's safe, and he won't let you leave until you help him."

Of course. The domovoy had a bride, and that was why he wouldn't come out of the room that Thea had given him. He was waiting for his bride to face her fears as well.

"Why didn't I think of that?" he muttered. "Of course, there's a reason he's staying in the house."

"And the domovoy will take your bindings with him," Brighid said. "Your father couldn't bind you to the house because that is simply not possible for one to do to the living. A house has no soul to bind. But he could bind you to something that he knew you would never release because he'd made it sound so terrifying to face."

"Until Thea came back into my life."

"Precisely why your father never wanted you around her. He knew she gave you a strength he couldn't fight against." The goddess grinned, and the expression was feral. "Women have a way of doing that to men. Your father was terrified of us."

One of the few things his father was terrified of, then. He should be thankful that there were women out there who followed in Brighid's footsteps. "Thank you, goddess."

"You may call me Brighid, Alistair. After all you've done for us, I think you've earned that much. Now go back to your beautiful bride. And I suspect she will be your bride soon, won't she?"

He knew a hint when he heard one. Brighid had made her point loud and clear. The goddess wanted them together, and she would stop at nothing to see that happen. For once, he wouldn't argue with one of the fae.

Alistair inclined his head and watched as the goddess pulled back the folds of the world. Beyond, he could see the faerie realm. Blue leaves with twinkling stars glistening on their razor-sharp edges. Tall Tuatha De Danaan waiting for her. And Bres, her husband, trying to catch a glimpse of Alistair beyond her.

Someday, he hoped he would see their realm. He wanted to walk into it, just once. Not only to see their kind but to experience how they lived. The honor would be his, of course, but he would never forget such a sight.

Then the curtain fell, and he was alone in that galaxy of strangeness. Lifting his hand from the water, he watched drops fall from his fingertips. Every drop contained its own small galaxy, and he was so enraptured by the sight. He couldn't pull his eyes away from the stars, even though he wanted to.

Alistair took a deep breath and let it out in time with the small drops, and then he felt it.

Life.

It started as a heat in his belly, then a tugging in his chest that felt as though someone was pushing him. Shoving him backward. Back, back... back...

He slammed into his physical form, and it knocked all the breath out of him. Or maybe there was no breath to begin with.

Ten faeries stood around him of varying types. Brownies, pookas, a couple of clurichaun, which he didn't trust were sober, all with their hands raised and their heads tilted back. They hummed on the same note, a strange sound that vibrated through his body and rattled his ribs. He had the thought that maybe the note was the thing keeping him alive. And that was a rather strange thought to have.

And then he could breathe again. His lungs sucked in a massive amount of air. He gasped, heaving in a great breath and wheezing in as though he had risen from the grave. Maybe he had.

Rolling onto his side, Alistair coughed and coughed until a black liquid poured out of his mouth. He gagged on it, vomiting more of the black sludge onto the ground until his stomach and body were purged of that poison.

"Marren," he hissed.

There was only one poison he knew that could kill him like this. That devious bastard had poisoned him, and now he intended to make sure that Marren never forgot why he shouldn't attack an Orbweaver.

"Help me," he said to the fae. "I need to stand."

And then it felt as though an invisible hand grabbed hold of the back of his shirt and lifted him upright. Horrified, he patted himself down one last time and then turned. No one stood behind him. The greenhouse was empty.

"Where is everyone?" he asked. And then he heard the screams.

He turned so quickly that his entire body rocked, and he almost fell back onto the ground. Except a furry body pressed up against him and held him in place. The pooka. The mangy-looking cat-like creature made sure he didn't fall over and then pushed him toward the door of the greenhouse.

"Out back," it croaked. "Hurry."

Why? Why did he have to hurry?

What else could go wrong? Thea had to be with the other people. She wouldn't have run away from here if he had been dying, and even then, they would have had to drag her away from his body. Wouldn't they?

Why wasn't she here?

The screams grew in crescendo, and he ran. Alistair sprinted through the greenhouse, slapping plants away from his face until he reached the end where there was no door. Only a glass wall stood between him and a massacre that he could not stop.

There was a small field in between the greenhouse and the home of the person who owned it. Three water fountains were topped with angels that held buckets pouring water back into the small pools. But the water coming out of the buckets was dark red. At least one person was laying face down in each of the pools, impaled with what looked like roots.

Thea stood in the back of the house with her arms raised. Vines grew out of the bleeding soil and twisted around those of the Academy, who thought they could run from her. A few of the people he recognized had gathered behind a wall of fire that kept them safe from her plants, but they couldn't keep that spell going forever.

Another person ran past the greenhouse but was stopped by a tree's roots that lifted out of the ground and dug into his chest. The man looked right at Alistair as tiny wooden spikes exited through his eyes, and then he fell flat onto his face.

Alistair had never seen power like this. He'd never even guessed that someone could be so destructive, so...

Thea turned toward him, and he watched in horror as plants wriggled underneath her skin. She called out for them with her fingers spread wide and a wicked grin on her face. She looked right through him, as though he wasn't even there. A tiny vine wiggled out from under her eyelid and a tiny rosebud formed over the bridge of her nose.

As he watched, a single red teardrop slipped down her cheek.

500

CHAPTER 46

She walked onto the back lawn before the house, intending to yell at them. She wanted to scold all these people who thought they were above Alistair and better than him. But then she saw them all *laughing*.

They enjoyed what they had done. They were merry about the fact that a man lay dead in the greenhouse next to a flower none of them even appreciated. So they continued on with their evening of pleasure and alcohol and good food, as though it didn't matter that he was gone.

She saw that, and something snapped inside her. Like athread had been held too taut with the loss of him, and their laughter had broken it. Already, magic swelled through her body. A voice whispered in her mind that they had no respect for life or the living. They needed to go. The world would be better with them gone.

She felt the plants wiggling under her skin. All the blooms and buds she'd devoured wanted to come out at the same time. There was so much power in her that even when she bumped into the first person who had laughed at Alistair's dead body, all she had to do was reach for his throat.

His neck snapped so easily. Too easily. And as she looked at her hand in horror when he fell from her grip, someone else whispered in her mind, "Another."

She kept going. The crowd ran from her as she opened her arms wide and let all that magic pour out of her body. Magic. Power. Raw life flowed through her veins in an unimaginable amount of pain. But it was her, and it was real. They had thought she was so weak, and now they ran screaming from her.

The pride she felt in that moment would haunt her for the rest of her life.

All that intoxicating pride cajoled her into doing what she didn't want to do. For a few moments, she reveled in that feeling of no longer being afraid but being feared. And then she blinked her eyes, and so many people were dead.

Three of the Academy's professors were tied to the ground with vines and roots squeezing them tighter and tighter. Their deaths would be slow and painful. Others were already face down in the fountains that now poured blood instead of water. A few people had sought safety behind a wall of fire conjured by one of the men who now feared her. They should, she decided.

It was good that they were afraid. For the first time in her life, she wasn't the young woman with a small gift. She was fearsome and wild.

"He was mine," she said, her voice deep and carrying over the lawn in the wind. "You thought you could take him from me, and then you succeeded. But he was mine, and I was his and I will not let this go unpunished."

Marren called out from behind the wall of flame, "You are only punishing yourself! Don't you see that?"

She turned her gaze to him and felt some wriggling next to her eye. "Marren, come out here."

"The rest of the Academy will soon destroy you. I am sorry for your loss, but you know it was what we had to do!"

She could barely make him out through the flames. The pale man stood with such confidence. Such certainty that she could never reach him.

Thea had been paying attention ever since she moved here, though. She'd watched the people who lived in Wildecliff, and she knew their weaknesses. They were selfish and cruel. They would do anything to protect themselves.

Lifting a hand, she gestured for the roots to lift three bodies next to her. Her heart wouldn't let her look for too long, but she could see their limp forms out of the corners of her eyes. They hung there beside her like her own personal army, waiting for her to give the order for them to fight back.

The wriggling whispers in her mind said that she could use them. If she wanted to puppet their bodies, then the plants could make that happen. All she had to do was ask for it.

But she couldn't. Not if she wanted to keep living after all this mess was over and done with.

Instead, she turned her attention to the leader of the Academy, who stood beside the man conjuring the fire. "Send him out, Headmistress."

"I will not."

"I'll let the rest of you go if you do." She tilted her head to the side, peering through a rose that slowly bloomed over her right eye. "I only want him."

The murmurs from the crowd should have made him nervous. A few of the people behind him were thinking about throwing him out to her through the flames. But the Headmistress wasn't about to be outdone by one of her own people.

She cleared her throat and then said, "You want us to believe that you'll let us walk out of here? Hardly."

Thea pointed toward the house. "You will run to that building and you will not look back. Anyone who looks back I will kill. And if you think of hunting me down, or trying to harm someone I love again, then I will smother you all in your beds. You know what death tastes like as the corpse flower devours your body. Do I make myself clear?"

The Headmistress nodded and then snapped her fingers. Two men behind Marren grabbed him under the arms and threw him out onto the lawn. He stumbled a few times, then caught himself. When he stood, flipping his disheveled hair out of his face, he looked at her with more confidence than he should have. "I will poison you again. Give me a reason to."

"You will stop talking." She opened her hand, and vines wrapped around his lips. They lifted him up into the air and dragged him toward her.

She only asked them to pause when he hung before her. And then she stared into those horrible eyes, waiting for when she would be lucky enough to see fear in them. That fear flickered to life like a candle flame, and he swallowed hard at her stare.

"What are you going to do?" he asked. "Kill me?"

"Thea, no!" The shout echoed across the lawn even as Alistair sprinted toward her. "Don't do it!"

He was alive?

The power in her quaked and surged like a storm had overturned the sea in her heart. He couldn't be alive. She'd checked herself, and he wasn't breathing. He'd left this realm for another where she couldn't follow him, and that was why…

She skated her gaze over the dead bodies and realized what she had done. The horror of the surrounding massacre made her heart squeeze in her chest. She hadn't wanted to hurt anyone; she had just wanted to feel like she was powerful for once in her life. She didn't want them to think she had a small gift anymore. All of this was for vengeance, to make up for the loss of him.

Marren sank to the ground as she shook her head in disbelief.

"No," she whispered. "He can't see this. He can't see me."

As her vines released their hold on Marren's arms, he pointed at her with a sneer. "The Academy will never forget this, witch. They will hunt you until the end of your days."

It shouldn't matter if the Academy saw what she did. Anyone could understand why she had done it. She thought Alistair was dead. He had died in her arms, and they were the ones to have done it! Surely anyone in their right mind would understand.

As she looked over at Alistair, she knew there had to be someone who saw her struggles. At least one person in Wildecliff must have felt what she felt when she looked at him. How the beloved wrinkles of fear on his face made her sick. The way he moved toward her with so much determination and love turned her anger into grief. Thea wasn't the only woman to have ever loved with her whole being.

Then Marren turned toward him and time seemed to slow. The pale man looked at her Alistair as though he were something to rid this world of, and then he opened his mouth. She had seen him spit poison into his palm, and she would not let him do that again. Never again.

She lifted her hands, and the vines surged. The flowers and magic she'd absorbed grew inside her, and her vision disappeared. She was nothing, could be nothing, for she was the world inside a small seed of a body waiting to bloom.

Roots and vines spread up through the ground, tunneling through the soft earth underneath his feet. She felt them surge out of the ground and bury into his skin. The wriggling, writhing, monstrous creations she had summoned would destroy this man who had only wanted to harm. And she felt no guilt. Not for this one.

Marren's spine bent as he seized underneath the weight of her magic. His arms spread wide as roots and branches grew inside of him and stiffened his body. Leaves slapped over his mouth and burrowed around his tongue so that he could no longer spit that poisonous venom. He would harm no one else. Not now that she had him in her grip.

As one last final measure, Thea closed her hand into a fist and twisted. Marren's head followed the same gesture as her hand, and his lifeless body slumped forward onto the roots.

"There," she proclaimed. "Now you are undone, and I am finished."

The magic drained out of her, and her feet touched the ground again. She staggered, her entire body feeling as though she'd been rolled through the dirt a couple of times. But that was all right. She'd survived unimaginable power. Now, all she could hope was that Alistair would forgive her for it.

She took two steps toward him, the shock on his face something she wanted to smooth with her thumb. She'd ease the wrinkles on his forehead and the lines around his mouth. He would see that she was all right. It was just... just... She looked down at her hands covered with blood and started shaking.

Had she really done this? Had she been so callous with her powers that she would allow so many people to die and not feel even a shred of remorse for their lives? It was unlike her.

It was wrong.

Hands covered hers up, and she felt the warmth of his grip sink into her soul. "It's all right," he whispered, drawing her up to her feet. "You can stop now. It's all right. Stop looking at them, darling."

"You were dead," she whimpered. "You died in my arms and I felt you go."

"I know. I know." He drew her against his heart and pressed a kiss to the top of her head. "But death isn't permanent for people like us. The fae spared me for saving them. They sent me back to you."

She curled her fingers into the hem of his shirt. Wrapping her grip around him so he couldn't leave again, she shook, her breath shuddering with each word, "I'm so glad. But these people, Alistair, I didn't think.... I didn't know."

"It was the corpse flower. You had no idea what it would do to you to consume that."

"I think I did," she whispered. "I knew it would make me crave death, and I wanted it. I ripped it open, Alistair, and the flesh underneath... It was... It was..."

Delicious. A part of her wanted to say. *It melted like butter on my tongue, and it tasted sweeter than wine. It made me want to scream with power, and it made me want to make men kneel at my feet while I drank from their throats.*

It was a power unimaginable and a power she should never have felt in her life. Thea knew there was no excusing what she had done. She would have to live knowing that she could kill and luxuriate in the power it gave her. But someday, she would roll this memory over in her mind and know that the corpse flower had wanted more from her. It had wanted death in the hundreds. The thousands.

That power drained out of her, leaking from her form like some kind of oil that had coated her body. Thankfully, they only bloomed once in a blue moon; otherwise... She shuddered to think of what she would have done.

"You did what you had to do," he whispered against her shoulder. "And I did what I had to."

But she could feel the quaking of his shoulders. He was horrified by what she'd done, and his eyes couldn't stop looking at the dead bodies of his coworkers. She'd murdered so many of them, and Thea could almost feel their souls streaking past them. Someday they would hunt her down, she realized. Marren might have been right about one thing. The Academy would follow her, even if they were dead.

She pressed her own lips against his shoulder, a kiss that lingered a little too long. "Losing you made me angry. Maybe that's not even the right term, but it made me go mad, Alistair. That madness consumed me until I was nothing but raw power. I wanted them to hurt. Like I was hurting."

"Shh." He pulled back and smoothed his thumbs along her jawline. "We don't have to talk about it right now."

"I do. I have to purge it from my soul because it's eating me alive. I killed them, Alistair, and I wanted to do it." She took a deep breath. "It wasn't me, but it was me. I was lost in an in between place and I didn't even recognize myself."

"I recognize you," he said. "I know this face as well as my own. There are exactly fifteen freckles on your cheeks, although they are hard to see. Your eyes are dark like the sea at midnight and your nose lifts slightly at the end. When you're very happy, you smile so wide that wrinkles form on your cheeks, but when you are blissful, your smile shows your gums. You are mine, Thea. Mine and mine alone, and I cannot claim that I would have been any better if they murdered you in front of me."

"They tried," she whispered. "They wanted both of us dead."

"And I will never put you in another situation like this again. I will protect you until the very end of my life, Thea Earthshaker. Forever." His fingers hovered over her right eye, lingering over the part still tinted with the shade of red. "May I?"

She nodded, although she wasn't sure what he was asking to do.

Alistair grabbed onto something that obscured her vision and tugged. She felt the last bit of that awful magic leave through her eye as he pulled out a lovely red rose by the root. He let the flower dangle from his fingers for a few moments before dropping it onto the ground.

"That was—" she asked, hesitating.

"You became something so much more than yourself, Thea. A terrifying witch with no small gift." He gave her that crooked half-smile she hadn't ever thought to see again. "You're more powerful than they ever could have guessed."

And she supposed she was.

Sagging against him, she turned her face away from the bodies and watched the pooka approach them. Home. Soon, they would go home.

epilogue

"A re you sure you'll be all right?" he asked the domovoy one last time.

The two faeries had prepared themselves very early in the morning. The monstrous, hulking form of the domovoy overpowered the kikimora, who they had finally pulled from underneath the stove. She had a rat-like face and a very long tail that waved underneath her pretty teal dress when she was nervous. Her long whiskers twitched at Alistair and then stilled when she looked up at the domovoy with love in her eyes.

That was all the answer he needed. They would be just fine, and he didn't have to worry about them anymore. The moment the domovoy left the house, the curse binding him to this building was broken. The domovoy wasn't within the walls of the Orbweaver manor, and therefore, Alistair was not required to remain either.

They'd keep the house, of course. It was a beautiful place for them to return to when they were needed in Wildecliff, but it would not be the home they lived in all the time. He'd rather sell the place than keep it, but Thea wanted their children to see his childhood home.

Not that they were having children anytime soon. At least, he hoped not.

The two faeries wandered down the street, invisible to all other than him and Thea, who had his whistle to her lips. And while the two faeries were ready for a new adventure, so were Alistair and Thea. Their bags had been sent before them down to the docks, and someone was waiting in Waterdown to pick up them and their bags.

They were going on their own adventure, Thea liked to say. Really, they both needed to leave the doom and gloom of Wildecliff. Maybe someday they would return, but not until they'd made new stories with each other.

"You be careful," Nora said, dabbing her eyes with a handkerchief. "It's a long journey ahead and two kids like you shouldn't be doing it alone."

He turned toward her with a grin and yanked her into a tight hug. "You're not that much older than us, Miss Nora. You know we'll be fine."

And as he released her, Thea pulled her into a hug as well, adding, "And you're joining us in a week once the butlers finish up with the last jobs to seal this place from the public."

"A week is such a long time!" Nora wailed. She blew her nose dramatically into the handkerchief and waved them off. "Begone with you two, or I'll never stop crying, and I still have to make lunch!"

He watched her wander off with a wry grin and then held his arm out for Thea to take. "Shall we?"

"Let's go home."

Atlas flew out of his window and landed on Alistair's shoulder.

Apparently their familiars had decided to get along with Thea.

Browning had never been happier than in his house, so the toad was rather disappointed to return to his quieter life on the other side of the river. Thus, he was in his sling at Thea's hip.

She glanced up at Atlas and sighed. "Are you still angry with me?"

In return, the bird angled his head and let her pat the very top. Just like she used to.

"I suppose that's better than nothing," she said quietly.

He marveled at how much his life had changed in such a short time. The carriage rocked them into a calm sense of peace. It would be left at the docks for someone else to take care of since the pooka wanted to join them in Waterdown. Neither he nor Thea had expected anything different.

Thea's expression had changed today. Perhaps it was the excitement of returning to Waterdown, or maybe she was just eager to see her family again. But there was still a worn edge to the way she held herself. As though the memories of what she had done wouldn't let go of her. He hoped someday he would ease those dark smudges underneath her eyes.

He knew it would take a while for her to heal. Though he would admit, once their things were on the boat and the fresh air blew across her cheeks, there was a color to her face that was much better than before.

Wrapping his arm around her, he said, "You look happy."

"Happier than before, yes." She leaned into him and put her hand over his heart. "They're excited to see you, you know."

He hoped they were. He had stolen their daughter and sister away, forced her to live in a house that terrified her, and then put her life in danger. Such things had a way of making a family not like him as much as before, but that would change once they all stood in front of each other.

Sighing, he pinched the bridge of his nose before looking down at her. "Are you sure about that? They have every reason to be angry with me. Even the old anger about the attack on Waterdown, my family, putting you in danger, then of course there's all the faeries that will be meddling in their lives from now on—"

Thea put her finger over his mouth, forcing him to stop talking. "They're going to love you, Alistair, like they did the first time they saw you."

"You think?"

"I know."

He swallowed hard and told himself to let courage flow through his veins. "Good, because I wanted to do this before we reached the shore, but I also didn't want to anger them overly much."

"What did you want to—"

Alistair sank down onto one knee and grinned up at her. Thea pressed her hands to her lips, eyes wide, looking more shocked and happy than he'd seen her in a long time.

Reaching into his pocket, he pulled out a tiny ring made of little metal leaves and a single ruby that sparkled like a little rose. "When I was a young man, I made a promise to you. That I would do whatever it took to marry you because I loved you. I'm sorry it took me so long to getting around to a real ring, but I want you to know that my dream of a future with you has never changed. Not for a single day. I love you, and I want to spend the rest of my life with you, no matter how difficult that may become. So, would you make me the luckiest man alive and be my wife?"

Tears welled in her eyes and slid down her cheeks. "Yes," she said.

"Yes, a thousand times, yes."

Relief welled through him. Not that he'd been all that concerned if she'd say yes, but... well, he wasn't so confident not to be a little nervous. He stood as she threw her arms around him and, oh, he loved her. He loved her with every fiber of his being, and he promised himself that he would prove that to her every day for the rest of eternity.

"I will always love you," he whispered into her hair.

"In this life and the next," she replied as she kissed him with her whole heart.

And as they floated in the river that had always stood between them, he knew he would be happy from now until the day he died.

518

Thank you for reading my heart book, I hope you enjoyed!
And if you did, don't forget to leave a review.

ACKNOWLEDGEMENTS

So much of this book wouldn't exist without a very special person in my life. My fiancé regularly gives me all the inspiration I need to write characters that make people smile, who support their partners no matter what oddities that person brings to the relationship, and how to choose each other even through the difficult times.

Thank you to the beta readers who have always sent me notes on each book, and to the new editor who jumped onto my team last minute and provided wonderful edits.

And of course, thank you to all my readers who make these stories a possibility every single day. I wouldn't be doing this without you <3

ABOUT THE AUTHOR

Emma Hamm is a small town girl on a blueberry field in Maine. She writes stories that remind her of home, of fairytales, and of myths and legends that make her mind wander.

She can be found by the fireplace with a cup of tea and her two Maine Coon cats dipping their paws into the water without her knowing.

For more updates, join my newsletter!
www.emmahamm.com

523

THESE BITTER BLOOMS

524

525

www.ingramcontent.com/pod-product-compliance
Lightning Source LLC
Chambersburg PA
CBHW031232310726
48971CB00004B/972